A START IN LIFE

Born in Nottingham in 1928 Alan Sillitoe started his working life at the bench of a bicycle factory and had no thought of writing until he was ill in hospital for a year after RAF service in Malaya. For some years he lived in France and Spain, bringing back to England the typescripts for two novels and some verse. The first novel was *Saturday Night and Sunday Morning*, of which Pan have sold well over a million copies and from which the film was made. *The Loneliness of the Long-Distance Runner* (short stories) followed a year later in 1959. Sillitoe's fascinating travel book about Russia, *The Road to Volgograd*, was published in 1964 and he has since been to Russia at the invitation of the Soviet Government. *A Start in Life* is his latest novel. He has also written three volumes of verse.

Alan Sillitoe is married to Ruth Fainlight, the American poet and has a son and a daughter. They live in Kent although Sillitoe's favourite pastime is travelling.

A START IN LIFE

Alan Sillitoe

UNABRIDGED

PAN BOOKS LTD : LONDON

First published 1970 by W. H. Allen and Co. Ltd.
This edition published 1972 by Pan Books Ltd.,
33 Tothill Street, London S.W.1

ISBN 0 330 02885 5

Printed in Great Britain by
Cox & Wyman Ltd., London, Reading and Fakenham

Part One

I remember childhood as an intense and wonderful love-affair that was stamped out by the wilful circumstance of growing up. So you can be sure I won't spend long on it.

It's hard to take things very far back, except to say that I came into the world without a father. A man must have been somewhere involved in it, but I didn't know who he was, and I felt for a long time that my mother hardly did, either. In this sense I married my mother at a very early age, so that until I grew conscious of the world, I lived the most perfect existence. But when I tried to stop rivals getting into bed with her, she slapped me, saying: 'Get out of the way, you little bastard.' If she hit me hard enough I did as she told me, otherwise I crawled under the bed and slept to the gentle rocking noise above.

She sometimes called me a foreign bastard, but there was no great insult to strangers in this, for it only meant I was foreign to her own body, which I could not help but be, having come right out from it. As soon as she thought I had reached the age of reason she stopped calling me these names for fear I should understand their exact meaning, or ask her to explain them to me. In this way I remembered the appellation till I was able to look up its significance in a dictionary at school.

She knocked me around, but fed me well and put good clothes on my back, so in the world we lived in there was no reason to complain. The war was on (don't ask which), and I took great interest in it from the wireless going continually. It seemed that every soldier in the world, on our side anyway, had to knock at the front door and, a few hours later, slip out of the back on his way up the line to death. They were stuffed with gin, and me with lollipops, while my mother seemed to thrive on fags and chewing-gum. As far as I was concerned that was how the war was won, and if children of mine ever think to ask: 'Dad, what did you do in the war?' I'll say, 'I kept my trap shut and loved every bit of it.'

Nothing lasts for ever, though you don't think so at the time. If it's bad you want it to go quickly, and if it's good you like it so much your heart marks time to hold it close, though you soon get tired of its dotty rhythm. A neighbour looked after me while Mother went to work and I played in the soil wearing clouts and rompers (and in summer nothing at all) till Mother came down the yard in her democratic overalls, an egalitarian jaunty fag at her lips, when I'd run to take her hand and we'd go together to the back door, me holding a biscuit she'd saved from the canteen at dinner-time, but unwilling to eat it quickly since it seemed the only visible proof of her love.

My father's side I didn't know about, for my mother never spoke of him. But she had parents still, so I got enough talk from her family to last for both sides. They lived in a house at Beeston, and she'd take me there, out of the streets and along Faraday Road as far as the bridge, where she'd pull me up to the top deck of the bus because she wanted to smoke. Then I could look out through clouds of it at wide spaces spreading left and right at the university that I thought at first was a hospital. One summer's day we went on foot, a short way along Cuthrough Lane which she always called Cut Throat Lane because as a girl she used to walk or cycle along its narrow and leafy path which was so secluded that it put her in that frame of mind.

Grandma was scrubbing the house and when she told me to sit down I did so where a chair was usually placed. But I fell in a bucket of muddy water laced with snakey and lukewarm floorcloths. I set up a scream – only drowned by my mother's of rage when she pulled me out of it. The house was dark with the shutters shut. It was bigger than ours and stood on a side lane off the main road, and had a walled garden. The tree in the middle was stout, an ancient elm that was rotten inside, but Grandad was frightened to chop it down because he thought it might crush the kitchen jutting out from the house, or smash through the wall and block the road. I tried to climb it at an early age. For a long time it defeated me because I was so small, but there were always other troubles waiting. I got into scrapes so much, not because I was unhappy, as people often believe, but because I was confident and full of hope.

Grandma used to say how cheerful I was, continually busy and knocking about, a handful of such brazen curiosity that I'd take some looking after, by God I would, which was the way of children who were *born like that*.

I ran out of her gate one day while they were drinking tea and eating cake. Across the road and by the kerb was a dark green motor van and I opened the door without thinking. Inside I found a new world of leather upholstery and dials, handles and knobs, as well as a monstrous wheel. Standing up I could look out of the wide front window and see down the sloping road. I was strong enough to pull the door shut after me, and then found force to grip another handle that suddenly fell forward with a clatter, causing the flesh of my palm to ring as it hit its limits somewhere forward. A rumble under the whole car told me all was not right with the world, and standing straight I saw my grandad's brick wall sliding backwards along the car. Then another house was in view, and, full of terror, I dropped into a bundle on the floor and cried out for my mother.

The car made ominous bounces down the road, ran across a junction at the bottom, and buried itself in a tall privet hedge, grinding its side against a concrete gate-post. A man came running, and when the door opened I felt a solid hand thumping at my head, and heard a voice calling me all the bad names that came to it, one of which at least was true. I cried, and thought my more-or-less pleasant world was coming to an end. My mother must have been told what was happening, for I heard her curses as she began bashing the man at any part of his body she could reach. Grandma pulled me out and soothed me, praising God I hadn't been killed, and shouting against stupid, dead-headed gets who left their cars by the roadside with open doors, and threatening to get the police and have the bewildered culprit sent down for murder and kidnapping.

But the man was in tears, because he'd saved up half his life to get a little van to take his wife and kids along the Trent for fresh air at weekends. He'd polished it faithfully every week, fed it with oats and water like a true yeoman of England grooming his horse, and now this act of God in the shape of

7

the Devil's imp had caused its shining flank to get sheered off.

I lived in the dark, and didn't know at the time the awful blow I'd dealt him, only felt the panic blows he'd thrown at me. The cries of humanity were being raised at the fact of my birth, and at the sight of me who was begotten in love – if in nothing else.

Whenever Grandmother cursed, she said it was the Irish in her. She had a great sense of justice, and knew exactly what was right and wrong. I got these feelings from her, and not my mother, who smoked too much to have them, it seemed to me, and who was too nervous ever to pass them on to me if she did feel them somewhere deep inside her. It was true though that my grandmother was Irish, for she told me later that her grandparents had come to England from County Mayo a hundred years ago. She talked about the Famine which was caused by the terrible English, something I took in silence because I thought that perhaps my father had been English (whoever he was) and that though my grandmother had the right to slur him I hadn't. When I hinted this she gave a great Irish laugh and said he might have been American for all any-one knew, and that, if he was American maybe he was Irish, in which case my boy you're altogether one of us. I didn't know what to make of this and didn't much care, because I lived in Nottingham, and that was the world to me.

I was spoiled as only a bastard can be spoiled, unless he's ruined by being despised. I sat on a wall and aimed pebbles at passers-by, dropping over on to a wasteground when they saw me. My grandmother told me to be good, but I didn't know what she meant because she couldn't show me. All she could do was open her mouth and let go sounds like a flood-warning when she told me what would happen if I didn't be good. But even this was so comforting in its tone of care and love that I laughed and asked for more cake, which she invariably gave me.

School was the torment of my life, and every morning my mother left me early by the closed gates because she had to be on her way and get to work by eight o'clock. She put a three-penny bit in my hand, and when I saw the shop opening across the street I'd saunter there and buy a lucky bag of sweets that tasted like honey as I sucked them, leaning against the school wall.

When the other kids asked what job my father did I said I hadn't got one because he'd been killed in the war – which may have been true for all I cared. But even at five or six I thought my mother hadn't married because no man would own me, and I didn't much mind this, for I was used to it, and anyway liked to have her to myself. Sometimes she bundled me off to Grandma's at Beeston while she went to Blackpool or London, but this was a glorious holiday because then I didn't have to go to school.

My grandfather was the best of men to me, though when he stayed home from work and drank a lot of beer he sometimes got nasty-tempered and called me a bastard – which is what I understood a boy to be whose mother couldn't find a husband to live with her.

One day when I picked up some marbles in the playground the boy cursed me by shouting I was a rotten bastard. I thought he'd rumbled my secret, and hit him so hard it got around I really was a bastard. Not that this grieved me because nobody had any proof, and also I'd become pals with a couple of boys who I felt sure were as much bastards as I was.

One was Alfie Bottesford who lived on Norton Street, and he had no father. His mother was fat and wore glasses, and she worked at Player's on a cigarette machine. For a long time I imagined her sitting at a bench with a little rubber-rollered fagmaker in her hands, turning up cigarettes all day that other women smoothed and put into the packets to be sold in shops. Alfie was her only boy, and his great passion when he wasn't at school, was playing marbles on the cobbled street. When he wasn't playing marbles with himself he was eating bread and treacle. I never saw him eating anything else. Sometimes when I went to his house after school his mother would give me bread and treacle, which I ate hungrily because I had an hour to wait before being able to go home and find my mother there. Mrs Bottesford would also give me a cup of tea that was so strong it smelled like iodine. Being a man of many colours I drank it down, and dreamed all night, dosed by the fire-and-brimstone of that awful meal.

I was taught to read and write at school, but not much else. The teachers pushed me to the back, and ignored me. But out of spite, and perhaps a desire to please, I got good marks in reading and writing. Then they kept me at the back of the class because I didn't seem to need the same attention as those duffers who couldn't even learn that much. At about this time, when I was seven, my mother and grandmother got wind of a nearby house that had been abandoned. Someone had done a moonlight flit to Birmingham and left a lot of stuff behind because the van was full. So my mother shuffled herself through the scullery window one afternoon and opened the door for me and Grandma. There wasn't much loot except a few old tats and pots, but I went into the parlour and saw that the floor was covered with large books of music. They were scattered everywhere and I sat looking through them, fascinated by the sheets of complex musical notation. They stood out black and plain – quavers and crotchets and minims, words I already knew from school – and I ran my fingers over them as if they were written in braille. I took two away under my arm, and was proud to own them, though later they disappeared to I don't know where, but for years afterwards those lines of soundless music went through my dreams stoked by Mrs Bottesford's iodized tea that you may have been able to stand a spoon in, as the saying goes, but could not have stood up in yourself.

My Beeston pal was Billy King, whose family lived in a cellar on Regent Street. He was unique among my friends in that he never asked me a single question during the year we knew each other, not even so much as what time do you think it is? or, are you hungry? This didn't worry me, because having a fatal flaw to hide, I felt that his taciturnity in this respect was all to the good. But I regretted it when in my natural and more exuberant curiosity I wanted to ask questions of him, only to be met by a mind your own business, or don't ask questions then you'll get told no lies, or, if he was in an affable mood because he'd been able to acquire one of his father's cigarettes, he'd simply say nothing at all, and dig both hands deeper into his pockets as he puffed ceremoniously away. I had to wait for him to tell me things of his own free will, and when he did it was like rich seeds falling on three-year fallow land as they took effect in my imagination, and the slightest event that happened to him achieved unwarranted growth. I mention this as a possible reason why I later became such a good listener, and often held back from asking the right sort of questions. People always tell you more when their boiling heart burst of its own accord, and I liked listening to stories, true or false, not out of idleness and the inability to tell my own, but because I am a gullible and good-natured man who listens to other people's troubles soothingly, and who, while hearing obvious lies and boastings, accepts the entertainment of them without questioning their morality – unless I fall a victim to their tricks.

Yet, how could I be a born listener if I had an Irish grandmother? The fact was that she told me few ancestral stories that I could repeat, at this early age or even later. Mostly she did little except laugh and shout, and occasionally threaten her husband when he got too drunk to dig the garden, and bawl after her daughter who hadn't been to collect me for three weeks. But I loved my grandparents even more than if they'd been my real parents, since it was two to one against. The proof of this is that when my mother left me at home to go to sleep at night because she was going up to the boozer with some boyfriend or other, I didn't cry or let it worry me. Yet when at Grandma's she and Grandad wanted to go for a walk or a drink I cried and all but panicked at being left on my own. The end of the world seemed close as the summer evening sun came into my bedroom and I had no one to share its light with. I wasn't a mother's boy, but a grandparents' boy, and if one wants to divide children up I suppose that isn't a bad way to do it.

I never went into Billy King's cellar when I called for him but shouted down the grating that spread its steel bars under my feet. He'd come running out of the house to which the cellar belonged. His mother and father, who lived down there with two other children, had rented it on the understanding that they'd only use it to store furniture while Mr King found another house. But having been thrown out, the family had nowhere to go, and so camped between its whitewashed walls. Once, Billy came out totally black and bruised, saying that a coalman had taken off the grating that morning by mistake and dropped a full hundredweight down the sloping chute on to the children's bed below, and if it hadn't been that they were curled together under the clothes in one snug ball then their heads might have suffered from that thoughtless avalanche.

The winter was the worst in living memory, and in an igloo built around my grandad's tree, Billy and I ate cakes and chocolate that we'd stolen from shops, looking out through a window-hole towards the gate in case anyone should come in after us. Our knees were wet on the floor of snow and soil, but it was our hideout that no one would imagine man or beast to be in, and we sat for hours in silence like two vagabonds waiting to be led off and hanged. The true and dreadful world was beyond the ice, and in our tomb of refuge we were untouchable because no grown man could crawl down that inlet of a hole – though at night in bed I dreamed of a pickaxe splitting through the ice-dome roof and barely missing Billy and me.

When spring came our house melted into the soil, till only a patch of black earth was left around the tree. Billy and I climbed over a wall off the High Street and found a fruiterer's cart inside that was loaded for his next day's outing. We threw as many tins as we could over the wall and packed them into Billy's barrow, pushing it away in the dark. We stopped by Billy's cellar to lift off the grating and roll down his part of the loot, which fell softly on to the children's bed. His underworld parents thought it food from heaven, and stowed it in the sideboard. Grandma was glad of my share, and opened two tins of chunks that night to have with our bread and butter.

I saw a policeman and the man who owned the fruit barrow come into the gate, and for the first time shot up Grandad's tree, to the topmost branches, without any effort at all. They begged me to come down, but I hung on like a cat, eyes paralysed at that half-circle waiting to drag me to the darkest prison as soon as my feet touched earth. But a bigger voice than mine had a say in what I did, for the branch snapped, and as it splintered somewhere behind my feet I felt that this was my plain death, that at lucky seven years I was bound for hell, and shouted in terror as I felt myself flying down.

Arms spread wide like a bird's wings, as if to clutch at the horizon and hold myself safe, I hit the ground before the branch, and felt it bounce by my side a half-second later. I was stunned and scratched, and some of my teeth were loose, but otherwise I was sound enough when Grandmother carried me into the house and sat me down; screaming all the while at the policeman: 'Murderers! Murderers! You'd kill a child for a few tins of fruit!' My grandfather went into the parlour with the policeman and the fruitseller, and settled everything with ten shillings recompense, and a few glasses of best Irish whiskey.

The next day I skulked around the garden before he got up. Grandmother had gone shopping, and I suddenly saw him at the back door beckoning me. 'What for?' I said.

'Come here, my boy.'

When I got close he gave me a ferocious slap across the face that bundled me against the shed. He picked me up and threw me half across the garden: 'Next time, don't get caught, d'you hear me? Never get caught.' He slammed the door and went in to eat his breakfast.

It was all right for him, but how was it possible to separate getting caught from stealing? If anybody could tell me, I'd listen eagerly. I was forbidden to leave the garden for a week, but got out before then by a bit of skilful climbing and ran off to find Billy King. Putting my face to the cellar grate I softly called his name, then louder when he didn't answer, and louder still. Neither he nor his family were there, and I could only assume they'd found a house at last. Wherever it was, it must have been a long way off.

All I liked to do at school was read. There wasn't much else. I didn't like arithmetic, and couldn't stomach writing. Reading took me right out of school, and into the world of the book-adventure, so it was like not being at school at all, and was the only way to avoid it without playing truant. The teacher caught me at it time and time again, but I always took the book back that he snatched from me, even when he lost his temper and thumped me. He was a young man, so it puzzled him, because he couldn't honestly call me the fool I probably was for not learning other things as well.

At home I wouldn't be seen dead reading a book, not until I left school anyway. If I did they'd have thought I was either mad or ill, and I didn't want them tucking me up in bed or sending for a doctor without good reason. When I did leave school, I read at work, and it was taken more amiss than before. After being sacked for this from a couple of factories (that I couldn't stand anyway because of the stink and noise, not to mention the *work*) I was careful to get jobs as an errand boy or messenger, pushing a bike with a high front loaded with cloth or groceries from one place to another. On my way back I'd lean the bike by the wall of a canal bridge and take half an hour at my book or comic. I was consequently looked on as intelligent because I never lost my way, but not very diligent because I always took so long over it.

On one trip I lingered through town and looked in a bookshop window. One of the titles which caught my eye was *The Way of All Flesh*. I stood in my overalls and gazed at it, and when a young girl also looked into the window I felt embarrassed in case she thought I had nothing but eyes for a book with a title like that. In a way I had, but I held my ground. I'd always liked books about sex, and this one I hadn't heard of, and as it was a paperback I went in to buy it. The girl had also decided to buy something, a young fair beauty of an office tart no doubt, and she stood by the row of books wherein I knew I would find the one I was looking for. So I held back, and glanced at a row of prayer books and Bibles, and I couldn't understand why they were in the same shop with the sort of book I longed to get.

An assistant asked what I wanted, and I told him I was just looking around, so the toffee-nose slunk back to his desk to wrap up parcels. I'd been out from my work-place too long to stay much more, and because the girl wouldn't move from the paperback shelves I made up my mind to come again the following day. This I did, handed the book to the man, who took my money and slid it into a bag so that no one would think I'd stolen it as I went out.

But I'd slid one book under my jacket, on the principle of buy one – nick one, which merely meant I'd got them both for half-price. I certainly wasn't a thief, to get them for nothing. The book I'd taken free was called *The Divine Comedy* because I thought that was dirty as well, especially as it was written by an Italian. I was so pleased with my haul I began reading by the fire that night after Mother had gone out. My eyes were avid and my mind eager as I propped both feet on the coal scuttle and opened *The Way of All Flesh*. I didn't imagine it would be easy, because I knew that in this sort of Penguin book you could hardly expect to read about anybody in bed together for the first fifty pages. But it turned out to be so interesting that I stuck at it, and by the time Mother came back at half past ten I'd forgotten what I'd expected from the book when I opened it.

After that, other good books were chewed into my maw, and though I never got the throstle-titillation that drew me to them in the first place (which is not to say I was always disappointed), I nevertheless saw that there was more to books than reading about sex and gangsters. I had always been unsatisfied by these two subjects, because the sex seemed unreal and always had to be paid for in some grisly way, and the gangsters were all rotten and made of cardboard and so got what they deserved at the first punch of the law. I can see how innocent I was, and though this may be usual in any ordinary youth it was no great advantage if you were a bastard. While labouring under my pleasurable education of reading, I began to see that all was not well with the life I had chosen to lead, because it was life itself that had chosen to lead me a dance that I did not want. To put it bluntly, I was fed up with work, with home, and with living the way I did.

I was eighteen by the time this slow fuse started burning, as if my litmus toes had been touched off and were smoking slowly up to my heart. When Mother asked what was up I said the sky, and grabbed my coat to go, before she could begin her carpet-bombing about how useless and dead stupid I was. She would have been right, and I couldn't stand that, so the only thing left was to wander up Norton Street and see if Alfie

Bottesford was back yet from the foundry office he worked at.

It was mid-week but he unlatched the door wearing a collar and tie, creased trousers, smart coat, and an extra polish to his glasses. 'Are you in?' I asked.

'I might be,' he said, 'but my girl is here.'

'That's all right,' I said, edging closer.

He opened wider: 'Come in, then,' whispering in the scullery: 'Her name's Claudine, and we're going steady.'

I boggled at this, and he introduced me (as he called it: I'd never been 'introduced' before) in the proper way, meaning he allowed us to shake hands, which was his first and last mistake. 'This is my girlfriend, Claudine Forks,' he said. 'Claudine, this is an old friend of mine, Michael Cullen.'

She sat back in an armchair by the fire, and I tried to catch her eye and give her the wink while Alfie was turning the record over on his gramophone. She had a small mouth and big breasts, and as she sat back I could see halfway up her thin legs.

There wasn't much of a welcome for me from either her or Alfie, and I supposed that his mother was out, and that they'd expected a frolic all to themselves before she came back. I wanted to spoil their fun, if not take it over, and when Alfie went into the kitchen to make a cup of tea, which he saw as the quickest way of getting me to go, I concentrated my gaze on his sweetheart, till she stood up and looked along the mantel-shelf for a cigarette.

'I've got some,' I said, flashing them under her nose. 'Make us a sandwich while you're at it,' I called to Alfie. Before she put the fag to her mouth I kissed her, and pulled her into my chest. She struggled, but seemed well practised at making no noise. 'If you say owt,' I whispered, 'I'll say you kissed me first.' Her eyes were like octopus lamps at this prime mischief, so I kissed her again and pressed her so that I could feel all she'd got.

I struck a match and lit her fag, and Alfie fried under his jealousy when he saw us so close. It baffled him, but Claudine took his arm and kissed him to prove that all was well, and encouraged by this he pulled her on to his knee and kept her until the red kettle on the gas stove whistled half-time and made him ease her off and rush into the scullery.

It was my turn and I lost no time about it. I sucked her mouth and closed those heavy eyes, my leg forcing hers apart so that she breathed hard and I thought I'd got her on my hands for life, until I remembered Alfie in the kitchen, at which I put my hand down and almost into her drawers.

She hissed like a snake and pushed me away. 'You dirty bastard!'

'What's going on?' said Alfie.

'He knows,' she said, tight-lipped and scarlet.

'I only asked if she'd got a sister I could be introduced to,' I said. 'But I know when I'm not wanted. You can keep your tea and sandwiches. I hope it gets cold and stale while you get stuck into your hearthrug pie and can't get out. I won't stay where I'm not welcome.'

From the scullery door I added a bit more, and Alfie hovered in a worried fashion, trying to get a word in, while his girlfriend stood with her face even tenser, as if feeling guilty already at any falsehoods I might throw into their den. 'Another thing,' I added, staring at Claudine so that Alfie turned pale. 'As far as I know I'm not the only bastard in this room, and maybe not the only dirty one, either.'

'Shurrup,' Alfie screamed, pushing me out so hard that I turned and pushed him back half across the room. I went of my own accord, slamming the door with less force than either of them expected.

I forgot about her in the next few days, because I was hard at it trying to get a date with one of the shopgirls at work who'd caught me reading a book in the warehouse and, on seeing what it was, thought I might be interesting enough to get to know. So one Saturday morning as I was walking up Wheeler Gate in the sunshine, I saw Claudine coming down the same side of the street, and I greeted her as if we were friends from long ago.

'What do you want?' she snapped, stopping nevertheless. She wore a purple summer coat and thick red lipstick, dark stockings, and a hairstyle puffed high.

My wanting her came back, and the fact that this might have been because she was Alfie's steady girlfriend didn't bother me a bit. 'I've been hoping I'd bump into you,' I said, 'to say I was sorry for running out on you the other night.'

'Is that *all* you're sorry about?' she said.

'If it comes to that,' I answered, 'maybe you ought to apologize to me as well, for what you called me.'

'What did you expect, shoving your hand up my clothes like that. I just came right out with it.'

'I didn't know what I was doing.'

'P'raps next time you will.'

'I hope so. I'm not usually a dirty beast. Only sometimes.'

'That's too often for me,' she said.

'Not according to Alfie,' and I watched her go so red I didn't notice the coat or lipstick any more. 'Did I say something wrong?' I added, as if trembling for my sinful way of talking. 'Alfie and me are old pals, right from birth. We talk a lot to each other. It don't mean much, duck.'

She got out a few words at last: 'He said he'd stopped seeing you, after that night. He swore he'd never talk to you again.'

'You know how it is,' I said, 'we're old mates. It ain't so easy for him. Maybe he meant to break it off bit by bit. Don't think Alfie's a liar. He's one of the best.'

'I'll tell him a thing or two.'

I asked her not to: 'It ain't worth it if you're going steady. Why break it up for a thing like this? Let's go into that Lyons on Long Row for a cup of tea.' She looked around, as if to find her mother there and ask if it would be all right. 'Everybody talks about everybody else,' I said, 'but nobody thinks any the worse. I could tell you a few things that happen at the place I work at, but I'm sure you've heard it all before, so why bother?'

Over a cup of tea, she said bitterly: 'I suppose Alfie told you everything about me?'

'Only that you were going steady, and that that made it all right, whatever you did between you.' I was anxious to get off this topic, because though it had served its purpose in bringing us closer together than I'd expected, it might now shove us apart if it went on too long. I wanted to get off with Claudine, not push her into a quarrel with Alfie which might only get them back into an even cosier hugger-mugger. Nor did I want to discuss their problems as if I was her brother. If we'd been in a more private place I'd have done something as daring as I had on the first night, just to bring us back to reality, and with this in mind I touched her wrist across the table and, when this wasn't repulsed, made a brief stroke at her knee under the table, but only for a second so that not having had time to push it away she began to wonder whether I'd done it at all. Which was all right by me because she didn't even blush, of which I was glad because when she did it made her look angry, an expression which took away the few good looks she had.

'I've just been around the bookshops,' I told her, 'but there wasn't much worth buying this morning. I usually call at them on Saturday. I like to get through a couple of books a week.'

'I didn't think you were like that. You looked a bit rough the other night.'

'That's because I wasn't wearing my best. I didn't expect you to be at Alfie's. It was a very pleasant surprise.'

'You didn't act very nice, either.'

'Don't get back to that, Claudine. I didn't know what I was doing. I can be polite – but not all the time. It's all right for Alfie, because he was brought up on bread and treacle, and iodine tea.'

She laughed: 'Was he? He never told me that.'

'I've known him since we was in nappies together.'

'What happened to his father, then?'

'He was killed in the war, like mine.'

'I was beginning to think he'd never had one,' she said. 'I'd never go with anybody like that.'

'Why didn't he tell you straight?' I said, riled at having to stick up for him like this. 'His old man was drowned off the coast of Norway. Mine was bombed in Egypt. Same thing.'

'That makes a big difference,' she said. 'He died for his country.'

'Lots did. It didn't do them much good, though. Have another tea?'

'I've got to go,' she said. 'I'm late already. I was supposed to do some shopping.'

'It's Sunday tomorrow,' I said. 'Meet me after dinner and we'll go for a walk.'

'I'm not sure about that,' she pouted with those dangerous red lips. When she smiled she showed her teeth, and I liked that.

'Bring Alfie if you like. We'll all go for a walk. He might like that.' She agreed to this when I put her on the bus, and I was in such confused and happy fettle that I went back to the bookshop and saw four titles straight away that interested me. Next day Claudine turned up alone, as I had hoped she would.

If there's anything better than reading books, it's going out with a young girl. A book takes you into another world, but a girl stamps you into the soil. Or, rather, you stamp her into the soil, or try to when you're on top of her behind some bushes and you're dying to go on that longest journey into the sweetest night of all. One time I would plead, the next I would bully, then I'd be silent and try pressing my own way onwards like a bull, but for months I never got anywhere. We lay between the trees in Shaws Plantation, away from everyone in the summer silence. I lit a cigarette, and passed it to her, then did one for myself. She was ruffled a bit, in her wine-dark velvet dress, and was glad of the soothing smoke.

'Alfie's had it often enough off you,' I complained, 'so I don't know why you're holding out.'

'Alfie and I are going steady, and that makes all the difference.'

'*We* can go steady if you like.'

'You only say that to get what you want,' she answered sharply, fastening the top button of her blouse which had come undone in the scrabble.

'So does Alfie, I expect.'

'He doesn't. He really means it when he says we're going steady.'

'Me too,' I protested, so thwarted I could have paralysed her, thinking that if I heard that mincing phrase about 'going steady' once more I'd kill whoever said it and lob myself off Castle Rock.

The kisses came soft and fulsome, but they weren't what I wanted unless they paved the footpath to the end which I had in view. She moaned and hugged and bit my ear but whenever my hand strayed close, her eyes opened wide with the stony lift of common-sense and she froze away from me. I was baffled, and didn't know how to go on, and more than once I left her late at night, feeling full of rage at the rice pudding down my leg. She worked in the City Combine offices, and scorned me for the fact that I was an errand boy. She could never love me because she didn't respect me, yet I wasn't the sort to show myself at her beck and call by trying to 'get on'. What kept her interested in me was my ancient friendship with Alfie, as well as my mysterious ability to read books that she could hardly understand. But I kept on and on at her in the hope that tomorrow or next week our love-life would take the great leap forward. I hung on like a drunken man at a one-armed bandit, always hoping for the jackpot. It occurred to me in my frustrated misery that maybe she was taking it out on me to keep herself going nice and lovely with Alfie. The only way I could get it was by straightforward rape, and though I was strong I didn't feel strong enough for that. Alfie didn't know about our weekly meetings, and at first, when I had hopes, I didn't want him to get to know, whereas in those early days Claudine wouldn't have minded if he had found out, because I think in some way she wanted to get her own back on him for having supposedly spilled the beans to me about their love-life. But as time went on, meaning weeks, but they seemed like years, I began to see that there might be some advantage in letting him know what was happening, or at least telling Claudine that this was in my mind. I was slowly brought to this, seeing that, as time still went on, the idea of Alfie getting to know appealed less and less to her, because of the precautions she began to take when arranging to meet me. Not having it while I was in full blood sharpened my wits and understanding, which is something to be said for it.

We sat in a coffee bar on Parliament Street, where both of us had met straight out of work. We had a cake to hold back the gnawing starvoes, and I was trying to persuade her to come up Strelley where we could fan out into the fields and woods. But, though it was dry and still daylight I couldn't make much headway. 'I don't feel like it,' she said. 'It's too much bother, going all that way. You can see me home, though.'

'Are you meeting Alfie?' I asked, a sudden suspicion.

'I want to watch television. Mam had one come yesterday. Bought it out of her savings. Dad would never buy anything because he don't earn that much.'

She wanted me to go home and watch television with her, seated between her struggling happy-saver parents, but I had another idea. 'I saw Alfie last night,' I said, in all innocence. At this, she had a very uneasy glint in her eyes. 'We just talked about this and that,' I added. 'Nowt unusual.'

'Is that all?'

'He did seem a bit worried. Have another cake? Go on. I'll treat you to it.'

She was too interested to eat. 'What was up with him? Did he say?'

'He did, but it was between mates.'

'Did he make you promise not to tell anybody?'

I smiled: 'He didn't need to.'

The cake had smeared her lipstick, and she took a mirror from her handbag to smooth it right. 'Was it about me?'

'He's got his eyes on another girl and he's wondering whether to chuck you up.'

Her lip trembled: 'You're a liar.'

'I told him he'd be a fool to pack you in. I talked and talked to him, so I don't think he will now.'

She looked around the coffee bar, as if to make sure no one might recognize us and clatfart the news to Alfie. If *that* happened, he really would pack her in. She stood up. 'I'm going now. On my own. Don't follow me.'

'You're going to see Alfie?'

She wasn't a very good liar, so didn't try: 'Yes.'

'You're wasting your time. He isn't in tonight. He told me he was going up Carlton to see his grandma.' She looked done for at this news, believing me all along the line, though I don't know how she could have been so stupid. I held her hand and pressed it so that she could feel my love. 'You might as well come up Strelley with me. It's fine out, and you'll enjoy a bit of country air.'

She sat down again, and I got her another cup of tea. 'I'm going home,' she said, 'that's the best thing.'

Now it was my turn to stand up: 'If that's how you feel. I'm fed up with this. I've got a date at half past six with a girl from our place, who comes in from Tibshelf every day. She's a smasher.'

'Don't *you* like me any more then?' Claudine said.

'Course I do. But I just want to get out of this dump and go for a walk.'

Half an hour later we were passing the Broad Oak pub on the lane towards Strelley, arm in arm. There were some two hours of daylight left, and a warm breeze blew in from the fields. 'Feeling better?' – and she answered glumly that she was all right. We turned left after the church and made our way into Spring Wood. A courting couple were snogging on the path in front, so I said: 'Let's get farther in off the path.' She didn't want to, so I thought it was time to say: 'Let's go and have it together. I'm dying for you, Claudine. You're the first girl I've been in love with, and we've known each other for months. It's all right now.' I pulled her to me, and we met in a wonderful kiss under the heavy rustling leaves.

'No,' she said, when I put my hand on her leg. I pushed them apart, and she wondered what was coming.

'I'm going to see Alfie in my dinner hour tomorrow, and I'll tell him what's been going on between us all this time.'

'Oh!' she exclaimed. 'How could you be so rotten?'

'Because I want you. You drive me crazy. But I'll tell him, and then he'll go to this new girl he's got his eyes on. *I'll* pack you in as well.'

She laughed it off: 'There's plenty of other pebbles on the beach.'

I laughed as well. 'The sea's a long way away, and at Skegness it's all sand.'

She stood silent for a while, then said solemnly: 'Do you mean it?'

I swore that I did, so she took my hand and said: 'All right, then.'

'What do you mean?' – I wanted it straight and from her own lips.

'You can do it to me.'

We found a place, and after passionate kisses she lay down,

head back on the grass and her legs open. She was warm and somehow her lips were peppery, mixed with the sweetness of her lipstick that seemed to be sliding all over me. I pushed up and took down everything, and after fingering her for some minutes my flesh-rod went sliding chock-a-block into her, and before I began going up and down I made her large breasts spread loose. Then after only a few goes I had the top of my head blown off with sweetness, and just after this she started to shift and bite, before I shrank out of her.

I felt sorry she'd only done this with me on condition I wouldn't spoil things between her and Alfie, and arm in arm on the way back I was jealous of him for the first time. But I needn't have been, for though I'd used false words to get her into that wood, the more I saw her after that the less she met Alfie, until we were going steady together, and having it marvellously several times a week in various fields and parks. When our hands clasped on meeting out of work we couldn't breathe till that smell of grass and full-grown leaves got into our noses. We'd thread our way through hidden paths, branching off from them and hiding absolutely from the world, living in our own house where we could all but strip naked under the trees, and I could bury myself deep into the first love of my life. Both of us wanted it, but she sometimes made it hard for me, so that I had to cajole and struggle, though this was doubly sweet because the end was certain.

After a few weeks of this man-and-wife play I got familiar and facetious, and on our way back from the woods one night I asked if she used to have it so good with my old pal Alfie.

She stopped under a lamp-post and looked at me very seriously: 'Shall I tell you something? Shall I, Michael?' Not waiting for me to say yes or no: 'I will tell you, though. I never had it with Alfie Bottesford. Never. I don't care whether you believe me or not, but I'm telling the truth. He'd never dare, because when he tried and I put him off (as Mam always said I had to do) he never came back for me but got downhearted and sulked. So in all the time we went together it never came to it.'

We walked on and I was all of a sweat. We were 'going steady' and the full force of these soul-treading words came to me now, because if she hadn't been having it with Alfie, then my little plan to ensnare her into having it with me had done nothing more than ease me into getting ensnared by her. It was hard to say who had set out to get who, but we had certainly got each other now, and that was a fact. She took my arm and leaned on my shoulder as if heaven were about to open and belt down the chimes of multiple church bells on to us. Passing a bus-stop queue I felt as if people were weighing us up in their different ways, thinking that there went another nice young couple to the altar in a few more months. An old man seemed to smile and smirk in the twilight and I felt like thumbing my snout and saying: 'That's what you bloody-well think, mate.' But I squeezed my sweetheart's hand, and kissed her when we reached the shadow of a hedge.

'I thought you was a bit quiet,' she said. 'I hope that made you feel better.'

'It did, duck.'

'Are you coming home with me tonight, Michael?'

'I don't think so. I'll miss the last bus.'

'Tired?'

'Not me.' But I wouldn't go to her house because that would put the seal on it, for if her parents liked us, we were as good as engaged, and this I couldn't stomach. There'd been a terrible rash of early marriages at work among the nineteen-year-olds, and I sometimes got the liver-jitters at Claudine's seriousness. It seemed as if I was being dragged towards a chute not too far in front, and that once on the brink I'd fall into a canning machine and come out at the other end with Claudine in the same tin marked IDEAL MARRIAGE. Where I got this terror from I don't know, though I suppose it was natural at such an age. Perhaps I didn't feel like getting tangled in something my mother had never entered into. She was one of those free and independent women who believed they were the equal of any man providing they didn't get married, so we got on well together as long as we didn't say much about the way we wanted to live. As a child she'd been thin in the frame, but now she was nearing forty and had put on weight. Men were still like flies around her, though she rarely brought them to the house. When she did I kept out of the way, for I was embarrassed at her getting from them what I was now so assiduously giving to Claudine.

I was absorbed in what I called the three -ings: reading, working, and fucking, and I did all three to the best of my time and ability. But now that I was beginning to feel too tightly held in my closeting with Claudine, I saw that after all one wasn't made as wise by reading good books as I had thought. I could read, but not at the same time learn, which made it all seem a bit of a gyp, till I laughed it off on realizing that good books were only as much of an escape from the world as sex-and-gangster stories. The solution to this was not to give up reading, which had hit me early as a cure to some disease whose name I did not know, but to go on getting more out of life on the one hand, and learning more from it on the other. There's no doubt I was mixed up in my feelings, but at least I wasn't crazy in it as well. Believing this only proved how crazy I really was, though the assumption that I had cool sense stopped me going round in circles, and at least led me to feel I was the most important person in the world.

In the factory, I was tolerated more than employed, though I must have been worth the eight pounds handed to me every Friday night. I carried bales of cloth from the stores to the cutting rooms, sometimes loading finished garments on lorries that drew up to the warehouse bay. The one advantage was getting suits of clothes at a discount, and occasionally for nothing when I worked up nerve enough to walk brazenly out with one wrapped in my overalls. In spite of my slackness, some intelligence had been noted when I suggested a way of speeding up the transport of cloth from one department to another, and the general manager asked one day if I wouldn't like to work in the office. Wallace Pushpacker had been a major in the Army, had a blustery face and a thick ginger moustache, and I believe he expected me to jump at the chance as a kind of promotion, but he was taken by surprise when I said in a voice as quick and sharp as his that I'd like to think about it first.

When I went off to load another trolley, having left Push-packer baffled and irritable, I was trembling with the effort of putting the pros and cons of his offer through my machinating mind. It would be a clean job with more money and shorter hours, but on the other hand I dreaded the effect on Claudine. Such news would only confirm that I had it in me after all to GET ON, and was therefore the ONE FOR HER. An engagement would not be more than a few weeks off, and if I didn't agree to it, it would mean the end of my delicious and fleshly privileges. So I told myself, and I may not have been far wrong, that having asked Pushpacker to let me think it over was considered so much of a cheek that even if I went back and said yes, he'd tell me the job was no longer available because I wasn't the right material to accept the discipline of office life that his Army rule imposed. In the end I left the factory altogether, and decided to look for some other work.

To Claudine this was as bad as if I'd turned down her suggestion of an engagement, because she looked upon me as a scatterbrained idler who couldn't keep any job for long. 'I only left to get a better place,' I said, sitting in her parlour one night when her parents were out. 'That was a dead-end joint, and I thought you didn't like me being there. Now I'll be able to get something better, maybe even in an office.'

She came across to me on the settee: 'Oh, Michael, that would be wonderful. I'd really know then that you were serious. You ought to look in the *Evening Post* and see what you can find. I'll help you.' She went into the kitchen and came back with the newspaper, holding it like a great white sheet, as if to smother me.

There was a homely passion between us that night, and we sat close and petted each other, though afraid to lay down to it in case somebody should suddenly come back to the house. Such clandestine satisfaction made the air deeper between us than if we had been in the freedom of the wood. I went home with six addresses of various city firms in my wallet, and promised faithfully to go bright and early to each one next morning.

I avoided decisions by thinking too far ahead, by wanting Fate to act for me. When it did I complained and cursed, but that was all right because by then it was too late. I didn't mind what happened to me, as long as there was no possibility that I could have made things any better. Because of that I learned early to have no vain regrets, and never to recall the lost chances that, had I taken them, might have made life easier for me.

True to my promise, I put on the best suit I had ever stolen, which would have cost twenty guineas if I'd bought it in a shop, and called at the first office by half past nine. I was fairly all right in my appearance, being five feet ten in height and, in spite of the lackadaisical style of work since leaving school, far from beefy about it. In fact what with steaming off so often with Claudine and walking umpteen miles a week with her, I could almost be described as slim, and perhaps this as much as anything else made me look as if I had some wits about me. There was also something in my manner that made me seem a year or two older than I was, possibly connected as well to my manly practices with Claudine, and augmented by that worry of getting in so deep with her that I wouldn't be able to shuffle out. Concern with worldly preoccupations was stamped quite clearly on my face, for I'd noticed it one morning gazing in the mirror before shaving, and since it suited me I decided to cultivate the picture it gave to my features, no matter how false it might be. This is only to explain that I got the second job I applied for, which was that of general run-about at Pitch and Blender's, the estate agents in town.

It seemed as if a river, five hundred yards wide, separated me from the last work I was at. At this new place I was never told what to do. I was always asked – though if I refused I'd have been thrown out on my neck just like in any other dead-end job. But I was puffed up with snakey pride, and on meeting Claudine after my first day, she had tears of dewy joy in her eyes. She talked to me, when she'd cleared her throat, about how I must be 'obliging' and 'show willing' in my new 'situation', said I must never be late, and always wear a clean suit. This was all very well, I informed her, but when I was told to run out now and again for tea or coffee from the nearby bar, I didn't much fancy the slops and stains that made my suit look like a map of the moon.

Yet it was so easy that I stuck it, and in a few weeks I was no longer sent to get tea because a new youth was taken on. I cyclostyled details of houses for sale in Nottingham and the country, as well as taking over Miss Bolsover's desk while she went to lunch (it was lunch now, not dinner) and answering the telephone. The blunt edges of my accent went in record time. I got through my first months by playing the silent man, as far as I could, listening to other people's speech, and copying the mannerisms of Mr Weekley, the boss.

I suppose I'm obliged to show how much I suffered at changing from one 'class' of job to another, how impressed I was at handling a typewriter and duplicating machine instead of a capstan-lathe or Jacquard-cutter. Maybe I ought to say what clothes people wore and tell of the witty things they said, how they talked about house deals and money, and making good marriages, and spending a pound on a haircut and five bob for a cup of coffee. But all this meant nothing – and in any case I've forgotten what effect it had on me. Swimming in the sea, all you want to do is keep the salt out of your mouth. You fix your gaze on the horizon, even if it's only a few feet away at the top of the next wave.

Yet when I met any of my friends who still slogged in factories I used my homeliest Radford accent, just to show that I wasn't being influenced by the toffee-nosed set I was now forced by my peculiar and unavoidable streak of perversity to associate with. This patronizing bonhomie, this twisted attempt to put things back as they were, when in a way it had always been too late, didn't usually go down very well, for I'd be met by a combination of cynical smile and blank stare, or a simple request to bogger off out of the way.

I often put on this broad accent in front of Claudine when I sensed she was thinking that, since I had been caught in the treadmill of getting on at work, she might now begin to draw me close into another sort of trap. At such times I could sound so low and ignorant that, judging by her look of unconcealed dislike, it seemed as if her heart had become a plastic bag full of ice cubes. At times it was the only defence I had, a thin red line of real blood holding me back from the land of milk and water beyond. Still, by all the rules of the heart (whatever they are: I still don't think I know) I ought to admit that I was in love with Claudine.

Because of something now and again in her appearance of the way that her intentions always turned out to be rea and her low-grade homilies being invariably right, I got the feeling that she was a lot older than me, and than she said she was, so that now and again I went to sleep in a sweat of panic. This was only my imagination, though the thought was so potent that I often felt people looking at us and wondering why I was going out with an older girl. Yet it was so marvellous making love to her, and I hoped she thought so too, that we soon felt we actually owned the woods and fields that had become so familiar to us. I was only put off this state of paradise by her nagging at me to get on. I didn't know where she'd got it from, certainly not her parents, because I found out that her mother was a member of the Communist Party and that her father drove a lorry and couldn't care less about anything except his twenty quid a week. Yet it only came to her in fits and starts, and as long as I stayed on the alert I felt I could handle it.

But it stuck in my craw, really, when she got on to me about saving money. This actually frightened me, not because I was incapable of it, but because I knew what she wanted me to use it for. The fact was, and she didn't know it because it was more than my neck was worth to tell her, that I'd been saving money ever since starting work four years ago. It was part of my nature to do so. I did it very carefully and secretly because if I let on about it to Mam she'd ask me now and again to lend her some. And how can you ask your mother to pay it back, or even accept it if she should offer to? So I'd had practice at keeping the fact to myself. Not that it amounted to much: just over a hundred pounds, but I guarded it like a miser without knowing what I would ever use it for. So when Claudine asked me to start saving money I was afraid that out of pride and to please her, I might in a weak moment let on that I'd already been doing so for a long time.

The one occasion I broke into my savings was to buy a superfine, capacious, pigskin lock-up briefcase that I took to work every morning and that cost twelve pounds. I made sure there was always a good book inside, provided free by the library, as well as my morning copy of *The Times* discreetly hidden. I also read books on architecture and surveying, not that I was hoping to learn anything and take exams, but merely to be able to follow conversations which took place around me. At first it had seemed as if I were living in the dark, because practically everything said was incomprehensible to me. I'd always had a horror of the dark, but in this instance I knew I'd be able to remedy it. I began to use my knowledge in conversation, and then the light really did shine on me, so much so that Mr Weekley suggested I might be far more useful to the firm than I was at present if I had driving lessons and got a licence. So for a while I took one every morning, at the firm's time and expense. When the instructor asked if I'd had any previous experience I didn't mention the time when, at the age of six, I'd let off the brakes of a man's van and got it trundling down the street into a privet hedge.

I may have been in the dark for a while, but never so much as the man called Wainfleet who turned up at our office every day looking for a house to buy. He was probably known at every estate agent's in the city, and had been coming to Pitch and Blender's for at least six months, so the others told me, calling several times a week and always at exactly eleven in the morning. An offer was made to put him on our mailing list, but he preferred the human contact of visiting us, in case anything good turned up, so that he could then get straight out and see it. A twenty-four-hour delay till the notification reached him might cause somebody else to get there first, and make a deposit while he was still reading the particulars over breakfast – which seemed to be the only nightmare he ever had.

He was more than forty years old, always wearing the same suit of salt-and-pepper drag, and a mackintosh of military cut, as well as a dark green hat with the faintest of feathers in it. His clean-shaven face was slightly flushed, with ordnance-survey veins on the cheeks, and his brown eyes turned anxious on coming in, as if he thought somebody might have been just before him and hared off to see the house that he himself had been dreaming about all his life. 'Good morning,' he'd say, putting a good face on it. 'I've called to see whether you might know of a country place for sale in the vicinity – eight rooms, up to four thousand pounds. Could go a chip higher for something special.'

He played it as if he were seeing us for the first time, and while I went through the books with him he chatted affably about how factory strikes should be illegal, and how bad the weather was. Now and again, he'd ask one of us to show him a house that sounded interesting, but he'd invariably come back dejected because he said he saw signs of wet rot, dry rot, rising damp, or death-watch beetle – sometimes all of them together. Or he found it too noisy, not sufficiently isolated, not enough garden, too close to a farmyard; or the ground was low-lying and might be subjected to river floods in spring. Sometimes it was too near an aerodrome, or he'd mention train whistles in the distance that nobody else could hear, or he thought that the presence of a colliery eight miles away might bring a risk of subsidence, so that one morning his bed would slide so far into the earth that a group of colliers with their picks and lamps would suddenly open their broad grins into his waking up. If all these conditions didn't exist he'd say it was a pity the house hadn't got central heating, or that he thought, on reflection, that he might after all need an extra room, or that on thinking it over the price seemed a bit too high.

For all these vacillations, he appeared to be, when coming briskly through the door, a man who'd been used to making quick and firm decisions all his life, and who perhaps still did in whatever his work was. Nobody had ever lost patience with him. Mr Weekley had once taken him over personally, and after showing him one very suitable property that no one else had yet seen, actually brought him to the point of getting him to make an offer for it, which was accepted. Wainfleet then had the house surveyed, and all seemed to be going through to the expected conclusion, but then he lost his nerve and pulled out, with the tale that his surveyor had told him the place would fall down if he slammed the door too hard.

'So we don't pay much attention to him,' Weekley told me. 'You'll get used to such people. They're serious, but can't make up their minds. They don't even want you to make up their minds for them. Years ago I saw one man taken from this office straight to the lunatic asylum. He'd screwed himself up so tight over the months he'd been looking at houses that he just exploded one day, challenged us all to fisticuffs, and then wrecked the office before he was taken off. There aren't many like that, mind you, but you get them now and again, and they plague the life out of us. Some of the worst are married couples who come around saying they are wanting a house, not the ones who were married last week, but those who've been married six or seven years and are looking for a place to stop the marriage breaking up. Estate agents run quite a service! Thank the Lord most people are able to make decisions, even though they are the wrong ones. But I expect we shall get rid of Wainfleet sooner or later, one way or the other.'

He came back after a fortnight, during which Mr Weekley lost his irritation, and began his search all over again. One morning another and younger client was going out, holding a foolscap sheet with the details of a property on it, and called to us: 'All right. I'll drive out and have a look at it right away. Sounds just the thing.'

Wainfleet stopped halfway to the counter, his face white, as if he had lost the only chance in his life by just five minutes. 'What was it?' he stammered. 'Is it something new?'

I laughed: 'It's only a bungalow near Farnsfield. Wouldn't suit you, Mr Wainfleet.'

It was, in fact, exactly what he was looking for.

'You're lying,' he cried.

I thought he was going to punch me, so jumped back a bit. 'Tek another step forward, and I'll brain yer.'

He went down at this: 'Sorry. Shouldn't have said that.'

There was nobody else in the outer office, and an idea came to me, vague and newborn as it was: 'Listen,' I said in a low voice, leaning over to him, 'I'll get you that house, if you want it. But it costs four thousand three hundred, and no offers.' I thought that in his quest for hearth and home he needed an extra bit of personal service to make him think that, not only was the house unique, but that the rest of the world was all right as well, since he who was doing him the favour (meaning me) knew his place in it.

My hands shook in case somebody came from the inner

office: 'The bloke who went to look at it in his sports car is bound to pay a deposit as soon as he sees it. He's been coming at twelve o'clock every day for the last three years. I don't know why, but he came at half past ten today. Still, don't worry, sir. If you really want it I should be able to pull it off for a good client like yourself. I'll meet you in the Eight Bells tomorrow at one o'clock. Keep the afternoon free to look at it. Got that?'

When he went I typed a sheet giving full particulars of the house, but putting the price at three hundred pounds more than the four thousand asked for, so that I could show it to Wainfleet next day.

Mr Weekley came in and saw I was trembling and as white as clay. 'My God, Cullen, what's the matter with you?'

'I don't know, sir. Seem to have the flu.'

'It's a bit slack, so you'd better go home.'

'I'll be all right after lunch, Mr Weekley.'

'Do as I tell you,' he snapped. 'Sleep it off.'

I sniffed: 'Perhaps you're right, sir.'

'Of course I bloody-well am.'

They thought a lot of me at that firm, but I was crazy enough to imagine they'd go on doing so for ever. Not that I had any intention of being there all that long, but at least I expected to leave only when I was ready, under my own good steam. Instead of going home I took a bus to Farnsfield to see Mr Clegg, who owned the house that was for sale.

It was a long job getting round to my real business, because first of all Clegg showed me over the house because I said I was interested in it, thinking that I wanted to buy it. If I'd had the money I would have, since it had good flower and vegetable gardens at the back and a landing-ground lawn at the front, as well as an orchard and paddock. There was no better spot for Claudine and myself to sport in as man and wife, without troubles and for ever and ever, not even an amen necessary to see us into heaven. Maybe it was the accidental sight of this Georgian fairy-box house that set my thoughts bending at last towards hers.

After lots of argy-bargy it appeared that the man in the sports car had offered the full asking price, and Clegg had accepted it. He told me that the house was too big for him, since his wife and kids had left. All he wanted was a small flat in Leicester, where he had relations, not to mention a few friends.

'You see, I'd been married twenty-eight years, and then my wife goes off with a man twenty years younger than she is, and I'm left high and dry with this house on my hands. I hate it so much I can't wait to get out of it. I don't suppose you'd understand, being so young, but after twenty-eight years it's as if the world's been pulled from under your feet. Too many memories. They're like poisonous snakes. Every one kills me. We were so happy, you've no idea. Happiness unlimited. I was an engineer at the pit, and retired last month. A lifetime of hard work and married bliss. Do you think a man can ask for more than that? He can't. You're too young to understand. It must be wonderful, being too young to understand. If only we could stay that way! I suppose I did stay that way, because when she said she was leaving a year ago I was so shocked I knew she couldn't be joking. At least she waited till my son and daughter were grown up and out of the happy home. I'll say that for her. Funnily enough, no sooner had she gone than I saw how right she'd been to go. The next thing was, I wondered why she'd waited so long. Number three thought came when I got angry at not having gone myself, before she did. Then during the long nights number four came when I cursed at the fact that we'd ever got married at all. Number five was when I wished I'd never met her. Last of all, number six, was when I sat here and wished I'd never been born. But I'm over that now, and just want to get out of this bloody house – and get the best possible price for it.'

I heard his life story while he made us a cup of tea, then put my question to him: 'How would you like to get three hundred more for your house? I have a buyer who'll pay that, if it takes his fancy. There'll have to be a little consideration in it for me, though.'

He didn't like this, threatened to go back to Pitch and Blender's and tell them, but I told him I didn't care if he got me the sack or not because I was all set to work elsewhere. I was just putting another two hundred in his pocket.

'Three hundred, you said,' he said.

'I did, but a hundred of it will be mine.'

After a bit more arguing he agreed, and I went away after saying that a Mr Wainfleet would come to view the place tomorrow afternoon.

I was so pleased that I walked half the road back to Nottingham. Next day I met Wainfleet in the pub, and over a glass of Youngers and a cheese cob, which he paid for, I told him to go and see the house. If he liked it he could get it for four thousand three hundred.

'And it's worth every penny of it,' I said. He was so excited he ordered a double brandy, and went on to tell me how he'd spent twenty years in the Army, and that he'd lived the last five years at Wollaton with his elder sister, whom he couldn't stand. I sympathized with him, and hoped he'd be able to straighten out his life soon, by finding the place that his heart was set on wanting. He said he wouldn't forget the favour I was doing, and that if he liked the house and got it, he'd be certain to remember my help. I told him I was only doing it out of friendship, and that he wasn't to mention my part in it to anyone at the estate agent's, because they didn't like me doing personal services such as this one, and this in his gratitude he agreed to. 'After all,' I said, 'they'll make fun of me if they know I'm soft-hearted.'

I went to Claudine's house. Her mother was at a meeting and her father had gone to the pub, so we made a play for each other even while still in the kitchen, moaning for it after the week-long separation caused by her blood-rags. The clouds were shifting and her breath smelled sweet. There was an instant rise in me, as if by some magic all the blood she'd lost had gone into my backbone. Not that I needed it, but it was plain that something special was on its way to happening, because into my intense kisses kept floating the vision of the country house I'd seen the day before, and in this picture there was a rainbow showing towards the Trent, the building itself under a shed of eternal sunshine, so that I was attacked by the sweet rat of sentimentality, so strongly in fact that I felt like fainting, as if actually getting the flu that I had shammed the day before to Weekley. I felt insane, but this view of that ideal love-house reduced me to tenderness. Her back was to the gas stove, and in my new-found consideration I saw that this wasn't comfortable, so steered her gently round the corner by the living-room door, and on up the stairs. She seemed frightened at where I wanted to go, but my soft kisses on every other step so surprised her that she daren't say anything.

'Where's your room?' I asked, my throat so parched I had to repeat it. But I opened another door showing her parents' double bed flanked by wardrobe and dressing-table, and we went in there.

'No,' she pleaded. 'No, dearest, not in here.' As if she hadn't spoken I went on kissing her till I could close the door behind us. I caught at a bedside light, which shone dimly over the counterpane. She felt terrible, I realized, having it on the place where her mother and father had always done it, and I was sorry afterwards that she hadn't enjoyed it as much as usual. But to me it was the greatest fuck of my life so far, tooling sweet Claudine on her parents' well-worn platform, as if I were getting the power and sweetness from their first ten years together. It seemed we were all in the room at the same time, wrapped and crawling among each other. Claudine's tense and tearful face had its eyes shut tight as if to get the full benefit of my kisses and tongue, as well as every other part of me. When she reluctantly came under my fingers, more tears and groans let out of her, as if it were the greatest disaster in the world, that we'd done it here – and would go on coming upstairs to the same place for it whenever we got the chance. When I lost myself in her at last, my backbone seemed to shift out of place.

We lay stupefied, not knowing what to say. Downstairs, she gave me supper of bread and cheese, and tea, which was all I wanted. The air was light blue, and it was the greatest food in the world. She sat opposite, sipping her cup of tea, and I became uneasy at her gaze. 'I don't mind getting engaged to you,' I said, 'but if we did we wouldn't be able to get married for a few years. We're both too young.'

She smiled nicely, and that was all I wanted to see, except that everything I did seemed like a trick. 'That'd be all right,' she said. 'We'd be sure of each other then, wouldn't we?'

So we decided to be engaged, though agreed not to say

anything for a few days to her parents, or to my mother who wouldn't have been all that interested anyway, except to call me a bloody fool. I made up my mind that when we announced it I'd tell Claudine about my good amount of money saved. By then I hoped to have collected the hundred from Clegg as an extra commission for helping to sell his house.

For the rest of the evening I made myself agreeable to her mother and father, so that Mrs Forks thought I was a dedicated Communist and hoped I might one day join the Young Communist League. Mr Forks pumped me about my job at the estate agent's, and I told him enough bullshit to make him suppose I'd become a big influence in the firm after I'd taken my examinations.

I missed the last bus home, but the two miles flew by me, and I didn't remember passing the usual landmarks, as if I were walking blind but on a sure radar beam that couldn't but lead me to wherever I wanted to go in the world.

The following afternoon I had to take a driving test. I was so affable to the inspector, yet careful, quick to know the rules, and at the same time go slow enough to keep cool and obey every dotted 'i' in the Highway Code, that I passed first time. This was considered a rare and famous feat in the office, and I was more stunned at it than anybody. They joked about me having slipped the tester a handful of pound notes, and we had a good laugh about it. I went to a pub with Peter Fen and Ron Butter, two of the older clerks, so that they could buy me a celebration drink, double brandies all round. We sat in the lounge of the Royal Children, smoking Whiffs I'd bought at the bar, and that I decided to smoke from then on instead of cigarettes. If I rationed myself to three a day it wouldn't be more expensive, and was bound to make a good impression. In any case, I liked the taste of them, especially with brandy, so I went to the counter for three more doubles.

Ron drove me to Aspley in his Morris, because it was on his way to Nuthall, where he lived with his newborn wife in a bungalow they'd got on a mortgage. I said goodbye and see you in the sweatshop tomorrow, swaying slightly as I made for the gate to Claudine's house.

She smelt it straight away, the ultimate sin of a man about

to become engaged, who'd strayed from his occasional half-pint and sunk to the degradation of 'shorts'. I took off my overcoat and sat down. 'It's not right,' she said. 'You reek of it. I never thought you'd start drinking whisky – at a time like this as well.'

'Brandy,' I said, lighting a Whiff.

'Please don't do it again,' she said. 'I love you, and I wouldn't want to marry anybody who drank like that.'

'I'm not *drunk*,' I said, 'honest, duck. Not on three doubles. I can tek a lot more than that.'

'You seem drunk to me.'

'That's because you're not me.'

'I'm glad I'm not, then. It's terrible, getting drunk like that.' She didn't look as nice as she had the night before, but I felt my love and sympathy too deeply for that to worry me. 'I've passed my driving test. I promise not to get drunk again.'

She said all right at this, and actually smiled. 'It'll be for your good, as well as mine, for *our* good,' was her conjugal way of putting it – 'if you really stop drinking.'

I said that in any case I didn't *like* the stuff, that it meant nothing to me, that the taste was rotten and burned my throat. All the same, she took my victorious driving test to be a great move in the war of 'getting on', saying I'd be so much more useful to the firm that I'd no doubt be given a responsible post in it soon.

Latching quickly on to her enthusiasm I went into a fantasy at how I might one day be able to save up for my own car, gloating to myself not only over the secret hoard of my savings but also about the money I was going to land from the sale of Cleggy's house.

We sat on the settee and kissed, but after a few minutes her parents came in and the television began shattering the room while supper was being put on the table. The old man thought I was even more of a lad when I told him about the driving test and the brandies, and yet, in spite of their friendly umbrella, I had a feeling of not belonging in this happy family that seemed all ready, out of the goodness of their souls, to treat me so well – even as a son. I was not really uneasy, because at the same time I felt a fundamental need to be with them and, while eating and talking, to remember the previous night when I had all but stripped Claudine and made love to her on their rich and wonderful bed. I was dead set to wallow in mother, father and wife, which was good for every string-end of me. Even though I felt an impostor who might be shown up at any moment for what I was and slung into the blustery autumn rain, I drank the unsuspecting familiarity they gave out. The thought that the real me had got at last what I actually wanted made me smile rather than become fearful as the evening wore on. I could bear this, and much more, and I felt so shifty and happy that I never stopped asking myself how much *they* could take, a vague sensation that drifted over from time to time. After several such evenings Claudine and I decided that we'd tell of our engagement on her twentieth birthday, which was to come on the following week. Everything seemed made to hold us together, even such a flimsy and insignificant secret as this.

A client came into the office and wanted to see a house that we had on our books at Mapperley, whose rough details had been advertised in the previous day's *Post*. Only Mr Weekley and I were in the office, and he had an appointment in half an hour, so when he tutted from his thin lips I offered to drive the parson-looking client to Mapperley. It appealed to Weekley: 'Think you can drive my car?'

'I passed my test, sir.'

'True. You'll never be as careful a driver as you are now, so close to your test.' He gave me the keys: 'Be doubly careful, then. It's my car.'

The fact that I had a passenger in the back gave me confidence for threading a way through the town traffic. While still obeying the rules I branched off from Mansfield Road and went on with the uphill climb, to a district of villas and large houses I hadn't much explored as a kid. Percy Parson asked: 'Have you seen the house?'

'Not yet,' I said. 'But it's supposed to be in good order.' It wasn't, though neither was it in an advanced stage of senile decay like some of the places we handled. The owners had left, and I took him from room to room, making doors shut behind me as best I could, because Weekley had always advised: 'When you're in an empty house, shut the doors of the rooms you stand in, because the client has a better feeling and can imagine how he'd live in it with his furniture. But if the house is still furnished, and the rooms cluttered with somebody else's rammel, leave the doors open, so that the client inspecting the house can see how big it would be when empty. Psychological tricks, Michael. Experience. Intuition. There's more to this business than technical qualifications!' I don't know whether or not he was right, but I always took his advice, though whether this particular bit was ever crucial in making a person buy anything I shall never know.

I felt in such a good state of mind that I showed the man over the house as if I'd spent my childhood there, and even as if my parents had grown up in it, but that now I wanted to sell it, though only with the most piercing regret, because my sweetheart lived in the delectable countryside, and I was gallant and loving enough to go and live there when we married each other. The story would have been as full of holes as the spout end of a watering-can, so I let it die a silent, undignified death.

On the way back I didn't speak, so that the client could make up his mind whether or not he wanted the house, my rhapsodies either to sink in or push him away from it for good. The fact was I had thoughts of my own, wondering when Wainfleet was going to come into the office and make his offer for Clegg's house at Farnsfield. It should already have been done, and I rehearsed an appreciative smile for when I came face to face with that hundred pounds Clegg had promised. A momentary uncertainty flitted into me now and again, and I cursed as I nearly had my lamp taken off by a delivery van moving too quickly out from the kerb.

It was expected of me that as soon as I left work I should make my way up by the post office and meet Claudine outside the Elite cinema, the point she would reach after leaving her place at the same time. It was an easy and pleasant rendezvous to keep, for a while. We would kiss and, if the sky was dry, walk up Talbot Street, leaving the city centre behind and below.

Sometimes we would go by the Ropewalk, stopping to look over the houses of the park and, on a clear day, gaze at the smoky valley of the Trent.

On one such evening, when the nights of autumn were drawing in, I felt the urge to get away from Claudine and go back home. This sensation of wanting to make a sudden escape confused me, because it was only part of my real desire at that moment, the other half of which was to go with Claudine and make love in her house. Our arms were fast and affectionately locked as we walked, and she was telling me some woe-tale of how the tyrant of a manageress at her office was threatening to make them work late as from next week if they didn't get through their day's quota by knocking-off time – or some such thing I was meant to drink in as if I were her twin sister. But I felt a definite twinge of panic drawing me towards my home, and when we reached Canning Circus I said: 'Look, sweetheart, I'll put you on a bus here. I've got to go.'

It was the simplest wish in the world, but she suspected a trick: 'Where are you going?'

'I've got to go home,' I told her.

Something was frightening me, but it only seemed to her as if I was up to no good: 'Why, what's the matter, then?'

I was foolish enough to be honest: 'I don't know, duck. I've just got to get home' – mad at myself for not knowing what was ratting at me.

'You're going to see somebody else, aren't you? Aren't you?'

I should have admitted that I was, in order to get away quickly, but I couldn't lie at that moment, because I was too disturbed, and I hated being like that, as if I were letting myself down at not being able to lie. 'Come home with me,' I said, 'then you'll see. We'll go on to your house after.'

But she wouldn't do this. I'd asked her before to come to where I lived, but she always made up some excuse not to, the truth being that having spent most of her life on an open-housing estate she was afraid of the dark cobbled streets of Old Radford. I might just as well not have spoken.

'All right,' I said, 'let's go on to your place. I won't go home.' In any case, the fear had left me, and I no longer felt the great alarm of a few minutes before. But every tack and move was the wrong one, because she now thought I'd really tried some deception on her, and that I'd only backed down when she had opposed it so firmly. All the way to Aspley she worried at me and wouldn't let go, trying to find out why I'd wanted to go off without her all of a sudden. The walk worked it out of her, yet it poisoned the whole evening so that neither of us enjoyed it. Even the kisses were tasteless, though at the last one outside her back door we both said how much we loved each other. She insisted on walking me to the bus stop, as proof of her love, but I knew it was because she wanted to make sure that I got on the right one, and didn't go off to see some other girl, even at that late hour.

When I arrived home my mother was at the table, still wearing her coat. There was a look of desolation on her face I'd never seen before.

'What's the matter?' I asked, sitting opposite without even bothering to take my mac off. She didn't answer, so I just looked, and tried to guess. The anguished premonition of my stroll through the Ropewalk with Claudine came back to me, and I held her hand.

She drew it away: 'My father's dead.'

As soon as I knew what it was my heart and stomach became normal again. My sense of wanting to die on the spot vanished absolutely and did not come back. 'Grandad?' She said nothing. 'What happened?'

'Had a heart attack at half past five. The police came and told me when I got home from work.'

'Where is he?'

'Grandma's. At Beeston. She's breaking her heart. I nearly fainted when I saw him.' She didn't say anything for a few minutes. 'They'll be taking him to Callender's funeral parlour tomorrow.'

I got up and put the kettle on: 'If you're going there in the morning I'll go with you,' I said, slashing three big spoons of tea into the pot.

'All right. You might be a help to us.'

'When are they burying him?'

'On Thursday.'

I felt fine, wonderful, and saw Grandad stretched out in the parlour next morning before they carted him away. He was sixty-five (or had been) and I considered he'd had a good life to reach such an age. From being a big man he now seemed like a doll, as if I could lift him up and sit him on my knee, speak for him like a ventriloquist. But his sternness was having none of it. He lay like an age-old soldier in a horizontal tailor-made sentrybox, but ready to get up at the split-fart of an Army bugle, or the smell of the rag they used to wipe up spilt beer on the bar with. His eyes were closed, so that he couldn't see where he was going, and though it looked as if some dreams might still be tail-ending behind his life, I knew he was surely as dead as I would ever see anyone and that God's heaven was not for the likes of him or me. We were both of us cut out for finer stuff than God's own heaven. I held his cold hand, hoping that I too would get the royal privilege of stepping into the be-all and end-all as soon as my heart stopped and the lights went out. I tweaked his ice-cold nose, kissed him on the stone forehead, and went out, to have Grandma throw her soft arms around me and wet my silk shirt through to the skin. She sobbed that I was just like him, and that no doubt I'd be as good as he ever was when I grew up. My mother was also weeping, but I thought: what the hell he lived to be old, and that should be enough for any man unless eaten up with the greatest greed of the world. They thought I had no heart and almost drove me away, till Grandma in all her soft wisdom said I was too young to let it tear me up, and that taking it like I did was the only way to show my grief.

And who knew that she wasn't right? Because in this frame of mind I did various useful errands connected with Grandad's sudden drop-out. There were payments to make and collect, various people to tell, as well as odd messages to carry to those who might come to the funeral, food to order for the party afterwards.

I went to the office with a black band around my arm to make me feel important, and Mr Weekley was sorry at my loss, impressed by such looks of grief that I could use when necessary, and told me I could stay off for a day after the funeral. I also got immediate sympathy from Claudine on telling her by phone at midday, and it blossomed to a full-blown envelopment of her body when I went to her house in the evening and found that her parents were out. It was marvellous, the grief people thought you felt, and how they were ready to shed your own tears for you, and the soft oily gratitude they gave you for giving them the opportunity of it.

Grandma wanted her dead husband to have a fair funeral, and Mother and I did our best to see that her wish was satisfied. There were three car-loads of friends and family, and I sat among them with my black suit on, seeing the occasional person by the roadside take off his hat as we went by. Standing in the rain by the open grave, and staring the box into the bottom of it, I had the mad desire, which I was hardly able to resist, to jump down and drag my mother and grandmother with me so that all three of us got buried at the same time.

I walked back to the gate and the waiting cars, and didn't care whether the world ended or not. This had nothing to do with my grandfather having died. It was almost as if I'd started something by suddenly beginning to live, but wasn't interested any more in going on to finish it.

I'd asked Claudine to come to the funeral, but she said she 'didn't like to' because she wasn't yet ready to meet my mother. The truth was that she didn't want to be connected to someone who had died, and nobody could blame her for this, because there had been moments when I hadn't been too easy about it either. Yet I wanted her to come, because it was the first opportunity in our courting that I'd been able to offer on my side something to balance the weight of her family that she had given to me from hers. It would in some way have equalized the intimacy of life between us, but she was too embarrassed to come, and I thought: so what? Why should she? Maybe she won't even go to her own grandparents' funeral, when the time comes. If I had a father of my own, I thought, instead of being the undoubted bastard that I am, I wouldn't have bothered to take so much part in it as I had.

I got really drunk that night, so that I didn't even have the stiffening left to get myself to Claudine's place as I'd promised. When I saw her the next day I said I'd been too blacked out with fond memories of my dear grandad to leave the house.

I'd hugged my bed, I told her 'in a paroxysm of grief'. She really understood that, and forgave me, giving me such comfort on the settee that I said I hoped I'd be able to do the same for her some day, if ever she needed it, though I hoped she wouldn't.

It took a long time to push house deals through, and I assumed that Wainfleet was having a surveyor go over the Clegg mansion before he made his offer. Nevertheless, I was beginning to wonder why I hadn't heard from either of them, and I knew that no news had come in at the office. Nothing would go wrong as far as I could see, and I stayed optimistic because before going out to work that morning (I hadn't yet steeled myself to calling it 'business' as they did in West Bridgford) I read my horoscope in Mam's paper which said: 'A day to remember. Financially good. Romantically sound. Don't rush it. Promotion in the air. Heady progress. Good for you.'

I went blithely to work and, as was only to be expected when I got there bright and punctual, Mr Weekley called out for me: 'Shut the door,' he said.

He didn't look good, and I wondered whether it wasn't his turn now to go down with some half-imaginary flu. He opened a folder in front of him: 'Cullen, you've been up to some monkey business, and it's the most clumsy piece of work I've ever come across in this line. If it had been a bit more subtle and underhand I might have been tempted to keep you on. As it is, you disgrace me. A bloody baby could have done better. Let me put you in the picture. Your Mr Wainfleet did offer Clegg a higher price for his house – four thousand three hundred instead of four thousand that Clegg originally wanted. I'm putting you wise so that you'll never make the same mistake again, behind the back of the person you might work for at your next job. Well, so far so good, but in comes the first chap who set out the asking price, and offers four thousand four hundred. Then Clegg plays him off in a dutch auction, and Wainfleet, red in the face, ups it to four thousand five hundred. Do you see what you started? You bloody jackanapes!'

46

I was boiling too: 'That's all right by you,' I cried, 'as far as commission's concerned, isn't it?'

'Oh, yes. But let me tell you the last of it. Then comes the bright young chap *again*, and jacks it up to four thousand six hundred. There it stops, and yesterday while you were away getting those ordnance-survey plans, enter Wainfleet absolutely frothing at the mouth, and accusing me of using innocent young you as a pawn to start a dutch auction, and positively screaming that he was going to make a complaint to the Society. Well, of course, I can take care of that. In any case that vile vendor Clegg wasn't entirely innocent when he saw which way the wind was blowing. But you've got to go, young Cullen. You can take your briefcase and umbrella, and remember next time to think before trying to push something so intricate. Oh, yes, I know, you nearly brought it off, but don't forget: there's always some swine a bit greedier than you are.'

'I didn't expect anything from Clegg,' I said. 'I was only trying to do the firm a favour so that you'd think highly of me and I could get on a bit. Anyway, they were both bidding for the house on the open market. What's wrong with that? It was nothing to do with me.'

'Don't lie, Michael. You make it hard for me, mate. I've got the particulars of the house here that you typed for Wainfleet, with your fancy price on it. Oh, all right, there's more to you than the others working here, but I can't keep you on. However, I'll give you a fair reference so that you might get a job somewhere else. But wherever it is, try not to pull such monkey business again. It'll get you a bad name.'

I couldn't be sure of a wink under his glasses, but wanted to thump his putty cheeks and grey moustache so as to stop the trembling in both my legs – except that I didn't want to end up in a cell at the Guildhall at that particular moment.

I took my fortnight's pay and insurance money, and said goodbye with regret to Miss Bolsover. 'It's a shame you got into trouble,' she said, 'but don't worry.'

I smiled. 'Glad to get away, really. I've been thinking of moving on to London' – another useless lie, for she was bound to see me around town sooner or later and wonder why I hadn't had the guts to go. She was a proud, grey-haired woman, well into her thirties, who I often fancied knuckling into because there seemed no hope of it.

There was only one person I wanted to see at that moment, and it was still early enough in the day to go out and find him. In fact a few hours in the country would do me good after the mental strain of getting the sack. I'd wheedled from Miss Bolsover the information that the bright young man had sent in his deposit cheque on Clegg's house for four hundred and sixty pounds, so I'd be due for at least a hundred pounds when the contract was signed, though I wondered now whether Clegg the egg would keep to it.

The fields and woods weren't half so pleasant, for a sharp wind was shaking itself out from Lincolnshire, and even a thick tweed overcoat didn't stop it finding my ribs. Walking through it from the bus stop, the full shock of getting my cards hit me, and I wondered whether in this life I was only destined to work in a factory where I could get into nothing more troublesome than walking out now and again with whatever was produced there bulging from my pockets. My natural move should have been to retreat, to get back and let my heart curl up in safety where no blow-through mistakes could get at it. But natural moves were already alien to me, and I was set on some course even more natural than my natural desires because I didn't think one bit about what I was going to do.

Clegg asked me into a room just inside the door, where he had a sort of office or study. He hadn't shaved for a few days and the stubble, like his hair, was grey. I sat down, when he asked me to, in an armchair. On the wall behind was a framed railway map of England. I was left alone while Arthur Clegg went hospitably into the kitchen to make some tea. I don't know what he thought I'd come for, because he asked nothing and said nothing, imagining perhaps in the quirky darkness of his mind that I just happened to be passing and had called in. But his grey shallow eyes showed him to be far more alive to the world than I was, and while he was busy with his teapot and old cups he'd left a record on his pick-up, playing part of what I knew to be Handel's *Messiah*. I supposed he spun this sort of music all day to stop himself going sideways up the wall till he got the hell out of his gloomy house. I wondered why I had come, now that I was here, and the voice was telling me that the trumpet shall sound, while I didn't know how to get to the point because I knew he knew he didn't have to give me a blue penny for the favour I'd done him.

He asked how I was getting on, and I saw that the only thing I could do was be dead honest and tell him I'd just been booted out of my job on his behalf. He smiled at this: 'That's the way of the world. What did you expect?'

I wasn't ready to let things go as easily, and said I was glad to hear he'd got four thousand six hundred for his house: 'That was due only to me, and you shouldn't forget it.'

'Oh, I won't, my lad,' he said, putting half a biscuit between his false teeth. 'Not in a hurry, anyway.'

'It'll take me a good while to get another job,' I said, 'and I'll need a bit to tide me over. A hundred and fifty would see me right.'

'You've upped your price?' he grinned.

I was beginning to dislike the way he too obviously played with me, and wished I'd brought a blunt instrument to threaten him with – though I knew that as a wicked thought, because it went out of my mind very quickly, especially when he said: 'There's many a slip between the first offer being made and the final payment falling into my bank. He can still back out, as you know. He's sending a surveyor over tomorrow, and if his report's no good, I expect the deal will be off, or he'll want a lower price. But if it all goes through as planned, I'll give you a hundred. That's what you said, wasn't it?'

'It's not much of a share.'

He poured more tea, looked me straight in the eye: 'It's all you're going to get. It's more than you deserve, twenty per cent, in any case, but I'll stick to our agreement. A pity you lost your job over it, though. What's a bright young lad like you going to do now?'

'I'm going to London.'

'That's even brighter of you. This town would soon be too hot to hold you, I suppose.'

'I haven't done anything wrong.'

'Nobody said you had. But you'll like London, if I know

you. You have the face to like it – though God knows, you must be careful.' He waffled on like this for another half-hour, while I sat at my ease and listened to him tell about museums and famous places he thought I should see down there.

When I left he shook my hand, held it and squeezed it, and his fingers were ice-cold so that I felt sorry for him, though I didn't know why. After all, he had no troubles any more, having got rid of his wife and kids, and being about to sell his house for a good fat price. He'd have nothing then, and he'd be free. Maybe this was why I had that faint shred of sorrow for him.

I got back in time to meet Claudine by the cinema. She was glad to see me, smiled as I took her hand and kissed it like an Italian count. 'You're in a good mood,' she said, 'have you got a raise, or been promoted?'

'Better than that. I've got the sack. I feel wonderful.'

She stopped so suddenly in the middle of the pavement that a couple of postmen going at a good pace behind bumped into us and almost knocked me flying. It was as if I'd buried the blunt end of a claw-hammer in her back: 'What for?'

'A good reason. A bloody good reason.'

Her stony anger flashed itself full into me. 'But why?'

I had to tell her something, or just walk away, and I couldn't do that. The real reason I'd got the push now seemed petty and stupid, and my pride buckled under it: 'I was in the office this morning' – persuading her to walk along so that it would be easier to talk – 'when Weekley asked me to type a sheet of information about a house. Then I had to cyclostyle it, but the machine was no good and it left off the bottom part. When he saw it he called me an idle bastard, and I said that if there was an idle bastard in this office then he was that idle bastard, the idle bastard. At which he calls me a thieving bastard, an illiterate no-good bastard from Radford, so I punch him one, and knock his glasses flying. Everybody in the office had to hold me down, otherwise I'd have pummelled him into putty. He sent somebody for a copper, but they couldn't find one near, so Weekley then said I wasn't worth taking to court because I'd go there soon enough on my own, being already a criminal who could only go from bad to worse. All he wanted was to see the back of me, which he did, because I got out as fast as I could. I'll never go near the place again. I hate it.'

I piled it on so high it nearly toppled over. 'Oh,' she cried. 'Oh, how awful.' We walked in silence while the full blood of it sank into her, and me, getting more horrible all the time. 'What have you been doing all day?' she asked.

'Sitting in coffee bars,' I said gruffly. 'What else could I do after that little set-to?'

'You ought to have been looking for another job. You might have had one by now.'

'I hadn't got the heart to.'

'Why do you do it? Oh, Michael, why did you do it?' she cried with such anguish that a man passing by laughed at the thought of what I'd done to her, the dirty bastard. It sounded as if I'd just killed her mother, or something. 'Well,' she said, when I didn't answer, 'we can't announce our engagement till you get another good job, and even then, I don't know.'

'Do you love me?' I asked, 'or don't you? Just tell me, for God's sake, so that I'll know where I stand.'

My sarcasm was mixed with a dash of bile, but she took me dead seriously: 'I don't know. I'm all mixed up. Oh, why did you do it?'

'I'll tell you,' I said, 'and I mean it: I couldn't stand working in that office with such a gang of four-eyed ponces for the next four hundred years, getting deader and deader and deader and deader, selling rotten houses to poor drudges who are even worse than dead but who just wanted a rose-painted kennel to die in, or a converted matchbox rabbit-hutch to bring their snotty-nosed kids up in. I've had my short sharp dose and that's enough to last me all my life. In fact I might die next year and I'd weep scalding tears if I'd wasted so much time saying yes-sir and no-sir to that lot of bleeders. I'd rather work in the blackest factory on earth than go through that again. I might be a fool and a thief but I've not yet been brainwashed enough to crawl into that sort of death with a lettuce up my arse.'

'Stop it!' she screamed. 'Don't swear. Go away. I don't want to see you. Don't follow me.' I stood, watching her get on to a bus that, conveniently for both of us, drew into its stop at that moment. It trundled towards Canning Circus, and for ten minutes I didn't move but leaned against the wall of the cathedral wondering what I'd done, why I had made Claudine so desperate and unhappy that she had to walk out on me. It was the finish, I knew, because knowing her heart so well, I could see that I'd split the ground under her feet, and that the absolutely unforgivable had been done and said.

I didn't think the oak and the ash and the bonny rowan tree was the best that the earth had to offer. A man of all colours is a man of the night as well as of the day, and because I acted merely, and hardly thought at all, I eventually began to see that the best the earth could give me was the wherewithal to support myself in bread and books without actually earning it. The nearer I got to my twenty-first birthday the firmer this belief took hold. Fortunately I had no moral teachers except myself. My mother didn't care, as long as I was clothed and fed. By this I don't mean to imply that we didn't love each other and wouldn't have died for each other. We certainly wouldn't. The fact was, I suppose, that I could never have found a moral teacher with whom to agree, certainly not in any of the people I knew both inside and outside the family. In this sense, a lot was put on to my shoulders, namely the task of finding my own moral way in a world where no adults were available to guide me. Of course, there must have been many who would have taken me on, but I'm sure that their qualifications for doing so would have been down below zero. Being young, I was left alone by moral hypocrites and bullies who'd only want to deprave or colonize me. A man of many colours can go a long way, as long as he keeps out of their way.

I walked home after leaving Claudine, feeling as if I'd been cursed, holding a weight of tons on my back. Mother was smoking a fag and reading the evening paper: 'You look as if you've lost your wages. What's up?'

'I got the sack.'

'That's not the end of the world.'

'My girlfriend packed me in.'

'Because you got the sack? She's not much of a friend.

You're well rid of her. There's some ham in the larder. Get a bit of it into your belly.'

I slumped down: 'I'm not hungry.'

'Come on, you bleddy fool. Get that light back in your eyes. It's down to twenty-five watts and it was a hundred yesterday.' She poured my tea, put out the bread and ham, with some pickles. 'Good God!' she said, 'you're crying! I never thought I'd live to see it. Come on, love. Don't bother about her.'

I was only nearly crying, if such a thing can be said. Tears were about to break through, and this was what she saw. After eating I went to bed, and cried there alone, and when I went to sleep I felt much better.

Claudine lost no time in getting back into the affections of Alfie Bottesford, if ever she had been out of them during the time we had courted together. I actually saw them a week later, walking through town and hanging on each other as if they were frightened of some black angel ripping them apart. Claudine turned her eyes at the offending sight of me, but Alfie gave a wink as I went by, amused at me not being able to stop and talk to them because they were determined that I shouldn't be able to. But I was glad nevertheless of this chance glimpse, because up to then I'd been thinking that perhaps I'd call on Claudine to see if I couldn't get us going again. Now I realized that, though seeing her with Alfie might give me more chance of success than if she'd stayed at home brooding alone and lonely over me, I was not prepared to risk it, because I didn't really want to become part of her cakewalk again – which might this time settle in for life. I began to recover from her, and enjoy my new phase of leisure.

I didn't try for a new job. Cutting myself to half-pay, I could last in idleness for a month. I bought a newspaper every morning, walked up and over the hill into the bowl of town. I found it impossible to lie long in bed. Idleness did not extend as far as to rot my spine. When Mother went out at half past seven I felt the emptiness of the house getting louder and louder in my blood, so in ten minutes I was dressed and down before the pot of tea had got cold. In scarf and overcoat I called at coffee bars and bookshops, looking at passing faces or in windows. A city is fascinating if you don't have to work in it, not the same place any more, but richer, and full of things you'd never noticed.

I went into the record shop on Clumber Street as if to buy discs, but played classical pops for an hour, then said I wasn't satisfied with the reproduction and went to spread out the next couple of hours in the reference library, before a cheese-cob and cup-of-tea lunch in Lyons. In the reading-room I went through the papers, but the news never really interested me, though I read it for a laugh and to while away time on such stuff as held everybody in thrall while on the bus to work or during a ruminative five-minute crap after breakfast. I rejected news, and even rejected the interest of it. I stopped buying magazines or newspapers, thinking the only news to be what was happening in myself, and this only came out in headlines flashing now and again across my brain, such as:

MICHAEL CULLEN GETS THE SACK. CULLEN THROWN OVER BY GIRLFRIEND. BASTARD'S GRANDAD KICKS THE BUCKET.

I usually went up and down the columns wanting men for work. Indisputable proof that I was needed stared me in the face till I went nearly blind. Before he lost his sight, I said to myself, he remembered that, now and again, for a few seconds, he would see a large patch of grey when he looked into the light. The Situations Vacant showed me the way people still lived, and the monkey's claw shot out at me to join them, but I held back the belly-laughs as I skimmed my eyeballs from one dead job to another, from van driver's mate to builders' labourer, loader, packer, welder, dishwasher, boilermaker, shop helper, bartender, and factory hand, a long sad hymn to real life spinning into me till I stopped laughing for fear I'd get the jaundice, and so switched to the crossword.

After three weeks I went to see how Clegg had got on with selling his house. Hedges were heavy and ugly with frost, and under a clear sky the fields rolled away white and sparkling like a sheet thrown off by a dead man on his way up to heaven. It looked grim and I wanted none of it, the countryside seeming alien to me in winter. I needed summer lushness with hot days and flowers, and I was reminded of how warm factories could be at such a time.

No one answered the bell so I walked to the back and saw Clegg taking wood logs from the shed and stacking them by the kitchen door. 'I was expecting you,' he said, straightening himself and coming towards me. I asked if he wanted any help, feeling suddenly bored with inactivity at the sight of him having a useful job.

He laughed: 'I can manage. I spin this work out, because what can I do when it's finished? I've still got plenty of packing to do, though. The sale's over. The survey was good, and the searches were made by the other man's solicitor. It was more of a rush than I expected. The whole price is paid already. Bit of a shock now I've actually got to clear out.'

'Better than standing still.'

'Aye,' he answered. 'I suppose it is.'

Remembering my first idyllic sight of his picture-box house, a great pang came back for Claudine, of the stupid daydream I'd had of us both living in this place. Close after it was the thought that thank God it was going to be sold, and that after this visit I need never see it again. I was frightened and put off by the surrounding frost.

Clegg asked me inside. He seemed older than when I'd first seen him, as if selling his house had been a big mistake that was too late to back out of now. His skin was lank and sallow, his eyes empty of all but an impression of water as if he were about to be ill, or as if the winter was threatening to do for him. A limb of the house had propped up his backbone, but still he smiled on telling me he'd be glad to get out of it. Perhaps he'd worked too hard at filling cases and stacking books in boxes when he should have left it all to the removal men. I offered to help him shift any heavy stuff, saying it not as if he weren't strong enough to do it on his own, but in a matey way so that he could get it done sooner. 'Perhaps you could,' he said, 'if you've no other work.'

So I stayed until after dark, clearing huge basket-cases from the attic. Because I was working so effectively he realized there was more to do than he had thought, so asked me to stay the night and get an early start next day. 'I don't mind,' I said, ready for any work as long as I got something to eat. Food wasn't important to me if I ate regularly. It needn't be a lot, but if it didn't come on time it put me into a very bad mood indeed.

Old Clegg took my hand and held it: 'Listen, Michael, whenever somebody asks you whether you want to do something, never answer by saying that you don't mind, because it's no answer at all. If you want to do something in the world, always come out with a straight yes or no, and then you'll be of great value to your fellow men, but also of even greater value to yourself.'

What could I say to such a sermon except nod my head? We went into the kitchen, which was warm because of an Aga cooker burning nicely – though the light was a bit dim. Clegg took out a plate of liver from the fridge, threw it into a pan of burning lard. With a tin of beans and a few slices of Miracle Bread, it made a good supper between us. He was disappointed that I didn't play chess, so we stayed at the table with a game of draughts. But it was too easy for him, and he was bored after an hour of it. When neither of us spoke it was so quiet I thought I was going off my head. So this is what it's like in the country, I said to myself.

Next morning I humped trunks and boxes from the attic and lined them up in the hall. It was a hard grind, which went on till after dusk, but I enjoyed it because I wasn't working for a boss. Clegg gave me the general idea, and I just got on with it. There was a bureau I had to bring down, and in one of the drawers were at least a dozen old-fashioned pocket watches. I looked at them, able to see that the numbering in Roman style was beautifully and thinly marked on their white clock faces. Maybe they were prizes or presents he'd been given in his life. One was a large heavy gold piece, complete with its own chain, and a cover that went over the face to protect it, fastening with a firm-sounding click.

To see whether its tick was healthy I wound up the top knob, and in my stupidity didn't give it a few twists but went on till I could turn no more without breaking it. I stood by the open drawer, gazing at the second hand strutting around in its small circle, till I heard the tread of Clegg on his way up. So I put it back and carried on dragging the bureau towards the door. When he went down I wrapped the watch in my handkerchief and put it in my pocket. He'd most likely never think of it again, and it was too good a piece of work to moulder away in that drawer for ever. The only thing was the powerful tick-tock, that I had no way of throttling short of snapping the main spring. Its noise, even from the far-off muffle of my handkerchief, seemed spiked into my veins, and my only hope was that Clegg was too deaf or absent-minded to notice, or that I could make enough noise when near him to drown it.

'I think we've just about broken the back of it,' he said, when we sat in the kitchen with tea, and cup-cakes I'd shopped in the village for.

'I'll stay here again tonight,' I said, 'if you think it's neces-sary. Nobody misses me in Nottingham.'

'I suppose you wish you'd never bumped into me, losing your job, and then your girlfriend.'

'What does it matter?' I said. 'Maybe it's all for the good. I didn't say that at the actual time but I always think so before a thing happens and after it happens. That's the way I am. I was born like that.'

'It's lucky you were. It never was any use crying over spilt milk.'

'You can say that again.' I said, pouring myself another dose of strong tea. 'I wasn't glad at losing my job just because I don't like work.'

'I can see that,' he said. 'I'll make it right with you before you go. That's a watch I can hear, ain't it?'

I held up my hand: 'This bobbin-ticker makes more noise than Big Ben. It was the cheapest I could find. I'm glad I got it though. Came out of my first week's wages.'

'It does make a row.'

'Yes,' I said, 'it was embarrassing when I sat with my girl on the back seat at the pictures. She used to think I couldn't wait to get her outside in the fields. Put her off a bit, this bloody timebomb.'

He laughed: 'It is that all right. Let's get back to it, shall we?'

I wondered what he meant by making it right with me.

During our short acquaintance we'd become as close as you could get without being related, or so it seemed to me. Due to my short-sighted power game, I'd done him a favour by getting an inflated price for his house, and all that remained was to see whether he appreciated it or not. If he didn't, at least I had the watch, though I would have regarded it as a shabby substitute for the golden handshake I'd grown day by day to expect.

I used the bathroom for a wash, and put on my coat. Clegg met me in the hall, and handed me an envelope. 'Take this, for your trouble. I always repay a kindness, and hope you'll do the same throughout your life, even when you do have bad luck, which I don't suppose you will, not very often, at any rate. But don't get into trouble that's all *I* can say. If you help people as much as you've helped me you should get on all right. In that envelope you'll find a note with my address in Leicester on it, so if ever you get that way, come and see me.'

'I'll be sure to. I was glad to do a bit of work for you.' After handshakes and a hug on both sides I went quickly along the lane to get a bus, feeling a right bastard with Clegg's best watch beating time to my heart in the arse-pocket of my trousers. On the top deck I furtively opened the envelope and counted a hundred and fifty pounds in five-pound notes. I could have jumped out of the window for joy, but instead screwed up the paper with his best wishes and address on it, and let that go into the blackness instead. All I can do, when I think back on it, is wonder at the irresponsibility of youth, while knowing for certain that at the actual time I thought about nothing at all.

In the isolation of my bedroom I took out my savings and totted up the total wealth, which came to the fat fantastic sum of two hundred and sixty pounds. It seemed impossible that I owned such money, and as if in doubt I held all of Clegg's five-pound notes up to the light to see if the watermark and steel strip were in them. I stowed it back under my mattress, and couldn't sleep. The moon glowed, so I drew the curtains, and I trembled, all of a sweat, afraid to sleep in case some robbing bastard should shin up the drainpipe, get through the window, flatten me with a bludgeon, and make off with my fortune. If anyone in an area like ours came to know of it, that would have been my fate. I tossed and screwed my face into the pillow, pressing my eyes shut tight in order to blot my heart into sleep.

Nobody did know of it, except me. The only safe way was to spend it, so next morning I put on my best suit and went to a garage that sold second-hand cars. The manager showed me a Ford Popular only four years old (or so he said) for a hundred and thirty-five pounds, and after a good try-out around the city, then over the Trent as far as Ruddington, I paid spot cash for it. With tax, insurance, and a tank of petrol I still had more than a hundred quid to my name.

I piloted the car home with a Whiff between my lips, windows wide open even though it was like Siberia. A bus followed me down Ilkeston Road, and I was afraid to go too slow in case it kept right on and flattened me. Fortunately, the traffic lights stopped us both, but I was still fluttering nervously when I pulled up at the kerb outside the house. I ran in for a tin of polish and a rag because there was a touch of rust on the front bumper, and worked till every bit of chrome reflected my happy and grinning face.

When Mother came in that night she wanted to know: 'Whose is that car outside?'

'Mine.'

'Don't be bloody silly,' she said. 'I asked you a civilized question: whose is it? If you don't know, say so.'

'It's mine,' I told her. 'I bought it this morning' – explaining how I'd got the money from Clegg.

'You are a dark horse,' she said. 'Has it got lights?' I told her it had, and she asked me to take her out in it. We drove to Grandma's at Beeston. There was a great wind going, and at one place along University Boulevard I felt it bumping the car side-on, as if with a bit more strength it would push us over. Mother enjoyed the ride so much she was singing all the way.

I bought some drink at a beer-off, and we supped a few pints in Grandma's warm kitchen. 'Be careful', my mother said. 'Don't put too much back.'

'I can only drive well if I'm drunk. Otherwise I'm frightened to death.'

'I'll do the boozing,' Grandma said. 'And you do the driving. That's fair, ain't it?' We laughed and stewed over it, and after the booze came tea and sandwiches as part of Grandma's generous service.

Halfway through this we heard a rending of rotten wood, the sound of a thousand twigs biting themselves in half, followed by a dull impacted crunch outside the house. Grandma screamed that hell was coming down on us. My heart almost burst, and I thought a bomb had fallen or a gasometer had gone up. A vision of my crushed and mangled car flipped over my eyes, and I charged like a madman for the scullery door, from which side most of the noise had come.

People were shouting, cars stopping, lights flashing. I felt the wind licking my face with its cold tongue. I couldn't get out for a wall of dry and tangled branches held me back. I was frantic, ripped and clawed my way to the garden where the greater part of the trunk had fallen. Much of the tree had smashed on to the wall, spliced halfway down it.

Mother was by my side. 'I hope no one was walking along the pavement. If they were, they've had it.'

'Sod them,' I cried, almost in tears. 'What about my car?' We pulled at the gate, but due to the buckling of the wall it wouldn't open. Grandma was laughing behind us. 'You sound as if you're off your head,' I shouted.

'Your grandad's tree's gone down at last!' she said, and went back to laughing so that I could have killed even her when I thought about my car.

It was buried under the rammel of branches. I held on to the wall to stop the stars going round. People were pulling at brittle wood and taking it back to their houses for kindling. I scrabbled like a maniac to get to the car, and a man said: 'Look at that greedy sod. Some folks aren't satisfied till they get the lot.'

'Appen it's his car,' another voice chipped in.

'Serves him right, then. Good job it struck the rich and not the poor.' But I reached it, and in no time the top was freed. The main weight of the tree had been taken by the wall, and far from the car being a write-off, it now seemed that apart from a couple of bad dints in the roof only one of the front lamps was smashed. Trying to hold back my rage so that all the nosy-parkers shouldn't have a good show for nothing, I got inside and saw that some split branches had punctured two jagged holes in the roof, as if God had fired two anti-tank shells for spite, vertically down from his stony heaven. I could have cried my heart out at such a disaster on the first day of my owning it, but later on, totting back a half-bottle of Grandma's Irish whiskey (that I'll swear blind she brewed herself) I didn't mind joining in the general laugh though only because I was drunk.

Next morning I got to work, and wiped up the water that had dripped inside during the night. I hammered the ragged lips of the holes as closed as they could get, then put a criss-cross work of stickypaper strips inside and out, and painted them from a tin of enamel I bought at a bucket shop. That made it as watertight as it would ever be again, and with the lamps fixed, the car was once more roadworthy.

I covered hundreds of miles in the next few days, till I was as good a driver as the rest of them, if not better, judging by the number of near-misses I had due to other people's careless-ness. I went past Cleggy's house one day and saw a couple of removal vans outside, but didn't go in to say hello in case he'd missed the pocket-watch, which I now wore proudly from my jacket lapel. I thought that perhaps I'd look him up one day in Leicester (I could get his address from the library) and give it back to him. This good intention agreeably stifled whatever guilt I felt, and even made me feel happy for the next half-mile. After the accident of the tree my car didn't look as spick and span as it had the morning I bought it, but my affection for it had grown accordingly. Such a vegetable baptism was all it would ever suffer, and I hoped that from now on whoever might be in heaven would look after us. I felt comfortable in it, safe, enclosed, as if it were more of a home than my own room. If I curled up in the back I could even sleep, and in fact often dozed there, parked by some narrow lane of north Notts when I was fagged out from the mental effort of steering it along. I had food in the car, a blanket, fags, tools, maps, and a Thermos filled with tea before setting out. I felt like a gipsy, but always went back home at night, as if I were still tied at the ankle by an invisible rope.

Driving through town at just gone five one afternoon I saw Miss Bolsover walking towards her bus stop. 'Gwen,' I called, using her first name now that we didn't work together. She heard me, I'm sure, but kept her head up and went right on, her broad arse shaking inside her loose grey coat. A van was hooting for me to get a move on, and she thought this was me also signalling her. So I flicked on my indicators as if I was going into the kerb to stop, but still crawled along it slowly, turned my window to the bottom and called: 'Miss Bolsover!'

She came over with a smile: 'Hello, Michael!'

'I'll drive you home,' I said. 'Get in.' The car sagged, not that she weighed more than most, but it seemed that the springs weren't in the best condition. Gwen Bolsover was what might be called a well-built woman of more than thirty, with touching grey hair above her delicate pink ears. Her pear-shaped face was always full of concern for others, and as far as I understood from office gossip she had gone through a succession of boyfriends, all of whom were said to have let her down. Why they had, nobody knew, but that was her claim, and such was the honesty of her face when she said it that no one dreamed of disbelieving her. This fact certainly made men go for her like flies when they heard of it.

Perfume filled the car, and I had to brace myself so as not to swoon under it because traffic was heavy, and I couldn't swear while she was in the car in case such words were misunderstood. I had hoped, in my over-optimistic way, that Claudine would be the first to waft perfume and smear lipstick over the upholstery. I'd intended calling on her when the month was up to see if we couldn't get back to our senses. And now Miss Bolsover had beaten her to it, a free gift suddenly out of nowhere, when she hadn't been in my mind for weeks. I knew already that you never got what you expected – or even what you deliberately didn't expect in the hope that you'd get it. That's why I lived on the minimum of hope and never expected anything. I certainly did as well as anybody else out of this system, and maybe, in some ways, a whole lot better.

Miss Bolsover asked where I'd got the car, and I told her I'd bought it out of my savings, that I'd been putting money by for exactly this since I was fifteen. 'Oh,' she said, 'I do admire such steadiness of purpose in a man. And you're still so young. I wonder what sort of a person you'll be in ten years' time? Or in twenty years?' She lived at Wollaton, and we were already caught in the rush hour to get around Canning Circus. 'How well you drive,' she said. 'It was good of Mr Weekley to give you those driving lessons.'

'I'm not that young,' I objected, 'Miss Bolsover. In fact I feel a lot more than twenty-one at times, I can tell you.' In one sharp turn she fell against me, soft arms and apologies, then asked me where I was working now, and I told her I was fixed up at Steke and Scull's, the biggest agents in the city, but that for the moment I was at their Loughborough branch. This seemed like a rise indeed, and she congratulated me on it. 'How wonderful for you.'

'It is,' I said, driving with one hand and taking out a Whiff with the other. I offered her one: 'Smoke these?'

Her laugh was loud, head thrown back: 'Oh goodness, no. Not yet, anyway.'

I lit up: 'You know, Weekley gave me the sack, but it was all due to a misunderstanding. I tried to do the firm a favour, and he thought I was going it for myself.'

'All I know,' she said, 'is that he thought you had done something that wasn't ethical.'

'Whatever that means,' I said. 'Maybe he just wanted an excuse to get rid of me.'

'I don't think so, Michael. He always spoke highly of you.'

'Well,' I said, 'he should have realized I was young enough to make mistakes, and not thrown me out like that.'

'It was a pity,' she said. 'I didn't realize you felt so bad about it.'

'I did, and do.' The fact was that if I'd stayed I could have made a lot more money doing exactly what I'd done with Clegg, but I'd have used my brains and not got found out so easily. To be able to do it, however, one had to work for an estate agent as a cover, and so as to get the necessary information. 'It was a great shock for me to get thrown out, Miss

Bolsover,' I went on, passing Radford station. 'Mostly, and I don't see why I shouldn't admit it, because I hated losing contact with you. It was the greatest treat in my life, waking up every morning and knowing that when I got to the office I'd be able to see you. Don't ask me why I'm telling you this. It's all too late now.' I looked straight ahead at the road: 'The reason I tried so hard to bring off that little bit of business for the firm was because I might be given more responsibility, and then you'd perhaps have thought a little better of me, because it seemed that in spite of my feelings you hardly knew I existed.' The words just tumbled out, without me knowing that they would. I was so controlled by them that I was slightly scared, but took a split-second goz at Miss Bolsover to see if there was any effect.

She looked in front, nose and mouth set to some thought that I wasn't party to, as if engrossed by other things entirely. But she was blushing faintly, so I couldn't be sure of this. In order to make it worse for her I said I was sorry, that I shouldn't have spoken, but that my heart was so full I hadn't had much say in the matter.

'You're a strange boy, Michael.'

'Normal,' I answered. 'I can't imagine anyone not liking you. But it's more than that with me.'

I said nothing else because no words came. She gave directions to reach her house, a small bungalow off a by-road near Wollaton. I let her get out by herself, and she stood with the door open. Play at being good-mannered too early on and you'll never get anywhere. 'Would you like to come in? We'll have a cup of tea,' she said. 'You've been so good, to drive me home.'

It was windy, and she was standing in it getting red cheeks, so I had to make up my mind. 'If it's a quick one,' I said, 'because I promised to take Mother to that symphony concert at the Albert Hall.' The lie was innocent, but I made it to put Miss Bolsover at her ease, knowing she was partial to that form of entertainment.

'I tried to get tickets for it, but couldn't,' she said as I switched off.

'You can have mine, if you like.'

'Oh, no, you can't let your mother down.'

'I can't really,' I said, slamming the door. 'She loves Beethoven. She'd never forgive me.'

Everybody loves a liar, I thought, but telling myself to stop it from that point on. I picked up a bottle of milk and followed her into the mock-Tudor pebble-dash matchbox bungalow, met by a smell of stale tea and damp upholstery. She asked me to sit on a deep plush sofa while she fussed in the kitchen, but I feasted my eyes on her from the doorway now that she had her coat off, as I often had in the office. It was marvellous, the way you had to get the sack before people would look at you.

She came back with a large silver tray, loaded with tea and a plate of fancy biscuits. 'I don't take milk' she said, 'but lemon.'

'Where's your family?'

'I only have my brother, and he went to Austria yesterday for three weeks, by car. He's a keen skier. Not that I see much of him when he's here.'

'A lonely existence,' I said.

'It *is*, Michael, but I'm very fond of it. I go a fair amount to the theatre, or concerts. Or I stay in and read, write letters, watch television. I think life is beautiful and fascinating.'

'So do I,' I said. 'I read a good deal too. Books are my favourite pastime. Girls as well, but my girlfriend packed me in because I lost my job.'

'Really? Sugar?'

'Yes, six.'

'I don't take it myself. But why? You got a better job. Didn't that please her?'

'She didn't wait for me to get another. She was very head-strong. But it's no use regretting it.'

'You're lucky to be able to take it so lightly.'

'I didn't. It broke my heart. But what's done is done. I can't live like that for the rest of my life.'

Miss Bolsover laughed: 'I hardly think you'll have to. But I know what you mean.'

There was a pause, and I took the opportunity to drink off half my tea. It was too weak, but I let that pass. 'Has it happened to you, then?'

She broke a biscuit in half and put it into her small mouth:

65

'At my age it's bound to have done. I'm thirty-four.'

'You talk as if you think that's old,' I said. 'My girlfriend was thirty-eight. She was like you in one way because she only looked about twenty-five. Not that she *was* like you, she was a bit too common if you know what I mean, and she'd been married before, but she had the same wonderful figure, the sort that I've always admired. When I was in London last week on business I had a couple of hours to spare, so I went into a gallery and saw some wonderful paintings with that sort of figure. I don't think anything else can be called a figure at all.'

She sat in an armchair opposite, blushing and smiling at the same time but not, she said, because she was in any way embarrassed at my frankness, which she thought was attractive in me, but because I took some interest in culture. This was true, and when I went on to talk about a few of the books I'd read she became convinced that there was more to me than had ever been apparent at the office.

Looking across the few feet of plush carpet between us I was swollen with the bile of lechery, and wanted to get her in my arms. She wore a thin woollen jumper, large tits shifting as she talked full of serious concern about the world and how good it was to be alive in spite of its ills and all the bad people in it. I agreed, till it occurred to me that too much agreement might not be a good thing. But I had no control over it, and was carried along by the sweet sin of listening and only opening my lips to say that she spoke the truth. Her eyes glittered, as if half a tear were buried in each of them, telling me that this was what she wanted to hear. Not that I doubted her intelligence, for under that soft exterior with the touch of sentimentality no doubt corroding it, she had a fine streak of rational perception. I leaned across and squeezed one of her hands warmly. She pressed mine, in recognition of the common ground we had found between us. Then she realized that I was pulling, as well as squeezing, and with a sudden shift she came over and sat by me on the sofa. 'Do I *have* to tell you that I love you?' I said wearily. My lips against hers pressed straight through to her teeth, because she opened her mouth as I went forward. Then her arms came around me.

After a few minutes we looked at each other, me with what

I hoped to be a gaze of honesty, and adoration, she with what seemed to be puzzled embarrassment and an excitement of wanting it that changed the curves of her face so that she hardly seemed the same person I'd known at the office. 'I love you,' I said, 'more than I've ever loved anyone. I'd like to marry you.'

She pressed me into her wonderful breasts. 'Oh Michael, don't say it. Please don't.' I decided not to, in case she started to cry, though that would be no bad match for the passion I felt in her. Nevertheless I said it again, and held her so tight that she couldn't respond to it. 'It would be marvellous,' I murmured into her shoulder. 'Marvellous.'

She shuddered at the touch of my fingers, then broke away: 'We really ought not to spoil it.'

'I love you,' I said, 'so it's the last thing I want to do' – which set off another round. This time she forgot to tell me not to spoil it, or perhaps she couldn't say anything at all, as my hand had found the warmest part of her.

We went into her bedroom at six o'clock, and didn't come out till eight the next morning, when she had to get ready for work. The whole night seemed no longer than five minutes, though I don't know how many times we worked up to the apple-and-pivot and cried out in the moonlit darkness. I shook like a jelly-baby while driving her to work, afraid of every vehicle that came close: 'I'll come and see you tonight,' I said.

'Please. I'll wait for you.'

'And I'll ask you to marry me again.'

'Oh, Michael, I don't know what to say.'

'Just say yes,' I said.

'You're wonderful.'

I set her down a hundred yards from the office, then drove home. The house was empty, and I undressed to get into bed. Unable to sleep, because I ached in every last limb, I wondered what I had done in tacking on to Miss Bolsover. Naturally, I wanted it to go on and on, never having tasted such loving before. Perhaps the fact that I had actually stayed all night in bed with her had something to do with it, though not entirely. There was really nothing to think about, but simply to lie there and regret that she wasn't still with me, only to hope that time would speed along before tonight, and that I would be able to get some rest before setting out again. I drifted into half-sleep, wonderful as only sleep can be when you know that daylight is pushing behind drawn curtains, and that the whole town is going full tilt at hard and boring work.

I don't know how long I'd been in bed, but I became aware of a battering-ram breaking through to my sweetest dreams. There was no rest for the Devil in heaven, so I put on some trousers and stomped downstairs with half-closed eyes, wondering who the hell it could be at this time of the day. At the back door, which we usually used, no one was there, and just as I was thankfully up on my way to bed the knocking came this time from the front. Any such sound at the door always pushed my heart off course, jacked-up its noise in the veins of my ears. We weren't used to people rapping at our doors. If a neighbour came to see us she usually called out my mother's name and walked straight in. A knock meant either a tally man, the police, or a telegram, and since my mother had never bought anything on credit, and neither of us had been in trouble with the police, and no one we knew ever felt in such an urgent frame of mind as to send a telegram, you can imagine that such formal visitations at the door were few and far between. When one did come, and I happened to be in on my own, the effect was of such intensity that it almost had me scared.

Claudine tried to smile, but ended up with a distressful saccharine expression that fixed me in speech and movement to the spot. 'Come in,' I said, after a while, and at my brisk tone she gave a normal worried look and followed me through to the kitchen. 'It's good to see you.'

She came back sharply: 'Is it?'

'Course it is, love. Take your coat off and sit down. I'll make you a cup of tea. I could do with breakfast, myself.'

'Breakfast? Do you know what time it is? It's just gone twelve o'clock.'

'We'll call it brunch, then,' I said from the kitchen stove. I cracked eggs into the pan, and layed enough bacon on the grill for two of us.

68

'You must be going to pieces,' she said, 'staying in bed so late. It's terrible. I always knew there was something funny about you.'

'The sun will never rise on me, and that's a fact.'

I spread a cloth and put out knives and forks, turned on the radio, gave her a fag, and pushed another lump of coal into the fire, not even wondering why she had come to see me, keeping so busy that I wouldn't be able to, while she went on and on about how useless I was. 'Still,' she said, watching me closely, 'you are a bit more domesticated than I ever thought.'

'I've often had to look after myself when Mam's been away, that's why.'

We pulled up our seats, but she didn't tuck in as heartily as I'd hoped. 'It's good to see you,' I said, 'but what's on your mind?'

'A lot that you ought to know,' she answered.

I thought I'd be funny: 'You're pregnant?' I said brightly.

'You bastard,' she cried, standing up. 'How did you know?'

I choked on a piece of bacon rind, ran over to the mirror and yanked it out like a tapeworm. 'I didn't. It was a joke.'

'It's no joke to me,' she said, eating a bit faster, now that she'd told me in this back-handed fashion.

'How's Alfie Bottesford?' I asked.

'What do you mean? What are you getting at?'

I stood by the mantelshelf, riled that she could go on eating at a time like this, till I remembered that she had two mouths to feed. 'I'm getting at nothing. But you and Alfie are back together, aren't you?'

'I won't talk about it,' she wept, eating her egg.

'Suit yourself. You walked out on me.'

She stood up and faced me: 'And can you wonder at it, Michael-rotten-Cullen? Look at the way you're living. Lounging in bed all day stinking with sleep. No job. No prospects even. What a deadbeat tramp you are. I can see there's no hope for me with you, even though I am having your baby. Oh, it's terrible. I feel awful. I'll do myself in. I shall. That's the only thing to do.'

'If you're serious about it,' I said, 'I'll give you a couple of bob for the gas, and a cushion to put your head on.'

'I really believe you would,' she said quietly, stunned at my response to her unnatural threat.

'You bet I would, if that's the way you feel. I love you so much I'd do anything for you.'

'You don't imagine I can feel very good, do you?'

'No, but don't come here palming a baby off on me when you've been going with Alfie Bottesford for the last month. I don't know what your game is, but I'm not falling for that one.'

'I thought you loved me,' she said, 'but all that went on between us meant nothing to you. As long as you got what you wanted. Alfie Bottesford's never in all his life done anything to me. He hasn't laid a finger on me, ever. And that's the stone truth, I'm telling you.'

I knew she wasn't lying – almost. The memory of Miss Bolsover's ripe body went out through my big toe, and I looked at the one tear of anguish and vinegar that came to Claudine's pale cheek. 'Won't Alfie marry you? You've only got to get him to bed once and he won't know the difference.'

She sat down, with both hands over her face, and I began to feel sorry for her, till she burst out: 'Oh, you're so rotten. I can't believe it. I don't know what to do. I'm afraid to tell Mam and Dad, and hoped you'd come home with me so that we could both do it.'

'You ditched me,' I shouted, 'didn't you? And now you want to take up with me again! I was bitter about you going off that day, I admit it. You walked out just because I'd lost my job. Do you call that love? And now that you and Alfie Bottesford have been rubbing up together so that he's got you loaded, you come moaning back to me. I'd like to know what for.'

She leapt up as if to knife me, but before she could say anything I took hold and kissed her: 'I love you. I'm going mad with love for you, Claudine. I'll do anything for you. Just tell me and I'll do it.' She kissed me back, and in a few minutes was more relaxed.

We stood in front of the mantelshelf mirror smoothing each other's cheeks with our lips: 'I came because it's your baby,' she said. 'I want you to come home tonight, and see my parents. We can tell them we're engaged, and that it would be best if we got married in a month or so.'

'All right,' I said, 'but I can't come up tonight. Make it tomorrow. One day more or less wain't mek much difference.'

'Why not tonight? It's as good as any other.'

'My car wants something doing to the engine,' I said, 'and a pal of mine who works at a garage can only do it tonight.'

She jumped away: 'Your car? What car?'

I told her I'd bought it out of my savings. 'Savings?' she yelled. 'You mean you had all this money in the bank while you were going with me, and you didn't tell me?'

'That's right.'

She broke down at this: 'How can I ever trust you?'

'Easy. You'll just have to believe me, then you can. I thought you'd be pleased to hear I'd got a car, but no. You look at me as if I've taken to crime. Every good thing I tell you turns out to be the end of the world. I suppose if I tell you something bad you'll think it's marvellous. Listen, you know when I said that my old man had been killed in the war, and that's why I hadn't got a father?' I couldn't stop myself even though I wanted to, though I'm not sure that I did. She looked at me, waiting for something special. 'Well, I never had a father, at least not one that I'd know. My mother didn't get married, and I was born from one of her affairs during the war – out of wedlock, as they say, or, to put it in blunt talk, I'm a bastard, a real no-good, genuine twenty-two-carat bastard in every sense of the word, so if ever you call me one again you'll at least be speaking the truth for the only time in your life, because I don't believe that you've never had hearthrug pie with Alfie Bottesford. The only thing I can't understand is why you come to me now that he's knocked you up.'

She roared and cried: 'I've got no one else to turn to, that's why.'

'I can't understand, you're courting Alfie, aren't you?'

'Yes.'

'And you come to me when you're pregnant. All right, if you want thirty quid to get rid of it I'll give it to you.' One of the men at the office had done it for his girlfriend, and putting the same proposition to Claudine made me feel big.

A bottle smashed over my head, a small compact square sauce bottle she snatched from the table. I grabbed her and slapped into her face. She cried out, and I thought that if this free-for-all went on much longer we'd have the neighbours in to part us. 'I came here because it's yours,' she said. 'That's all.'

A thin red line trickled over my nose, and I knelt down to wipe it with a corner of the tablecloth. 'If that's the way you feel,' I said, 'I'll be at your house at half past six tomorrow night.'

'Tonight,' she demanded.

'Tomorrow. I must get my car fixed. It's the only chance I've got. He goes to Mablethorpe first thing in the morning to see his aunt. So it'll just have to be tomorrow. I promise.'

'If you aren't there,' she said, 'I'll come with my father and mother. I will, and I mean it.'

'You won't have to,' I said, with my best honest smile. 'I love you. I really do. I've never loved anyone else. I'm already beginning to see how nice it'll be to live in a married way with you.' She sat on my knee, and my old passion came back for her: 'Let's go upstairs,' I said. After a little more persuading she agreed. We lay in bed till four o'clock, and then she left, thinking that all was well again. I went back and dozed in the marvellous rumpled sheets until it was time to drive to Miss Bolsover's.

'How long can it last?' Gwen wanted to know.

'Years,' I said. 'Why?'

'I always ask myself that, and it's a bad sign.'

'If I love someone it's for ever – unless I'm ditched. Then it's not my fault. But you don't need to ask it with me.' We lay on the rug in front of her electric fire.

'I ask it with everyone,' she said, 'then I can't blame it on the fact that I asked it – if it goes wrong. But I ask it. I can't help it.'

'If that's the way you like it,' I said, 'but as far as I'm concerned I love you, and that's that.'

'Oh Michael – you're so strong and simple. You're so direct. That's what I love most about you. I can understand you, and I've never had that feeling before.' It was hard to take this as a compliment, though I saw that in one way she was right.

I'd felt for a long time that I couldn't do anything at all unless I was simple, so in order not to be paralysed I fought to keep that simplicity. And Miss Bolsover's approbation of it was flattering in this respect, but if I loved her for saying it, it was only because she had said something at all.

She made a short meal of meat, chips and salad, and served us both on a small table in the living-room. She had a huge bathgown over her, and I wore her brother Andrew's smoking-jacket. I stroked her hand at each mouthful, which made me feel like a husband, and also as if I owned the house – both new sensations for me. Afterwards I smoked a Whiff, and talked her into a few puffs of it. Then we went to bed, not at midnight like grown-ups, but at eight o'clock, driven there by a pure and marvellous lust to get back to the centre of things.

But as usual lust did not mean force, because Claudine had blunted me, so we romped for an hour, though Gwen (if I could by now be permitted to call her that?) tried to pull me on immediately, and when she saw it wasn't possible started to mother me. I cured her of this by a few slaps on her fat behind, which she didn't object to, and then our loving continued through a couple of deep and meaty encounters. When I began to get dressed, she asked what was the matter. 'I love you,' I said, 'but I must go. I have an appointment to meet a client early in the morning. I was late yesterday (for the most wonderful reason in the world) but if I don't get in at the right time tomorrow, it'll look bad.'

She embraced me, her warm naked body against my shirt and trousers, or rather she grasped me, and turned her full lips for a big kiss, which I gave with my heart bursting. 'Tomorrow night?' she said.

'Yes,' I answered. 'I'll be here. You can bet. You've got me for ever, you know.'

'I don't want you for ever,' she said. 'I only want you for now. Always is not good for anybody.'

'Don't worry,' I told her, 'we'll be together in that rough old spring again. It's a sidereal mantrap that gets us all, you as well as me.'

I was weeping in tune to her creaking heart when I got into

my car, but I cheered up as I drove home in the moonless night. I made my tunnel through the black dark, fumigating my cluttered mind so that by the time I pulled up at the kerb it was obvious what I should do. It was necessary to act in haste, so that one never had cause to repent, because if you act in haste there can't be anything to blame yourself for, and that is a state of mind I relished. I had been acting like the Caliph of Baghdad in the last few weeks, and now the time had come to stop all that, to reform and go my own ways. Perhaps I had a sense of sin after all, for I wanted now and again to be pure so as to boost my self-esteem for when the time came around to sin again.

It was one in the morning when I looked at my gold watch in the dim bedroom light. I took the suitcase from my wardrobe, and lay it open on my bed, which still had the perfume smell of Claudine on it. I buried my face there for a second or two. But there was no time to be lost. I put on a clean shirt and my best suit, and packed my other clothes neatly in. Looking around, there was nothing else but a line of books along the washstand, and they would have to stay. It surprised me that I owned so little, though at a time like this it was a pleasant discovery to make. After all, I did have a car and a watch, as well as a hundred pounds. What more could anybody want? There was also a small transistor radio and I saw myself speeding along the main road with it lying on the seat beside me, thumping out some great symphony. It was small, but powerful, and Mam had liked the tone very much when I first showed it to her.

I was careful to make no noise in case I woke her up, but the door suddenly opened and there she was. 'You're off, are you?'

I put in two pairs of pyjamas, one clean and one dirty. 'Yes.'

'Where to?'

'North, east, south, and west.'

'That really does sound as if you know what you're doing, I must say.'

'I'll let you know where I am,' I said, botched at the throat, and all the way down into my bottom gut.

'That's something, anyway.' I was going to give her half my money, but didn't because it spared her the dignity and embarrassment of telling me to keep it. I was sure to need it more than she would, and in any case her wages were sufficient for all her wants. 'All I ask from you,' she said, 'is that you take care of yourself. That's all I'd like you to do for me.'

I tried to smile, but could only lie: 'I'm not going for good.'

'Don't lie to me,' she said.

'I'm not lying – that's all I can say.'

'It doesn't matter,' she said. 'Only don't be cheeky, and get going if you're going to. I'll go back to bed. If you're around in the morning I'll make breakfast. If you're not, I'll get it on my own.'

I kissed her. 'You'll hear from me.'

'Don't be so bleddy sloppy,' she said, breaking free and going to her own room.

I set the alarm for six and lay down in my clothes. It seemed only a second later that it jangled my ears, and then I remembered what I was up to, so jumped out of bed and went downstairs with my case. I left my transistor radio on the table with a note saying I wouldn't need it while I was away. Then I made tea and lingered for an hour, until I heard her moving upstairs, getting dressed for work. I went out, quietly closing the door behind me.

The streets were empty, I noted, getting into my black all-enveloping travel-bug car. It wouldn't start. The night had been wet, but now the clouds were shifting, and I lifted the bonnet and dried the contacts with my handkerchief. Not being mechanically minded, and lacking motorized experience, I knew nothing about cars, and I was swearing in case it should let me down at such a critical laughable time. It would be unjust, because I had no plans for it to waylay and spoil. I was acting without any plan whatsoever, and that was enough to make me innocent in the eyes of prankish worn-out motorcars. Still, I cranked it up, in case conciliation was necessary from a trickster like me, and when I sat in it once more and twitched on the ignition I felt the sweet shake of life under me, and after a few parting roars to the empty street and the benighted morning, I was off, slowly at first up the cobblestones, and then swiftly along Lenton Boulevard, skirting the city centre, by the valley of the Leen that took me under the heights of the Castle.

It was still dark, and only my own lights and the roadlights led me away. There was no heater in the car, and my greatcoat was wrapped around me, a scarf muffling my neck and chin. Because I was still so tired from the last few days, my brain was clear. I remember it well, a familiar feeling. At the same time I didn't think ahead, or tell myself where I was going. I knew, but I didn't tell myself. It didn't even occur to me not to tell myself. I was in that balance of knowing, but not wanting to know, and maybe I was helped to maintain it by the disturbing physical action of driving the car.

I went slowly across Trent Bridge and glimpsed the sky to the left, eastwards. The dawn was mixing in, all fiery and noble, watery and red, so I stepped on it and took the first turning left, on my way to join the Great North Road to Grantham.

Part Two

It is a common belief, after being hurt by them, that simple people are not so much wise as cunning. This is wrong. They are neither. They have the knack of becoming united with their souls at certain inspired times, that's all. Even then, they do not know what harm they have done. It is like a snake that has poison available when it is forced to strike. A simple person never strikes unless he has to, for he is basically lazy. Thus when he is driven to strike he uses far more venom than necessary because he was dragged unwillingly out of his simplicity and sloth which is, in effect, laziness. Something like this was in my mind when I remembered Miss Bolsover's view of me as simple. Though it should have flattered me, and in some ways did, I could never forgive her for it. Thus I felt no blame, as I drove towards Grantham, at having left her for good. Claudine at least knew better than to think I was strong and simple, and for that reason it was rather more difficult to get her out of my mind.

But I was never a victim of too much thought, at least not to the extent that it did me any good, so I lit a cigar and got the pedal down at Radcliffe by-pass, until my speed was touching fifty, a fair lick as far as I was concerned. There was no reason for hurrying. A slight rain spat down, and my wipers tackled it sluggishly as if the batteries had been low and still weren't charging properly. The engine was healthy, however, so I trundled on, beginning to make a road map of England under my wheels – though the winter didn't seem too good a time for it, and now that I was on my way I didn't love my freedom as I'd thought I would. In fact I began to feel a bit too much on my own, not only as if I didn't know where I was going (which was true) but also as if I didn't know where I had come from (which was false). But, I told myself, you can't make a move like this without feeling as if a compass needle is struggling to find a way out of your guts. It would have been more natural if I had stolen the car and was making a getaway. There would have been some point in it then, but unfortunately I hadn't been brought up to be a thief, so I couldn't have the dubious benefit of that. And if I'd make-believed it to be true, just to get a kick out of going away, it would have been telling lies, and I hadn't been reared to be a liar either, at least not to myself. So nothing was on my side except bleak reality, and for the moment I had to make do with that.

I felt better with Grantham left behind and me dipping south along the Great North Road. The land was black and bleak and waterlogged, and the tarmac cluttered with lorries so that I got scared yellow overtaking with hardly the speed or charge to do so, which made me realize for the first time that my cronky old car wasn't exactly the high-powered javelin I'd supposed it to be at first, out of heartfelt affection for it. I told myself though, that I mustn't lose faith in my piece of machinery, otherwise it might be tempted not to do its best, or even let me down if I got discouraged without real cause.

A heavier rain drifted in from the Fens, and one or two drops came through the makeshift patches in the roof, though not enough as yet to have me worried. But I swore at having forgotten the roll of sticky paper. Against the roadside stood a solitary figure in a cap and mackintosh, a small case at his feet. He lifted his thumb, so I drew in and stopped, forgetting to flash my indicators. A lorry close behind, weighing several thousand tons, pressed its horns in rage, making such a noise that the top of my head nearly unscrewed itself. The man smiled: 'He's in a bit of a hurry. They always are, though.'

'The bastard,' I said. 'Where are you going?'

He was about thirty, tall and thin, gnarled hands as he put them on my window. 'South.'

I liked his succinctness. 'So am I. Get in if you like.'

'I will,' he said, 'if you don't mind.'

'My name's Peter Wolf,' I said, as he slammed the door so I thought it would drop off.

'Likewise,' he said.

'What do you mean,' I asked, 'likewise?'

'Mine's Bill Straw,' he said, with the most obvious idiot grin I'd ever seen from someone who was plainly alert and all there. I was nervous with another person in the car, in case I had an accident, so till I got used to him, I drove like a man of sixty-five who'd been a careful saver all his life. 'Come far?' he asked.

'Derby,' I said. 'You?'

'Leeds. Business or pleasure?'

'Business,' I told him. 'I work for an insurance firm. Just spent three days in Derby wrapping up a contract for Rolls-Royce. Hell of a job. Cigarette?'

'Please. Thanks. Going down to look for work, myself.'

'What do you do?'

'Anything,' he told me cheerfully. 'Just done two years as an interior decorator. That's why I'm so pale. It's a lousy job among all that paint. Don't know what I'll do in London. It's a big place.'

I nodded. 'You can say that for it.' The one time I had been was on a school trip as a kid of twelve, when I'd seen Buckingham Palace (from the outside) and the Crown Jewels at the Tower of London (also from the outside). 'There's plenty of work there.'

'There's work anywhere,' he said with a glum wisdom, 'and that's a fact. But I'm going south because it's healthier. Can't this grim bus go any quicker?'

'If you're in that much of a hurry,' I said, 'get out and walk. 'Appen you'll pick up a Bentley to get you there for lunch.'

'Come off it,' he laughed. 'I wain't desert you.'

'Take your pick. I'll be stopping for a cup of tea and a swiss pudding soon.'

'I could do with a bite as well,' he said, in such a way that I knew he hadn't got the money to pay for it.

The transport café was full, with a line of men at the counter. I felt their sarky looks at my collar and tie and best grey suit, as if I had no right to be getting in their way, so I handed Bill Straw half a crown and said: 'Get two teas and two cakes,' while I sat at a table and waited. There was a *Daily Mirror* a foot from my hand, and I reached for it to read the front page, but a huge driver coming back from the counter with his breakfast of eggs, chips, sausages, bacon, beans, tomatoes, fritters, and fried bread bawled out: 'If you want a paper, buy one, mate, like I have to.'

He loomed over me. 'All right,' I said, 'keep your shirt on.' I stood up, as tall as he was, though not quite as meaty. 'Nobody's trying to make off with your paper. I was moving it out of the way so's I could have somewhere to put my tea.'

He recognized my Nottingham accent: 'I just thought you was one of them posh bleeders trying to save threepence.'

'Not me,' I said, as he chopped and scooped at his breakfast. Bill Straw came back and sat by chance where I could get a better look at him. 'You didn't sound much like an insurance nob to me just then,' he said, 'when you stood up to that pansy lorry driver.'

'Keep your trap shut, for Christ's sake, or he'll have you on toast.'

'He won't,' Bill said. 'I'll carve *him* up. I've done it before and I'll do it now.' I believed him. His face was thin, as though he'd fought with a razor now and again in his life to get what he wanted. Yet he had a few days' growth of beard, and I thought he should use one at his own face to start with. His suit was threadbare in all places at once, and his filthy shirt was drawn together with a tie so old that it had a hole in the front. 'Good of you to treat me,' he said. 'First bite since yesterday.'

I pushed another half-crown across: 'Get something else, then.'

He jumped up: 'I shan't forget this,' and almost ran to the front of the queue, so that I expected to see him get churned into little pieces and spat out through the windows. But he bustled at the nearest men, and gave them a strong sort of funny look, and it must have made things all right for him, because within minutes he was back with two eggs on fried bread which he scoffed almost before the plate was down. 'You're number one,' he said. 'You might not know it, but you've saved my life. It's the turning point.'

'Stow it,' I said. 'Forget it.'

'I shan't,' he said. 'I never will. You're the good sort, I know, who'd like me to forget it, but I wain't. Never.'

I was surprised at the colour it put into his cheeks, and

offered a fag to complete his meal. 'You don't seem to have earned much as a painter and decorator.'

'Maybe I wasn't doing that sort of work at all,' he smiled. 'When we're on the road again I'll tell you a story. It's so bloody long it'll keep us going to Timbuctoo, never mind London.'

From outside came the sound of a lorry about to drive off, and under the noise of its engine I heard the ripping of tin and a crunch of gravel or glass. Someone at the counter said: 'There goes Mad Bert. I expect he's chipped somebody's wagon.'

A man went to have a look, and came back laughing, while Mad Bert in the meantime seemed to have gone on his merry way towards Doncaster. 'It's all right,' he said, 'it's only a little black Popular. He's taken the front bumper off, dented the side, and smashed the lamp. I expect Bert's all right though.'

I jumped up and went outside, all eyes staring me through the door. The rain blinded and choked me. Apart from anything else I wondered why I'd chosen today to start on my travels. It was even worse than had been reported with such poker-faced glee. The left back wheel had been buckled, its tyre flattened and ripped.

Bill Straw followed me out. 'The destructive bastard. Got a spare wheel?' I nodded. 'Let's change it then,' he said. 'I'll not desert you, don't worry. You looked after me, now I'll help you. It ain't so bad. She'll go like a bomb again.' He bent down and pulled the bodywork straight so that the fresh wheel wouldn't catch on it. The meal seemed to have given him strength, and I was glad of that at least.

In ten minutes we had the new wheel on. 'The other's buckled,' he said. 'You might as well throw it away. Ain't worth a light.' I agreed, and he bowled it towards a fence and left it there.

'Let's have some more tea,' I said when he got back. 'Maybe we'll find out the name of the bandit who did it.' There was a sharp pain in my heart, and tears mingled with rain under my eyes. No one knew who Mad Bert was, or said they didn't, so after throwing a few curses over our shoulders we humped out. 'That's the solidarity of the working-class,' Bill muttered. 'Very strong among lorry drivers.'

'Well, fuck it,' I said, 'we're working-class, aren't we?'

'Not at a time like this, cock.'

In spite of its fearful wounds I felt a swamp of affection for my car as we went down the road. I was in a state of shock from my first automobile accident. All I wanted was peace and quiet, and didn't much fancy any talk from my passenger. In fact I was beginning to wish I'd never picked him up, and made up my mind that there'd be no more lifts from then on. I was brooding so badly that I almost got to blaming him for what had happened, till I realized how cranky this was, and laughed. 'What's up?' he asked.

'We're on our way,' I told him. 'The rain's packing in. It's light over Stamford.'

'We could do with it. But what's that smoke coming out of your headlamp?' Through the drizzle it was like a gnarled finger going a little way into the air, as if diffident about the prospect of finding God's arse. 'What now?' I cried.

'Pull in when you can, and I'll fix it. I'm a dab-hand when it comes to cars.' His voice had such conviction, such solemn wisdom, that he sounded as if he'd lived for three hundred years and knew everything. When I stopped on a grass verge he jumped to the front of the car and peered into the lamp. 'Switch off,' he shouted. 'Now put your lights on. Put them off. Now on. Off. On. Off. On. No. it's no good.'

'What is it then?' I wanted to know.

'Don't worry. You'll reach London today, as long as we get there before lighting-up time.' He was wrestling with the whole headlamp, as if it had threatened to come out and do for him. His two hands gripped it, a sort of spiteful look now on his face.

'Leave it,' I cried, getting out. 'Stop it.'

He fell back with it in his hand and, as if it could still sting, threw it with mighty strength clean over a hedge.

'That wasn't bloody-well necessary.'

'Didn't I say I knew about cars? Listen, I was a garage mechanic for three years. All the wires in that lamp had fused. You'd have had a fire on your hands if it'd bin left in. Got a fire extinguisher on board? Of course you bloody-well haven't. I'm not stupid, so don't think so.'

'Keep your shirt on,' I said, beaten for the moment. 'Let's get going.'

True to its promise, there was sun beyond Stamford, and we both became more friendly at the feel of it through the windscreen. 'I'll get on with my story,' said Bill.

'I'm listening,' I said, skating around a lorry and feeling for a moment as if neither of us would come out of it alive. But Bill hadn't shown a tremor, seemed to have absolute faith in my ability to get him to London. I began to have faith too, in him, glad now that I'd picked him up, in spite of the terrible (though necessary, I had to suppose) piece of brute surgery on my brand-new second-hand car.

My name isn't really Bill Straw,' he said, 'but don't let that bother you. What's in a name, anyway? I was born in Worksop thirty-seven years ago. My old man was a collier at the pit, and a weedy little get he looked as well, though he was hard enough for the job, but not so hard that he didn't die of dust on the windpipe when I was ten. I remember going with my mother to the Co-op to get fitted up with a black suit, the first one, and I'd have been proud of it if I hadn't been up to my neck in salt tears for my father. My two brothers and a sister followed Mother out of that shop like a gaggle of black crows, and next day we went to the cemetery, with fifty-odd colliers who were mates of the old man. It was a sunny day in September, and I remember being shocked and feeling sick because I'd always been told that most people that died, died at the end of winter, and I thought God had done this to my old man out of spite, and from then on I told myself I'd have nothing to do with Him. Kid's talk, because it don't matter whether you think about Him or not. Makes no difference, so you might just as well set your brain on to other things if you've got any brain at all.

'At school I didn't sing the hymns, just stood there with my lips firm, and though I got the strap for it I still didn't sing, not bloody me. I got it again and again, but I never gave in. The teacher complained to my mother about it, and she asked me to be a good lad and do as I was told, if not for her sake, then for my father's sake. That did it. I was more determined then not to give in, and they could do eff-all about it. It's no use mincing matters. We starved for the next ten years. The only time I didn't was when I got sent to an approved school for nicking a bike lamp. I wanted to go round the dark streets at night, and shine it into the sky. I must have been loopy to want to do a thing like that. Anyway, I went into a shop and took it from the counter, but the shopkeeper had a little glass panel in his cubby-hole door so that he could see anybody who came in. I was caught halfway down the street, and the police were called. So for a couple of years I got regular meals, even though they weren't much cop, and when I came home at fourteen I'd grown tall and well set up. I made up my mind never to be so stupid again as to get sent away.

'I got a job, and for fifty hours a week in a shop took home eleven shillings on Saturday night. I won't go into whether it was worth it or not, because I'm trying to tell you how I come to be in your car, not complain about my life. Mother took in collier's washing, and between us we kept the house going. Though I'd vowed never to nick anything again, I got into trouble a few years later. My youngest brother was still at school, and one day he came home with marks all over him where the teacher had pasted him. If we'd got a doctor and a lawyer on to our side we could have had this teacher thrown out on his arse – though I don't think so, somehow. You see, I don't believe in justice. I'd known him in my day as being a cruel bastard, but now I saw what he'd done to my own brother. Peter was the youngest of us, who'd hardly known his father, and for this reason we tried to make life easier for him than it was for us. He was also the weakest, and the brightest. A bit cheeky now and again, because perhaps he was spoiled, though he still had a hard enough life. Mother went to see the headmaster, but he shouted at her to leave the education of children to them, and get on with her own work. Something along those lines. You can imagine. Next day I left my job early and waited until that teacher came out of school. I caught him near the gates, and told him I was Peter's brother. He pushed me aside. In front of a lot of the kids I smashed him in the chops, knocking him against the wall. I hit him twice before he got over the shock and came back at me. I went a bit potty, and in spite of his cracks (he was strong as well) I split his eyes and lips, and made enough of a mess before the police arrived and dragged me clear. You can imagine what happened.

'The magistrate said I was a dangerous creature – that was the word he used – who ought to be put away from decent society – meaning that schoolteacher, I suppose. He said he'd have sent me to prison if I'd been old enough, but that under the circumstances, Borstal would have to do. I said nothing to all this. What was the use? I'd done the best I could to get my brother's own back, but at the same time I had no use for revenge. My bitterness sank to the bottom like sand in a bucket of water, and I went into Borstal like a saint. I was a good lad, and gave no bother. Once my storm of temper was over I wanted peace to come back on me. I went through it like a zombie, which is the nearest thing to saying that I was let loose on the world, at the end of three years, a reformed character. That Borstal was a tough place, though. You had to fend for yourself, even if you wanted to get through it as easily as you could. But it didn't seem too hard to me, I must admit. We all boasted as much as our imaginations let us. The stupid ones would claim that their brother was a racing driver or a champion jockey, but I used to entertain them with stories about gangs of young colliers from Worksop and Retford, who'd go to a lonely place in Sherwood Forest on Saturday afternoon to have fights with razors and bottles, just to pass the time, I said. I told them that even though I was young I'd been elected to the ranks of the Worksop Choppers because of my prowess at the pit face (where I'd never worked). They believed me, I don't know why, and these stories made them wary of me when it came to persecution. They never knew when I wouldn't go as berserk as a Worksop Chopper, and have at them in such a way that a few would bleed to death before they could overpower me. That didn't save me from getting mixed up in a few midnight scuffles, but I soon learned that as long as you go on hurting somebody, then they can't hurt you. If you stop, expect it, get out of the way, jump clear, mate.

'In this frame of mind I came out of Borstal. Being set free made me feel like a piece of straw blown about in the wind. On the way home I stopped in Worksop market and pinched a big tin of pineapple chunks so that we could celebrate. It was a drizzly evening, but I found the house empty, because Mother had gone to see her sister, and had mis-read the date in my letter. I got in by the scullery window, made a good fire and sat down to wait. I looked at the tin of chunks in the middle of the table, my only contribution to the household in three years. To stop myself crying at how hard so many people in the world were done by, I got a tin-opener and took the top right off. They were well-packed, sweet fruit that all of us could enjoy. Pineapple chunks had always been a luxury, even though they did taste like turnips and sugar. I emptied them into a basin and put it in the cupboard. The circular tin-top had come off so neatly it looked like a razor, and I turned it round, running the ball of my thumb along it. I thought: why don't I cut my throat so that that will be that? Being nineteen I felt I'd had enough, decided that I was good to no one and no good to myself. It was possible to do it, but when I thought that if I didn't do it then, I would never do it, I lost heart and didn't do it. It would make more trouble for my mother and the others, and none for myself. That was what stopped me, not because I hadn't got the nerve. I wanted to do it because it seemed the only sensible thing I'd ever thought of, but to be sensible like that you needed to be the most selfish bastard in the world. The others came back an hour later, and they were so happy to see me, you'd have thought all their troubles were over now that I was in the house again.

'It was hard to get a job, just out of Borstal. I tried till my eyes went beady at the newspaper columns, and my legs rickety with walking. What references had I got to flash before their Bible-spiked noses? Still, there are some good souls in the world, and such a person was the rich old man who wanted a bloke to push him about in his wheelchair. When I called at his big house for the job he was sitting in the garden, and one of his servants showed me out there. A gramophone record was playing and I had to stand a couple of minutes till it finished, then, out of the goodness of my heart because he couldn't reach, and not because I was sucking up to him, I lifted the gramophone head and stopped it. "I've had twenty young fellows here so far," he said, "and I'm tired of it. Any special qualifications?"

'"No sir," I told him. "I'm fresh out of Borstal." He was eighty years of age, and so shrunken and small that when he burst out laughing I thought he'd fall to pieces. I hoped he would, then I could blow away the dust and go on with my search. But there was something about him that toned down my hatred, specially when he said: "I'll take you on, then. When can you start?"

'Because of my shabby clothes I was led off by the butler who showed me a row of uniforms upstairs, and by luck we found one that fitted. It wasn't the best sort of work, but I got thirty bob a week, as well as my keep, which wasn't bad at that time of day. For the first time in my life I not only had a room of my own, small as it was, and right under the roof, but also the chauffeur gave me an hour's driving every afternoon while the old man took his sleep. On my half-day off I went home, and gave all the money I earned to my mother, except a bob or two for fags. It wasn't the sort of job you could ever boast about in Borstal, but at least it kept me alive, and rigged my brothers and sister in good clothes from time to time.

'The man's name was Percy Whaplode, and he owned a lot of land with farms on top and endless coalmines underneath. As I pushed him for an hour in the morning and an hour in the afternoon around his garden and park he'd chat to me on the beauties of life, but mostly as if I weren't there, cataloguing what he was going to miss when his head finally hit the tin lid. Often he really did talk to people he knew, or had known, but who weren't there, or were no longer there. If they could have heard him they'd have been shocked, I can tell you, and many a time I was so doubled up with trying not to laugh at his fanciful language that I was frozen at the handle and not able to push. Now and again he'd speak to his two sons who'd been killed in the Great War, telling them how they ought to do their lessons, and study well when they got to university. Or he'd tell them, as I pushed him along the path by a stream, how good it would be for him and their mother (already dead) when they got married and had children of their own. Sometimes his stepbrother came to see him from Yorkshire. He was twenty years younger, and always shouted at poor old Percy if he wasn't able to hear him properly.

'When it rained Percy had to stay inside, and I'd push him for half an hour up and down the ground-floor corridors, because he couldn't bear to be still. For the rest of the time he got me to read to him, and this was torture at first because he'd curse and shout and all but crack me with his stick if I was too slow or made a mistake. But sometimes he could be patient, and that helped, so that after a month or two I got to be a good reader, since it seemed to rain every other bloody day. All in all, we were quite friendly, and in any case I was forced to take his banter in good part because he was paying me for it. The chauffeur said he hadn't seen Percy in such frequent good moods for years, and hinted that maybe he'd leave me a few quid in his will if I stuck at it. I took this as a joke, a bloody good one on the chauffeur's part and a poor one on mine. Money would never come to me like that. I'd either have to earn it, or steal it, and I didn't yet know which was the harder way.

'I grew to feel at home there, wallowing in the easy hours and comparatively mild work. The housekeeper and the chauffeur were actually quite kind to me, talked to me from time to time like a human being, and fed me like a turkey-cock. My driving lessons went on so well that during my time at that job I was able to get a licence, paid for by the house. The chauffeur took Mr Whaplode for a drive every week around the Dukeries, and it was said that I might one day have a go at this, as if it were the greatest honour I could ever hope for.

'The housekeeper's name was Audrey Beacon, a plump woman pushing forty who came from some place near Chesterfield. She dressed plain in her job, but was good enough looking for the chauffeur, Fred Cresswell, to claim having had her a time or two, though I didn't altogether believe him because she'd got the sort of mouth and seemed the kind of person who wouldn't have let him go so easily. He claimed she wasn't bad, except that there was a bit too much meat to plough through before you got to it. It took me some time to realize why she was feeding me up so well. One afternoon when I was lounging in the kitchen she came up behind and pressed her topwork into my back. I'd had one or two girls on the tumble, but nothing as grown up as this. She was kissing me at the shoulder blades, even though my shirt was on, and I was burning so much I daren't turn round. When I did, I looked into her grey eyes, and put my arms about her shoulders. We got to kissing, and before anybody could come in and part us she told me to come to her room that night. I must have looked at her gone out at this, but she said, sharp: "You know where it is, don't you?"

'To cut a long story short, if she was a meal (and she was, I can tell you) I had a slap-up feed from it, because every time the plate emptied it was filled up again. It went on for months, so as far as that job went there was nothing lacking in it. What more could a young chap want? I had work, money, food, love, and shelter. I swear blind I've never had it so good since. And yet, I can't think now how it was possible, but I got tired of her. From one day to the next I just didn't go to her room. Something happened to me, and I don't know what it was. I just closed up against her. I started going to Worksop more often, just to call home for half an hour in the evening. I'd have a pint at some pub, or a cup of tea somewhere, then walk the few miles back and crash into bed. I didn't even meet another girl. Audrey tried to get me out of my mood, but found it was more solid than that, so she turned against me, and wouldn't rest till she got me into trouble and saw the back of me.

'This was difficult, because there was nothing in which she could fault me. I was, as they say, a man of sober habits who even, by now, liked walking around the house and looking at Percy's paintings and sometimes dipping into his library when I got the chance. The old man was fond of dogs, and had a few slouching idly around the house. Now and again a red setter would follow us on our walks. Dogs are only valuable if they're useful, but I had nothing special against them, even so. For his eighty-first birthday one of his great-grandchildren (no doubt thinking about his position in the will) sent him a Yorkshire terrier. The old man shed tears at this tender thought, and considered the dog to be his greatest treasure. In actual fact it was a bloody nuisance. It ran about and pissed all over everywhere and, worse still, took a strong dislike to me. It's hard to say why, because I left it alone, and never so much as looked when it barked at me (and backed away) as I walked through the house to collect Percy for his outing.

'One day it snapped at my ankle, and I thought: this has got to stop. I did nothing, but just walked on. Then I felt a rip at my flesh. Audrey Beacon was on her way by, but the pain was so sharp I let out a bloody good kick. I should have been man enough to ignore it, or just laugh, but I lost control, and the kick got it right on the arse. In fact the dog went skidding three-quarters of the way back up the corridor where it had come from. I suppose this might have been all right, but unluckily it let out a great yelp that echoed through the house. It was quite close to the room Whaplode was in. His deafness came and went, and this time he heard everything as clear as a bell. He called out as if he'd been stabbed, and I went in to see what was the matter. "The dog," he cried. "What's happened?"

'I told him that I'd accidently stepped on it in passing, but he didn't believe me, pulled the bell and went on roaring for the others. He threatened to sack everybody if he didn't get to the bottom of it, but Audrey Beacon, as cool as a stone at the bottom of a stream, told him all she had seen. So I was ordered off the premises, Percy holding his pet dog, tears in his pot-eyes that didn't look at me at all. I showed him the teeth marks on my leg and the rip in my trousers, but it made no difference. I walked from the place with four pounds in my pocket, on the lookout for something else to do.

'I picked yesterday's newspaper out of a litterbox and noticed that the war had started. It didn't take me long to get a job. Luckily my driving licence came in handy because I got van work taking bread from a bakery to shops in the town. My family never wanted for it, because I dropped three or four prime loaves there every morning on my way by. The trouble was that I didn't think. It still is, but my experience of the last few years has taught me a lot. The world's got no use for people who don't think. If you can't think, then you can never be like they want you to be, and that's no good, either for you or them. Maybe I'll be able to steer a course between the two, and if I can do that, there might be no object to what I can get out of my life – in spite of myself.'

The sun warmed us. While he talked we smoked through my supply of fags. It was like listening to the radio, which I didn't have because I'd left it with my mother. The car cruised at about forty, and Stamford was right behind. The morning was getting to its hind legs, and I was well and truly on my way, snapping the strings and ribbons one by one. I was glad they stretched such a long distance out with me, because as they broke each strand flew right back, giving the impression of being severed for ever. During the break in Bill Straw's story, when he seemed to be gathering himself to tell more of it, which would no doubt increase the lines of his worried face because he was nearer to the end, I brooded on Claudine and how I still loved her. After all, she was going to have my child, and I decided to write a long and passionate letter when I got to London. I smiled at the thought that everything was going according to plan, the only trouble being I didn't know whose plan it was, and I got brooding on this when suddenly the radiator blew up.

'Pull in,' Bill Straw shouted. I did so but, jumping out before him, lifted the bonnet to see how my lady did. 'You've got no water,' he said. 'Burned up. Not a drop. Don't you know the first thing about cars?'

'She was full a couple of days ago,' I said.

He had a hand clasped to his face: 'Something's wrong, then.'

'Why don't you ever tell me a bit of good news?'

'I will when I've got some. You walk down the road for some water, and I'll wait here,' he said. 'Just give me a fag to keep me company.' I gave him the last out of my packet and set off.

After about a quarter of a mile a lorry passed me, and Bill Straw was waving and laughing from the cab. Then it was out of sight. That's the last of him, I thought. Now I shan't hear the end of his story. He'll be in London soon, at that rate.

Easy come, easy go. I suppose that's what life is like on the road.

There was neither house nor filling station for another half-hour. I walked quickly, and the least exertion made me sweat, which was why I'd never taken to hard work, because I didn't like to sweat. Not only did it smell, but it made me afraid that some vital part of me might melt away, if it ran too freely. But after a while walking became pleasant. I relaxed and slowed my pace, in spite of traffic pounding a few feet from my right elbow. Between such noise I heard birds and smelled the whiff of fields, and knew how free one might feel if there was no car to anchor your heart to its engine.

In the distance I saw someone walking towards me, and I would ask him where I could get water for my car. The face was familiar as he came close, and then I saw that it was Bill Straw carrying a jerrycan of water. 'I thought you needed a walk,' he said. 'It's no use sitting cramped up in that driving position for six or seven hours without stretching your legs. Makes you safer at the wheel. And it's good for the liver. Come on, let's water our horsepower.'

We walked back together. 'I suppose you thought I'd left you?' he said with a laugh, holding up twenty Player's. 'Here, have a fag to keep you company! I took them from the counter when his eyes were elsewhere. Don't feel bad about it. You can pay him for 'em when we pass. I promised to take the can back, anyway. A very obliging bloke. If you need petrol we ought to buy a few gallons off him, just to show willing.'

'You have everything buttoned up.'

'Not yet,' he said, alluding to something in his own mind, 'but I shall have soon.'

'What do you mean?'

'Ask me in three months.'

'Christ,' I said, 'where do you suppose we'll be in three months?'

'Down among the tadpoles, for all I know. Where do you expect to be?'

'I don't know. I'm on my own.'

'I thought you said you was an insurance bloke,' he said. 'Not that I believed you, with a car like that.'

'I'll tell you all about it,' I said, 'when you've finished your story.'

'I'll soon do that, when we get to that bloody car. Still, I'll see it through, though it's cutting hours off my life.'

I poured water into the radiator, screwed back the cap, and started up. Steam rose from the front, but I thought this was the residue of the previous heat, though Bill in his way of facing the truth with the eye-teeth of reality said that this wasn't possible, because it could have cooled twenty times over while we'd gone for the water. By the time we reached the garage the radiator was empty again. Discouragement came easy to me, and I could have wept as I looked at it, wondering whether I shouldn't abandon the car and tramp to the nearest railway station. I could be back home in a few hours. 'You can if you like,' said Bill Straw when I mentioned it. 'But what's the point? It's such a tiny setback.'

'How bloody tiny is it though?'

He held out his hand: 'Give me five bob – no, make it ten – and I'll settle everything.' I'd taken to him, bonded by his story, and the look of self-assurance that came on to his face whenever there was an emergency – which was beginning to mean all the time. Yet also, in my black and superstitious way, I couldn't help wondering whether there'd be an emergency at all if he weren't with me. But I gave him ten bob. 'See what you can do then.'

He left me leaning against the car with the caution not to press too hard in case I fell through it. He came back with the jerrycan full of water, which he'd bought from the proprietor, as well as a roll of sticky tape, and a packet of chewing-gum. This last we masticated rapidly, its foul mint taking away the fag-smoke and fresh-air taste patiently built up since leaving home. 'Give it all to me,' he said, which I was glad to do. He squelched it into a plaster, then got down to the radiator, plugging the hole and reinforcing it with tape. 'That'll hold for a while,' he said, standing up to fill the radiator. 'Meanwhile, we'll be living on a diet of chewing-gum till we hit London. It's good for the digestion, anyway, if you treat us to a dinner in half an hour.'

'I'll be sure to,' I said, and we set out once more.

He lit two fags and passed one over, before going on with his story: 'One day I stopped my bread van near a park and fed half of my load to the birds and ducks. I wasn't as stupid as you imagine, because I'd already taken my daily quota home, and enough for the next few days, as well, if my mother wrapped most of it in tea towels as I'd asked her to do. Then I drove back to the office and told them I was packing the job in. When the manager said he'd fetch the police I laughed in his face. He thought I was a bit cracked, so gave me my wages less a quid for the loaves I'd fed to the birds and fishes. It was an awful winter, snow and ice piled everywhere, and I can't see anything starve.

'I went from one job to another, till I was called up into the Army. This wasn't as bad as I'd expected, after the training, because I was posted to be a driver at a camp in Yorkshire. Much of my two bob a day went to my mother as a sort of pension, but I begrudged it a bit now because I needed more to smoke. I had a night shift for a week, then a day shift, for my job was taking a lorry-load of rations to a special signals camp a few miles from the main base. It was regular, and it was easy. One day I was thumbed for a lift by a corporal, who asked me to take him on to the signals depot. He was short and fat, and had wavy hair spreading from a parting down the middle of his head. He'd been a wireless operator in the Merchant Navy, but had left it and joined the Army because he was fed up with the cruel sea. He asked if I'd like to earn ten quid, by picking up a load one night and driving it ten miles to the nearest town. It was a good chance, and I took it. The family was having a hard time, because Peter, who'd been next on the list for work at fourteen, had managed to get to a grammar school and needed cash for his clothes and books.

'On the night in question, having delivered the rations, I was flagged down beyond the camp gates by this corporal, and we went on to the signals school. "Now stop," he said, while the road was still in the middle of nowhere, though I soon saw that it was only ten yards from a lonely part of the camp fence. A gang of swaddies were staggering through the gap, and began loading my lorry up with two hundred typewriters – though I didn't know what they were till afterwards. I drove the corporal to town, and the goods, shall I say, were unloaded. Money was put into my hand, and I got back to my hut without anyone being much the wiser.

'The only time you are in heaven and don't know it is those few days between doing something wrong and catching the first glimpse of the police coming to ask you questions which are going to start the long slide down on your arse to prison. You walk lighter on your feet, breathe sweeter and better air – so it seemed after the lead weight had just fallen. Life is marvellous, and you are not only good-natured with everyone, but they are also friendly to you. You don't even think of the past that was no good, or wish to live for ever because you feel so wonderful. Nothing matters but the exact minute, which you ignore anyway. It's a state of grace, and the strength that you get from it is the easiest sort to carry. I know about this, because it's happened to me a few times, which made life worth living more than anything else. But that was a long time ago, and I hope I've got over the need of it now.

'Half the signals school must have been involved in that great typewriter grab, and a dozen of them got sent down, including me for eighteen months, for I was said to be the key man in it, the lynchpin of the whole operation. It passed the time on, and taught me a thing or two. The war was a little bit more on its way towards peace, though not far enough, for when I got out I was dragged back into the Army, and ended up in Normandy, with too much battle for my sort of stomach.

'I got the Military Medal for driving a load of ammunition to some blokes who had been cut off by the Germans. I didn't know I was doing it, you can bet. Normally I was shit-scared when a bomb went off five miles away, and skulked around at base so that I wouldn't get any dangerous jobs, but this one time I forgot to hide, and was sent to a village that nobody told me was almost behind the bloody lines. I thought as I drove along: what's that whizzing and whistling noise? The wheels shook, and when soil fell over the windscreen I must have been miles away in my woolly brain because I just put on the windscreen wipers, which naturally made knock-all difference. In any case the lorry was off the road, skirting the lip of a crater, but I kept the wheel steady. Shells were croaking like great frogs all over the place, but I got back to the road.

'When I reached the village I wondered why the butcher was working in the open air. Then I cottoned on. It was a shambles, and the twenty or so blokes still alive and unwounded were ready to lynch me. One of them pointed a Sten, but the others didn't want to carry things that far. All hell had been blasting for hours, but I'd reached them during a lull, so called, when the Germans hadn't seemed too keen on the fight either. Our blokes had been short of ammunition, and the officers had been pooped off, so they'd decided to surrender and get taken prisoner. Then when I showed up with ammunition it meant they'd have to go on fighting to the last man, as it were, and that's what made them just about ready to do me in. You should have heard the curses! The flower of the British Army. Some of the poor boggers were in tears. I sulked, and offered to drive them back in my lorry, which was the least I could do. A sergeant got on the radio to company headquarters and asked for permission to pull out, and back the answer came from a solid dug-out: "Fight on, you idle bastards," and he was ready to put his boot through that piece of machinery. We had a meeting, and formed a plan. He asked HQ to arrange an air attack on the outskirts of the village because German tanks were moving up. They agreed, and said it would arrive in five minutes. At this, we threw off the arms and clambered on the lorry ourselves, packing it tight. At the first sound of planes I drove like a madman away from that village, shot at from all sides. Behind us the planes did their job so well, as we'd known they would, that the whole place went up in smoke and flame. "That was the end of us," the sergeant beside me in the cab shouted.

'We got back safe, telling how the Germans had attacked in such numbers that we couldn't help but piss off out of it. Three of us got a medal for that brave job, but I kept a long way from exploding shells for the rest of the war. Even the pilots who blasted the village got a pat on the back for wiping out attacking Germans who were nowhere to be seen. My brain swims when I think of it, which I don't, any more. I was twenty-three at the time, but felt fifteen because, after all, it was a childish throwback sort of game, playing at war, a fact which everybody realized at the time, though nobody said as much.

'Later on, I was out of it, and my medal went over the side of the boat coming back to Southampton. At home I found I had one brother in the Army, another at work, my sister in the family way, and my mother in a mental hospital. Within a few weeks I was back in prison, and feeling as if I'd been born there. Those months were so black in my mind that I don't even remember what I got sent down for. I was haunted by the looney-bin look on my mother's face, which it seemed she had always had, but I hadn't noticed it before. I never want to be twenty-five again, that's all I can say. I breathed a sigh of relief when I was twenty-six, determined that from then on my life would take a turn for the better. To make sure this happened I did two things which made sure it never could: I got a job, and I got married.

'We met in a pub, Jane Shane and me. Her middle name was Audrey, which she favoured most, Tawdry Audrey from Tibshelf, who got off the bus one Saturday night in Worksop market place. During an hour of comfortable drinking I saw she had smoky short black hair and diamond eyes, pale cheeks and thinnish lips, a real beauty until she opened her raucous chops. She'd had a baby by another man, but I wasn't to know this until after we were married, and in those days I thought an agreement with a woman was something you couldn't break no matter what the other party had done. After a quiet wedding at the registry office, she brought her kid to live at our house. My mother, now out of the looney-bin, went absolutely soft over the little boy, so that he soon loved her far more than his own mother who, in fact, totally ignored him except to kick and shout whenever he unluckily crossed her path.

'Getting married seemed a good thing to do, but it wasn't long before I got to Cuckold's Cross, so one day I didn't go to work but took a train to London instead. There were plenty of odd and casual jobs there, but they didn't pay very much. One day I met a man who asked if I'd knock a car off for him, and take it to a certain garage in Bermondsey. There'd be a good load of money in it for me, but on delivery, he said. I asked what sort he wanted. We stood side by side in an arcade pumping tanners into a slot machine. He laughed because I'd given him a choice: "Get me a Jaguar."

'"I suppose you want it for a job?"

'"Shut your mouth," he answered.

'"I'll deliver it late tonight, then. Tell them to expect me."

'Back in my room at St Pancras I put on my best clothes. Then I bought a couple of window-cloths from a bucket shop, and put myself on the Northern Tube. It was a rainy day, spring, so I had my mac on and walked the streets and lanes of Hampstead with eyes wide open. I spotted two or three likely ones, but waited at a corner till I saw a well-dressed bloke get out of a flash Jag, a real beauty, and walk to a block of flats down the road. With a bunch of flowers and a parcel, he looked set for a long visit, or so I hoped. I started cleaning the windows of his car with my new orange cloths. A side window was half an inch open, so I took the newspaper from my pocket, smoothed it as flat as a board, and by sliding it through and then down was able to press the button that released the latch. I could get in whenever I liked, but showed no hurry. Even if the owner came back I could say I was down on my luck and only wanted to earn a bob or two by polishing his glass. Who could object to that?

'But the time came to act, so I lifted the bonnet and started the engine. I snapped it down, got in, and was off, moving from the kerb and turning for the opposite direction to the one I'd seen its last owner vanish in. Like a newborn fool I'd left the dusters on the bonnet, just under the windscreen, and when I stopped the car to get them in, the engine stalled. Sweat roped off me, but I fixed it again, tightening the wires and burning my fingers. This time I was definitely away, taking the ring road and getting into Bermondsey from the south.

'When the garage door closed behind me Claud Mogger-hanger came out of a cubby-hole office and tapped the car at certain vital places. "Last year's. I'll give you fifty quid for it."

'I didn't like the face of him because he looked not only all brawn but all brain as well, middle-aged, half-bald, a man who'd had enough prison and so much good living in his life that he'd kill you rather than argue. "It must have cost fifteen hundred quid," I said.

'"Take off the purchase tax, wear and tear, and the fact that it ain't yours, and you're lucky to get forty."

'My blood was up: "You just said fifty!"

'"Its value goes down by the minute," he smiled, while the three other blokes behind him laughed. "Thirty now."

'I gave in: "Fifty, then, and I'll clear out." He nodded, and I looked at the fivers to check on the silver thread, and make sure the head wasn't upside down, or that the ink was dry. Even then I wasn't sure. A couple of experts were unscrewing the number plates and dragging out spraying equipment, as if they really had a rush job on. Moggerhanger glared at me for hanging around, so I went away, spitting and cursing.

'I got work with a group of blokes washing cars in St James's Square, which in good weather drew in about twelve quid a week. I didn't tell a soul about my fifty quid, but stitched the whole of it into my jacket to save till I was in need and no one could wonder where I'd got so much money. One day I was washing an Austin, and the rough Geordie who was more or less in charge told me to go to the other side of the Square and scrub down the Daimler that had just come in, a rush job for a regular and generous customer. It was a warm day so I took off my jacket and laid it on the car next to the Austin, then went over right away to do the Daimler. When I came back, an hour later, it was gone. I looked at the empty spot and a black wave floated over my eyes, going away just as quickly. I leaned against the car, then jumped into a frantic search in case I'd moved it at the last moment and forgotten where. I found Geordie, and asked if he'd seen my jacket. "No," he said. "I've got one."

'"I left it by the Austin."

'He laughed: "I hope you haven't seen the last of it. Ask Johnny Spode." Johnny had vanished, and never came back. I found my coat stuffed under a bush, the money ripped out, so that I was practically penniless once more. If I had suddenly been able to get my hands on the thieving bastard I'd have choked the shit out of him. It's all right robbing the rich, but when one working bloke robs another it makes high treason look like a parking offence. I was reduced to washing up in cafés, which kept me so broke that a fortnight later I went to the garage in Bermondsey to see if they needed another car. I'd have sold them a Rolls-Royce for twenty quid if they'd said yes, but the place was derelict and boarded up, so I'd only wasted my bus fare.

'To deaden the long drag back I bought a newspaper, sat up front on the top deck to get the feel of being on my own while I read it. At one piece of news my head rattled. I pulled the paper on to my knee before I could fix it firm enough for reading, not knowing whether to laugh or get off the bus and run for my life in case the coppers had already got the hint to come after me. Johnny Spode had been charged with trying to pass false fivers at a pub in the East End, and I knew of course they could only be those Claud Moggerhanger had given me for the stolen Jaguar, and that I'd stitched into a secret pocket of my working jacket, and that Johnny had nicked from me. He'd been remanded in custody, which meant they were trying to make him squeal where he'd got them. I hoped it was the last of the bunch they'd found him with, for then he might argue his way out of it by saying some toff whose name he couldn't remember and whose face was covered with smallpox had given it him for cleaning his car. In which case it could be I was in no danger at all.

'I didn't believe it, not on your life. It was better to be on the safe side, and flee. I got to my room and packed my small case, then spent my last few bob on a packet of fags and a bus ride to the south-west. This only took me twelve miles but soon I got a lift in a car going to Salisbury, which was lucky for it was starting to rain. My exhaustion, my downhearted ruin seemed certain and complete. My only need was sleep, but the chap driving wanted to know why I was heading for Salisbury.

'"Going to see the Cathedral?" he asked, "or have you got friends there? Myself, I'm off to Dorchester, to look at a house I'm hoping to buy. What's your work?"

'I told him I was a gardener who'd heard there was work at

Salisbury, and so I was on my way to find it. I didn't spin any hard-luck yarn, though when he set me down in the middle of the town he opened his wallet and gave me ten bob. My thanks were never more sincere, at that time, and maybe it was an omen of good luck, because I stayed two years in Salisbury. Nobody bothered me during all that while, and I was known by a few people well, and many people slightly, and they saw me only as a quiet person who'd come down from the North. I gave out that I had worked as a miner since I was fourteen but that now, nearly twenty years later, having been menaced by a soot-kiss of silicosis, I had to get out of such drudgery. What's more, my widowed mother had died, and being the only child of an only child, there was nothing in the line of duty to keep me in the North Pole of Nottinghamshire.

'I worked as a van driver and odd-job man for a market gardener, so that I was soon seen to be getting my health back, much to everyone's touching concern. I lodged with a widow who had a moonshine face, and who (so it was said to me later in the pub) had been married for a fortnight fifteen years ago to a man gone into the Merchant Navy at the beginning of the war. Before the end of it he had just vanished, so after a while I shared her bed at night because, believe me, there was still a lovely amount of juice in her.

'But one morning, for no other reason than waking up with a headache (or it may have been stomach ache, I forget, and in any case, it doesn't matter which it was) I kissed her goodbye as I always did on going to work, and came back an hour later when I knew she'd be out shopping. I had forty quid put by, as well as a watch and a small radio, and with my suitcase and overcoat I walked to the station and took the mile-a-minute train to London. I wondered whether I hadn't done the wrong thing when I saw the desert of Surbiton out of the window, but stepping from the train at Waterloo, I walked along the Thames to Hungerford Bridge through the air of summer dust and smoke that made me shout with happiness. I crossed the footbridge, sweating over my case, though it wasn't that heavy, and stood looking at the green water oiling its way against the supports below, and passenger boats loaded with people setting off downstream for Greenwich. The line of the shore pressed itself into me, and I was disturbed from looking at it by the whole bridge shuddering as a train punched out of Charing Cross. I was so happy I dropped a shilling in an old man's cap who was playing a tin whistle. The city seemed made for me, a land of treasure I'd never felt so close to before.

'When you feel like this on coming to town there's only one sort of life you can lead, and that is a life of crime. I own up to it. Knocking around Soho I heard of a garage that took stolen cars, and I lost no time in selling a few I found by the roadside – usually cars of the medium-expensive kind – and this time I got a better price for them, I might tell you. As is only right and proper, one thing led to another, and I began to help in robberies, usually as the driver of a getaway car. In this I was expert because I'd studied the map and was familiar with much of London. I could do a zig-zag course with such speed and skill that I'd throw anybody off the scent. To bring my story right up to press I was one of the four who did a job that netted eight thousand pounds. The trouble was that I got caught, while the others didn't. We were getting away, but the cops were closing in because we had a radio with their wave length on it and could hear them yapping to each other. So I let the others out, and set off towards Croydon on my own. I was nabbed, and the beak gave me five years. I've just finished four of them, and got out yesterday, heading for London now so that I can claim my two thousand pounds. Don't tell me it's hopeless and that I won't find it, because I know I will. I could have got off with a lot less than five years if I'd given the other three away and put the police on the trail of the loot, but I didn't. I held out and said I'd done nothing except steal sixty-two cars, and finally that was all they could get me for.'

The end of Bill Straw's story brought us north of Biggleswade. Rain was coming through the roof, and the South wasn't living up to its promise. With so much damage done to the car, I was driving on borrowed time. Both of us felt it. The engine was coughing like a man in the last stages of TB and it was Bill Straw's opinion that, as the car seemed to need not only a new body but also a new engine, I might be wise after all to abandon ship and leave it by the roadside to rot. 'It doesn't sound good,' he said, 'so you might as well cut your losses. Anyway, let's have our dinner and give it time to cool down. A bag of damp hay might encourage it. Do it the world of good, and we'd benefit by something to eat as well – at least I would. Can't seem to live on fags like you do.'

'You're always on about food,' I told him, 'when you're not running down my car, or boasting about your past exploits.'

'You should feel privileged,' he said, 'to be driving me to London. I'll be a rich man when I get there, and then I'll pay you back tenfold for all you might still spend on me.' I had a strange feeling when he said this, not at all distrustful of him, as if he really might turn up in the future and demonstrate some blinding shaft of truth out of all the lies he'd been telling.

I parked as far as I could from the lorries, and followed Bill in. He stood at the counter, eyes turned up to the menu as if it was the light from heaven. 'What'll you have?'

'I've already decided,' he said. 'It don't take me long to make up my mind when it comes to food.'

'I like a man of decision and character,' I said, in a sarcastic way which finally annoyed him.

'You're getting a bit too bloody familiar. If you want to eat alone, you can. If you want to drive on your own, you can do that as well, but you'll end up walking to London with that wreck on your back.' He laughed so loud at this that the girl behind the counter asked him what he wanted. He rattled off a poem to the empty stomach: 'Tomato soup, my lovely, then liver, sausages, onions and mashed spuds. Then steamed pudding and custard, a couple of them jam tarts, a mug of tea, four slices of bread and butter, twenty fags and a knife, fork, and spoon.'

'Steady on,' I said, 'I'll be bankrupt.' He didn't hear me.

'Is that all then?' the girl asked.

'Except for a bit of you,' he said, jutting his scruffy, but confident face over the counter. She blushed at this, stepped back and smiled: 'Cheeky devil! I'll call you when it's ready.' She turned to me: 'What about you, then?'

'Beans on toast and a mug of tea.'

'You won't carry that car far on that!' Bill laughed.

'You're getting a bit too bloody familiar as well,' I snapped, paying out the best part of a quid on his monumental scoff. 'Nothing's gone right since I picked you up.'

We walked to a table and sat down in silence. A slim, dark-haired woman of about twenty-five was at the other end of it. The fact that she looked bored with her solitude made her more fascinating than she might have been if seated in a convivial atmosphere such as the midst of a gay family gathering. But in any case I was halfway struck by her as she smoked a tipped cigarette over the remains of an apple pie – while I waited for sufficient wit and perhaps courage before opening my mouth to say something. I knew I had to speak before the food came, because it would be bad manners to talk on a full mouth.

Bill Straw must have had similar ideas, for he opened with: 'Will you pass the sauce, duck? I must have a lick of something or I shall die. That dinner I ordered's taking ages.' She slid the half-filled bottle along, smiling at his common and slimy wit. He took the newspaper out of my pocket and offered it to her: 'Like to read this while you're waiting?'

'No,' she said. 'Thank you.'

'I don't blame you,' he said, drinking the sauce to the bottom. 'It's full of lies. Do you want a lift to London, with me?'

I hoped she'd get up and kick him in the shins, but she didn't: 'I am going that way,' she said with what could only have been a smile of gratitude. 'Is it in a lorry?'

'Car. We've come from Grantham. I don't know why the mean bleeders don't put sugar on the table. I could have a dip if they did. That sauce just set me going.' When the waitress arrived she set each plate before him so that most of the table was covered. 'Will you join me?' he offered. I might have said the same, but what can you do with beans on toast?

'I've eaten already.'

'Sure?'

'Of course. I set out from Leeds, and so far I've made good time.'

'Well,' he said, ladling the soup into his lantern-chops, 'we'll get you there in a couple of hours, more or less, if we all get out and push. My name's Bill Straw. What's yours?'

'June. Do you live in London?'

He didn't answer till the soup was gone, then stabbed his finger towards me. 'He does, I don't.' The further he got into his meal, the more clipped his answers were, though he still left space between his lips for questions to get out: 'Are your parents alive?'

Her eyebrows wrinkled with surprise. 'What do you want to know for?'

'Just wondered, love.' It was hard to say whether he was the greatest card of them all, or just plain stupid. He took life too easy for a wise man, it seemed to me, and that might be dangerous if we got too close, so I thought it would be best to avoid him when our mutual journey was over. 'You live in London?' he asked her.

'When I can.'

'That's a funny answer' – onions streaming out of his mouth.

'It's expensive. Makes it hard. But I like it there. Life's interesting.'

'Doing what?'

'Hey,' she cried, 'who are you, anyway? You're so genuine you act like a plain-clothes man.' It was something I'd never have thought about.

'That's a lark, for somebody like me. The best joke I've heard in ten years. I just wanted to know what you did.'

'I work,' she said. 'What's your sweat, then?'

'Painter and decorator. I'm fed up with Notts, so I'm going down south. Left my wife and kids in Mansfield yesterday. Spent last night with my girlfriend in Nottingham and now I'm off to fresh fields and pastures new. Where will I be to-night then, eh?' he ended with a leer. She said nothing to this, as if to show that he had gone too far. He accepted it, but only because he could then devote complete attention to his meal, which he gobbled so that anyone would have thought he'd fallen in love with that now, in his flippant, one-sided way.

I don't know what sort of car she imagined we had, but when she saw it she didn't show too much interest at getting in. Bill said he'd better fill the radiator now, which would save us doing it during the next three miles. Still, she put her small valise in the back, and got in when I held the front seat forward. 'It don't look up to much,' said Bill, 'but it pulls itself along all right. Slow but sure.'

I turned on the ignition. 'Let's go.' Nothing happened, so Bill leapt out and flung the bonnet up, taking a piece of rag from his pocket to dry the contacts, which he thought might have got wet from the water he'd splashed too freely when filling the radiator.

June drew her coat around her in the back as if sitting in a refrigerator. 'Shall we give it a push? The road slopes a bit here.'

Bill's trick worked, and the engine coughed into life. 'Push the choke in as soon as we get going,' he said, 'or it might stall.'

'Whose car is it?' she asked, when we were trundling along at a fair forty.

'Mine,' I said, before Bill could put his false spoke in. 'Or my brother's, I should say. He lent it to me to go to London for a holiday. I work for an estate agent in Nottingham, and I've been so bored the last few weeks that I thought I needed a break.' Every hundred yards a noise went out of the exhaust pipe as sharp as a pistol shot, shattering the nerves of any car or lorry driver who happened to be nearby.

'The engine's bunged up,' said Bill. 'It sounds as though we're armed to the teeth. Anyway, you can tell me your life story now. I've told mine.'

'I can't talk while I'm driving. It puts me off.'

'That's a bloody fine get out, ain't it? I was looking forward to it.'

'Some other time. What about June?'

She said nothing. Bill, who had managed to forget her existence for a few minutes, passed her a lighted cigarette: 'All for one, and one for all. It's sheer communism in this car, ain't it, Michael?'

'Seems like it,' I said. 'What's yours is mine, and what's mine is yours, but I'm the only one that's got something.'

'Don't be like that. You'd be back there in the mud, trying to start this box if it weren't for me. We all earn our keep. Eh, duck?' he called significantly to June.

She stirred. 'Oh, well, I suppose I'd better tell you all about myself, if that's the way it is.'

'If that's the way you want to pay,' he said in a mocking and disappointed tone. 'But no lies, you know. This is a game of truth. The pot on the bloody fire, love.'

'I never lie,' she said. 'I don't see any point in it, especially in front of strangers.'

'I thought we were friends?' said Bill.

'You can take your choice,' she laughed.

'All right, as long as the miles roll by under this fusillade of shots. I'll have to interrupt you now and again to tank up that thirsty radiator. You're a real sport,' he went on, licking his chops, inside as it were, 'to join in our fun and games.'

'You think so?' she said, in such a tone that I knew she wasn't joining in anything at all, though only time would prove whether Bill or I was right. There was a strong whiff of petrol in the car, but the others didn't say anything, so I decided to go until they did. Not that I doubted my nose, but I just didn't see how it could be dangerous. In any case, I had always found the smell of petrol rather agreeable to the senses whenever I was beginning to be just a little bit tired.

'I had a perfect childhood,' June began. 'You see, when my parents got married they wanted a girl, and I was a girl. Even they couldn't mistake that. They were as happy as they could be that things had begun so well. At the time I didn't realize this, and though they told me as soon as they thought I was able to understand, it wasn't till I was sixteen and began to have a mind of my own that I realized what a responsibility had been put on to my shoulders, especially since, after having me, my mother wasn't able to produce any more. What had kicked off for them as a blessing ended up for me as a curse.

'I was a girl, and therefore they indulged me in everything that had to do with girlishness – though you've got to remember I'm talking from hindsight and not so much from what I felt at the time. I was up to my neck – unwillingly – in dolls' houses, dolls, ballet clothes, sewing machines, and embroidery sets. Whatever I wanted, I had, providing it was just just the thing for a little girl, the girl of their dreams. They weren't very well-off, mind you. My father was a booking clerk at the railway station, but in providing so well for me they acted as if they were thanking God for having sent me in the first place. It was an act of worship. God's altar was little me.

'I suppose somebody should have told my mother that children were born from my father's penis that in a moment of dark confusion got mixed up in her womb – and not in heaven. But they didn't, and my ideal life went on for a few years more. My hair grew in dark ringlets down my back, and in looks I seemed to satisfy them as well, though they found me a bit quiet, which they put down to intelligence, and the much hoped-for fact that still waters run deep. But I only remember feeling sly and miserable, because though children can't tell you what they feel they certainly know enough about what they feel to be able to remember it when they're grown up. Being the apple of their eye they didn't let me play with other girls on the street, thinking they were too rough for me and that they might initiate me into games of doctors and nurses, so I was reduced to dismembering my dolls with a kitchen knife when my mother's back was turned, or cutting their hair with scissors as if they'd been found in some sort of unmentionable collaboration with a dirty hooligan down the street, or I'd make a hole between their legs and stick spent matches there. In actual fact, my mother was bored with looking after me, after she had lost her enthusiasm for petting and spoiling, so she was only too glad to see that I was pensively playing on my own for an hour. When my father came home he would slobber all over me for half a minute, then rush out to his railwayman's club to play darts.

'A few years went by before my mother realized that it would be impossible for her to have another child, and then a year or two more passed before they began to regret that they hadn't had the sense to wish for a son first, since now it was too late to have one. They seemed to think, then, that their wish for a girl – me – had been the prime cause of the first child being a girl, and because of this their attitude began to change. I was at school, so at least I had another form of life to cushion the shock of it. But still, it was hard. I'm not blaming my parents, because I think those who blame parents for things they think were done against them as children are being a bit unrealistic. All you can do is state the case. Maybe I'm only saying this because I've got a seven-year-old daughter now.

'Anyway, whereas before they loaded me with all the feminine things at a time when I wanted to know something about what boys had to do with the world, they now took everything like that away and brought me guns, Meccano outfits, chemistry sets. This might not ordinarily have been much of a shock to me, but the fact was that I'd actually been so weighed down with little-girl things from birth that I'd long since given in and grown to like it. I was a little girl, and that was that. My father would now teach me how to shoot a pop-gun. Once, he came proudly home from the club with a great parcel in his arms, which turned out to be an electric train set he'd won in a raffle. He set it up for me, and played with it for more than an hour while his supper got cold, and I sat boggle-eyed and not understanding a thing.

'My parents were so selfish and gentle that they were totally ignorant. But when my father tried to dress me up in a cowboy suit, my mother drew the line, and at last got a glimmer of what confusion was being spread in me. So she went out next day and came home with the largest doll I had ever seen. I was eight, and didn't like dolls all that much, anyway, as I'd often said, and when I pushed it aside in disgust so that it fell off the table and cracked its skull, she was so chagrined that she smacked my face for the first time in my life. All I could do was go back into my corner, and indulge in the age-old consolation of playing with myself, which I did, for at least by doing that I could see I was definitely and for ever a girl.

'Though my parents may not have realized it, I already knew about the facts of life, because at school we talked on this topic continually. In fact I remember feeling that because my knowledge was so much more recent than any similar knowledge my parents could have had, mine was so much more accurate, while theirs must be right out of date. The fact that my nose was always up in the air because of this made them lose hope of their little girl ever growing up into a beautiful-dutiful daughter. From time to time they tried by an act of kindness to do something about it, but one or other of them usually ended up by cuffing me or pushing me aside in a despair that I knew wasn't genuine.

'In spite of this, and maybe because of it, I did well at school. From first to last I was top of the class, and though they made a show of being glad, this also puzzled them. Up to the age of ten my father had helped with my homework, but after that it became too complicated and I was left to deal with such mysteries on my own, which I was capable of solving. But my mother thought I was only doing it to spite my father, so as to make trouble between them. This wouldn't have been difficult at the best of times, but they stood together by saying how ungrateful I was at them sweating blood half their lives to give me the ideal conditions in which to enjoy and take advantage of my education. It was awful, really. I hardly understood what they were saying. Going to sleep at night I'd made up stories to myself saying I hadn't been born to them at all, but that gipsies had sold me to them as a baby, and that my real care-free wild parents were at that moment bending over a smoking fire in the mountainous part of some Balkan country waiting for the supper pot to boil so that they could feed themselves and the numerous children scattered around in the darkness who were all my real brothers and sisters. I even spread this story at school, not from spite, but because I wanted to appear different to the rest of the them. I didn't hate my mother and father, I swear I didn't, but to me they were more like other children than parents, whom I would try to fight on equal terms. I went so suddenly between love and hate when I got to the age of thirteen that in calm moments I'd picture myself running away from home. Neither of them thought twice about knocking me about, and a time of violent rows began that lasted till I was seventeen.

'They used to take me to spend my holidays with an aunt at Southport, so that they could go off for a fortnight's peace at Bridlington. It was lucky I liked my aunt, who was my mother's elder sister and therefore a very different person. She managed a hotel, and never lost her temper with other people, not because she held herself in, but because she was altogether more good-natured and easy. She'd been a keen reader all her life, and every time I came home I brought a few books from her library. This annoyed my parents who thought they were losing the control over me that they didn't know they no longer had. My room acquired these, and other books, because I'd gone by scholarship to the grammar school. They were proud of me for having done this, and when my father told me so in one of his rare bouts of confidence I was filled with happiness. The trouble was, if it can be called trouble since it is so normal, that we were a close group most of the time, and there was enough love floating around to keep us human, but not enough to keep us warm.

'So you can see how uneventful my childhood was, and you can't get nearer to perfection than that. This isn't as sarky as you think, but the certain fact is that, being so perfect, it had to have the right sort of ending. My father accused me of becoming a precocious schoolgirl, though God knows where he picked up the phrase. I think he was the saddest person I've ever known. He had no idea how sad and ordinary his life was. He had given everything up to the purpose of rearing me, and that should have soothed him, but as an ideal it had cracked quite early on, and from that point he had nothing else in life – except my mother. And a man who has nothing except a wife can only make everybody's existence a misery he comes into contact with. I'd never seen a man so trapped, yet I couldn't feel sorry for him, because I happened to be his daughter.

'Even now, when I can at least begin to have some respect for his crushed life, there's nothing I can do for him. Whenever we meet he asks me continually when I'm going to mend my ways and settle down with a suitable husband or job. He says his friends are always asking about me, wondering what I'm up to, but I tell him to drop dead or wrap up because I can't be bothered to try and break through the knot that ties him to wife–job–house–club. If only he was happy in it, I wouldn't mind him getting at me. But he's not. He sees me, only a woman, doing some of the things he's often dreamed of imagining himself doing, such as lighting off to London and working there, living in my own room, sometimes with men, now and again with another woman, having a child and not caring that I wasn't married. A life of freedom is no more marvellous than a life of slavery, I sometimes think, but at least I don't feel that society is forcing me to live in the way it wants me to live.

'At eighteen I went off to London, already pregnant, and became an unmarried mother. It's about the easiest status for a girl to acquire in life. I fell in love with a boy I'd known at school, a dark-eyed secretive bastard who wrote poetry, and could talk his head off without giving anything away. But he was so handsome that nothing could keep me from him, and though my dear father shouted and bullied me for staying out late, my hours actually got later and later. I'd started a temporary office job, and was doing a secretarial course in the evening, which my parents wanted me to take in order to get on and become self-supporting. But because of it I was able to stay out late and be much of the time with him. We'd go to the cinema to see French films, or up on the moors so that he could read his poems to me. I tell you, it was a dream life, and I lapped it up because I was not only getting what I wanted but was doing what my parents had forbidden me to do. Something to hurt them with was handed to me on a platter. I could hardly believe it. My mother, in awful and mysterious tones, had warned me never to let boys and men *do anything to me*. She never really said why, but I don't think it would have made much difference, anyway. So behind a sheep-wall and in the balmy air of summer, my flooded membranes tingled under Ron Delph. We couldn't be kept apart, but by the time autumn came (it always does) Ron began to see that I was only one of many.

'I don't want to say that I got jilted or let down, because I was cooling off from him as well. His poems were all about me "giving myself" to him, and him "taking me". They were like apples that went rotten after they'd fallen from the tree – meaning him. After our first big quarrel, full of heartlessness and spite on both sides, I woke up next morning and spewed into the bathtub. A girl at work laughed and said maybe I was preggers. What could I do but search out Ron Delph and tell him? He went almost crazy from fear and rage but I had no idea of getting him to marry me, because I couldn't think of a worse fate for either of us. I only wanted to talk to him about it and maybe get a bit of advice. But even that was beyond his intellectual capabilities. We were in a pub, and after half a pint of beer he went out to the gents, and didn't come back. I'm learning fast, I thought.

'Only anger stopped me from the pouring tears. I wandered around in the rain, stunned that my first love had done such a thing. But after a cup of coffee it no longer had the power to devour me. I actually began to feel happy. A sense of lightness came up in me and pushed all gloom away, and it seemed wonderful to be living. I wished Ron hadn't run like that from the pub, and then if the evening had been warm and dry we might have gone up on the moors and laid down together, because that's what this feeling made me want to do. I didn't hold anything against him, because my love was coming back strong, and I thought that perhaps the same true feeling was happening to him too. But I couldn't be sure, and wanted to find out. Knowing where he lived, I went there. I suppose it's crack-handed to talk about the turning points of one's life, but be that as it damn-well may, this turned out to be one of them. Ron Delph was enough of a poet to know that I might consider going to his house when I got over the shock of his vanishing trick, so his obvious ploy was not to show up there himself. In my mind he'd gone home to his mother as fast as he could, and she'd hidden him in the farthest attic or coal cellar. But no such luck, for by the time I got to the door I felt like rooting him out from wherever he was, and giving him a good scratch across the eyes.

'His mother stared, and asked what I wanted. The house was a semi-detached villa with three steps leading up to the front door, the sort of place where, if you want to be on a level with the people inside, you have to go round the back, up the entry and through the dustbins. She was a small woman, and pretty at the age of forty so that I had to ask if she was Ron Delph's mother before I believed her. From all his lies I expected a bleak six-footer dressed in a sugar bag with a face like a rusty frying-pan, because he'd told me terrifying stories about her wild temper, and of nervous breakdowns which she'd had from the age of twenty-six. When he was four she'd throttled a live chicken in front of him – that was one of his tales, but to look at her now I knew she'd never done any such thing. I realized all this in a flash, and saw how things would improve if I went away. But I'd asked for him, and it was too late to back out now. "Whatever do you want," she said, "with my son?"

'"We've been seeing each other for the last four months," I told her, "and I wondered if he was at home."

'"Well he isn't, you fast young madam, having the nerve to come knocking at the door for him! I always thought this would happen, him being out at all hours and never telling me where he's off or what he's up to."

'A man's voice called from inside: "Who's that, Alice?" I felt as I'd always felt at the bottom of my spine, that I lived nowhere and belonged nowhere, was always set on the door-step between house and street, and that in this home town at any rate there was no hope of ever getting to any fireside where I could really feel safe from the elements. I didn't even belong to myself, never mind to a house, and I knew that I didn't deserve to because all my life I'd not only had it too easy in being cradled with every comfort, but that at the same time I'd been trying too hard to get myself into something that didn't exist. I wasn't one person, I was two, if not three or four, and nobody in their right minds would want such a disturbing gang at their fireside.

'I was set on a quiet getaway, but in answer to the man's question she called back: "Oh it's just some young trollop calling for our Ron."

'The street was dark behind me, but one or two people were walking by. "Is it?" I shouted. "Well, your darling son Ron has been getting off with me, and he's been up me a few dozen times. He's got me pregnant, and that's why I'm here. I'm going home now to tell my parents, and they'll be back in the morning with my six brothers to settle you lot."

'I was shouting and crying, then felt a sharp pain across my face where she'd hit me: "I'll teach you to show us up in front of the neighbours. If our Ron's got you pregnant you'll have to prove it."

'I broke free, and walked off. It happened that I wasn't even pregnant. We started going with each other again, and then I was, beyond any doubt. So I took my fifty pounds of savings from the post office, and packed a suitcase, leaving the house early one morning without saying goodbye, and not even telling Ron what I intended to do, because I didn't really know myself.

'That was seven years ago, and as for my work in London, we'll leave that for another time. I've just been to see my parents, and I spent all my money there. They would have given me my train fare but I preferred to be independent, and have the fun of hitch-hiking. I do it now and again for kicks. Not that my life can be called dull, but as I said, that part will have to wait till we meet again. It's rare, I suppose, but so far in my life I've never bumped into anyone I've not seen again. It's impossible for me to lose track of anybody, even if I want to.'

'It's taking us so strenuously long to get down this London road,' said Bill Straw, 'that I vote we stop for a drink at the next inn that's still pumping.'

'That's a bright idea,' said June. 'I could do with cheering up after my sad tale. That's the first time I've told it in a long while.'

'It almost brought tears to my eyes,' said Bill.

'It's all very well,' I said, 'but if I get drunk I shan't be able to drive, and I want to reach my destination in one piece.'

'That'll be a miracle, in any case,' Bill said, 'in this crumbling hearse.' He was right, perhaps, because in the middle of June's story, part of the exhaust pipe had snapped away, a great sudden clatter that sent the chill of disaster up my spine and left haloes of sparks on the road behind. But Bill's suggestion of a drink was pleasant nevertheless, and I felt that one or two would do none of us any harm. Besides, it was so near midday closing time that there'd be no opportunity for tanking up later.

The brakes were failing, so as soon as Bill yelled that there was a snug pub to port, I dropped the gears one by one and gently trod the pedals so as to slow down in good time. Even so, I swerved too quickly into the parking lot and bumped into the far wall, jerking the three of us at the neck and bringing grumbles of protest.

It was a place where they served luncheons, and as we disembarked from the car a well-dressed middle-aged man came out of the dining-room door and spewed all over the gravel.

'Good home cooking,' said Bill. 'Still, the whisky can't be off. I'd rather die in there than on the road.'

'It bodes no good though,' I said, and while arguing, we watched the man, pale and harrowed, walk unsteadily to his car and get in, then fall asleep over the wheel.

'I expect he'll run some kid down on a pedestrian crossing before the day is out,' June said with disgust. I liked the moral tone she was taking, because she'd be a safeguard against me having more than one drink. Bill wasn't with us, and when we went in he was already at the bar.

'I've ordered,' he said, 'so get your wallet out.' Three double whiskies came up. 'I'll get your bottle now, sir,' the publican said, sliding away to his secret and extensive cellars.

'What bottle?' I said, expecting the worst.

'Don't get gloomy, comrade. If that car of ours breaks down far from civilization we'll want something to keep us warm and happy. Cheers!'

'Cheers!' June said, turning on her stool to look at a middle-aged man sitting over a brandy glass in the corner.

'Do you know him?' I asked. He had a thin bony face and a high pink bald head, wore a cravat instead of a tie, and hadn't shaved for a couple of days.

'It's a writer,' she told me, 'called Gilbert Blaskin.'

'Go over and say hello.'

'I don't know him that much.' She turned back to the bar, and swung down the firewater in one gulp of her beautiful throat.

'I've heard of his books,' I said. 'I even read one, but I don't remember anything about it. It's the first time I've seen a real writer, even from a distance.'

'Don't stare at him,' she said, as if having a reason for not meeting him now, 'or you'll embarrass him. He's very sensitive.'

'Poor bloke! I suppose that's what comes of being an author.'

The publican put a bottle of White Horse before me, then

two packets of Whiffs and a consignment of Player's. 'Make it three more doubles as well,' Bill cried, sliding his glass over like a lord.

'Yes, sir,' the publican said, with such obsequiousness that I wanted to put my boot into his lardy face for hating us so much after he'd said it. It helped me to pay up with a smile, treating June and Bill, my boon and travelling companions. There was nothing else to do, since I had money and they had none. I could hardly have walked out when we had grown so friendly with our story-telling in the car, and in any case I didn't want to.

'Drink up,' I said, 'and have another. I'll order this time,' but when I did the three glasses put before us came with no 'yes sir' for me.

'You don't have the personal presence yet to get that,' said Bill, who noticed everything. I blushed at hearing this in front of June, and cursed Bill for an inaccurate and bloody liar, feeling I would certainly have got that sort of treatment if he hadn't been there.

'Let's go,' I said gruffly, 'out of this clip joint.' Bill saw a one-armed bandit by the door and, going over to the publican, asked for ten bob's worth of sixpences, nodding across at me. I paid, and stood behind him as he almost pulled his arm off, but without getting anything back. When he'd wasted half I asked him to let me have a go, and held out my hand for some sixpences, but he told me to push off and get my own, which I did, and at the first pull I heard a dozen tinkle down into the space-mouth below.

'You see?' I said jubilantly.

He pushed me aside, trembling with greed: 'I'll get that fucking jackpot yet.' But he lost every last sixpence in the next half-hour, and just as I was getting into my stride to do the same, and we'd knocked back a few more doubles, the publican bawled that it was time to close the pumps, making us feel like real bloody mugs.

That short stay at the pub cost me the best part of five quid, so I was glad to get out of it and back on the road, even though thick clouds were belting across the woods and steeples and it was starting to rain. June regretted not having got a lift in

Gilbert Blaskin's Jaguar as she huddled in the back expecting the worst, but Bill and I felt quite cheerful at such a mild attack of weather. I felt a bit drunk, with a rubber face, and steel arms broken in six places, but once we got going it didn't seem much of a disadvantage. In fact we were all so tight that the car went better than before. The only letdown was when I nerved myself at last to switch on the windscreen wipers. They both shot sideways out of the car's path and were never seen again. Bill made me stop while he crawled around in the wet for a long search, promising he'd be able to fix them back. 'You know,' he said, buttoning his saturated coat when he got in beside me, 'I'm beginning to think that this vehicle isn't roadworthy.'

'Don't be pessimistic,' I said, when it started like a dream. Rain drummed down. I was driving on the ocean bed, and expected to see herrings and goldfish making boggle-faces at me. In spite of being drunk I was afraid to go faster than thirty miles an hour, and even twenty at times, so that lorry drivers hooted and cursed as they swung out to overtake. I was sweating with the work of it, a fanatical stare of concentration baking my stomach as we jogged along. By some incredible scissor-feat of the body, Bill managed to transfer himself into the back without knocking my driving arm, murmuring that he was going to make a party of it. June was nervous, but joined me and Bill in smoking a Whiff so that, what with their frequent swigs of whisky, the place stank worse than a pub on Saturday night. I suddenly realized that their lives were in my hands, so my stone-cold soberness came back quicker than it would normally have done.

I passed the map over my shoulder to Bill and asked him to find out where we were, but he laughed, wound down the window, and threw it outside. It must have opened and got laid by the wind across some unlucky bastard's windscreen, because the scream of two or three hooters broke into me. I didn't mind that so much, but when Bill tried to get the window back up it wouldn't come, and gusts of rain ran around the inside of the car and sprayed us all. He and June (I could see them in my mirror) had their arms around each other, and started to sing 'Oh it ain't gonna rain no more, no more'. I wanted to get back there and throttle them, but couldn't see out of the car behind me and so was afraid to pull up in case a lorry trampled us all to death. Apart from my wonky brakes, oil and water made the road as slippery as a frozen lake. Rain made it so dark that cars coming by had their headlights on, but I couldn't do the same because I didn't have any lights left. I thought of getting into a lay-by and stopping this mad journey, but I didn't want to hear Bill's scorn that I was yellow and had no guts. As long as they were happy I didn't mind going on. June had the goodness of heart to light a cigar for me now and again, to lean over and put it like a kiss between my lips.

The rain eased down and normal daylight came back. This seemed to depress those in the back, so they dozed for a few miles. I pulled in and wiped the windscreen with a sheet of newspaper. Now I could see again. A bit of sun shone on their angel faces, and I felt I was driving the Lazaretto express as I got nearer to London. My recent fling with tender Miss Bolsover seemed years away, and my concern at having left Claudine in the lurch had turned into mild curiosity when I wondered what she'd do now I had well and truly gone.

I felt myself falling towards the middle of the road, though it was obvious to my senses, lost in sentimental recollection, that I was still in the car. Bill woke with a great shout, and June screamed, as a noise of scraping metal seemed about to cleft the car in twain, and dig all our graves before we could slump into them. An overtaking van braked and swerved, got safely by, and went on without stopping to see what peril we were in. My head hit the windscreen but did not break it. I applied all my skill to stop the car. The front right wheel had fallen off, we discovered, on getting out.

Bill scratched his head. 'That's rough. Are you a member of the AA?'

'You know I'm bloody-well not.'

'It's not so obvious,' he retorted. 'Your badge might have fallen off. Everything else has. I can't imagine when this car last had a service. The next one will be a church service.'

'You're too bloody funny. What are we going to do now?'

'Get the wheel back on, then continue our journey. The first thing is to find it.' This was done in a few minutes, and while June was stationed to warn other cars of our obstruction, Bill got tools from the boot and lifted the car up. All the nuts had vanished from the wheel, so he took a nut from the other three to fix on the erring one. The thread of the bolts was a bit raddled, but he did not consider this to be dangerous. In less than half an hour we climbed back in and set off. 'That was a close call,' he said, tilting his head to get the full benefit of the whisky bottle.

I laughed hysterically. 'You can say that again.'

'The wheels are all right now. I suppose the roof will blow off next time.'

'I don't think so,' I reassured him. The wheel had buckled slightly when it flew off, so it wasn't easy to steer. Sometimes I had to use all my strength to keep the car on the proper side of the road. Nothing had gone right on this trip, I brooded, fighting for my life and dreading another phase of rain. The sky in front was dark enough to promise it. When Bill came out of his drunken doze I asked if he knew a garage in London where I might have my car repaired.

'Get rid of it.'

'How much do you think I'd make if I sold it?'

'At a rough guess,' he said, 'fifty bob.'

'You're cracked,' I told him, feeling that my sense of humour was no longer to be trusted.

Bill slung the empty whisky bottle through the open window. 'Take my advice. Abandon it at the first Tube station we come to. Park it somewhere, and finish your journey by public transport. You can always go back for it at a later date, if you're still hankering for a final ride of death.'

'I'm coming to the conclusion that I definitely don't like the way you talk,' I said. 'It's not that I mind pessimism as a line of patter, but with you it's pure malice. What's more you try to pass it off as humour, and that's the dirtiest trick of all.'

'I'm only trying to keep your spirits up.'

'The car goes better when you stay quiet,' I said, pressing the horn at a van too close in overtaking, and finding as I spoke that Fate must have cut its throat while I wasn't looking.

'Do *you* want to drive for a while?'

'Not me,' he said quickly. 'It knows you best. A machine is human enough to know its own master, and you're it, in this special case. Might kick me in the guts if I have a go.'

'Can *you* drive?' I asked June.

'Yes, but you have to *ride* this one, and I've left my saddle at home.' So, clapped-out as I was, I was on my own, and had to stick it out, which I began to think might be possible since we were only twenty miles from the middle of London. As the afternoon grew dim beyond Hertford, I knew I'd just about get there before I was called on to use my non-existent lighting system. Orange sodiums already canopied the road at intervals, though it wasn't officially lighting-up time. It turned dark blue and smoky, as if snow were going to pour down. I felt cut off from where I'd come from, and where I was going to (wherever that was), and also from Bill and June who appeared to be snogging in the back. I was more on my own than I'd ever been, fighting my lone and maybe losing fight to keep the car going and on the road. It didn't feel good being the one person between my friends and injury. All that stuff was so much crap, I thought, about responsibility bringing out the best in people. Certainly, one slip and we'd have been under the wheels of an articulated dragon coming in the opposite direction.

Traffic was thickening by the minute, and at the next box of lights a London swine wheeled down his window and called across at me that I should buy a new car. I was too done-for to respond, but Bill, straight from a refreshing doze against June's precious bosom, poked his nut out of the gaping windowless window and shouted in his best, vicious jailbird's voice that if the other bloke didn't stop his feeble insults he'd take him and his instalment-plan tin-lizzie to pieces and pelt him with the rusty bits after he'd been tied to a traffic light with a fanbelt. The trouble about insulting somebody in a car is that you can't see how big they are, though it was certain that no person could be bigger than Bill Straw's big mouth.

The lamps were still on blood-red stop, so this chap swings his door open and comes over, aiming a punch at Bill that Bill dodges so that it grazes June. The light changed to amber so I shot forward as fast as my battered car would go, swinging across to the inner lane so as to put a line of protective traffic between me and the hefty swine now set to get my liver. This was a feat in itself, but soon his souped-up Zodiac came gliding sideways on, so close I felt a bump as he got me at the place where my fender should have been. 'Let's stop and fight it out,' said Bill. 'There's a razor in my bag. I'll cut him in bits.'

'Maybe he's got one too,' I said. 'It looks as if his boulder-head has been in a few avalanches.' A wide front view with flashing headlights filled my mirror, and he then swung to get me in the flank. Bill mumbled something about having seen that face before, but couldn't think where or who it belonged to. When I caught a glimpse of it looking at me, it seemed the sort that never forgot the face it looked at. My steering was so erratic that maybe he thought me a skilful manoeuvrer against his attacks – if a trifle reckless. But I hit the high kerb, and one of my wheel hubs spun along the gutter. It was the last I had, and made me want to get out and kill him. Several glimpses showed him as well dressed and about fifty, with a huge red-stoned ring on a finger of his hand that gripped the wheel. 'I'll know him if I ever meet up with him,' I said. 'I'll never forget that face.' He tailed me again, came close for another bumper-knock, trying to open my car like a sardine tin but do no damage to his own. He cruised alongside for a few seconds, and Bill also got a good look at him. As the thump tore against my front wing June said: 'Bill's fainted – or he's seen a ghost. He's as white as a sheet. If we can't rustle up some smelling salts or another flush of whisky he'll pass into the eternal fields.'

'I know who it is,' he croaked. 'Why didn't I guess sooner?'

I made a suicide dive to get back at him, feeling my car so battered that I'd nothing left to loose. 'Who? For Christ sake, tell me!'

A police car with wailing sirens and a blue light flashing pushed by us both, and my attacker slowed down in front as if steel wouldn't melt in his mouth.

'It's Claud Moggerhanger. I sold a brand-new car to him for fifty forged quid a few years back. What a nut I am, getting on the wrong side of him. I'll never open my big mouth again.'

I thought he was going to burst out crying. 'Not in this car you won't, anyway. Just call next time he comes close and say you'll apologize. Maybe he'll let up.'

My engine started to bang like a machine gun that shot nuts and bolts, and I thought the end was close, even without Claud Moggerhanger. Strangely enough, it picked up speed and whizzed its howitzer way towards Hendon. As I crossed the North Circular I hoped vindictive Claud would veer off east or west, but he didn't, and came in for another bang just beyond. It was like a dogfight, but he missed. Thinking he'd done the worst, and leaving my engine to do the rest, he turned off before me.

I reached the traffic island in Hendon, and instead of going round it to the middle of London, I took a wild swing to the left, pulling up to the kerb as soon as I could without killing us all. When the car was still, and a reasonable silence reigned, and before anybody could comment on our miraculous deliverance, the engine dropped out.

'We just made it,' said Bill, opening the left-hand door, which also fell off. 'It was exciting while it lasted, though.'

I sat with my head in my hands, over the steering wheel, reflecting ruefully (that's the only phrase I can use) on the fact that I'd bought the car especially to come to London in, and that such a simple journey had cost me a hundred and forty quid. At that price I could have hired a Rolls-Royce and chauffeur and eaten caviar and drunk champagne all the way down, and still stayed the night in Claridges or wherever the best doss-house was. 'I thought I'd never see my little girl again,' said June, pulling her valise out.

'Come on, love,' said Bill, 'we'd better get going. I expect Michael's going to stay here a while and make arrangements to have his car reconditioned.'

'Go away,' I said. 'Vanish.' It started to pour with rain, heavy drops drumming on the roof, homely and comforting now that the car had stopped, streams of water going down the perspex windscreen.

'We can't vanish,' Bill said, 'without the Tube fare.' I gave him a ten-bob note. 'What about a quid for a cup of coffee?'

'Perish,' I told him.

'A right bloody comrade you are,' he threw at me. 'Come

123

on, June. You can see me any night of the week at the Clover Leaf if you want to. Maybe I'll buy you a drink.' They ran along the road towards the Tube station, and fifteen minutes later, by which time I'd been able to recover from the awful fact of having to abandon my first and beloved car, I took up my suitcase and went in the same direction. A coat collar didn't help against the blinding rain, and my legs were weak and wobbly, like a sailor just on shore after years at sea. I'd had a few months with a car, and was now back as a normal member of society, a bloke in the descending piss lugging his suitcase towards the Tube station, standing at the ticket box and asking for a one-way fare to King's Cross. As the train rattled south I laughed at having done that simple journey so perilously, crossed that no-man's-land after a red sky in the morning, all hundred and twenty-five miles of it.

Part Three

A catchy tune was playing all over London, and I don't remember the name of it any more, not even the tune itself. Sometimes it half comes back to me, but before it can turn fully on, I blot out my mind and fight shy of it, as if I really don't want to remember. It was a gay, jumpy, tuneful, deathlike-trancelike tune which seemed to be everywhere, livening up the wet winter, and giving people a reason for thinking they were alive. But conductors and window-cleaners whistled it, hummed it, thrummed it on their bells and buckets as if determined to prove themselves made of flesh and blood. I first heard it on the Tube train from Hendon to King's Cross. A long-haired youth had a transistor radio, and it broke into my speculation as to what I should do now that I had reached the smoke.

In spite of losing my car, things weren't as bad as they might have been. I had a hundred pounds in my pocket, and supposed most people came to London with less in their wallets than that. It felt like a fortune that would never run out, to be lived on in affluence for endless weeks. I found a hotel beyond the station, that was full of old ladies and foreign students, where I could get a decent bed and breakfast for thirty bob a night. My name was Donald Charles Cresswell, and I gave my address in the book as 11 Stoneygate Street, Leicester. Why, I don't know, because I didn't even feel I was doing it till I had (which is always the case), though I considered only a minute later that it might one day come in useful.

My room was the smallest space I'd ever been in on which a door had closed. There was a bed, built-in wardrobe, chair and small table, and above in the ceiling was screwed a one-candlepower bulb. It really made you feel welcome, but I was in such high fettle at being in the big town at last that after a wash and brush up I went down the stairs whistling the same one-eyed tune I'd already heard with such scorn.

The counter clerk asked what time I'd be back as I handed

him the key and I said: 'Why, will I get locked out?' and he stared at me as if I wasn't playing the game by popping that uncivilized question.

'No sir, but if you come in past midnight you'll have to ring the bell.'

I thanked him very much, and stepped into the burnt air. A woman asked me to go with her but she didn't look much good, and I thought I ought to be a bit wary of these London tarts in case she had the shirt off my back and gave me a dose of the Baffin Land clap. It was only yesterday that I'd been to bed with Claudine first and Miss Bolsover second, and that would have to last me for a while, if I weren't to call myself greedy. Also I was flayed out with tiredness, and reckoned only on a short walk in the surrounding streets before going back to my matchbox for a hard-earned kip.

I said goodnight to her and wandered till I came to a place to eat. A cat slept in the window, but the meal was good enough, considering the price. While I got stuck into my stew, an old grey-bearded ragbag came in selling almanacks, and I bought one, giving him half a crown and telling him to keep the change. His brown eyes glinted out of all that bush: 'Thank you, *sir*!' he said, with the heaviest sarcasm I'd ever heard.

I could have kicked myself that such goodness of heart had been spurned by the bug-eaten old bastard, but by the time I was ready to throw a sharp crust of bread in his face the door rattled and he'd gone. As I chewed through my minced-up mutton and cat I wondered where he'd come from, and a low feeling gripped me when I thought maybe he left Nottingham forty years ago full of hope and promise. Perhaps he'd worked well at a good steady job, but then he'd felt the strain and taken to having a few drinks now and again. He'd got into bad company, overspent, embezzled, been sent to prison. Then his wife left him, his kids grew up not knowing him and disappeared, and he'd gone from one job to another, bad to worse, beer to meths, sleeping under bridges and on wastegrounds, walking the streets with a sandwich board on him, and finally he'd taken to pubs and cafés selling almanacks so that he was known to everyone, a bit contemptuously, as

Almanack Jack. I shook off the black mood and ordered coffee, the best part of the meal, and from a good long swig I looked up to witness the return of Almanack Jack.

There were three other people in the place, but as luck would have it, he shuffled up to me: 'You look as if you could do with a bit of advice, hearty.'

I held out my hand: 'Going to read my palm?' He stood by my table, tall and hefty, and not at all as old as I'd thought him at first sight. 'Sit down, and have a cup of something.'

'Tea,' he said, 'and a piece of bread and butter,' when the waiter came over. He stank rotten, so I lit a cigarette. 'You're too generous,' he added.

'How else can you live?'

He sat down and faced me. 'I've known lots of people who know how. In this piece of bread you can see the greatness of God. It gives power to nature. There's no other way I can put it.'

'I don't believe in God.'

'Neither do I,' he said, 'but I believe in the power of bread, and that's the same thing, as far as I'm concerned. I like to feel the greatness of God in my belly.'

'You're welcome,' I said. Hoping he was a vegetarian, I added: 'You can have a piece of meat as far as I'm concerned.'

'I'll dwell on that,' he answered. 'Meat is the Devil, and bread is God. But since man is compounded of God and the Devil at the same time, and I don't deny my truly human nature, then I'll take you up on your kind offer.' He snapped his fingers for the waiter with such experienced aplomb that I began to see a reason for his looking so healthy, and well built. He ordered stew and rice, and when the waiter brought it I asked for another coffee.

'I don't suppose you get much of a living flogging alma-nacks.'

He smothered his volcano with salt: 'Enough. How much do you think a man needs if he isn't God?'

'I wouldn't know,' I said, lighting my last Whiff.

He looked ruefully as I crunched the packet up. 'You can live on much less than you think,' he said. 'I buy my almanacks at fourpence each, and mean people give me a tanner, while others pay a shilling. Occasionally I get half a crown. I have been known to get a pound from someone who mistakenly feels sorry for me.'

'You seem to have got yourself a nice little corner,' I said, realizing that he was no fool, because the longer he talked the more the educated edge to his voice came through. His beard was not so much grey, as reddish-ginger, and it was obvious that in fact he couldn't be a day over forty-five.

'Not that it adds up to what a young fellow like you might call a good wage, but it gets me a room and a few simple eatables.'

'Don't you feel a bit of a shitbag though,' I said, 'not doing a hard day's work? You're living and scrounging on the backs of those who sweat their guts out, and that's the truth.' A piece of stew got tangled in his beard, and I wanted to pick it off and eat it rather than see it go to waste by falling on to the floor as he shook his head violently from side to side. I felt that he had no right to waste even that much food, the idle bastard. Then he gripped it in the pincers of a piece of bread and put it into his mouth.

'You think that, do you? And why not? If you didn't I wouldn't be eating this meal at the moment, and that would never do. My existence like this is only possible because people like you believe in doing a fair day's work. That's putting it mildly, though. You see, ninety per cent of people are of such low intelligence and intellectual perception that they'd go crazy if they had no work to do. Let me show you the system, dreary and accurate though it may be. The vast teeming majority couldn't exist without work. Their spirits would shrivel up, their bodies would perish. You need vision to be idle. But at the same time they want to hear that one golden day in the future they'll only have to do ten hours' work a week – but that right now civilization will go under if they don't pull their weight.

'It certainly will when they only work ten hours a week, and thank God I won't be here to see it, because it won't happen for another three hundred years. The first government that allows it will have revolution on its hands in five minutes. Oh, no, the longer and harder they work the better. That's what people want, though you've got to tell them they don't want it and that it's a bore just so that they'll go on doing it. God dreads idleness, you goddam bet he does, and with good reason. He'd better, otherwise the world will be full of Nimrods shooting up arrows to drag him down from his golden fur-lined palace. And it's not only factory, farm, and office slaves who must sweat to keep alive. No, it's also doctors, artists, lawyers who wither if they don't get enough to do. You have to have a particular, peculiar, God-given bent to exist without work. I'm a great benefactor of humanity, because though I'm often a bastard in my behaviour I've never been as much of a bastard to actually deprive anyone of work by joining the task force myself. I deliberately abstain in a great spirit of self-sacrifice, even at the risk of destroying my own character. It's an experiment I've been carrying on for a few years now, though not for so long that I can see how it's going to end or who is going to get the ultimate good from it. Oh no, don't think my life's an easy one, though I suppose I like it, otherwise I'd change it.

'If those who felt like me (and there are quite a few of us) suddenly decided to demand jobs, the social structure would collapse. Maybe that would be no bad thing according to certain people, but I'm no revolutionary. If ever any government threatened me with work I'd put on my dark glasses, take up my stick and kidnap a dog, tie a label on me saying "Blinded by Work", and tap my way to the nearest seaport so as to make my getaway to foreign parts. I've no desire to take any man's job, which is most likely his only reason for being on this earth at all. And if you're appalled at the unparalleled extent of my self-sacrifice, maybe you'd like to make amends by buying me a cup of that marvellous Turkish coffee they sell here.'

'How could anybody refuse after that little talk?'

'People do,' he said. 'They're vicious at times. Don't think I made my decision to run this kind of life lightly. I didn't. I was forty, in the prime of life, with a wife, two kids, a big flat, a mistress, two cars, a country cottage, as well as being near the top of my job in textile designing. It was a very comfortable and satisfying existence for the type of person I was then. I didn't even feel that because things were so perfect there was nothing left in life for me. My decision to turn the other cheek wasn't that shallow. But immediately I made up my mind, from one minute to the next, that the present life was no good for me, then I was a different person, and it was no longer satisfying, but a torment until I began to change it. The only thing I regret was not doing it the easy way by making the break clean enough. I was a liberal-humanitarian, so I did it by stages, thinking that this would be more effective, and that it wouldn't allow me to change my mind, and that it would cause less pain all round. I wasn't very strong-willed, you might say. My faith at the beginning wasn't too strong. It had to develop, through the fire. So within the space of a few months my domiciles had come under the hammer, my wife was in a looney-bin, my children were in care, my mistress was having psychoanalysis, my job was filled by one of the hungry generation with sharper teeth than ever before, and I was in hospital with double pneumonia. But I knew that when the dust settled everybody concerned would be able to live the life they'd always wanted to lead.

'It's always better to act. Never stifle what you feel to be a fundamental impulse. If it causes chaos, so much the better, because maybe the right sort of order and happiness will arise from it. It can never come out of anything else, and that's a fact, my friend. You look young and inexperienced enough to believe all I'm saying and maybe to benefit by it. At least you deserve to, because I'm enjoying this coffee, even the mud at the bottom. Will you be in here to eat tomorrow night? If you are I'll buy you a meal.'

'God knows where I'll be. I've got to start looking for a room in the morning.' I felt at the bottom of a pit, dying from lack of sleep, so I paid my bill and trudged back to the hotel.

I must have got to sleep because it was suddenly morning, and when I looked at the fine-faced ticker-watch nicked from Clegg, it was nine o'clock. I dressed, dragged a razor over me, and went downstairs for breakfast.

It was a good meal, and I stuffed everything into me within reach, so as to get my money's worth, and to save buying much for a midday meal. I shared a table with a melancholic blond Scandinavian from a town called Swedenborg who said he was writing articles on London vice dens. He had no appetite, so it was double toast and butter for me. He grumbled at not being able to work, because at each vice den he succumbed to much that was offered, which meant that he didn't get back till dawn and had no time to crank up his typewriter and compose his piece. I couldn't spend much sympathy with him, but wished him better luck, lit up a Whiff, and went out.

It was a raw morning, and though it was foul I liked it because it was in London. At the nearest newsagent's I bought a street atlas and a copy of the local paper, two pieces of literature to see me through the day. It felt good to have my legs working again, and I was determined to walk them back into shape, for they'd grown soft in the glorious weeks of having a car. At Russell Square the ache was so sharp at my calves that I considered jumping a Tube to Soho, but gritted my toes and traipsed on, pausing now and again for a flip at the map. The girls looked lovely in their muffed-up coats, and fine sharp noses turned in the air. My eyes said good morning to each one passing, but a frosty nip was darted back as if even their cunts were cold.

The smell of the city was like Brilliantine and smoke, chicken and iron filings, and I fed on it as I walked along, even smiling at the curses of a taxi driver when I nipped too sharply on to a pedestrian crossing. You couldn't take your rights too much for granted here, I thought, and was even glad of such cold comfort, for my backbone was made of optimism. Two million people were in their factories, shops, and offices, all endowed with the heavenly privilege of work, as Almanack Jack might have put it, and here was I for the moment at least cast in the mould of idleness that only their massive labour made possible. The very idea of it made me want to stop at the nearest bar for a cup of coffee, but what I wanted most was a piss due to the monstrous amount of tea I had put back at breakfast. I didn't know a soul in London, and that as much as anything made me love it. With so much money I felt like a prince. I'd saved up to squander it in just this way, and to worry about it seemed more unnecessary than ever as I found a place on Tottenham Court Road to unload those pots of tea in.

That first day I walked and re-walked the whole middle area of London, and by the end of it, when I headed back in the direction of the hotel, I knew that it wasn't as big as I'd always heard it was. The next day I did the City, and for a fortnight, till my money was near enough done for, I got familiar with most of the sprawl. At first the far-off places were known only from the Tube scheme. If I was at Bond Street and wanted to go to Hampstead I looked at the underground map and said to myself: 'I'll get on the Central Line to Tottenham Court Road, then turn left on the Northern Line, and go up until I see Hampstead on the station label.' Often I'd fiddle my way down by bus until, eventually, if some foreigner (or even Londoner) stopped me in the street and asked where a certain place was I'd be able to tell them in five cases out of ten. This made me feel good, and was all very well but, as the dough ran low, it didn't tell me how I'd latch on to any more. Not that I was obsessed by this, because I felt if it came to the worst I'd be able to do something like Almanack Jack, or get a job for a week or two, until something more money-like came along. What it would be I had no idea, and didn't much care, because exploring this gigantic and continuous prairie of buildings during the day, and wandering around the West End like the Phantom of the Opera until late at night, didn't leave much time or energy for serious speculation. In other words I was living the full life because I felt no real connexion to what went on around me. If I had, or began to, I should become buried in it and wouldn't be able to see anything at all. Which was why I clung as long as possible to my arduous free wandering.

Opening my map one day near Leicester Square I saw a good-looking blonde girl coming down the street. As if puzzled and halfway lost I spoke when she drew level, asking if she could kindly direct me to Adam Street. 'Unfortunately not,' she said. 'I'm not familiar too much with London because I come from Holland.'

'Sorry,' I replied, 'but I thought you might have been able to tell me. You look like a typical London girl to me. I'm a stranger here as well, because I'm from Nottingham. I'm studying there at the university, doing English Literature. Watch out, or that car will take your arse off. Pardon me, it's only a colloquial expression. I'll explain it to you if you come and have a cup of coffee. I'm down here for a few weeks, staying at a hotel, but my mother is coming to see me tomorrow to make sure I'm not getting into mischief. It's going to be a bore showing her around, but she insists on keeping me under her thumb, so what can I do?' Just when she was beginning to find my gamut had a bit of a hook to it, she noticed that we were standing outside a strip club with framed photos hung up of bare women whose faces you couldn't see for their breasts. From the pious distaste on her face she might have thought I'd try to drag her inside, drug her, and rumble her off to a miners' club in Sheffield. So I put on an honest, half-bewildered expression, folded my map, and took her by the elbow.

A few minutes later we were sitting in the Swiss Centre having cakes and coffee. 'You a student, then?' I asked. She wore a nice white blouse with a brooch at the neck, looked icy and demure, the last person it seemed possible to go to bed with, so why the hell had I picked her? She blushed, though I didn't know why, and said: 'I'm working in this London, as an au pair girl. But I'm also studying to make my English fluent.'

'That's hardly necessary,' I told her. 'Your vocabulary dazzles me. It scintillates.' My only chance of maintaining hold of her was to keep the talkpot boiling with words that she understood but hardly knew the meaning of. If it was English she wanted, English she would get, and since I was born talking the lingo, who could give it to her better than old Jack Spice? I said how perfectly good her English was, while at the same time using words in such a way that she thought she'd never heard them before. 'My family dwell in a mansion-hall near Nottingham,' I went on, 'a place my mother had me in, with its own hallelujah-garden where an old monk chapel once stood, and where we used to see silent films as kids. A private tutor taught me, up to the year of twelve, and then I was sent to a boarding college, though I kicked up the hot dust of hell because I didn't want to be pitched out like that. But our family is bound by the steelropes of tradition. That's England all over, and also what's wrong with it. There was no gainsaying them. Yet it had its advantages, because me and my three brothers, as we came of age at fourteen, were taught to drive in a dual-controlled Rolls-Royce in the private grounds, which was a useful experience. That training Rolls has been in our family for generations.

'The more you know me the more you'll hear about my family, because families are like iron in this country, very important, worse luck. I've been wanting to kick mine off like a salty boot for as long as I started to dream, but it's no use. In any case what's the point? When I'm twenty-one in three months' time I'm going to get a quarter of a million in sterling cash, and a tax-free income of fifteen thousand pounds a year. So it's hard to let that slip out of my hands. Not that it would worry me if I never got it, because I'm quite capable of being independent and earning my own living. In fact I'm seriously considering giving my money, when it's due to me, to the Charitable Organization Inching Towards Unspeakable Suffering – otherwise known by its initials as – well, anyway, it's such a scorching brain problem with me, my dear, that its intensity sometimes threatens to trouble my studies. However, I imagine people do have worse worries, though I can't visualize what they are, because this certainly seems real enough to me.'

I spoke such as this, and more, not in a swift, manic, lynx-eyed way, but slowly and mellowly, as if throwing it off in a familiar drift, casually, blowing out nasal cigarette smoke and sipping my coffee. I told her my name was Richard Arbuthnot Thompson, but that I was called Michael by my friends, when they hadn't cause to use my initials, but within an hour she was tearful and wringing her hands over my dreadful dilemma of whether or not I should accept my share of the family fortune and be imprisoned within it for life, or whether I should be poor, independent, and territorially unsung. I knew which side she'd come down on in the end, if we knew each other that long, but I let her get all deliciously upset over my non-existent problem because it drew us together like liquid dynamite. In two hours, and a different café, we were gazing into each other's eyes while our cigarettes burned low and our vile coffee got cold. I said that in case I did repudiate the family coffers I was already practising the holy art of self-abnegation, and though I'd be delighted if she'd eat with me, it had to be in Joe Lyons at no more than five bob a head.

So we had lunch, and I told her how much it meant to me, having found someone who actually had the greatness of mind to understand my problem and not laugh at it. Then we went into the National Gallery (free) so that I could show her what pictures were fakes, because the real ones existed in the northern wing of Nondescript Hall, which was the name of my family and ancestral home. The more I posed at being noble, the more noble I felt, and it occurred to me that you are what you tell yourself you are, not what other people tell you that you are. You've only got to insist loud enough, and the clouds open to let in the sort of sunshine you've always been looking for.

Later that afternoon my new-found girlfriend, whose name I made out to be Bridgitte Appledore, said she had to go to the house she was working at because a night of baby-sitting had been arranged. Such had been my all-day gabble that she'd told me nothing about herself, but I hoped that would come later when I'd got more of a toe-hold into her confidence.

She worked for a doctor and his wife, who lived in a big place near the BBC. When they'd gone out she came down and let me in, and up I went by lift to the fourth floor.

I'd not been into such a flat before. It was so rich it didn't even smell rich, but was full of good furniture and paintings, books and carpets. Bridgitte told me to sit in the living-room while she put a few finishing touches to the little boy of six who still crowed from his bed. I poured a cut of the doctor's whisky and relaxed on the long deep settee, half listening to the inane story being read to the kid, who interrupted every phrase. I spied a box of Romeo and Juliet Havanas, and lit one – a far cry from a common Whiff – with a heavy effective lighter which had a solid base of pure silver. I was tempted to put it in my pocket, but for the time being resisted it, not knowing Bridgitte well enough to betray her. She might give me away if I nicked something so early on. But I was boasting to myself in even entertaining the idea of making off with such a thing, because I wouldn't know where to sell it without getting caught. In any case I never had been and never would be a thief because I considered that there were better methods of making your way in the world than stooping to that. I just contented myself by taking half a dozen more cigars.

She came in from the kid's room, hot-fer-dommering in Dutch that little Crispin had jumped out of bed and shat on the floor just to annoy her. He did it almost every night and she'd found no way to stop him. She'd told the doctor and his wife but they'd laughed and said it was only his cute little way and that he'd grow out of it soon. Meanwhile she had to be patient with him. There wasn't much else she could do because the job was easy, the pay high, and the flat in the middle of London. She came back from the kitchen with a bowl of water and a bundle of cloths, a cigarette in her mouth to stop herself being sick at the mess. 'Is he still awake?' I asked.

'Oh, yes. He likes to look at me cleaning it up.'

'Let him wait,' I said, 'for a few minutes. Sit down and finish your smoke. Let him go to sleep before you clean it up. If he misses the show he might not bother again.'

'You're so clever, Mr Thompson,' she said, but halfway through her cigarette Crispin called: 'Come to me, Bridgitte. My room smells awfully. I can't go to sleep until it's clean.'

'Ignore him,' I said, pouring her some whisky.

'I don't drink,'

'Try it. It's good for wiping that up.'

'Perhaps you are right.' She took a little, but made a pain-face over it. Then she swallowed more, and finished off the glass. I poured her another.

'Come in here,' Crispin shouted. 'If you don't wipe my *shit* up, I'll do it again.'

'Go to sleep, you little—' I shouted.

'If you don't come and clean it I'll tell Mummy and Daddy there's a man in the flat, then they'll send you away, Bridgitte.'

I went in to look at him, an angel standing up gripping the bedrail, a long white nightshirt covering down to his feet. He had a thin, well-formed face and ginger hair. I went back to the living-room. 'They call him Smog,' said Bridgitte. 'On the night he was expected they couldn't get his mother to the hospital because it was smoggy, so he was born in the ambulance car on the way there.'

He began to cry. 'Come and wipe my shit up. Please. I'm tired.'

'You don't live here,' he said, when I walked into his room. 'Are you a burglar?'

'No, I'm a plumber. I've come to fix your windpipe.'

'What's a windpipe?'

I noted where he'd done his mess. 'You're a very intelligent child,' I said. 'Very clever indeed to do it down there.' Girding my stomach I got on hands and knees and put my face close to it. 'What's this in it?' I asked, in a pleasant voice. 'Oh dear! It's full of half-crowns. My God, it is, and all.'

He leapt off his bed and knelt by my side. 'Where? Where?'

'There,' I said, 'can't you see 'em?' His face went close and I gave it a push so that he fell right into it. Bridgitte came running in at his scream. 'You've got a bit on your face!' I said to him. 'What a thing to do to yourself. Bridgitte, get him into the bathroom and clean him up. He won't do it again. Will you, Smog?'

'You fool,' she said.

I sat down for another drink, and in ten minutes she came in to say that Smog was fast and peacefully asleep. 'He'll not do it any more in such a hurry,' I said. 'You see if I'm not right.'

'If he tells his parents,' she said, half a smile coming back to her, 'I won't be here to see whether he does or not.'

'Plenty of other jobs. Perhaps Mother could find a place for you at Nondescript Hall. I have a brother who needs looking after just as much as Smog, and more or less in the same way – from time to time. He's ten years older than me and his name is Alfred. Had a nervous crisis at twenty-one because he couldn't face inheriting so much money either. It's the disease of our generation. Slashed his wrists, took fifty Aspros, and put his head in the gas oven, but the cook found him and snatched the pillow away because she couldn't bear to see it getting dusty on the floor because she used it when sitting down for her tea or elevenses. So Alfred woke up with a gurgle, and then she saw the blood and called my mother, who gave her a minute's notice on the spot and phoned the family doctor, who brought Alf round and kept the whole thing quiet. Alf has the constitution of an ox, like most of our family. Tough as nails, all of 'em, except me – and it's one crisis after another with people like that.

'I had tuberculosis at sixteen, and it took a year or two to get over it. Now I've got this question of conscience coming up, and I don't know what to do about it. But let's not get stuck too much on my troubles. I'm sure you'll be as right as rain now with Smog. You can come up with me to the Hall if you get the sack. We'll tell Mother we're engaged to be married if you like. It won't make her very happy, but she'll have to take note of you. I'll also introduce you to Alfred. When he's lucid he's the most charming fellow in the world. Spends most of his time rowing around our own lake and fishing in it. He catches so much that Mother's thinking of opening a canning factory for him – tinned pike and salted minnows from the Dukeries. Good for the export trade – go all over the place.'

Her large round blue eyes were turned full on so that I continued jabbering till they dimmed a bit, then I reached over and kissed her. I was surprised that she glued her lips on to me. From that moment the wagons rolled. We wriggled around that opulent sofa, shedding our clothes like mad animals their skins. We fell on to the floor, and when I was well into her juice-tunnel, the telephone shattered my erection as if it had been made of glass. But she wasn't put off by it, and I managed to stay in her and set myself going again. She reached for the phone with one hand, and held my shoulder tight with the other. 'Hello?' she said, over my grunts. 'Yes, it is. Dr Anderson is out. Do you want to leave a message? You phone in the morning? All right. I'll tell him.' Then she began to gobble me up inside, and dropped the telephone as she fell back.

Later we sat in the kitchen to eat cornflakes and jam, then bacon and eggs. I was lucky to be in such a well-provided household. I pulled her up from the food, dancing belly to belly and back to back to Dr Anderson's hystereo music in the living-room. She was out of breath and laughing, then stood rigid when Smog appeared at the door, looking at us with tired but curious eyes. 'Can I do it?' he said.

'Go back to bed,' said Bridgitte sternly. 'You'll catch cold.'

'He wants a bit of fun just like the rest of us, don't you, Smog?'

'Of course.'

'All right, get that shimmy off,' I told him, 'and we'll all dance together.' In spite of his dirty habits, and I hoped he was cured of at least one, he was a good sport, and hop-trotted between us both to Dr Anderson's unique collection of bongo tunes. Then he sat high on my shoulders, licking a spoonful of honey while I slid around to his shouting and laughs.

'Will you come tomorrow, because I like you?' he said, when we'd got him on the high stool in the kitchen eating scrambled egg. 'I like dancing, and music, and midnight feeds.'

'If you're a good lad to Bridgitte, I'll come here often.'

'If you don't, I'll tell Mummy and Daddy.'

'It's not midnight,' I said, 'but you'd better go to bed or your parents will be back, and if they catch us, it's out in the street for all of us.'

He made a face as if to cry: 'Even me?'

'Maybe,' I said, 'but we'd look after you. You'd come with me and Bridgitte.' He laughed, and said he hoped his parents would catch us in that case, but Bridgitte slipped his nightshirt on and carried him against her bare breasts to his room. When she came back the party was over, so we got dressed and cleared up the mess. Exchanging telephone numbers, soft murmurs of undying love, we finally let each other go.

The manager at the hotel started to trust me, so that instead of paying my bill every three days, it was all right now if I left it for as long as a week. He was thin and pink-faced, and what was left of his fair hair was also thin – the sort of a man who would have been melancholy and sad if he hadn't gone into the sort of job where his living depended on him being bright and cheery. He called me Mr Cresswell, and seemed mystified by by comings and goings. One night at the bar I bought him a double brandy and gave him a Havana cigar I'd lifted from Bridgitte's place, and from that point on we were as friendly as his job would allow him to get. I didn't tell him anything about myself, saying I was down on business for my family, which involved a bit of research at Somerset House. This impressed him, so he left it at that, giving me a wink now and again to hope that things were going well, as if we were in some secret together, or he thought I might be coming up for a lump sum in a will. It was hard to say what he thought, for it seemed to me that the less words passing between us the better, and the more nudges, hints, and winks, the closer I'd get to winning his confidence.

Dr Anderson led a busy social life, and I was able to see Bridgitte nearly every night. In our carefree rapture we humped around on the matrimonial bed, though it needed all our stern persuasion to stop Smog joining in. As long as we promised to let him come in the kitchen afterwards he didn't mind, happy to lay on his bed playing with bricks and rockets. But once he strayed out and stood in the doorway while I had my arse in the air, and later I had to tell him what we'd been doing. Bridgitte turned away laughing as I explained about playing at love – which was what grown-ups often do. He wanted to know if Mummy and Daddy did it too, and I said I expect they did now and again, because it's also a way of making babies. Then I had to tell him how babies were made, and he took to me for this, sitting affectionately on my knee while he thought up other intelligent but embarrassing questions. When he finally did go back to his room he went to sleep happy. Bridgitte hadn't done any wiping-up work since I'd rubbed his nose in it, and whenever I saw him now there was something about his earnest, unprotected face that made me feel sorry for him. I wanted him to grow quickly to be eight years of age, safe out of this vulnerable age. I knew he was all right in the way he lived, but nevertheless I was impatient and wanted to be sure, to see him suddenly older, with his face maybe cruder and tougher against the world, his body more stalwart.

There were only a few pounds left in my pocket, so I had to get out of the hotel. I owed a bill of about ten days, though this put me in some danger because I had nowhere near enough funds to pay if the manager should demand it. As far as I could make out he never slept, which maybe was why he was so thin. Even when I came in at midnight or later he'd be sitting behind the desk, and whenever I got up early in the morning he was sure to look in through the dining-room door while I was having breakfast. The idea of getting out unseen with a bulging suitcase seemed impossible.

The day I chose for my lift-off was very cold. I sat at breakfast with the Scandinavian journalist, and wondered how I would be able to say goodbye to him without betraying my intended flit. This was out of the question, so I just made polite inquiries about the article he was writing on sex and vice in London. The work itself didn't seem to be going well, but he was nowhere near so melancholy as he had been at first, because he had become totally immersed in the subject itself. He preferred to live, he said, rather than write. It was cheap in London, but he was sending home for money till he had exhausted his subject, or until the subject had exhausted him. He'd been a different man of late because he now consumed the whole of his breakfast and, on occasion, had even tried to encroach on mine. The more his cheeks sank, the more he stooped when walking, the more he ate, the happier he felt. I asked what place he found so convivial in London that he liked so much, and he told me about The Golden Frog, so I said I might see him there some night. 'I'll buy you a girl,' he said, a wide thin-lipped smile as he reached out for a piece of my toast. 'Myself, I sometimes have two girls. Better.'

'I always thought you were a bit of a Turk,' I said.

In my room I stripped off and started to put my luggage on. There were three sets of clean underwear, which padded me fairly well so that I'd at least save another shilling if the gas ran out. Then there were my three best shirts, which was awkward, for I could barely fasten the buttons of the top one. Luckily, walking such distances over the last month, not to mention my antics with mistress Bridgitte, had thinned me down a bit, so it wasn't as bad as it might have been. It was more difficult to get on two pairs of trousers. The first I fastened into my two layers of sock, and drew the second over them. The zips didn't quite come up to the top, and when I tried to stand up from sitting on the bed I fell back again.

Sweat was pouring off me, and it all seemed doomed to fail because once I got in the fresh air, if I ever did, I would be sure to get triple pneumonia. I pulled myself up by the bedrail and felt my face puffed out like a red balloon. Then I almost wept, because my shoes had still to be put on, and I'd have to sit down again for that. But I pulled the chair over and jerked my foot on it. This was by way of an experiment, to see whether it could actually be done, and when I saw that it could, I slid my foot down again. As the shoes were on the floor I let myself subside gradually to them, holding the bedrail and bed-leg to stop a bump on to the threadbare carpet.

So far so good. I smiled at the achievement, reaching for a shoe. That was easy, but the next step was to get at the foot, when my arms and legs were encased in wood. The shoes were several paces away, so I rolled on my side and crawled, till I held them triumphantly in my hands. This, I thought, pondering on how to get them on, is real life, a test of ingenuity that one might be asked to do at any time in the future. It's as well to get it over with, to suffer the experience once. The first time is always the hardest, I've no doubt of that. I could too easily have given the whole thing up, gone out in one set of clothes and abandoned the rest, but with tears of effort and frustration I was knotted in the stomach with the obstinacy to get one shoe on at least. I could always hobble to the Tube station. I smiled with relief. I would get the other one on as well.

There was a knock at the door. Faces flashed through my mind: Claudine, Miss Bolsover, my mother, Mr Clegg come for his watch back, Bridgitte, even Smog to ask more questions on how babies were made, all or one of them at this crisis of my life intent on passing the time of the day. 'Who is it?' I croaked.

It was the voice of the Scandinavian: 'Kundt,' he said. That's what his name always sounded like to me, though I'm sure he wasn't one – certainly not more of one than I was.

'I'm washing at the sink. Stark naked,' I cried. 'See you later.'

He opened the door and walked in, looking down at me: 'Oh, you've fainted, Mr Cresswell. I'll tell the manager to get a doctor.'

'No,' I said, trying to smile, 'I'm all right.'

'You look all crimson.'

'Put my shoe on,' I said, 'and I'll be eternally grateful. But close the bloody door first.'

He did so, and laughed. 'You Englishmen wear too many clothes. Not like the women. They have very little. I get too quick to it.' While he talked about submissive English women he rammed my shoe on and tied it, then lifted me upright like a slab of timber. He sat down. 'I'm in love with a woman,' he said, as if holding back gallons of melancholy tears, 'and she went away last night. I didn't know I was in love till this morning, and I want to write her a letter. You can help me with that.'

'Why don't you just go to her?'

'She's with her husband. But she'll be back in a week.'

'Your English's good enough to write a letter,' I said.

'Yes, I know, Mr Cresswell, but I want to talk to you about it.'

'I'll see you at the Tube station at ten o'clock,' I said. 'We can have a cup of coffee over it.'

'All right. I'll go now, and wait for you. But first I must shave and need one razor blade.' I told him to take one and he went away smiling.

The next thing was to get two jackets on my back. The sleeve-lining of the second one tore, but they both fitted more easily than I expected. I put a pair of socks in each jacket pocket, and my razor and toothbrush in the lapel pocket. Finally I got into my overcoat, put a scarf casually around my neck, and pulled on woollen gloves. Over all, on top of my head, was a cap. The great problem was: how to move? I walked across the room like a wooden dummy, and fell down. I was so padded that it caused no real noise, but I was far from the bedrail and had no way of getting up. The doorknob was close, so I got a grip on that. I heaved slowly, going up the door like a great fly, and almost made it, when the knob came off and I fell back with it in my hands. This is a pretty kettle of fish, I thought, instantly checking my blind rage. The next nearest thing that caught my eye was the sink, which had strong-looking steel supports underneath it. I took off my gloves for a better grip. If this is life, I thought, then roll on death. The sweat of it seemed to be already pouring off me. I'd always thought of myself as being strong, but it was an impossible job to get back on my feet, which it was essential to do if I was to walk free and unfettered from that hotel. But I weighed enough to cause the sink to slowly ease itself from the wall and hang by a thread on its curving bars just above my head.

I slid back in despair, crawled around the floor like a dog that had lost its bone. By the bed I sat up, then swung myself on to all fours, then on to my knees, then, by using the good old faithful bed once more, I gradually escaped my dreadful impasse. I stood, free and upright. My gloves were on the floor, but with grandiloquent contempt I decided to forget them. In any case it might look more natural if I sauntered nonchalantly through with my hands in my pockets. But could I saunter? I could only walk like a monster newly created by its master, stiff and wooden, looking for some innocent to crush or strangle. This was no good, for I had to get myself out of that place looking more or less as I did every other morning.

I spent half an hour walking up and down the room, keeping the window open to get cold air in. The effort was awful. I felt as if I had no limbs at all, as if they'd been shot away in war, and I was a hero who had been given artificial limbs of the crudest sort, but who with fiery indomitable courage was sweating out his life in order to walk and work normally with these limbs, only to get back into his fighter plane and shoot down more German bombers. It was a real man's life right enough while I was doing this, and after the first ten minutes I was drawing in strength and self-control I never thought I had. What was London and all the world doing while I was locked in this totally absorbing struggle? I didn't know, because only I was concerned in it. After twenty minutes I seemed to be getting close to my ordinary walk, but I still wasn't satisfied. I wanted it to be more than good in case I was tempted into a too optimistic assessment of my skill. I could take no chances, and knew it was my insistence on this that separated me from the run of people who might by now have given up. Not only were part of my earthly belongings at stake, but my honour and self-respect had got involved as well, to such an extent that I'd never recognized them in this way before.

As a last gesture of bravado, when I was all set for a perfect going away, I picked up yesterday's newspaper from the table, folded it under my arm, and strutted out. I whistled the crazy jig-like empty-brained tune that everyone else was whistling, locked my door, and stepped down the corridor. I hadn't reckoned on the stairs, and felt my laminated interiors creaking and groaning like the timbers of an old ship as I took the steps as quickly as I could without capsizing. The manager at the counter greeted me in his usual friendly manner. 'Off again, Mr Cresswell?'

'A bit late today,' I smiled, 'but I had a report to write.'

'It's a hard life,' he quipped.

'Some have it harder,' I said. 'I'll be back for dinner.'

'Oh, I have a bill for you,' he called as I turned to go out. 'All made up.'

'I'm off to the bank,' I said. 'Settle it when I get back.'

He smiled. 'No hurry. Just ask for it.' I laughed at his good nature, and he wished me good morning again. Then I dropped my newspaper.

I gripped my panic by the throat and forced it back. Because I was heavily enough dressed and must have weighed half a ton, I pushed it under the coat rack with my foot. 'It's yesterday's, anyway.'

He hadn't seen it: 'What did you say?' – looking up.

'It's cold this morning.'

'Bitter,' he said. 'It's going to be a bad winter, they say.'

At the first stationer's shop I bought sheets of brown paper and a ball of post-office string, meaning to reach a toilet where I could change, and make my surplus padding into a transportable parcel. It was later than ten when I stopped outside the Tube station, but Kundt was no longer there. He waited for no man, not Kundt, for time was precious to him. He was on his own ship and caught by a storm that made him sweat and that never let up. Every meaningful tick of time counted as he hatched and planned the delicate machinery of his gadabout life, which was probably wilder than any in London, so I knew I shouldn't have him bothering me when I zombied in my crude way up to the station map.

I travelled as far as Leicester Square, and couldn't sit down because of the crush of people. Neither could I get my arm up for a bit of helpful straphanging, so I was bumped around when the train stopped and started, and a man in a bowler hat swore I was knocking into him on purpose. 'If you want a punch-up,' I said, 'follow me when I go out. If you don't, shut your arse-tight mouth.' He looked at me, but finally didn't brace himself to taking me on, which is just as well, for I was so boarded up he could have pushed me over with one finger.

I came out of the gents carrying a big parcel and wearing my normal quota of winter clothes, feeling as if I were dressed in tissue paper. I shook and shivered and walked quickly, though I had nowhere to go. The double clothes had protected me, and now I was back on the Earth from Space, a babe unwrapped in the biting frost. I went into a phone box and dialled. A child's voice answered: 'Who is it?'

'Put Bridgitte on,' I said.

'She isn't here.'

'Listen, Smog, this is you-know-who. Get her for me.' I heard him laugh, and the phone clattered down. When Bridgitte came I asked what the score was for that night. 'They're staying in,' she said, 'so I can meet you somewhere.'

'Make it the Cramborne, at six exactly,' I said. 'I'm having lunch with Mother. We've got to decide what to do about Alfie. He burned down the canning factory and sank his boat. It's the straitjacket for him this time as far as she's concerned, but I want to talk her out of it. I don't believe in that sort of thing. By the way, I've changed my hotel. Mother came last night and made me leave. Said it was too sordid. I liked it, but what can you do?'

'You have a marvellous life,' she said. 'I've got to go now because Smog is kicking me. He's pushing a hairgrip into a light socket.' There was a click and our talk was over.

I breathed and walked better at having come back into the world as a thinner man. As I struggled in that small toilet to get my surplus off, it felt like being born, bringing the real meaning of freedom home to me. I regained a narrow contact with people who were also thin, and was able again to walk on the streets with reasonable speed and flexibility. I wandered into Soho, and passed by the Clover Leaf. I'd called there in the last month hoping to see a friendly familiar face in the form of Bill Straw, but there'd been no sign of him, and Straw by word of mouth seemed not to exist. Of course I hadn't for a minute believed that to be his real name, because no man with such a past would be daft enough to give it. I supposed him to live, like myself, under the sky of his own flimsy lies, but only to make himself easy to know when he talked to other people. He used lies to explain himself, not to hide behind, and I knew that to begin such a process as this, one had to falsify one's name.

It was more of a casual look than a search, some thread to remember as I walked around, that still took me back to the Great North Road. One night I dreamed about that car journey, coming down in an old-fashioned charabanc with a dozen other people, and Claud Moggerhanger in his private silver-sided bomber flying above, diving time and again till we were running through fields and the bus was a flaming ruin in the middle of the road. My dream-slime was trying to make a complete past of that day's journey, and it was as if only something so crazy could explain the greater splintering of now.

I sipped black coffee, and wondered what news theatre to kip in until meeting Bridgitte at six. But I couldn't bear sitting in popcorn and spit, fag ads and Flash Gordon, so walked around more streets. When I was flush for money I hadn't the courage to descend the cellar of a strip club, but now that I was on my last few legs I didn't hesitate, paid my membership fee and entrance fare, and sat down with a score of other deadbeats, most of them middle-aged, or foreign tourists out to be shorn like the sheep. A tart tried to get me to buy her a drink for us both, but I just sat tight waiting for the fun to start. The audience was muttering and shuffling, but the management were hoping to pack more in. Another reluctant youth was pushed down the steps, and then a dash of music from a concealed speaker marked the opening of the curtains. A wall behind had a notice on it which said: 'Miss Felicity Lash,

Beauty Specialist for Ladies and Gentlemen.' One of the men in the audience let out a high sort of squeal, then an elderly girl came on wearing clothes of a hundred years ago. There was a bed by the wall, and when she'd straightened it neatly she began to undress. I was half asleep, but when she was naked a fire started in the building, and a fireman in full rig came in. They began a bit of parley in mime, and he pointed to the flames when she didn't want to come with him. She panicked and screamed but he gave her arse a couple of smacks, at which she quietened down and winked at us all as he carried her off over his shoulder.

That was the first half, and it bored me so much that I would have left, except for the fact that I had nowhere to go. I think it was more of a show for women than men, though the men around me enjoyed it in a mild sort of way. In the next part a well-brought-up young girl was reading a book that looked like the Bible, and it seems that, as they say, her thoughts wandered, because a few feet away, in another part of the room, a man and woman were undressing each other. She became more and more excited at this, and eventually closed her book and reached for a candle, with which piece of tallow she started to toy with herself.

The only interesting part for me in all this was the girl of the couple who were stripping each other, because I had seen her before – and not very long ago at that. In fact she had sat in my car for several hours coming down the Great North Road, and it was none other than June. I sweated under the fact of recognition and couldn't wait for the show to end. When the lights went up I called one of the waiters and said I'd like to buy that wonderful actress a drink. He said he'd tell her, and that she'd be out in a minute, but would I buy one in the meantime for him? I told him to drop dead, but he indicated that he wouldn't dream of doing such a thing. So I said in that case he ought to come upstairs and we'd fight it out outside, but he ignored this and said that if that was how I felt I needn't buy him a drink, and that he'd tell Miss Booth anyway, and that he wouldn't take what I said in bad part because judging by my voice and language I was no more than one of the boys in the place.

June came through a curtained doorway, and was led to me. 'Oh,' she said, knowing me immediately. 'I thought it was a millionaire, and that my fortune was made.'

'I hope you recovered from the car ride,' I said.

'Almost,' she laughed. 'I was shattered for a week though.'

I felt glad to see her, almost, on my side anyway, as though we'd been through death together. She was the last plant I had smelled out of the North, and now the first flower I had met in London – not counting the Dutch tulip. She had dark hair held back in two strands by ribbons, and a blouse tied in a knot at the waist, leaving a bit of bare skin between that and the short skirt. 'How's your little girl?' I asked.

'She's wonderful. Goes to school in Camden Town. My flat mate meets her in the afternoon, and I take hers and mine in the morning. It works very well.'

'Sounds intelligent. My mother was that sort of woman. Still works in a factory.'

'I'm on again soon,' she said, 'but stay around. I'll tell the boss you're a friend. We don't get crowded at this time of the day.'

'By the way,' I said, before she could dash off, 'whatever happened to Bill Straw?'

She turned her saucer-eyes on me:

'Who?'

'The bloke you travelled down with.'

'Him! Oh, my God. I'll tell you about it later. So don't go yet, will you?' She had me on the hop, and there was nothing I could do but stay. When a story was in the offing I was all ears, like a man in chains. One listens, another talks so that nobody else can get a word in edgeways, and up to now I fit into the first bracket. The worst bother takes place between those who listen and those who talk, because the one who listens all the time is sly, and the one who talks all the time is over-confident, and if they ever come to grips, or when they do, it's the Devil take the hindmost, with the listener never able to properly lose, and the talker never capable of really winning.

But my cogitations broke at the touch of a boot, because during the next performance a man sitting two seats to my left

149

started shouting the show was a cheat and he wanted his money back. 'They're whores,' he bawled, about June and her companions, standing up as if to charge on to the tiny stage. 'They do these things better in Manchester, anyway.'

The manager got to him before I did, and was knocked through the curtained doorway like a shot skittle. I pulled the heckler from behind, gripped him in a half-nelson, but even so I was almost hauled like a flag up the mast of his back, could feel my arm giving and my feet trying to lift off. But I held, and gripped, and whispered in his big left ear that he should calm down or it would be the worst for him because they had Jack the Ripper on their payroll who would sell him to Pastry-cooks Incorporated for making into meat pies when he'd done with him. I let go, and his whole body slumped. By this time another bouncer, borrowed maybe from the joint next door, came running down the steps. The manager was with him. What had happened to the girls behind the drawn curtain I did not know, and was just beginning to wonder when the huge man from Manchester straightened in one sudden movement.

'You bastard!' he cried, so that everybody heard it, and shattered me with a body blow as well.

At the sound of that cruel word my heart and stomach stayed intact for a vindictive comeback, and I slammed him so that his whole bulk dropped away and tripped on a chair. He spun like a tombstone against the manager and his bouncer friend, falling on top and putting them out till they could heave him off and get free. When he did, I remembered his insult, hit him again so that he was knocked out cold. They screwed twenty quid damages from his wallet when he came round, otherwise they'd get him to the copshop, the manager said – a tall, thin old-school-tie bloke with the right accent. Then he came back and thanked me. 'Nothing,' I said. 'I thought the drunken bastard was going to get at the girls, that's all.'

He brought me a drink, while the show went on: 'Do you want a job? All you do is stand around the place. Twenty pounds a week. We've been short of a man since we opened. You'll have to be okayed by Mr Moggerhanger, but you'll pass, on my recommendation.'

I gagged at the name, but asked in a cool way: 'Do you get many fights?'

'A few,' he said, very reticent. 'But it's not too exciting on the whole.'

I wondered why not. 'When do I start?'

'You've started,' he laughed. 'If that was your audition you passed with flying colours.'

June congratulated me: 'You'll be all right working here.'

'I'd better take the job, then,' I laughed. 'It'll be somewhere to leave my parcel.'

'I wondered whose it was,' she said.

'It's my luggage. I've got to find a room by tonight.'

She gave me her address: 'If you can't find one, you can at least sleep on the floor – under the gas stove in the kitchen it'll have to be.'

'You're very kind,' I said, not too keen on such accommodation. I'd never been brought as low as that before.

'One good turn deserves another,' she said, biting me in half. The manager's name was Paul Dent, and I told him I'd start at two the next day if that was all right by him. He said it was, so after hanging around another half-hour, I got out on the street, feeling a free man because I'd left my parcel down in the club. All the same, I didn't like the idea of having to work for a living, because that wasn't what I'd come to London for, though there seemed nothing else for it at the moment. Almanack Jack wasn't the only one who believed in fucking up the system. He might have been right down in it as far as his neck, but I intended to earn a living out of it as well if I could. In his confused brain he was still so chuffed at having made the bloody and ragged break from his former life (and who could say that it wasn't a pack of lies he'd told me?) that he couldn't see like I could that all he'd succeeded in doing was cutting his own throat, so that he was already more than halfway back there.

I met my delicious Bridgitte at the place and time of our telephone choice. We sat in the pub, she at tomato juice and me with a brown ale, and I saw that tears were about to drip from those luscious blue eyes that shone with a prick-stiffening mixture of depravity and innocence. 'You *must* tell me,' I said, when she didn't want to. 'After all, I've confided in you entirely. All the intimate secrets and scandals of my family. If Mother knew, she'd go pig-crazy. But she doesn't,' I laughed. 'So drink up, my butter-love, and have another dose of that intoxicating fomentation.'

'It's nothing, really.' She smiled. 'The doctor's wife went away for a couple of days, and last night Smog came into my bed. He sometimes does, for warmth, and when he's asleep I put him back in his own. But before I could do so, the doctor walked into my room, and pulled the clothes right back off me. He thought I was alone, and I don't know exactly what he wanted to do. But he got a shock to see Smog curled up against me with his thumb in his mouth. He was full of anger, and dragged Smog up in the air like an animal and carried him to his own bed. Smog was screaming all night, but I couldn't go out to him because I know the doctor would have got me, so I had to stay behind my locked door with Smog crying and the doctor playing his bongo music. I think he is more insane than his patients. This morning at breakfast he told me if I didn't mend my ways I would have to leave. So I think I must start to look for another job. But I will see if anything happens tonight. If it does I shall go from there.'

'When's his wife coming back?'

'I don't know. Maybe she left him.'

'Is he going out tonight?'

'I don't think so. Otherwise I would have stayed in. He's writing in his study.'

'I'll go back with you, and get into the flat. I'll stay in your room and protect you. I know that sort of person. You can't trust him. He'll rape you and cut you up. You're in England now. There's a long tradition of that sort of thing. You remember I told you about my brother Alf? Well, he had a psychiatrist at one time who used to come to the Hall. Got quite friendly with the family in fact, and was liked by everyone, especially my mother, so that he became almost a resident headshrinker. One night he made a vicious attack on a sixteen-year-old cousin who'd come to stay with us. Fortunately, the gamekeeper saw him and raised the alarm. But it was a close call for her. You've got to expect it. They've all got a touch of the Rasputin in them. Otherwise they're nice people. I've got nothing against them at all. You've just got to be on your guard if you're a simple girl staying in their house. So it'd be best if I stayed with you.'

'Yes.' She nodded. 'It may be that his wife will be back to-morrow, and then there will be no more danger. But if you get in all right, how will you get out?'

'We'll cross that barbed wire when we come to it. The main thing is to see you right. Nothing else matters. I was supposed to see Mother later on, but it's not too important. She'll be at the solicitors' till quite late because they're old friends, but I needn't be there if I don't want to be. In fact I think she'd rather I wasn't, but she was too polite to say so. The trouble with her is that she's shouting fiercely at me one day, and the next she's so tactful and considerate. It's difficult, but I suppose we all have others' foibles to put up with.'

She touched my wrist: 'I love you.'

'That makes me very happy,' I said. 'Let's go for a walk.'

At half past ten we went up in the lift to the flat. I took off my shoes, and followed her inside. She walked along the corridor to her room. All the lights were on, and I highstepped after her. She closed the door. We'd made it. The excitement of getting secretly in with the doctor only a few doors away in his study made us turn spontaneously to each other with relief, and we made love there and then on her single but firm bed, a bit of a bang that got us both into a sweat, even though we stripped to our ribs. I lay back smoking while Bridgitte went to let Dr Anderson know she was in, her intention being to cover a large food tray for us in the kitchen, and bring it back. I lay with my knees drawn up, a Dutch newspaper opened on them like a lectern, trying to read the swaddled and compli-cated words. Even backwards they didn't make sense, so I took a pencil and fiddled with anagrams, till I'd worn out three fags and realized that my sweetheart had been gone too long for my good, and possibly for hers. So I slipped on shoes and opened the door, seeing the lighted corridor and nobody in it. There were pictures along the wall, of a Scottish castle wrapped in a muffler of mist, then one of a tall façade of Glasgow slums on washday, then a picture of an English

cottage. At the front door I bumped into a hat-stand and made
such a clatter that in two flips I was back at Bridgitte's room.
'What do you want?' said a little voice I knew so well.

'Don't you ever sleep, you little bleeder?'

'I don't bleed,' Smog said. A door snapped open, so I
pulled him inside. 'I want a cigarette as well,' he said, scratch-
ing himself.

'You can't smoke. You're not seven yet.'

'What are you doing here?'

'Waiting for Bridgitte.'

'I expect she's sitting on Daddy's knee,' he said, innocently.

'Does she often do that?'

'Only when he pulls her on.'

'Oh,' I said, relieved, 'does he pull her on often?'

'Only when Mummy isn't here. She doesn't like it. That's
why she's gone away. I think she's gone into hospital to get a
divorce.'

'Is there anything you don't hear and see?'

'Not much,' he said.

'You know, Smog, I think I like you.'

'I like you,' he said.

'So will you go to bed now? Bridgitte will be cross if she
finds you here.'

'Are you going to dance tonight?'

'Your daddy wouldn't like it.'

'That's because he can't dance.'

'Nevertheless,' said I, 'give us a kiss and go back to your
room.'

He sat beside me on the bed. 'It's so boring there. I like to
smell smoke. But not cigars. They make me choke.'

'Go and see where Bridgitte is.'

'No,' he said, 'Daddy will see me. He said he'd destroy me if
he saw me out of bed, but he was only being funny.'

'Wait here till I come back then. Don't move an inch.'

I went out along the corridor, looking into every open door.
Bridgitte stood by the kitchen stove waiting for coffee to boil.
I went by without her seeing me. The next room was lined
with books, and a man sat writing at a desk. He had a round,
pale, irritable face, with a bald head and a small moustache.

Wearing a bow-tie and no jacket, he looked sober and studious, as if set for an all-night stint. By his arm was a tray with teapot and cup on it. I was about to move when he looked up and saw me: 'Who the hell are you?'

'Just passing by.'

'Well bloody-well pass out or I'll call the police.'

'I'm Bridgitte's boyfriend.'

'Oh, are you? Well I suppose that's different. You'd better say goodnight then and be on your way.'

'Is it in order,' I said, 'if I finish my cup of coffee in the kitchen?'

'Do what the hell you like. Only close my door. I'm busy.'

I shut it, and went back to Bridgitte's room. 'You shouldn't wander around,' she said. 'The doctor might see you.'

'Never. I walk too quietly.' There was salami and cheese, pickles and jam, black bread and coffee, as well as a cigar she'd brought out of the living-room. Smog joined us in the feast: 'Are you going to get married?'

'We are married,' I said. Bridgitte blushed, as she might always have done in front of Smog, but didn't.

'You aren't,' he said. 'But you make babies, though.'

I lit my cigar. 'Let me know when you've finished, then we can tuck you up nicely in a coal scuttle. Not this one, either. Go on, get down.' He grumbled, so I sat him on my knee till Bridgitte had done with her supper.

She came back from putting him to sleep: 'I don't think there's going to be any big peril from the doctor tonight, so you can go to your mother if you wish.' This wasn't much to my liking, for it meant kipping down in June's flat under a perfumed gas stove.

'No. I'll stay. You never know. I took a peep at him just now, and he seemed in a very agitated state. Unless of course you don't mind taking a chance on being all alone with that brain butcher.'

'Oh, no,' she said. 'Please! You can stay.'

Paul Dent was right. Life at the stripperama wasn't all whisky and kickshins. I went at two in the afternoon, and left about one the next morning, with a couple of hours off about tea-time. There was no saying how long I'd stick it, possibly as long as I didn't get used to it. There was an occasional punch-up, which was the part I liked least. Not that I was afraid, though any sane person might have been. I just didn't fancy ploughing like a charge of lightning into some stupid bastard who was either so insane or drunk that he could also get fleeced for ten quid because of non-existent damages. Yet that's what some of them wanted when they came into the place, a punch in the gob, a knee in the groin, and then the added jolt of paying actual money for the underground pleasure they'd gone through. In that way they didn't lose on the deal. Their next move after leaving the club was to go to a prostitute and have the job finished off. I made up my mind to quit as soon as something equally aimless came along.

After a while I stayed with Bridgitte all night again, and told her the sort of work I was doing. The doctor had gone out, to see his mistress, and Smog was sleeping soundly after an exhausting day at school, and five tantrums since teatime. 'I parted company with my mother today,' I said, lighting up a Havana, 'and I feel good about it. I've given up everything, my fortune and all connexion with the family. She wanted me to sign papers but I flung them in her face. I couldn't ponce on the working class for ever, live off land and property. For, my one and only heart, it just wouldn't do. Of course, Mother was furious, because it went against everything she stood for. It was unprecedented. No one had ever done it so blithely before. Even poor Alfred had gone mad rather than do a thing like that. She threw that in my face as well. It was hell while it lasted, but I stood my ground. The upshot of all this is that I'm suddenly without a roof over my head, without money. But luckily I got work this afternoon helping out at an enter-tainment club that an old friend of mine is running. It isn't much, and it's long hours, but I'll be able to keep my inde-pendence and that's all that matters to me now. In actual fact I know I could get a couple of thousand a year off Mother whenever I liked, with no strings attached what-so-absolutely, but even that I don't want to dirty myself with.'

I was beginning to feel that Bridgitte must be a bit mentally deficient because she believed everything I said, until it occurred to me that perhaps I was a good liar. But I was only a good liar to her, and maybe this meant that we had fallen just a little in love for them to be so effective. It was that feeling of trust we had in each other that made the lies I told so unimportant.

I went to the club every day, but got more time off the longer I worked there, and this bettering of my conditions made me less keen to give the job up, though I was still determined to. The other bouncer was Kenny Dukes, who'd been a middleweight boxer in his younger days. But now he was gone to fat and viciousness, with pink skin and half-bald fair hair, smelling of scent and immaculately dressed. The girls who worked there were afraid of him, though he had an air of gentleness, almost tenderness, about him. I could imagine he kept canaries, reared them with great love, but only for the pleasure of breaking their necks when he was in a temper about something he thought the world was trying to do to him. Then he could have a good cry and feel a new man after it. June said he was afraid of nobody but Claud Moggerhanger, but then, she added, everyone was afraid of *him*, though she personally didn't know why because he was always charming and courteous as far as she was concerned.

'He was the man who tried to run my car into the wall when I was coming into London,' I said. We sat in a pub when some of our time-off coincided, both of us with a brandy.

She laughed. 'I know. I knew it then, but didn't say anything. He was only trying to run you off the road as a bit of a joke because he saw me in the car.'

'Christ,' I gasped, 'what's he to you?'

'He's my boyfriend.'

'Well,' I said, 'I'm not afraid of him, I'll tell you that. If I see him on the road again and I'm in a good-sized car I'll try to do the same to him.'

'It was his idea of a bit of fun,' she said. 'Honestly. Anyway, he's the man you're working for now. He's a good person, even though he has got a bit of a name in this area.' Since he was her boyfriend I couldn't say much more against him, so I shut my trap on that topic.

'You remember Bill Straw?' she asked. I nodded. 'Well, when we left you a broken man at Hendon, he came to the Tube with me, and insisted on seeing me back to my flat in Camden Town. I told him not to, but he wouldn't take no as a warning, and when we got there, Claud was already waiting, sitting inside. Bill tried to kiss me at the door, and when I told him not to be so stupid he pushed his way in. Claud stood up and came towards him. Bill's face turned into a whited sepulchre when he recognized him. He stood gaping, still holding my valise that he'd kindly carried for me. Claud took out a couple of half-crowns and gave them to him as if he was a porter, then pushed him gently through the door so that he fell on his back. I haven't seen him since.'

I couldn't help but reflect that it served that Bill Straw bastard right, after he had so gleefully left me in the lurch with my ruined car. 'I expect he'll turn up,' I said. 'He was hoping to lay his hands on a few thousands in ready cash when he got here.'

'I hope he doesn't show his eyes when Claud's around,' she said. 'He's very possessive. He might even get upset if he saw me in here with you, but not so much because he knows about me getting that lift in your car. He doesn't like me to have any other boyfriends, though he doesn't care how many girlfriends I have. In fact I think he actually gets a kick out of it, the bloody Turk!'

Talk of the devil, and a few days later Claud Moggerhanger came into the club to see that all was going well. He saw me standing at the door, and recognized me, I'm sure, from the hard stare he gave. I met it, and sent it back. Ten minutes later the manager tapped me on the elbow to say that Mr Moggerhanger wanted to see me. 'What for?' I asked, sharp of voice.

'I don't know,' he said on the way down: 'Maybe he's got work for you.'

'I've already got some.'

'You'd better be on your best behaviour,' he said, so pale and serious that I laughed.

Moggerhanger filled the cubby-office, and you could tell he owned it. 'I remember you, Michael. Do you remember me?'

'Yes,' I said, 'I got a good look at you.'

'Well, Michael, we'd better get our relationship all correct and right from the very beginning. I think I can trust you. At least Mr Dent tells me I should be able to. Also, as I already know, you're a good hand at driving a car. I'm going to let you into something personal: my doctor says that my ulcer is playing up, and though I enjoy driving, he advises me to get a chauffeur. I'm offering you that job – providing you've got a licence and haven't any convictions.'

I was going to tell him he needn't worry about that, but he lifted a hand full of rings and said: 'Shut up and listen to me. First of all, you call me sir. OK? Then you have a room at my house in Ealing. Right? Then you get the same pay as you're getting here. Agreed?' I'd had no time to say anything, but I did get a brief nod in now and again. 'If you consider this in the nature of a promotion,' he said, 'we'll get on fine. I don't ask much, except superlative driving and absolute loyalty. That means no talking. See all, hear all, and say nowt. A loose lip means a cut lip. I only let the silent sort of chap close to me. Understand?'

'Yes, sir.'

'Good,' he nodded. 'A lad like you might go a long way.' And that was that. I'd become the personal chauffeur to the biggest and richest racketeer in town.

Mr Moggerhanger fixed me up with an attic room at his big house in Ealing. My quarters, as he called them, were a room with a sloping ceiling against which I continually bumped my head, unless I went around doubled up like a collier. There were a few oddments and throwouts of furniture spaced about, which were enough for me. The floor was bare boards, covered with jagged splashes of white paint where some maniac had decorated the walls and let flip with it everywhere.

As soon as I got there Moggerhanger told me to take out the Bentley and drive it around for an hour to get the feel of it. It was like driving somebody's living-room. You could almost stand up inside it, and touch it along at over a hundred miles an hour when you dare. I had no other thought in my head when I'd lifted off except to keep it unscratched and in one piece. My main aim was to have it out on the A4 and into the country, because I didn't want to run it against too much traffic on my first hand-in. I acted gingerly, until I found that its acceleration and speed, not to mention its presence, over-awed most other drivers. All I had to do was flash straight for a souped-up sales rep in his new Cortina as if I were intent on smashing him to bits, and he'd get out of the way sooner or later. Sometimes it was later, but he slid from my path never-theless. The only danger was those people with foreign cars, owner-occupiers who were so convinced of their superiority over anything English that they were insane or fanatic enough not to get clear under any circumstances, and in that case I had to pull back. But I didn't hate them for this, for in many ways they were right not to give in just because I drove a Bentley, which was after all somebody else's.

When Moggerhanger sat in the front with me, he made remarks as if he were at the wheel himself. 'Go on,' he'd say, 'step on it and you'll get across before the lights change. Overtake that Cooper. You can see the bastard thinks he's God Almighty. If you keep on, you can flatten him as you turn the next corner, get him up against the kerb.' At night, when we were coming back from his ranch in Berkshire he'd say, 'That nut should dip his headlamps. Flash him, Michael. Do a swerve and shake the shit out of him. Scrape him like a box of matches, so that he goes up in flames. I'll foot the bill for a tin of new paint on our car.'

'Yes, Mr Moggerhanger,' I'd say, doing none of these devilish things to other road-users, unless they were absolutely in the wrong and I could teach them a lesson with no danger to myself. But Moggerhanger enjoyed talking like this, and that's all that mattered. If I'd followed him to the letter I'd have been out on my arse in no time, of that I'm sure, and so I just gazed straight ahead with the poker-face I was developing fast, and said nothing except yes, Mr Moggerhanger and no, Mr Moggerhanger.

The trouble was that he belched all the time, and it stank rotten in the car. I wasn't allowed to smile, so had to put up with it. He seemed a bit apologetic about it at first, because he said once or twice: 'I'm only healthy when I'm belching, Michael. It's the breath of life to me.' He didn't even laugh when he said it. Mostly he sat in the back with a briefcase on his knee, and a bundle of newspapers. Whenever I had to wait an hour outside the lawyers' office I'd get stuck in and read these, every morning paper you could find, so that I caught up on the news and scandal as part of my job.

On long drives, Moggerhanger might break into a long bout of talking: 'The only luxury in life,' he said, 'is to have more than one place to live. Nothing else matters. You can eat bread and oil, wear a sack, but if you've got a few places scattered around, plus half a dozen passports, nobody can touch you. The trouble is, I can't wear a sack because people wouldn't be impressed by me, and I have to eat four-course lunches otherwise they'd think I was dying and about to lose my grip. And I can't walk everywhere or take buses because then I'd never have time to get anything done. But at least I have a flat in town, a place in Berks, a bungalow in Cornwall, and a chalet in Majorca – not to mention the abode in Ealing and a little place in Kent. That's property, Michael, that is. And there'a a car at each place. I could live off that for the rest of my life in a quiet sort of way if anything went wrong, fundamentally wrong I mean. Of course my wife wouldn't like it, and my spoiled daughter would gripe even more, but I do have a bit of cupro-nickel stashed away in Switzerland to stop their mouths if that should ever come about. I've got it all weighed up, except the weight of my fist. Only others can tell me about that, and they never do because they'd get knocked for six. Not that I think that's the only way to deal with people, Mikey-boy, because it ain't. I'm not inhuman. Violence never got anyone anywhere, at least not all violence, and not everywhere. I used to lean a bit too much that way, but then I saw that most of it wasn't necessary. The reputation of being rough was all I needed to get me what I wanted. I had to punch or slash some poor bastard once in a while whether he deserved it or not, just to show my kidneys were still hard. I gradually got better with the quick lip and the flash look, and nowadays I hardly ever have to prove even to myself that I'm as tough as I once was. Life's like that. If I say it's funny I'll spit blood. If I say it's hard I'll swallow my teeth. I don't say anything except talk about the way it is. The war made me, or helped to.

I was nearly thirty then, with such a criminal life behind me that even the Army turned up its nose. It came at the right time as far as I was concerned, though I wished it never had come when it finished and I saw what it did to so many in Europe. I never bargained for that, Mikey. None of us did. But what else could I do but take advantage of it? I was made that way, by myself and by others. I wasn't unpatriotic. Don't get me wrong. I'm as English to the bone as the next man – though not to the marrow perhaps. I just helped to channel certain food supplies in the right direction, and to organize exotic entertainments that might not otherwise have been available. All much of a muchness. Property was dirt cheap, and I snapped up a few big places. Went from worse to bad and bad to better, and when I find it hard to get to sleep at night I keep telling myself over and over again how much money I'm worth, in round figures, of course. Believe it or not, it actually soothes me. It's a great big cushion I float on to. I think I'd turn queer if it weren't for all this money! It's all right, Mikey-moo, I shan't, so don't shift over. In the prime of my fifty-year-old life I'm beginning to get an ulcer, and it's hard to say what's giving it. All my life I've only needed to glance at a person to tell whether I can deal with him or not. But this spot-on ability is what built up my ulcer – over the years. So it's my ulcer now that tells me whether or not I can treat with someone. I feel it jump, not much, sometimes more than others, but it jumps, and I can feel it. If I look at a person and my ulcer's quiet, then he's OK. If it jumps, then I put on the big stuff to help me to get what I want. A perfect ulcero-meter, Michael. I must patent it. Maybe everyone should have one in their guts. You've got to turn everything to your own advantage, especially the bad things, because if the good things help other people it's the bad things you've got that help yourself. Not that I'm having everything out of life. Far from it. In the first place I don't even know what I want. I only know what I haven't got, which might sound like the same thing but isn't at all. One thing I haven't yet got is a son. I don't drink my spinal fluid over it, but it bites me now and again. I've got plenty of daughters, but only one by my own wife. I've never had a son, though they do say it takes a real man to go on making daughters. I've had so many here, there and everywhere that I always know a child is mine, just because it's a daughter. If one of my women had a son I'd know she'd been treacherous. I'd slash her till she looked like a circus tent after a stormy night, not to mention what I'd do to the real ponce-headed daddy. But it's all talk, Michael. I don't do much more than talk these days, I can tell you, but it's enough, and if it wasn't I'd soon turn to a little blunt persuasion.'

Not long afterwards he tried some of this, and was arrested on a charge of extortion. At first I was glad that the great Moggerhanger had come crashing down at last, even though I'd listened to his talk with a lot of admiration. And I thought goddammit here goes my job, but suddenly he pours into the house from a taxi, having got out on five thousand pounds bail. And then I was pleased to see him. His wife clung to him as if he'd already done twenty years in prison. 'I wish you'd retire, Claud,' she said, 'and not get mixed up in things like this any more.' She seemed to have the idea that he was the managing director of a straight factory who'd got taken in by dishonest underlings.

He gave her that impression as well: 'No, Agnes. Who'd run things without me? Everything would fall to pieces. There are too many relying on me. Don't worry, love. It'll all blow calm again. There's nothing they can put on me, and they know it. They try a little frame-up now and again in the hope that it'll stick. They haven't got a chance. That Detective Inspector Lantorn just won't be sensible and let go. He's got to show willing now and again to Chief Inspector Jockstrap, otherwise he's a decent enough bloke. In many ways I've got a lot to thank him for, but we won't go into that now, especially a few years ago when . . .'

He saw me listening, and though I'm sure he trusted me, some inborn caution told him not to go on. It was true that we had become quite friendly, though with a certain distance always between us. He talked to me as if I were himself, and though this sometimes made me feel as if I were no longer myself, it did make it the most interesting job I'd so far had. He had a certain flinty wisdom which I was too young to see myself as ever having. I won't say I wanted to be like him, because I was too frightened of him for that, but I admired him nevertheless.

There was a suite of kennels outside the house. Apart from a brace of Dobermann Pinschers which served as guard dogs to his property, Moggerhanger kept a couple of champion greyhounds. One was run under the name of Long Tom, while the other was called Abel Cain. He'd bought them six months ago, but already they'd won a few races and were high up in the lists. They would have turned any Nottingham collier green with envy, if such people still kept whippets, which I wasn't sure of, because I'd never seen them doing so in my short life.

The only blight on Moggerhanger's arrest was that, as a condition of his bail, he was not supposed to leave town, and this came at the time when his sporting heart was set on letting Long Tom and Abel Cain race on a dogcourse in Devon. He not only stood to win fair money, but to increase the fame of his prime animals – which would jack up their price when they were worn out and he wanted to sell them. He fumed about this unreasonable confinement as I drove him from one to another of his clubs by day, and to a certain place in Knightsbridge at night outside which I had to wait in the car for several hours till he came wearily down, snappy with me, but pleased with himself. Cursing his ill-luck in this way was Moggerhanger's method of clarifying his thoughts towards a certain plan. He proposed to invite Detective Inspector Lantorn over to dinner, and I was sent to the appropriate police station at seven o'clock to bring him back to Ealing.

He had a face that was distinguished by being utterly unrecognizable. He was as tall and thin as a ramrod. His look was thin and expressionless, and with the grey suit he was wearing and the glassy stare in his eyes he could perhaps more than in any other country have vanished like a fish in water, because if there were any features at all in his face I saw that they were getting uncomfortably close to those of a fish the more I got the opportunity of glancing at him.

I sprang out and opened the back door for him as he came down the steps – as I'd been told to do. He got in and sat down without even a thank you. What went on at the dinner I shall never know. Walking the lawns outside, I certainly heard a lot of glass clinking and gruff matey laughter. I don't suppose many people can claim to have been dined and swined at the Moggerhanger's, but when I drove Lantorn back to his Wembley home that night he was singing *Kemp Town Races* all the way, even when I'd let him out and watched him go crump at his matchbox gate.

Two days later I was called at six in the morning to drive them to the racecourse in Devon. For an hour neither Lantorn nor Moggerhanger spoke a word, but sat well back behind, arms folded into their overcoats, not even glimpsing out at the ominous fish-red dawn. Two sleek greyhounds sprawled on the upholstery at their feet, opening their scissor-jaws now and again for a yawn so wide that they seemed capable of swallowing the whole car. That's the picture I got when I heard the sharp whine of it above the purr of the engine. The sky as I went south from Wembley was purple and red as if God had slit His own throat, and was spilling Himself over the whole world. It seemed a normal, raw, unkindly London dawn, and I was glad to turn my back on it when we swung on to the Great West Road at Heston.

I cruised at fifty and sixty where I shouldn't have done more than forty, but this was to see whether the big copper in the back would stir up and say anything. He didn't, so I hoped a patrol car would tail us and pull us in to see why we were going so fast. Then I'd see an exchange of looks that might be interesting. There wasn't much traffic on the way out, and I thought how good it would be to have a few hundred miles of road all to myself. If I were king I'd issue a proclamation saying that all subjects were to be off the road on such and such a day, and then I'd get into a souped-up Rolls with my prime minister, minister of war, and chief of police, and speed along freely wherever I wanted to go. As it was, any honest chauffeur making a living risked his life on England's arterial lanes. It was good practice for my self-control, not being able to curse blind because of my passengers, as I went through town after town and there still seemed no end to getting out of London. But those at the back didn't worry, and when Moggerhanger let out a reverberating belch Lantorn stirred and asked: 'What did you say?'

'Not a word,' said Moggerhanger. Long Tom jumped on his knee at the sound of his voice, but he eased it off with the back of his hand. Moggerhanger was getting his own way and that's all that mattered to him and his underworld. He'd asked Lantorn if he couldn't waive his metropolitan regulations and let him go off for the day to race his favourite dogs in Devon. At first Lantorn refused just to show he had some weight to throw about, but then he relented on condition that he, James Lantorn, could go along too to keep an eye on him, and maybe win a bit of money into the bargain on these dogs Moggerhanger boasted about so much. Moggerhanger swore they were certain to win every race, and I for one knew him to be right. I was prepared to bet every pound on the dogs because they couldn't help but win. I'd seen Claud put the dope and syringes into his small case before leaving that morning, which was something Lantorn might or might not know. But as I drove along I saw I was stupid in thinking he didn't know, when it was obvious he knew very well, because it seemed to me that James Lantorn and Claud Moggerhanger were two of the biggest crooks in the world – as I opened up and went at sixty towards Basingstoke. If there was an angel in the car at the moment it must have been me, and I kept saying it to myself in case I should fall for the trap of being proud of it.

Lantorn must have been awake because I heard him say, when a Jaguar overtook me: 'That bastard's doing above seventy. I'd pull him in if I was in a squad car.'

'It's terrible, the sort of people you get on the roads these days,' said Claud. 'If it was up to me every car would cost ten thousand pounds cash, and them that couldn't afford it could walk, or take a bus. That'd keep the decks clear. It's getting bad, and it'll get worse.' He took out a bottle of brandy and a silver cup, poured a round, and passed it to Lantorn, who silted it down without a word. 'Cards?' said Claud. There must have been a nod in his direction, because I heard the case come open, and the crisp efficient shuffle of a deck. Cigar smoke filtered through, and the rattle of money. Small stakes, I thought, as laughter at some surprising hand or other dinned my neck. There were light-hearted curses, a slapping of thighs, and an occasional harsh: 'Get down, you bastard,' as one of the dogs tried to barge its long head in, or when they hadn't even moved but Claud had lost and wanted somebody to take it out of.

I stopped at a town traffic lights and half turned my head to see what was the score, and Moggerhanger rapped out: 'Keep your eyes to the front, and your ears to the front. That's what I pay you for. Not to drive. Any ragbag can drive.' He laughed at this, and Lantorn joined in, but I shot forward on green so that the deck of cards moved. Surprisingly, Moggerhanger didn't bury a razor in my neck or sack me on the spot. Apparently his bad hand had suddenly become a good one, and it was Lantorn who laughed on the other side of his face when he couldn't get things back to the way they'd been before. When we stopped for a sandwich Moggerhanger looked more like the copper to me, a real hardback if ever there was one. But we felt in a better mood after eating and a mug of tea. The dogs were brought out for a piss as well, to stretch their long and lovely legs that were set, when specially primed, to win us so much goo.

At eleven o'clock, and not far from the course, I heard them packing the cards away. Moggerhanger was in a grumpy state of mind because he'd lost five quid. Being a millionaire he resented it more than a man whose last money had slipped away. 'You'll get it back on the way home,' said Lantorn in a friendly manner, seeming to feel that this bad mood between them wasn't worth such a measly sum.

'I bloody-well will,' said Moggerhanger, an unrealistic prophecy that seemed nevertheless to cheer him up. 'Let's see to the dogs, anyhow,' he added. 'Hold the buggers.' I heard a couple of yelps, then a few slaps at the arse to get the stuff into circulation, so that both my passengers considered that all was right with the world.

This turned out to be more or less correct. I was told to wait in the car park while they went in and did business. I asked Moggerhanger if he would stake ten of my own quid on Long Tom, since I couldn't be at the race myself. He snatched it and said he'd do his best but that I'd no right to ruin myself getting into the gambling habit. I'd do much better, he said, sending it to my mother who no doubt could do more worthwhile things with it. The dogs, full of pep, pulled him away, otherwise the sermon might have gone on for an hour. Moggerhanger was still full of surprises to me, which may have been why I put up with so much from him.

I went over to a restaurant and got myself a plate of steak and mashed potatoes, cabbage and bread pudding. Travelling with such people there was no telling when I'd be able to eat again. They didn't seem interested in food, with such dog flesh and high finance on their hands. Afterwards I sat in the car and heard music on the radio, read a newspaper, smoked, lay full out along the seat and slept for an hour, a far-off announcement of winners coming over from the stadium, with the tremor of cheering and noise now and again.

It was four o'clock when Moggerhanger and Lantorn came out, flushed and half drunk both with booze and the success of their outing, regarding it as more or less over and done with. 'All right, Michael, home we go,' Moggerhanger said, bundling the deadbeat dogs inside like so much window-leather. 'Step on the petrol,' he crowed. 'Sink the golden boot in. We cleared the decks, eh, Jimmy' – nudging old Lantorn when they were seated. 'By God we did. You should be of good cheer, Michael, because you're a couple of hundred up on this little journey. Good, eh? He's a lucky lad, ain't he, Jimmy?'

'I'd say so,' said Lantorn with a chuckle.

So we sailed away eastwards towards threatening clouds. We stopped at some Wiltshire market town called Pigminster and had tea at the hotel. The dogs, who had slept like two stones since leaving the course, woke up and followed us into the lounge, and the manager was so impressed by them, being a fervent greyhound man, that he let them lie like royalty beside our table. Moggerhanger took my saucer and his own and put them on the floor, full of tea. They lapped up pint after pint, and several pots were ordered because we were all thirsty. Neither Moggerhanger nor Lantorn were sober, and their laughter gunned around the large and otherwise empty lounge. Moggerhanger threw whole cucumber sandwiches across at the dogs, whose huge jaws snapped over them like crocodiles. By their eyes, and the way their ribs trembled as the food came flying, they looked as if they needed that sustenance, to stop them caving in altogether.

It pepped me up too, and I drove on across the Plain. Moggerhanger got his friend back on to the cards, but the game had lost its spirit now that they'd made so much at the races. I tried to speculate on the amount, but didn't get very far. If I'd won two hundred they must have made ten times as much. This thought was cut off when raindrops poxed up the windscreen, and I reached for the wipers. Grey clouds rolled low across the countryside, but the road was fairly empty and I bowled along near to seventy miles an hour, which wasn't bad on such a narrow and rotten road.

The dogs stood together and scratched at the carpets. 'They want to piss,' said Claud, scooping up a few pounds he'd won. 'Pull in when you can, Michael.'

There was a lay-by close to Stonehenge, and as soon as I opened the door they shot out with such force that I went down into the wet grass. They found a stump a few yards away, and I thought that if they emptied themselves much more they'd go down flat like balloons. Moggerhanger sat in the car and watched them proudly through the open door, while Lantorn lay with his head back after the hard day's work and was on the point of going to sleep.

When I went to get them in, Long Tom jumped in the air, spun like an acrobat, came down facing the opposite direction, and went off sniffing from tree to tree. Abel Cain snapped at my hand to bite it when I got close, then thought it might not taste so good, and ran after Long Tom. They romped and scampered happily, and for a while I thought maybe they had a right to ten minutes of fresh air and frolic, albeit wet, before coming back into the stuffy car.

But Claud thought differently: 'Get them in.' I knew it was no good running, because how could I hope to catch them when they'd just won me two hundred quid against the fastest dogs in England? I crouched, and went up slowly, calling them pretty names, my hand held out as if a piece of raw steak were spread in it. They looked tempted, but only to torment me, because they turned and ran through a hedge and into the middle of a field. I chased them, aware of Claud's bull-like roaring behind. Together with Lantorn, who had now been roused, they fanned left and right while I was beating up front. My shoes and trousers were saturated, and rain started to come down heavier.

There was no sign of the dogs, but we kept up the advance, knowing they must be in our flimsy net somewhere. I heard Lantorn coughing on one horizon and Moggerhanger cursing on the other. The afternoon was heavy and quiet but for the dogs' names being shouted, and the occasional thin drone of a car going by on the road we were fast leaving behind. We were worried in case the dogs should double back and slip through on to it, where they'd be in danger from traffic. But as far as we knew they were still up ahead in the expanding distance. I began to reflect that this job had its good and bad points, to see that if this went on much longer I wouldn't be able to keep my date with Bridgitte for that night. Owing to the unexpected demands of Moggerhanger I hadn't been able to see her for a few days, and missed the occasional nestle into her naked body.

The raw wind and the blight-rain put such pretty thoughts away. I waded ahead calling for the dogs, unable to curse and wish them in hell because they had just won me two hundred quid. The great blocks of Stonehenge rose on the other side of some railings, Long Tom and Abel Cain sporting around and under them. Without considering, I lifted myself up, tearing my trousers at the arse and ankle, but doing the great feat of getting over, nearly breaking my abdomen when I landed on the sacred earth of the other side. Long Tom came up to me, and for a second I touched his collar, but he snapped free and ran back to Abel Cain, his mouth open and choking on moist wind as he snapped at his pal's back legs.

I ran under the stones, around the supports, my lungs creaking and rending. I leapt forward and fell, sprawled along the soaked gravel and soil, damning the painted, perverted druids for all I was worth. Moggerhanger and Lantorn waited at different parts of the fence. 'Get him,' Claud called out. 'Come on, Michael. There's a bonus when you've got 'em in. Good lad. Good lad.'

I swerved, zig-zagged, ran, switched back, reached out, spun, ran again, circled, cut my arm on a supporting pillar so that the blood ran salty in my mouth when I licked it during a pause. Rain poured down. Lantorn had gone back, told to bring the car closer so that the dogs could be bundled in more easily when we caught them. They mocked me, tricked me, tried to bite me. I was their mortal earthly enemy, and they were my devils, cut out of Stonehenge stone and waiting for me to exhaust myself before they could turn and rend me. I fell on to Abel Cain by a ruse, but he snapped so fiercely with his ugly teeth that I was frightened and let go.

The bastards were turning ugly. As far as I was concerned they could take the two hundred quid and pad their rabbit-ribs with it. I thought of giving it up when Lantorn and Moggerhanger came into the enclosure, followed by a keeper who, however, didn't take part in the round-up but only stood by grinning. I envied him and saw how sensible he was, but the drug that had been pumped into the dogs must have worked off because they seemed calmer. I hoped they were becoming exhausted, so that we could then lift them into the car like so many sleeping pieces of meat.

Moggerhanger spoke to them affectionately, but their eyes were mad and hollow, not of the world beyond the stones of Stonehenge, and with no effort they rallied their energy and were right away from us. Then we were all running without any purpose. I was dreading that they'd extend their field of freedom by getting outside the Stonehenge enclosure again and spreading over the whole of Wiltshire. If that happened they'd be lost for good, because Moggerhanger could hardly advertise in the papers that he'd lost his dogs, when he was not supposed to be out of London. At least I couldn't imagine Lantorn allowing that, for it might be more than his job was worth – unless Moggerhanger were prepared to employ him at a similar sort of salary.

We ran our guts out till it got dark, and at the end only captured Long Tom, who was kicked savagely into the car by his loving master. Abel Cain was never seen again. We searched and sweated through the mouldy perishing dusk, driving to all points of the compass, then walking inwards like a military search operation. In fact it would have needed an army to track down that lousy dog which was worth its weight in gold to Moggerhanger. At nine o'clock we gave up, sat glumly in a pub saloon hardly able to talk.

Lantorn's long face was grey with exertion, while Moggerhanger's was pasty from shock. I just felt knackered, hardly able to get down my sandwich and tomato juice. Moggerhanger said we'd have to come out tomorrow at the slit of dawn to carry on the hunt, but Lantorn said this wouldn't be possible while he was on bail. I thought Moggerhanger was going to slit him there and then, and both of us make a break for it, but his white gills relaxed into a smile as he downed another brandy and began to look human again. 'It'll be worth a few hundred,' he said, 'on top of the thousand you got today.'

But I could see Lantorn's face from where Moggerhanger couldn't, because he was sitting by his side. Lantorn had remembered what firm he was working for, and his face now showed it. 'Couldn't,' he said, 'old sport. The super's back tomorrow and it's more than my life's worth.'

Moggerhanger tried it from all angles, but the more he did so the more did Lantorn dig his heels into the soil of his heart. It wasn't that he couldn't let Claud off the hook tomorrow. He could, and he knew he could, and do it with safety. And Moggerhanger knew as well. But for no reason at all Lantorn chose not to, and nobody could do anything about it. In this black mood we travelled back to London, and it was more like being in a boat than a car because the rain poured down all the way. Being so late, there was no thick traffic, though I was driving with my nerve-ends on the final run, which came just about midnight. There was no cardsharping, or brandy swigging, and the silence almost sent me to sleep. At one point I went straight across a red traffic light, but nobody was the worse for it. The only break was an occasional whine from Long Tom who by now was beginning to miss his mate, and perhaps still felt the boot marks that Moggerhanger had planted on it. Lantorn must have felt the most hated man in the world by the time we got home, and I sensed that his only aim left in life, if he had anything to do with the prosecution (and I knew that he had), was to get Moggerhanger the longest possible sentence for whatever he'd done wrong in the eyes of the law. Moggerhanger knew this as well, and I hoped there was something he could do about it, because out of the two rogues I was driving home I knew whose side I was on, without even having to make the choice. I suppose this was one of the reasons why Moggerhanger had taken me on and, having weighed me up, had not found me wanting in this respect. Still, I could not bask in such a man's approval, even though I was young, because the fact that he might approve of me had nothing to do with me approving of myself – though maybe it was fast becoming so.

The next day Moggerhanger handed me a bundle of notes, and I thanked him as I stuffed them into my pocket. 'Count them,' he said.

'I trust you, Mr Moggerhanger.'

'You're a bigger fool than I thought you were. Never trust anybody. If you do you'll make the fatal mistake of one day trusting yourself. And any man who trusts himself is asking for trouble.' He was in the dining-room having breakfast. 'Pour yourself some coffee,' he laughed, 'and sit down when you're talking to me.' The Spanish servant had let me lie in till ten, so I felt refreshed after my eighteen-hour day of yesterday. I drew a large cup of coffee, with a dash of milk. 'And while you're drinking it,' he insisted, 'count that money. I shan't be offended.'

'It's all correct,' I said, flattening it into my wallet.

'Got a bank account?' If I hadn't, he said I ought to open one, and offered to recommend me to his bank, which I accepted. 'Put that two hundred on deposit,' he said, 'and forget about it – until you can add to it.'

'I was thinking of buying a car, to take my girlfriend out in.'

'Who is she?' he asked, sharply.

'A coloured girl from West Ken, student at London University. We clicked on a bus to Hampstead. Very platonic, though.'

He smiled. 'Good luck to you. But don't buy a car,' he said, 'till you've got the price of one ten times over. Then find a good one, and have the best out of it. I'll tell you something else. Don't get a second-hand car. Only a rich man finds a bargain, because he can get it under his own time and conditions. I didn't have a car till there was fifty thousand quid in the bank. Then I bought a new one, for cash. I walked or used taxis till then, and it didn't interfere with my work, or my self-esteem. It'd need a lot to do that. I run my life on ten of my own commandments. I worked them out month by month in prison as a young man, though they were a bit different to what they turned out to be later. Life smooths all edges. Pour some more coffee and I'll run through them for you. Number one was: don't do anything against a friend who can still help you, or an enemy who might soon be talked into doing you a good turn. Not bad, eh?'

'Very sharp,' I had to admit.

'Two: don't kill for money, spite, or love, but only to get what somebody else has got but what you consider to be your own.'

'That's rough.'

'Ain't it? Number three: when you put money into the bank don't do it like a happy saver, but feel on top of the world, as if you're throwing it away. But hoard your gains, because money is power over others – though never over yourself.'

I was struck by his sense, not to say flabbergasted, and hoped I'd remember all he said. There was no stopping him.

'Four: treat the police as well as you would like to be treated if you were one of them. They are put there by society to help you keep what you have got no matter how you got it. They're only human. Five: when you don't know whether to say yes or no, always say yes. Six: train yourself never to love, and never to hate. Seven: if you want to make money, sell people what they need, not what they've been told to want. Then you'll have earned it. Eight: people are always stupider than you think. If you don't know this, you'll hardly ever act. Nine times out of ten you'll be right. But polish your powers of intuition, and plot every step intelligently. Note where there's a chance of your being found out, and prepare to turn it to your advantage if this should happen. Nine: never be afraid, neither of God, man, nor beast. The others are always more afraid than you are. Ten: be law-abiding in every possible way, except when it stops you getting what you want. Eleven, and the last: honour thy father and thy mother. If it weren't for them you wouldn't be here, and if you live by these rules they'll certainly do well by you.'

'Sounds all right,' I said, 'but they're not so easy to follow.'

'Takes time,' he admitted. 'If you try hard you can do it by the time you're thirty. But even if you only try, you're a thousand times better off than those who don't know about them.'

'Do you want me to go out to Stonehenge today and look for Abel Cain? He might still be somewhere in the neighbourhood.'

He stood up and fastened his jacket. 'I know when something's good and lost. He's stashed away in somebody's barn or kennel by now. We'll never see him again, at least not under the name he's been known by. Thanks all the same. I'll be off to see my lawyers in half an hour, so get the car ready. I'm going to wrap this case up so neatly in its warp and weft that that bastard Lantorn can wear it around his neck as a scarf for the rest of his life.'

In the next few days I worked day and night at the beck and call of Moggerhanger's eleven deadly rules. One journey was to take a box of groceries to the house of his eighty-year-old mother in Hendon. I didn't get a glance of her because the maid took them from me. Moggerhanger spent much time talking to lawyers, and during these weeks he must have dropped a couple of stone in weight, though he was loud and cheerful through it all.

Bridgitte accused me of going cold on her, and once when I went to see her Smog cried as I was about to leave. It seemed that Dr Anderson's wife had come back, and so he had started licking his way towards Bridgitte again. This didn't worry me, because I wasn't the jealous sort. But Bridgitte said I ought to do something about it and that if I wasn't jealous it proved I didn't love her. Smog snuggled up to her and said: 'I still love you, though,' and she clutched him as the tears ran down her apple cheeks, her beautiful button nose an island in between. I told her that the day after tomorrow Moggerhanger's case would be over. Then I'd make sure to spend more time with her. If he went to prison, I'd be out of a job. If he was free he'd go for a holiday, and so would I. 'In the meantime,' I added, when Smog had gone to his innocent dreams, 'if that dirty bastard Dr Anderson tries to slip his hands up your clothes again you should go out and buy a lipstick that neither you nor his wife uses, and put it under her pillow so that she can find it and cause a rumpus. Then she'll leave again, and he'll brood so much on her going that he won't be able to paw you.' I threw off this idea more or less in an idle moment, never thinking she'd act on it. At least I left her calm that night, which settled my mind for all the Moggerhanger work still to be done.

The case against him was thrown out of court for lack of evidence. The headline that night said: MOGGERHANGER ACQUITTED – and I caught some of his satisfaction in the guts as I drove him from the lawyers' on Chancery Lane. On the steps of the court he had shaken hands with Lantorn, an immortal picture for me if ever there was one. He sat with me in the front, saying nothing, looking far grimmer than he'd done while waiting for the trial, as if he had in mind some sort of cataclysmic revenge on those who'd tried to get him. The only thing was that he belched more frequently than he'd done lately, as if now that it was over his stomach could relax.

At home all was set for a quiet celebration dinner with his wife and beautiful dark-haired daughter, and his brother Charles Moggerhanger, who was the managing director of a department store in the North, and who looked after Claud's property up that way. Charles Moggerhanger was quiet, sarcastic, and suspicious, a lightly built man of medium height with a quiet tread, a bald head, and finer features than his brother. All in all it was hard to say who would be the worse to get on the wrong side of.

While they were knocking back champagne and calling every two minutes for the Spaniard who looked after the table, I slipped away to visit Bridgitte. I hadn't bothered to phone beforehand, and when I got there, going up in the lift and full of anticipation at getting her lips and body wrapped into mine, there was no answer to my ringing. That was bloody funny, I thought. Somebody at least had to be in, because they couldn't all have gone out and left poor Smog alone. I rang again. I even knocked. Then I went down into the street, and phoned from the nearest callbox. My eyes were wide open, glued to the mirror, hypnotized by the continual buzzing that was never going to be answered. I unlatched myself, without getting my button-B money back.

It was raining, so I pulled my mac around me, heading for the club I used to work at. I was in time to see June at the end of her act. Paul Dent called to me like a firm old friend, and even Kenny Dukes tipped me a no-hard-feelings wink. I had heard from June that he'd smouldered with dangerous envy for a week or so after I'd got my rather special job with Moggerhanger, but at the moment he seemed convivial enough. He even offered me a drink.

A few minutes later June came to the bar: 'Isn't it wonderful about Claud?'

'A foregone conclusion,' I said. 'Whisky?'

'They were really out to get him, though. Tomato juice, love.'

'He knows how to tie them up.' We drank our doses and I sat in a stupor the rest of the evening, chatting her up between the times she was on.

In the early hours I offered to get her home in a taxi, and she accepted. 'Sometimes my working day goes like a dream,' she said, nestling close when we were in, 'but today was a drag, waiting for Claud to get off.'

'Are you in love with him?' I asked her, my arm over her shoulder, the other in her lap.

'He's the only man I have anything to do with properly. But don't talk about him. Kiss me.'

I did, and she clung to me as if I were the last man on Earth, opening me and feeling me so that I began to be a bit embarrassed in case the driver turned round, or saw us in his mirror. I tried to do the same to her, but she wouldn't have it. We were gasping and half choking, and I suddenly let go of myself completely, at which she gave me a final kiss and drew away.

On the steps of the house she lived in I asked if I could come up to her flat. 'No,' she said. 'I've got a girlfriend I'm rather sweet on at the moment. Thanks for the nice ride, though.'

'I'll come up and serve you both if you like.'

She smiled, giving the final rub-off: 'I'll serve her myself.'
'As long as you enjoy it,' I said, walking away.

Sodium lights flared and glowed down Camden Road, and I walked in the blackest of hugger-muggers back towards town. It would have been better, as things turned out, if I had gone to sleep it off in my room at Ealing, but my feet wouldn't move that way. That bastion of all-devouring Moggerhangers had kept me in thrall for more than I should have let it these few months. As far as I was concerned he could rot on the dungheap of his self-invented rules, because tonight I wanted to shake it off for a few hours and roam at my own will.

Before I'd gone half a mile I dialled Bridgitte's number again, but, like before, there was no answer. I went through multiple speculations as to what had happened, but every one of them was a tragedy, and so none sounded like the truth. There was nothing to do except wait some unspecified amount of time before getting to know what had happened, and it gnawed at my guts. I wanted to go to the flat and quietly break in, but when I got there the big front doors on the street were locked more firmly than those of a castle in the middle of a brigand-infested wilderness.

A few taxis circled Leicester Square, and a copper eyed me as I passed a closed-up picture house. I walked down Villiers Street, then up the steps on to Hungerford Bridge. The water below was circling slowly as if only a foot deep. A skyline of buildings stood under the halo of their own light that seemed to be generated by the faint traffic noise. London was beautiful at night, when most of the eight million people were asleep and I could have the feeling that all of it was for myself.

I lit a Dutch cigar and strolled on over the bridge, telling myself how good it was to be alive once all things that held me down had vanished from sight. In a corner at the top of the steps a body was hunched away from the breeze and drizzle, trying to sleep. At the noise of my footsteps his head lifted and said: 'Got a smoke, mate?'

I stopped, and passed him one. 'That's all I have on me' – wanting to tell him off for being out on a night like this, give him a lecture on not providing for himself, and maybe at the end of it recite Moggerhanger's rules. But I sensed that this might not mean much at such a critical stage of his life.

'Eh,' he said, 'a cigar! I'll take a puff, though it won't be any use on an empty stomach.'

I'd heard that voice before, that complained with such professional confidence. 'I suppose you want a couple of bob for a sandwich?'

'That's cheap at the price,' he said. 'With five shillings I could get a bowl of soup as well.'

I looked close: 'If I'm not mistaken I'm talking to the well-known and notorious Almanack Jack.'

'Are you a copper?' he said, a well-developed snarl. 'If you are, I'm an innocent man. I've driven a few people into the looney-bin in my time, but apart from that nobody can point a finger at me. Still, we've all done that sort of thing. If you're too young for it you've got plenty of time yet.'

I told him who I was. 'I don't want to disturb your good night's sleep, but I haven't had a bite for fourteen hours, so I'm probably hungrier than you are. You can come to the market for a feed if you like.'

He jumped up, surprisingly agile for a man of beard and rags. 'I got rolled,' he told me as we walked along. 'Some young toughs from Lambeth jumped on me and took my almanacks. They scattered them all up Northumberland Avenue, then drove off in a souped-up Zodiac. It's happening too often these days. I'm going to fix myself up with a knife. That'll keep the young bleeders at bay.'

I told him I was working for Moggerhanger, and he gave a whistle to show he was impressed. 'I hope you hold your job. They say nobody works for him long.'

'We get on fine, the two of us.'

'Keep it that way, then you can buy me a meal now and again.'

'I'll do my best,' I said. He gradually straightened up while walking, till he seemed at last to be a little taller than I was.

We found a place, and indulged ourselves at my expense. Bacon and cheese sandwiches got washed down by innumerable bucket-sized mugs of tea. The place was full of porters and lorry drivers, as if I were back in a Nottingham café near a factory, where the blokes go because they can't stand the better food of canteen dinners. It was warm, smoky, steamed-up, and timeless, and I began to feel as tired and done in as Almanack Jack looked. In spite of his bang-about life he seemed better fleshed with food than I was, and in the end he was thumping me on the shoulder and telling me not to look so depressed. Then he fell forward on his arms and went to sleep.

He heard me stand up to get more tea and sandwiches, and when I came back he was wide awake, and started snapping into it. 'I don't know why you sell almanacks,' I said. 'You only frighten people half to death with the prophecies inside.'

'That's what they want,' he said. 'They wouldn't buy them otherwise. They're only human, after all. If you can't have a good earthquake or war to look forward to in somebody else's country, life isn't worth living.'

'You don't believe that crap.'

'No. But *they* do. I think war is stupid as well.'

He leaned back, lit a cigar of mine, and sent the first smoke out slowly, like a calculated trick, as if knowing that he could bring it back again when it began to stray too far. The unfamiliar smell fetched disapproving looks from a couple of men nearby, but Jack was enjoying himself, as if the smell of a cigar brought back a lucidity that he'd had, once upon a time. 'Those that indulge in war,' he said, 'seem to like it so much that once they start they can't stop, like two people fucking. In fact war is a male homosexual act between consenting nations, carried out in full view of God. Otherwise it wouldn't have gone on so long. My almanacks make no difference, whether it comes or goes. Ever tried prophesying peace? You wouldn't sell a single copy. You'd be a bloody liar, what's more.'

I didn't like this idea from him, that I was a liar, but my hard-earned food was making him light-headed, so there seemed no way of stopping him, short of walking out. And I couldn't do that because I still had half a mug of tea and a sandwich in front of me.

'I can pick up your thoughts like a man in the park stabbing bits of toffee paper with a sharp stick. Ever since you saw me dozing on Hungerford Bridge you've been thinking I ought to have a shave and get a job. Don't deny it. But just because you've become someone's bodyservant, don't get feeling so superior to me. If it hadn't been you on the bridge just now who'd felt guilty at seeing me shivering to death and got me something to eat, another mug would have turned up sooner or later. I feel superior to you, mate, because having slipped off the social scale altogether, I've got nothing to feel guilty about. You can't get any higher than that in the world, take it from me. So when you do me a good turn, I'm not too grateful because I'm doing as much for you as you are doing for me. The unemployed should be treated as great gifts to a nation, because if they didn't in their largeness of spirit agree to be unemployed, all the other toffee-nosed bastards who've got jobs couldn't hold them. The unemployed should be fed and pampered, given double pay to what they'd get if they were working. There should be special centres where they could queue up for a daily ration of cigars. One prominent motto of my Democratic Republic of Euphoria would be: Hail to the unemployable, because they should inherit the earth in payment for letting the guilt-ridden neurotics of the world work.'

I suddenly felt the weight of Moggerhanger at one end pulling, and Almanack Jack at the other. His head fell forward, and in a few moments he was properly asleep. I got up and walked out, on foot all the way back to Ealing, brooding on the black ingratitude of such sly bastards as Almanack Jack. I took time off to phone Bridgitte's place again, stood in a callbox at four in the morning, listening like a madman to that regular brain-sawing rhythmic buzz, feeling that if anyone were in the flat they'd have to get up and answer it or be driven as crazy as I was beginning to feel.

I wasn't called till midday, thank God, and then only for a short visit to the lawyers. Moggerhanger didn't want a holiday after his strain of waiting for the trial. He wasn't that sort of man, and I should have known he wouldn't be. In fact he was more ebullient and bullying than ever, and I began to hate his guts, though I didn't want to quit because I liked the job so much, wanting at least to hang on to it while the mystery of Bridgitte's disappearance was clawing at me. I also found that my heart in some way was missing Smog, which made me wonder what sort of a person I was. He'd latched so much on to the secret life of Bridgitte and myself that it almost seemed as if he were our child and not Dr Anderson's.

My work was so hard that Moggerhanger should have had three chauffeurs instead of one, because now I was going at it from eight in the morning till sometimes ten at night. After his acquittal, business was surging. Clubs, brothels, and gambling pits were opening all over the place, and in spite of all regulations Moggerhanger was a law unto himself. The police had tried to get him, but he had beaten them with their own rules, and in consequence they treated him with far greater deference than before.

I was going fifty miles an hour along Bayswater Road at ten one night when a motor cyclops stopped us. When he peered in he said: 'Oh, sorry. I didn't know it was you, Mr Moggerhanger.'

'That's all right. I was busy at these papers and didn't know he was doing half a ton. Go a bit slower, you damned fool,' he called to me. When we got going again he apologized: 'I had to do that, Mike. They like to keep face, these coppers. Go as fast as you like beyond the Gate. We're late already.'

From the Arch to the Gate, through the Bush to the Scrubs, and my daily zig-zags continued. I felt a marked man going into some of the more bizarre clubs that Moggerhanger had under his thumb. There was a striptease joint in which men peeled off to the buff in some corny act or other. The spectators seemed mostly lesbians, hefty women in rural drag up from the country, or grey-haired bony-faced executive business women, too drunk and bawdy to go back to work after three in the afternoon.

After a tour of such clubs and properties Moggerhanger told me to come to the house because he'd like a word with me. I was too dead tired to wonder what was up. We went into the living-room, and he didn't tell me to sit down. 'I hear you were at the club last week?'

I nodded.

'I also hear that you left with June, and that you took her home.'

'I saw her to the door.'

'Maybe. But you didn't get back here till five in the morning.'

'I walked around.'

He laughed: 'You've cooked your goose. I can't have my chauffeur messing with my girlfriend. You can get out. I'll pay you a month's notice. Now. Tonight.'

'That's not right,' I said.

'Go in the morning, then. If you're here when I get back for lunch tomorrow they'll find your body – or part of it – in the Thames by the time it gets dark.'

'It's a bit sudden,' I told him, trying to sound contrite so that he might let on who had told him about me and June. 'What are you going to do for a chauffeur?'

There was a flicker of doubt regarding my guilt: 'Kenny Dukes is taking over.'

'Is he then? He's always been envious of my job, the fat snake. If he can get it as easy as this, then good luck to him. There's never been anything between me and June.'

'He tells me no lies,' Moggerhanger said, as if losing my living was no more than a game to him. 'He kept me informed, which is what he's paid to do.'

I felt like going berserk in his contemporary mansion, but turned and went out, wanting to put as much distance as possible between me and Moggerhanger. I didn't think this would be so difficult, but regretted losing my job, though it couldn't be said that my life crumbled because of it. My new suitcase hadn't had time to get more than half filled in the time I'd been there so I carried it with ease towards the bus stop and headed for town, leaving the reddest sunset behind me that I'd seen in years.

Part Four

The fact that I had nowhere to go and no one to see didn't worry me a bit. That is to say, it did worry me, because I was only human, after all, though it didn't put me off doing what I had to do. The only flaw was that I had no idea what I had to do, or even what I wanted to do. But I was on a half-empty bus going east, and at the moment that was enough for me, because if there was one thing I liked doing in life it was watching buildings and people from the safe top deck of a bus, especially after having worked for a few months as a chauffeur, in which I'd been so engrossed in driving a car that it'd been impossible to see a thing. I felt like a king, able to smoke and relax, and touched my pocket to make sure the table lighter was still there. I'd lifted it on my final plunderer's run through Moggerhanger's downstairs hall, and it now weighed heavy and fat in its silver lining, something he'd never see again because I'd pawn it at the first opportunity. It was a lovely piece of work, and I'd had my eyes on it for some time, but now that it was in my pocket I began to wonder whether I'd done the right thing. The arm of Moggerhanger's vengeance might reach a longer way than I imagined. He was the sort who valued even the most trivial of his knick-knacks, and the one that currently nestled in my pocket was a bit more than that. Still, even with Moggerhanger, possession was nine-tenths of the law, and I was after all only following the gist of his jungle commandments which, shuffled up tight into one slick pack, said that you must get anything you want no matter at what cost to others. Maybe he wouldn't miss it till Kenny Dukes was well and truly taken on, and then would blame him for it, slit his throat like the no-good pig he was.

I dropped off the bus in Piccadilly, and stood looking at the lights, but I hadn't the sort of heart that got glad at them. I preferred faces, because they could at least look back, and who knows? I thought, one of them might recognize me at the same time that I recognized it. I walked on into Soho. Not that I was lonely. That would never do, and I'd deny it to my dying breath, but I did wonder again where Bridgitte Appledore had gone, and even cast my mind back to the days of Miss Bolsover and Claudine Forks. I stood by a pub bar with my case at my feet, supping a bitter pint and slewing a sly eye now and again at the women's faces, but bringing no response. Even the men who were with them weren't jealous enough to resent my stares. So I went into another house, and then up a curving alleyway somewhere off the Strand, careful not to get drunk because I wasn't in the mood for that.

One crumby pub was bunged up to the gills, but along the bar was a face I'd seen before, though for some moments I couldn't say where, not knowing whether it was from months or years ago. He was a tall man, dressed in a high-necked sweater and an expensive tweed jacket, the sort of casual gear that must have cost far more than a good suit. His face was, I suppose, sensitive because of the thick lips, putty skin, and pale eyes. He wore a hat, but in spite of this I was struck by the length of his face and head, which did not, however, make him as ugly as it should have done. In observing to this extent what he looked like, it came to me quite quickly that I'd first glimpsed him in the pub where I stopped with June and Bill Straw on my way down from Nottingham, and it was sharp-eyed June who told me he was a writer by the name of Gilbert Blaskin. If I was mistaken in any way, it was only that I remembered him as not being quite so tall as he certainly was now, but I felt no doubt as to who it was because faces are about the only thing I have much memory for, except remembering what's happened to me in the past – which I was able to do from a very early age, as soon as I realized that a certain amount of time had been put behind me in which events had occurred that I could look back on, especially those that in some way joined me to other people.

As I looked at Blaskin's face I went off into a reverie, thinking that the longer I lived the richer became my past, though sometimes things were too hectic for me to find time to reflect on it, and that was bad, for in those moments I usually committed my most foolish actions, for I forgot to think about my past, which was the only thing to tell me who I was and where I was, and why I was where I was. But while I pondered on my past, there was the added and built-in disadvantage that it didn't allow me to consider whatever future might be coming to me. So I never had time to think seriously on what I was about to do, and this was not a good thing in someone as witless and reckless as myself. But thinking so much about the past (not being a philosopher, there never seemed much else worth thinking about) should at least – one would imagine – have guided me in a friendly and wise way to formulate some rules of conduct from which I could benefit. You'd have thought so. Perhaps because I never finally trusted the past, it didn't stand by me to the extent of doing me any good at all.

So I edged nearer to hear what Gilbert Blaskin was saying to the girl who looked on with such respect as every word came out. She was small and thin, with a pale doe-face and glasses, hair shorter than mine and freckles around the bridge of her nose. The author himself had a double brandy at the elbow, his back nonchalantly to the bar.

'I have an aunt who lives in Knightsbridge,' he said, 'but I have to forgive her for that. Otherwise she's one of those monstrous people you never wish to meet. She helped me when I was young and struggling, when I lived on letters telling me what rubbish I wrote. I ate at least one a day, plain, and stirred the rest into an omelet. No, she couldn't bear to think of me scrounging. So she helped me, and not long ago I gave her a present to mark the publication of my tenth novel. A little dog, the most disturbed and snappy little brute I could get my hands on, which cost me all of twenty pounds. She loved it, until it started to bark. The trouble was, it didn't like her, and went on barking. It was hysterical. I called on her after a week, and it was still barking, except when it was eating its steak. I told her to have it put to sleep, but she couldn't do that, looked at it lovingly. Then it got more hysterical. It was well behaved as far as house-training went, but this continual barking from her favourite chair was having its effect. She dug out a record of Hitler's speeches, and the ranting of that madman stopped the dog, so that it listened, entranced. After that, whenever it went into a fit of barking she'd put this record on, and right away it was reduced to silent admiration. Of course, where she found that record I'll never know, but I admire her ingenuity.'

The girl, whose eyes seemed to get bigger and bigger throughout the story, reached for her shandy, while Blaskin burst into a great peal of horsey laughter, and pulled back his arm so violently that he knocked his double brandy over. 'Fuck it,' he said to the girl, wiping the sleeve of his jacket. 'I'll never forgive you for that.'

'Let me get you another, Mr Blaskin,' I said. 'A double brandy and a pint of bitter,' I called. 'I hope you don't mind, but I'm a great admirer of your books. I've read every one of them. In one way, they actually stopped me going crazy. I lived in a place called Nottingham, and they inspired me into getting away from it, especially that terrific book you wrote about the man who lived up that way and became a writer. I thought that was great. I felt exactly like he did, in some parts. I can't tell you what a lot of good it did me to read it.'

He must have been used to this sort of thing, because he offered me his hand to shake, and said how pleased he was that his work after all was having some effect on people like me. I went on telling him how good his books were, though in fact I'd only read one of them, or tried to, because I couldn't get more than halfway, and had given it to Claudine for a birthday present, which made her see how different I was from other boyfriends, because none of them had given her a book before. She'd read it to the end and thought it was wonderful.

I told him I'd seen him in a pub on the A1 road but had been too shy to talk, and he said he remembered the place, being on his way back from Sheffield where he'd been to give a lecture on the modern novel and its place in society. He'd also spent a week cooped up in his flat with dysentery after the meal he'd eaten at the place I'd seen him in.

'It's a wonder you didn't get anything worse,' I said, 'the things they dish out on the roads in this country,' and he said how much better it was to be driving around France in the car, and I said I hadn't had that pleasure yet. He introduced me to his girlfriend, who had lost much of his attention because she idolized him too much to make positive statements of admiration as I did. Her name was Pearl Harby, and I noticed her looking at me with big eyes as well. He didn't explain who she was or what she did, but in the next opening of his brandy-mouth he wanted to know what I was doing in town.

'I'm a chauffeur,' I said, 'or was until tonight. I left the job because the bigshot I drove was in such a hurry to get back from the country today that he told me to go over the speed limit through a built-up area. I thought it was dangerous, because kids were coming out of school. A big argument followed, and when we got back I told him I didn't want to stay any more.'

Blaskin laughed: 'You're brash, and young, otherwise you'd have found some way out of it. What other jobs have you done?'

'Estate agent, clerk, bouncer at a strip club, garage mechanic, to name a few. I've done most things.'

'Can you type, dearest?' he asked Pearl Harby.

'No, Mr Blaskin.'

He turned to me. 'Can you?'

'Yes.'

'Good speed?'

'Any speed.'

He ordered more drinks, all round. 'I want somebody to type my novel. My secretary walked out on me because I was randy and tried to drag her into bed when she brought me my breakfast this morning. My wife left last week so she can't type it, and the publisher's clamouring at my shoulders. When can you start?'

There could only be one answer to that question: 'Now.' This pleased him, as it pleased everyone, and when he asked me where I lived I said where my own two feet are touching the ground.

'You lucky bastard,' he said jovially.

I stiffened: 'Nobody ever calls me a bastard and gets away with it' – my hand gripping the beer mug to rip him open with.

He laughed: 'Well, let me be the first. Let's be jolly and gay. I hate serious people. They take to politics and ruin everything.' He dipped down and put his arm round Pearl Harby, dragging her close for a big kiss. I couldn't very well smash the glass into his bald head, so held back till he stood upright again, but by then it was too late. My anger had gone and for the first time in my life I thought what the hell does it matter if someone does call me a bastard? It's only in fun, and they can never know the truth anyway.

Most of the people in the room began moving towards the stairs. 'We're going up for a poetry reading,' Gilbert said. 'Come and listen. There may be a fight – you can't tell, once poets get together.'

I pushed down the rest of my beer and joined the crush, making a way through with my suitcase. A girl in front didn't like this at all, for she glazed me with the fire of her blue eyes and tut-tutted sharply. All I could do was smile, and change it to a flat look when her boyfriend swung round to find out whether I was trying to get off with her. Gilbert and Pearl came up the stairs in the gap I made. 'What do you carry in that case?' he asked.

'Ashes,' I said. 'Mother, Father, two brothers, a sister, and four cousins.'

He held me grimly by the shoulder: 'Listen, you aren't a writer by any chance, are you?'

'I've got more to do with my life.'

'And you haven't thought of becoming one?' We were stopped at a small table and had to pay half a crown to get in.

'Forget it,' I said. He smiled with relief, while I paid all the fares and we passed into a large room with rows of wooden chairs laid out in it.

He leaned across Pearl Harby: 'There's a big attraction to-night, a working-class poet from Leeds.'

'You don't say?' I said.

'Ron Delph. The club invited him to read his poems. It's hard to get poets to read their own work, but we're hoping things will improve.'

'Does it pay much?' I said.

'Five pounds, and expenses. Delph won't live in London. He works in a brewery office, and won't leave. Here he is!'

As soon as the name of Delph was mentioned I saw June's face again while she'd told her story, that flash of it in my driving mirror. I was interested to know what he looked like after her information that he was the one who'd jaggered her with a daughter. He stood up front by a table, stared at everybody for a long two minutes. Then he took a bus or train ticket out of his pocket, and read in a loud monotone something like:

> 'Freedom is blue
> A white scarf in it:
> In the end it is a woman's hair.
> In the end, a flag.'

We enjoyed that, because though it might have been ordinary, he made it sound good. He tore the ticket into quarters, and threw it like confetti towards us. He was tall, had dark flat hair, and looked like a conjuror, because next he took a roll of toilet paper out of a shopping basket, and began undoing it, tearing it off sheet by sheet, and with everyone saying 'Shit', which he went on to say about a few hundred times.

We were held, hypnotized, pushed into silence – except for a few ignorant bastards who let out a giggle now and again, and someone who called: 'Pull the chain, Ron, pull the chain' – and nearly stopped the show. The tension was hardly to be borne as he got to the end of the roll, and especially when, with the final tear-off, he didn't intone the expected word but spelled it slowly, letter by letter, S–H–I–T. A great noise of clapping spread in the room, as if a wooden ship of long ago were grinding itself up a long stretch of seashore rocks.

His next poem was about a man who accidentally stepped on a butterfly and killed it, and ends in tears of remorse for his savage act. 'After the last General Election,' Ron shouted, 'my mother became Minister of Culture. She changed her name and put in for a new past, then marched down Whitehall to the marital music of a grenade of budgerigards.'

'By God, he's got talent,' said Blaskin, lighting a cigarette and resting his head back on fag-smoke air, the schizophrenic's pillow he always carried about with him.

'But I'm not a poet of the niggling moral doubt,' Delph shouted, picking a button off his jacket (which I'm sure he'd loosened deliberately hours before) and throwing it into the mouth of someone on the front row who yawned. 'I'm in it for the quick quid and all expenses paid, and I want everybody to know it. I'm not a death-wish beetle eating away at the fabric of society. I'm just looking for a patron to buy me a coin-op laundry so I can sit in the warmth of it and spread my bed while my living goes on earning itself all around me. So if anybody knows a millionaire with the right incline I'll note his post-office box in my little black book and—'

'Poems,' a voice shouted from the back. 'You're a self-indulgent prole. Let's have a poem.'

Delph stared hard in the man's direction. 'I'll put you on my death list, if you aren't careful.' He held us all by sleight of hand and slight of brain, took a pound note from his lapel pocket and passed it to the front row so that it could be certified as real. Taking it back, he held it by the tips of two fingers, as if not wishing to be too much contaminated by it. Then he drew the ashtray to the middle of the table, fished out a box of matches, and lit the banknote, holding it upright so that it burned slowly, shouting a slow incantation before the flame got to his fingers and he let go:

> *'Smoke is no joke when you choke on it.*
> *It's even less funny when you're burning money.*
> *The smallest weevil knows that it's evil.'*

He crumpled the charred paper of the note with an asbestos thumb, then blew the black powder of it towards the audience: 'Go, little turds, God give thee good passage—' And for a moment I wished I had stayed at Moggerhanger's because then he went on to recite a poem called *Elegy on the Death of the Pennines*, which consisted in reading all the words from a pocket dictionary beginning with P, and this went on for about twenty minutes, so that I began to think I was going crazy, which may have been the effect he was aiming for, because I had a suspicion that under that crackpot flamboyant style was a sly and cunning bastard who had weighed up the balances of every pickled word. One or two people in the audience did in fact break under this sustained barrage and shouted out as if their hearts had cracked, but the teeth and tank tracks of Ron Delph's subliminal intelligence went on and on to the very end, so that they just had to sit back and sweat it out. Gilbert Blaskin's shanks began to twitch, and I thought maybe he's going to split at the fleshpot mouth, and then where will my typing job get to? – but the look on his face was rapt and angelic, and his zipped-up tailor-made boots beat time to that demonic shunting forth of just plain words. I stayed above it all, after that first shiver, sidestepped it, and kept my eyes wide open and my heart well dyked against the waves of pure emotion building up in the room. They were rapt and stoned while I was able to look around me at their ossified faces in the grip of this mad hypnotical impostor.

It took a few seconds for them to realize that he had finished. They were stunned. From the seabed where he had held them they started to cheer and clap and rave, getting themselves up to some sort of air again. He was sweating, worn out, haggard as he stood like a totem post in front of the table. Blaskin pulled along the row, ran to congratulate him.

When they stood talking together later, I heard him mentioning manuscripts, and a publisher for them. Delph flipped his ash at random and didn't seem much interested. A girl with green eyes and yellow hair had an arm through his, and giggled at Blaskin whenever he spoke. Delph patted her on the head, as if to encourage her. 'My Pandy,' he said, 'she perpetually takes the piss out of you metropolitan ponces' – unable to slip from his groove of the letter P. 'She's a proper Persian pussycat is our Pandy, and I'm planning to get my pump into her, aren't I, pet?'

'Oh,' she pouted, 'what a plague you are.'

'It's just that I'm hungry,' he said. 'Let's pile downstairs for a pint.' The wave of the audience went with him, and it was my opinion that he wanted a pasting, but to hint as much to anybody else would have got a leg torn from me. So I picked up my case and pushed down after them.

'I don't write *all* my poems,' Ron was saying with a sandwich in his mouth. 'I find some of 'em, pick 'em up, practice 'em, polish 'em – purloin them from time to time and purvey them to you pansies down South. Pot of port, love?' he said, at Pandy. 'Last time I came down I gave a great show. I read a Tube map, pure and simple, name after name, round and round. Went off. I was as cool as a landmine. Burnt my fingers on that map because some ice-cold swine in the audience ups and shouts. "What about copyright? London Transport wrote that poem." So I read it again, went right back to Cockfosters and crept in little circles till I got to Ealing, and by that time he was on the floor with the rest of 'em frothing to death.'

'Oh, Ron,' said Pandy, 'you're perky tonight.' He slid another sandwich in his mouth, followed by a pickled onion: 'I'm still steamed up, the pistons wumphing away. Allus like that after a perf.'

It became clear to Blaskin that he'd never get a word in edgeways so he said: 'Let's be off.' I picked up my case and went outside into the lamp and starlight. He walked ahead down the alleyway, and Pearl Harby took my arm in hers. She was suspiciously quiet with me, but I didn't fancy a gang-bang with Gilbert Blaskin. It felt comforting nevertheless, and I was sorry when she let go as we hit the wider spaces of St Martin's Lane.

He was rocking a bit, after a few hours on double brandies, and when he swayed at his car door, trying to open it, a policeman who'd watched him from the shadows said: 'I hope you aren't going to drive that Jaguar.' Gilbert swung round, a look on his face as if about to let go a flow of bad language or vomit.

'I'm Mr Blaskin's chauffeur,' I said, 'and I'm taking him home.' I pulled open the door, and Gilbert, having second thoughts on sending his richest prose against the copper's clock, bent to get in.

'That's all right,' said the policeman, and walked away. Pearl hunched in the back, and soon I was steaming through Trafalgar Square. 'I thought I'd save you a bit of bother,' I said.

He seemed sober enough now: 'Perhaps it's just as well. I had a nasty bang a month ago, though it wasn't my fault. Some unthinking advertising yobbo pulled out too suddenly and I crunched him, spun off, bounced against a lorry, ricocheted into another car, scraped a bus, and hit the back end of a van.

Came to rest halfway up a lamp-post. Hardly got scratched. The police were mystified at this, thought I must have been drunk. I enjoyed every minute of it, till I suddenly realized it was real, and that I might actually have been killed.' He held an arm over to the back seat, and in my mirror I saw Pearl take it with both hands and kiss his fingers passionately, not a word passing between them.

We went up to his fourth-floor flat near Sloane Square. He switched on a tape of Duke Ellington, but low so that we would be able to hear him talk if he said anything. Standing by the hall door he took off his hat and coat, and invited me to do the same. I was struck by the length of his absolutely bald head, a shining pink up from the palest of eyebrows, over the top and down to the back of his neck. Along the middle of his dome was a neat and curving scar caused, I was to hear later, by a murderous husband who happened to have a cleaver in his hand when catching Gilbert and his wife. The long-healed wound, which I thought must almost have killed him, made his head, especially from the back, look like nothing less than the limb that had got him into such trouble in the first place.

He sent Pearl into the kitchen to make coffee: 'That's what women and disciples are for,' he said, sprawling back in a wide armchair, 'to clean your glasses, fill your pipe, and tuck you up at night when you go to bed slightly drunk.'

'I believe in treating them better than that,' I said, deliberately sanctimonious so as to draw him out.

'That's because you're young,' he laughed. 'You'll learn.'

I was always being told that, and it riled me. They said it in order to bring me round to their opinions. As far as I was concerned I'd learned already, but I had yet to find out how wrong I was. 'They stay longer if you treat 'em better,' I said.

'Who wants them to stay? There are plenty more where they come from. They never get wise, either, so don't tell me that.'

Pearl came in with a tray. 'Do you take it black or white, Mr Blaskin?'

'Better give it to me black, Pearly dear. That's the way I'm feeling tonight, so watch your bum when we get to bed. I'm the sex maniac incorporated tonight.'

Her face went vermilion at this, so she turned to pour coffee for me. 'Do you want me to leave?' I asked Gilbert. There was a row of small pictures along the deep-blue wall behind his chair, of horses floundering to death, and jolly huntsmen in their bloody jackets lying on top of them with gritty smiles.

'Not yet,' he said, 'unless you can't stand my personal remarks to Pearl. You don't mind, do you, lovely?'

She didn't speak, tried to smile, but the coffee went down her wrong throat and she coughed to clear it out. I offered to start typing his novel right now.

'The morning's better,' he said. 'I can't be bothered to find it. I think I put it in the bread bin. Or maybe it's under my pillow. Or in the airing cupboard. Anyway, don't bother me with such supremely unimportant questions. I think I'm going to have a thought.' He lifted himself a little, and one of his profundities splintered the room.

'It's all very well,' I said, 'but how much are you going to pay me while I work for you? I was getting twenty a week at my last job.'

He threw his cigarette towards the electric fireplace but it landed on the carpet. 'What's all the hurry?'

'I've got to go out and find a room for the night.'

He glared at Pearl, who still had her nose in the coffee: 'Stay here,' he said. 'There's the spare room if you want it. We can talk terms in the morning.'

It didn't seem a bad place to hole up in if Moggerhanger should think to hunt me out for the theft of his cigarette lighter. 'Darling,' Gilbert said to Pearl, singing like a canary, 'are you going to sit there watching a hole burn itself in my best carpet? One of my great great-uncles looted it from India, and that would be a sad end for it.'

I found the spare room, and on my way called at the kitchen, taking half a cold chicken from the fridge, as well as a few slices of Miracle Bread from the bin, and a tin of orange juice and two bananas. So I lay in bed and puffed myself on Blaskin's goodies, while he was in the main room doing his best to stuff Pearl Harby.

I woke in the morning to the noise of Handel's *Messiah*, which seemed a mockery to the confusion I felt inside me, because for a while I didn't know where I was. Then the music made me want to laugh, because it was so great to hear first thing up from the dreams of oblivion that no matter where I was I felt glad to be alive and wanted to go on living for ever. Looking out I saw a great façade of drainpipes and back windows, lit up by the sun. By my pocket watch it was almost ten o'clock, and the smell of breakfast filtered under the door, together with the music singing 'O my people' which, the longer it went on, made me want to cry with joy, booming as if the world was full of drums and voices, so that when I lay down again, with my eyes closed, it began to pull me backwards by the feet, back towards some great river I'd never get out of.

I dressed to my shirt and trousers, then hungrily followed my nose. Blaskin was sitting in a grandad-armchair at the end of the kitchen table, a wine-dark dressing-gown looped around him, frowning over the various plates of breakfast that Pearl had laid out. 'Life,' he said, 'is serious in the morning. In the morning you realize with deadly dread that the past is the present, because whatever has happened in the past is part of now. To know this gives you an angel's grip on life, but it's a bitter pill, just the same.'

He began eating, and Pearl, whiter than the night before and far more haggard, wrote quickly in a pad by the side of her cornflakes, maybe what he was saying, though I couldn't be sure, because at the same time she breathed heavily as if she were making up a shopping list. 'My next novel is to be called *Motto* by Gilbert Blaskin. People may think I've gone crackers, using a title like that, but it's the thought that counts.'

I launched a thousand cornflakes into a dish of milk. 'I'll give you two pounds a week with your room and food,' he offered.

'Two pounds fifteen,' I haggled.

He glared at me. 'Two pounds ten.'

'That's all right,' I said, thinking to take it for as long as it suited me.

'My novel is about a man who came out of a Christmas cracker, and lived by the same motto, through thick and thin, until he gets run over by a bus while being chased by the police for firing an air-gun at a horse-guard's horse. Pearl, the bacon's cold.' I couldn't see myself lasting very long in this place, though I thought that if I was here for the next half-hour I'd be all set to hang on as long as I liked.

She stopped writing: 'What *was* the motto, Mr Blaskin?'

'You'll have to search the novel for that. It's a quarter of a million words long and based on the Oedipus legend told backwards. It consists of four fateful words, but it does for our hero. Two will be hammered into his feet to lame him, and the other two will put out his eyes. That's how he gets run over. He can't see. Also he can't run, but he hobbles very well. They find a copy of the Factories Act in his pocket, which is the only pornography he ever allowed himself. Also, of course, the pertinent question may be brought up as to how a blind man can aim an air-gun at a horse. The fact was, he didn't need to run at all, would merely have been bound over, or patted on the head and given a safe seat by the Conservative Party. Such is life, he said, as they lifted the bus off him a few seconds before he expired!'

I got up and put the coffee back on the stove, while he chewed the fat of his insane liver that lived off the fat of the land. I wished I'd been working in a factory so that I could have told him to belt up and get some real work done.

His novel, a pile of paper tied up in purple cloth, was taken from a locked safe in his study and carried to my room as if it were the royal baby, and set on a table where I was to copy it on to a typewriter. I did ten pages the first day, but after that I speeded up to thirty or forty. It was better than I thought it would be, after all the gobbledegook he spouted when he wasn't actually writing, and at the end of each day I quickly read what I'd done to make sure I'd missed no part of the story. Pearl sat in the living-room copying his notes, and writing her own book on what the great man said, and what his ideas were. She must have been more of a genius than he was to fathom that lot out. And while we were busy Gilbert himself was in his study, writing to the record of Handel's *Messiah*, which he played over and over again. He said that with such music he fancied himself in the wilderness, with no other soul nearby for a hundred miles, and that's what he liked because it kept his thoughts on an inspired and elevated level. Sometimes when he was in the kitchen or living-room eating in silence he would get a glazed look over his eyes and cry out: 'Pass my pen. And some paper. I can feel it. Something's *coming*!' Pearl would usually hustle to do his bidding, so that he was able to scribble a few lines of whatever it was, then get back to the serious business of eating or throwing back brandy.

There were times when Gilbert Blaskin went into what I came to recognize later in life as a mood of cosmic despair. It seemed to me, nevertheless, only right that an author should subside into this misery, even though it might be self-induced for the benefit of his work – as I sometimes suspected it to be. In order to work himself into it he had first to have an audience which, because they were black days for him, consisted only of me and Pearl. He also needed to say something funny, not necessarily so to him, but he had to see us laugh before he could get really depressed. I told myself I was only staying there to escape the wrath of Moggerhanger when he discovered I'd filched his heirloom, but partly, and maybe even mostly, it was because I couldn't contain my curiosity regarding the inner life of this weird person. I didn't like myself for it, either, and said ten times a day that I'd slide out as soon as I'd had my fill.

One night Gilbert Blaskin (who hasn't heard of him?) was booked for the Royal Court Theatre nearby. He dressed in his best suit and bow-tie because it was a first-night performance, and before leaving he went – all spruced-up as he was – into the kitchen, looking for his lighter, which he found, and put into his pocket. His eyes then caught sight of a full cool bottle of milk, so without thinking he pushed in the top, upended it at his mouth, and began to gurgle it down. I was on the other side of the table cutting into a steak that Pearl had just grilled for me, and saw that half the milk was spilling down Gilbert's immaculate togs. I was too fascinated by this spoliation to say anything, though I know I should not have been, but ought to have opened my mouth about it at the beginning. By the end he didn't need to be told, though I did tell him, for he felt his saturated front with horror. Then he shrugged, wiped it with a tea towel, and went out cursing his luck. This depressed him for a start.

I couldn't stand the flat, so went for a walk towards Victoria, drinking in the drizzle as if it were the best and freshest moisture in the world when it fell against my face. The station held me in its movement, and I drifted along one platform after another, till I wandered on to one from where trains left for Paris and Italy. People were kissing and saying goodbye before setting off towards the coast. It made London seem smaller and less important, and myself less rooted in it, thrilled me to realize that I had enough money in the bank to get on one of those trains whenever I liked, and go a long way, not only there, but even back if I wanted to, or had to. It calmed me, and I walked home through Eaton Square.

It was still early, so I went into the kitchen to make coffee. Pearl hadn't heard me come in, because she was standing at the stove with only a thin pair of pants on and nothing else, not even carpet slippers. 'You look marvellous from behind,' I said, 'but turn round, love, and let me see the front.'

For the first time her face had an expression on it, of discontent that was near to tears, so I went over and tried to comfort her, though my eyes weren't too long on her face. There were scars on her back and sides, as if she'd been stitched up for some good reason or other. When my fingers touched one she shrugged them away pettishly. Then she nestled close and said: 'Why didn't he take me with him? I've known him for a month but the only time we went anywhere together was to that poetry reading where we met you.'

'Maybe he's meeting somebody else,' I said, kissing her forehead. 'But don't let it worry you if he is. He can't help it. He's just rotten. He has to be, otherwise he wouldn't be able to write his books.'

'I know,' she said, 'that's what I keep telling myself. I didn't expect anything when I first met him, and then when I didn't get anything I began to expect something. It's so stupid of me.'

'It is,' I had to admit. 'I don't really know why people expect things of each other in any case.'

'Well,' she said, trying to smile, 'it's not as bad as you make it, because I don't expect anything from you, but you're being kind and trying to comfort me.'

'Don't let that worry you,' I said. 'I can't help it. It's my nature to be kind to people.' She was right though. I had no thought of getting her into bed just because she was Blaskin's mistress. For that's what she was no matter how he snubbed her. However, she stood a bit too long leaning her naked top into me, and soon I began to kiss her lips, and out of her tears she began to respond.

'I'll put you to bed,' I said, and when she nodded, I walked her into the main bedroom. In case she was feeling cold because of her tears, I filled a hot-water bottle, but she said she didn't need that sort of heater, so I let it drop and took off my clothes to lie by her side. In fact I found her to be burning like a big hot coal, and of its own accord my piece found its way there, and of its own accord her birdcage welcomed it till my vulture sank its head for joy and flooded her to the brim so that I was also scorching. I was flushed with love, but she wouldn't let me kiss her lips or touch her on the tenderest spot with my fingers, so after a while I got out of bed and dressed, left her content as far as I could tell, and went into the kitchen to look for something to eat.

While I was chopping off slices of salami she came in wearing a thick sunflower dressing-gown: 'I'm hungry, too, now that I've got over my fit of melancholic jealousy.' I made her a sandwich, thick with German mustard, and she ate greedily, which put me off her a bit because though I like to see a woman eat (it gives me more of a kick than if she had loosened her own blouse) I don't like to see one as voracious as Pearl Harby now was. So I turned my back on her and got the coffee. In any case, she was eating so quickly that she reached out for the salami before I could offer her some more, and soon there was none left for me. Never mind, I thought, she's been disappointed in love, and that explains everything, or is supposed to.

'My father worked in the railway yards at Swindon,' she said, sitting herself comfortably on my knee, 'and one night he was killed by a German landmine that lit up his life beautifully before it blacked him into a thousand pieces. I was six at the time and there was no funeral because he didn't exist. It must have landed right on the parting of his hair. A year later my mother died of bronchitis, and I was taken to live with an aunt and uncle, who already had a little girl of their own, called Catherine. The man, unlike my father, had got on in the world, as they say, and he was a solicitor in Cowminster, a small Wiltshire market town. He was very respected, but apart from having done what he regarded as his duty by adopting me, he really had no love for me. He was cold towards me, as if he thought I was going to jump into his bed and force him into an unnatural crime, or as if I was going to alienate him from his own daughter. In my bewilderment I was a bit afraid of him, and it took me a good two years not to be, and to adjust to the new situation. He could tell I was afraid of him, and resented it because he thought it meant I didn't love him as I should for having had the kindness to take me in.

'Well, he didn't realize that I was a child, and had no consciousness. I only loved him, for a few minutes, when he was giving me something, and so he resented it too, that I didn't love him all the time, even though he didn't really love me. But neither of them knew that for several years I was still grieving for my real parents, and I wasn't able to tell them this. They spoke about them now and again, but in a very matter-of-fact way, almost as if they were still alive, and as if I were on holiday with them. Of course, they loved Catherine as their true daughter, and nobody could blame them for that or expect it to be any different, but I felt it sharply. To make up in some way for my desolation I fell in love with Catherine, because much of what she got from her parents she gave to me, because she was very kind and sweet. She was two years older, a girl with blonde hair and grey eyes, slightly fat from overfeeding and too much indulgence, but we were good friends, and my life after a year or so became much more settled, and I eventually did get to think more tenderly of my new parents.

'The mother was kind to me, and tried to love me, and helped me a great deal. Most of all, I grew up in a mildly intellectual atmosphere, which could never have been the case with my real parents, and this certainly did a lot to make my life richer. The house was full of books, books read, books talked about. I found out later that most of them were no good, all second-rate except for writers like Dickens and Thackeray, Jane Austen and Shakespeare. So I read those avidly, because I was soon able to tell what books were good and what were trash. Catherine went to a grammar school, and I followed her there as soon as I was old enough. If only she had been my real sister, then I wouldn't have gone through so much suffering because of her. All the love I had in me I put on to her, and when I saw her getting a crush on somebody else, whether boy or girl, I got so jealous and tormented that I thought I'd have to kill myself to get over it! It was crazy, and bad for both of us. Not that she didn't love me as well, in her way, as a friend, though at times this was almost enough to make me happy and satisfy me, but mostly she was interested in everything and just wanted to get on with her self-absorbed life.

'Our parents noticed how I mooned after her, but they thought I had only the same worshipful regard for her as they had, because after all she was their only child. I always felt that I was nowhere near as good-looking and well favoured as she was, which wasn't all that true, but that's what I felt at the time. It's terrible being a child, when you don't know what's happening to you. You're just at the mercy of these super-charged underground emotions that gnaw you away like black midnight wolves, and you suffer because you can't tell what's happening to you. You're able to see it more clearly when you get older, but by then it's too late to do any good, and in any case underground emotions are still taking you to pieces and not putting you back together again, just as they were then, and you still don't have the detachment to know what's happening. In fact I suppose it's even more dangerous because you think that you do, and actually get the illusion that you are in control of yourself. I have the horrible feeling this goes on all your life, and that at death the final question whose answer can solve everything and tell you everything can only be answered after death itself, which really is too late. It gives me the horrors, throws me into despair if I go on thinking about it for too long. But as there's no answer, I try to block it out, though I'm not always capable of it.

'For a year or two Catherine went cold towards me, and I was put into a walk of death by it, getting thinner and, it seemed to me, smaller so that I was only a few inches above the earth. Once when I was walking alone along a lane I thought I was small enough to get into a pothole in front of me, curl up and go to sleep in it so that I'd be perfectly safe even if a car went over it. But I did very well at school, and surprised everybody by being best in the class at almost everything.

'Catherine had been used to having her own way, and she'd been seeing a boy for a few weeks. I think they'd been making love because a group of us used to go out on our bikes at the weekend, and sometimes Catherine and her boyfriend would creep off for half an hour. Then he went away with his parents and didn't write to her, and she was shocked as she'd never been before. I found his address and wrote, telling him how upset she was, but nothing came of that, which was good I suppose. She used to come into my room at night and weep, and get into my bed for some sort of comfort. Now it was my turn to put on weight, and for Catherine to get thinner – but only for a time because soon she more or less forgot about him.

'We became very close to each other after that, and she loved me as if I'd been through her experience, as if it ran in my blood as well as hers. We were both young women by now, and our parents, apart from pushing us gently along the educational railway, more or less left us alone. They were generous with pocket money, so we were able to buy extra dresses and what paperbacks we needed, and go to the cinema now and again. Neither of us went with boys, though we were well looked at by any we happened to meet, and many of the boys in the sixth form were friendly with us. But I think we were both mad for a time. We talked crazily about books, films, paintings, plans for the future. We were going to become teachers or doctors and go to Africa together. It was a marvellous age of innocence. We took our baths at the same time. We often slept in the same bed, not being able to stay apart after an enthralling conversation. We even started to learn Swahili, so that we'd know at least one African language. If I told Gilbert any of this he'd mock me to death, but I know I can tell you. Our parents thought we were model daughters, because we helped in the house whenever we could, though this really wasn't necessary because we were well-off enough to have an Austrian maid, and a man to look after the garden. We went to Wales or France for holidays, and life was good for all of us.

'The boy Catherine had known two years earlier came back, and she went out with him. He left again after a month and she was pregnant. We didn't know what to do. She was let down, and horrified. We talked for hours, wondering whether to try and find out how to get rid of it, or tell our parents, or whether she should say nothing, but just go off to university and perhaps have the baby in secret. The weeks went by and we even prepared an elaborate plan for both of us to kill ourselves. It was as if I were pregnant as well, I felt so much a part of her. What we did was worse than anything. We decided to run away together. We discussed it with such enthusiasm as the final, sensible, unalterable answer to the disaster, that all our troubles seemed to be over. I shall never forget the illumination I felt during those few days. I walked as if I were sanctified. It's crazy. It was crazy, absolutely mad, yet it's the most wonderful memory.

'There was seventy pounds between us, and we decided to go to London, find a room, get jobs, and pool whatever we earned. It seemed as if she were no longer pregnant, for in our keenness to escape we almost forgot the blow that had caused it all. I had the insane idea of driving to London in our father's car. Some nights he and Mother would go to see friends on the other side of town, which meant that if we went away in it it would have to be in the evening. Catherine had taken some lessons, and drove rather well. I had seen her, and I couldn't drive at all.

'We hurriedly packed our cases and put them in the car. She drove though the open gate, and both of us were trying not to laugh out loud at this easy getaway, all set as we were for a long and happy life together. It was a fine summer's evening, with a few hours of daylight left, as Catherine took the car slowly but confidently along the lane and towards the main road. There was hardly any traffic, and she seemed radiant. But there were tears on her cheeks: "Do you think we should?"

'"What else can we do?" I answered, touching her wrist. "It's wonderful to be leaving everything behind."

'She smiled: "All right. It is." From the other side a car was approaching the brow of a hill, not going very fast, and at the same time a lousy motorcyclist was overtaking the car. He actually missed us, but his sudden black appearance startled Catherine so that she screamed, and our car went through a hedge and down a slope. The world rushed over me like a blanket, hammers beating at me though the woollen padding. Then I was being pulled clear.

'The blackness came back, and I opened my eyes in hospital. I asked about Catherine, and was told she was all right. She was in a better state, in fact, than I was. Both my legs were broken, my ribs were smashed, and I'd been concussed, apart from sundry other wounds. When I left hospital Catherine was married to her boyfriend, who'd been made to admit his part in getting her pregnant. She went to live with him near New-castle, and now they have three children. I was able to say goodbye to her, but we hardly knew each other. I was said to be the evil one who had led her into bad ways, and I didn't deny any of this. It would at least give her something to remember me by.

'I haven't seen her since, and we never write. I did my time at Bristol, and worked as a private teacher. Then I got the bright idea of doing some postgraduate work on the modern English novel, though whether I'll ever get beyond Gilbert Blaskin I don't know, because I've fallen in love with him. Not that that's rare, because I fall in love rather easily. Don't ask why. I miss my real parents still, and because I didn't get that jealous and possessive love from my second parents, I'm still looking for it. But what you look for you never get – or so I'm beginning to think, and the idea frightens me a bit. But I can't help looking. It's a sort of heartless search that's been built into my nature. I fall in love because I want something, not because I have something to give, and that's what men see, and what puts them off when they've finally got to the end of me in bed.'

'You shouldn't worry about anything,' I said. 'Everybody gets what they want. I'm convinced of it – even though I might not.'

'I don't want pity,' she said, a wonderful smile which showed that she was no cynic about her life, though she'd try to convince everybody that she was.

'You'll get no pity from me,' I told her. 'I only feel sorry for people who haven't got enough to eat, or who've got an incurable sickness.'

'How right you are,' she said. 'I wish people often said that sort of thing to me.'

I felt good at hearing this. 'It's true,' I went on, 'the body has to be seen to first. If that goes, there's nothing left. If you're fed and healthy you've always got a chance of getting through somehow.'

'It's easy to say that,' she said, 'but you're right. I know you are.'

'Forgive my big mouth,' I said. 'I'm worse than Gilbert in my own narrow way. But I know that what I say is true.'

'Keep on saying it,' she said, 'so that I'll believe it. Sometimes I feel like walking off the edge of the world because everybody I meet agrees with me when I say things are terrible, and I can't see what the point of life is.'

I got up to boil water for coffee. 'If I ever write a book I'll call it *How to Stop Worrying – and Drop Dead*!'

She squeezed my hand affectionately, as if it were real love she felt: 'Gilbert doesn't know I love him. I'd never tell him. As soon as you tell someone you love them, they can then do their worst to you.'

'But if you don't tell them, they may never know.'

'Maybe he'll find out,' she said, hopefully. 'I've given lots of signs. Things can't be worse than they are now, but it's when I think that things might start to get better that I get frightened, because that's when the worst really happens.'

She had me sweating at these twistings and turnings, burning through my flimsy front of simplicity and common-sense,

so that I started to imagine that whatever she said was right,
'I mistrust myself and my emotions all the time,' she went on.
'but only so that I might be able to get to know myself, not in
order to destroy myself – which seems to be where it's heading
me.'

'It's a way of destroying others,' I told her, a bit too strongly.
She lifted my hand to her mouth, and I thought I was all set
for a tender kiss. Her eyes closed, as if what I said was a revelation to her instead of the deadly insult she took it to be. Her
small sharp teeth ground into the gristle of my wrist.

'You bastard!' I shouted, never having called anyone else
such a thing in my life before, shooting back from the bloody
witch. 'What was that for?' I had to move because the pain
was killing me, so I walked over to the stove, but the kettle
wasn't yet boiling.

'You deserved it,' she said, beginning to smile. 'I never
wanted to destroy anybody. People can only destroy themselves.'

'I'm not so sure,' I said, thinking about revenge. 'Coffee?'

'Please, love.'

'Do you often bite people, or is it just when you're hungry,
like?'

'Oh, stop it, can't you?'

'Drink this, then, you bitch.'

Gilbert came in, slumped down in such a way that I knew
the play had been no good. 'The kitchen sink,' he said. 'A slice
of life. Full of dirty dishes. They didn't even throw them at
each other. Very good dialogue, though. All talk.'

Pearl put a hand on his shoulder and let him sip her coffee.
'Do you want something to eat?'

'Had supper,' he said, 'with the man who wrote the play.
He thinks my novels are trash, and I think his plays are bunk,
so we drowned our mutual comradeship in wine. I was going
to show a bit of solidarity by saying we were both writers after
all, but he started talking about decorating the house he'd just
bought, and wondering which was the best car to buy.'

'But *you've* got these things already,' Pearl reminded him,
unnecessarily, I thought.

'So's he. But he wants more and more. But God forgive me,

he'd be all right if only he'd write a play with a happy ending, and leave me to write my tragic novels. Still, I can't expect to corner the market forever. I'm so incriminatingly selfish. What have you two been doing in my absence? Fornicating on my best bed?'

'Wandered like a ghost around Victoria Station for a couple of hours, then walked up West.'

'I see she's bitten you,' he laughed. 'Somebody ought to punch some sense into her, the bloody vampire. Or am I talking to the woman you love?'

'Bollocks,' I said.

'Like that, is it? Never mind. I had a letter today to say that an admirer of mine had produced my fourth novel in an edition of illuminated braille, so that it would be seen as a beautiful object while being read. Can you imagine that? But then somebody told the visionary who'd done it that the blind couldn't see, so he shot himself in despair. I sympathize with him because he was trying to light up the darkness of the world, and though he was foolhardy and mad, as it turned out, it was a commendable thing to do. Light up your hearts! That's what I'm for, to persuade people against their better instincts that life is worth living. Do not despair, says Gilbert Blaskin. He'll do that for you. Gilbert will lighten the loads of all of you. But who, dear God, is going to lighten his load? Life falls twice as heavily on him, ladies and gentlemen, but he's not supposed to notice it because he's helping you not to notice yours. The trumpets shall sound, but Gilbert will never be able to unload his load, caught as he is in the desert between Pimlico and Earl's Court.

'I saw my wife at the theatre with a gaggle of friends. I never left her, but caused her to leave me. I wanted to leave her for years but couldn't bring myself to do it, so I made her life such a misery that she was forced to clear out to stop herself going mad or getting strangled. I wanted to get rid of her so as to have a free hand with my girlfriend whom I intended to marry. But as soon as my wife left me I lost all enthusiasm for my girlfriend. Don't ask me why. The bullets of introspection don't go that far. Maybe they do in the characters I conjure up, but not in me. So I broke things up with my girlfriend, and asked my wife to come back. But she laughed at me and wouldn't, having discovered that she'd wanted to leave me for years, but hadn't been able to do it till I'd forced her to. And now I'm here in these rooms of memory which even my delectable and scorching Pearl can't rub out. And if she can't, there's no one else who can. The trouble is I'm not even in love with my wife, and if she came back I'd only get rid of her again after a month – no, a week. By God, Michael, life's not easy. If you think it is just jump in the toilet and pull the chain after yourself. They say the sewers in New York are full of alligators because people have flushed them down there when they no longer want to keep them as pets. I think God or some swine has flushed a few into me to keep me lively and kicking. I'll pop somebody into my mouth one day armed with a quick-firing double-barrelled rifle to hunt those alligators out, even though I die over it.'

He went on like this, slooshing his tripes with brandy now and again, till he fell off the chair, and we had to drag him to bed. I left Pearl to tuck him in.

I sat in my room making plans for departure. Gilbert hadn't yet read the typed copy of his novel. When he did there'd be a shock for him. It wasn't that I hadn't made a good job of it. The typing was clear and firm, the paper white and clean between the lines, and maybe even some people would consider it to be a novel. I'd started off with Gilbert's true text, but halfway through I got bored by the story, and at the point where his hero was sitting outside a Paris café and wondering whether to go back to his girlfriend in London, or down to his boyfriend in Nice, I reached up to the shelf behind me and brought down *Roderick Random* by Henry Fielding[*] and typed twenty pages of that, which, if anything, lent a bit of quality to Blaskin's thin-blooded crap. More pages were ploughed in from other novels, though I understood that this wasn't exactly what the author wanted. Considering that I'd spent three weeks over the work, he might have been irritated by this and given me the push, so I decided to take fate once more

[*] Michael Cullen's mistake. As everyone knows, this novel was written by Tobias Smollett – though Cullen is by no means the first to make such an error. *Author.*

into my own hands and light off before he got wind of the disaster. Then I thought I was being too hurried about it, that if I didn't lose my nerve, and stayed, maybe he wouldn't bother to read the novel before sending it to his publishers. And once it got there maybe nobody would tumble to what had been done, and print it with the fond thought that Mr Blaskin had at last set off on better and richer ways, something they'd been secretly hoping for ever since they'd mistaken his first novel for a work of art. Maybe the reviewers would even praise the newly emerging quality of his invention. In which case he'd actually have something to thank me for – if I was still around.

I decided to move on, though not at midnight, because it was always better to look for a bed in the morning, when the memory of one was still with you. Another thing was that I needed a room of my own, an absolutely set pad where I could come and go of my quick will. I'd dallied long enough at Blaskin's for Moggerhanger to have given me up as lost, if he'd even bothered to miss me or imagine I could ever be found, which I was beginning to doubt now that my hope and initiative were coming back, blinding me to all caution. Another fact was that Blaskin had given me no money, when he'd solemnly promised fifty bob a week. I'd reminded him of it in good terms a time or two, but like all people who are ultra-sensitive in everything, and don't miss a splinter of what goes on anywhere, it went over his head completely – or at least he acted as if it did.

When I considered that all were asleep I crept out of my room and found his coat hanging up in the hall. I removed two five-pound notes, which I thought to be honest payment for all the work I'd done on his novel. There were sixty pounds in the wallet altogether, and I could have lifted all of it, but I knew in my heart that Blaskin would call the police without hesitation if he thought I'd robbed him unjustly, for he was one of those people who loved the world as long as the people in it interested him. After that, it was back to the jungle for all concerned.

I had to get out of the flat while he and Pearl were still asleep, and to save time packed my case the night before. I stood with the light off and my curtains open, watching the opposite buildings. A woman leaned in white underwear, and a man's arms pulled her to him, out of my sight. Then the blind went down. A huge dog, as big as a man and with a head twice the size, pressed at one window, and seemed to be barking, though I couldn't hear it, pawing the glass as if it were locked in and there was no escape. I wished someone would pull that beast away so that I couldn't see it any more. I turned my head to another range of windows. In some, there was washing, because most of the rooms seemed to be kitchens. Light bulbs were often bare, a few were shaded. A shadow moved across a window now and again, too quick to see whether it was man or woman. I wondered how many of them had to get up in the morning and go to work. I felt hatred of those who didn't, as if I was the only person in the world with the right to be idle. Just as I could never feel sympathy for anyone unless they were without food, so I would never go to work unless I were starving. But as I looked at those massed windows covering the whole sky, I felt this sentiment crumbling. It just wasn't worthwhile. It cut me off too much, from all those people in the world I most wanted to know. It was as if I had to break my own bones in order to join them, that was the only trouble. The longer it went on like this, the harder it would be, though at the same time I devoutly wondered whether I'd have the brains to stay away from their terrible anonymity without falling as low as Almanack Jack. To join them, all I had to do was switch on my own bedroom light, and stand there, imprisoned in the oblong of window so that they on the other side could then see that I was a prisoner like the rest of them. But I got into bed in the dark.

A few hours later, with something lurking at my window that looked like morning, I was awake, croaking for a pot of liquid to drink but knowing I'd have to wait till I got clear and found a café. I dressed in two minutes and, taking one last glimpse around the flat, made for the door with my case attached to my hand. I shivered, as if I'd made too many departures in the last few months, and wasn't sure that I wanted to go. I wasn't even getting kicked out, but that didn't seem to matter, for I was moving, and, at this time of the morning, that was that.

A man standing by the door, about to press the bell, got as big a shock as I did. He was tall, well built, had thinning hair, and wore a pale short mackintosh. I tried to keep my voice down: 'What do you want?'

He lisped: 'Mog wants his flash back.'

I didn't know what he meant. 'You've got the wrong house.'

'Moggerhanger sent me. He wants his lighter back.'

'I haven't got it any more.'

'He wants 'is flash back.'

'I ain't got the thing,' and shut the door behind me: 'Shift out of the way. I'm going down.'

He bumped me so hard that I dropped my case: 'Mr Moggerhanger wants 'is flash.' He took a cut-throat razor from his pocket, opened it, and grinned: 'He told me to make the sign of the cross if you don't hand it over.'

I saw that glint, and took the hint, and bent down to snap open my case, scrabbling under a heap of shirts and dirty underwear. 'I was going to call in and bring it back today,' I said, pushing it into his hand. He pressed the fuse, saw the flame, looked at it as if he thought it a pretty sight that he could gaze on all day. After a final grin at its beauty, he blew it out and put it in his pocket, the razor held all the time in his other hand.

'That all right?' I said, trying to stay calm and smile. He lifted the razor and drew it across my face, without touching flesh. I cried out, but he laughed, kicked my case down the stairs, and walked through the mess.

I picked up the bits and put them back. On his progress he'd trodden on a tube of toothpaste and squashed it flat, so that a white jet of it had shot across the carpeted stair. A cold sweat was all over me, and my hand trembled so that I could hardly put a necktie back into the case. I knelt to do my work, and thought of going into the flat, to fall asleep and tell myself afterwards, when I got up to a good breakfast and decided to stay, that this had been a mere bad dream. But the door was locked and I had no key, and in any case I would not have done it.

The longer I sat the better I felt, and I suddenly urged myself to close the case and stand up. In my pocket were cigarettes and matches, and when I found that my feet weren't yet ready for me, I smoked casually as if resting before my long journey down to the street. It was eight o'clock by my watch, and apart from feeling sick I wanted some breakfast, so with a good heave I was standing at last, ready to descend.

The air smelled good, smoky and full of petrol, the very stuff of life, as Gilbert Blaskin might have said. People were already going to work, and I wished them luck and a long run as I walked my case towards King's Road. I found an eating place and stuffed myself back to health and strength on bacon and pancakes and coffee, soon feeling cocky again after my fright from Moggerhanger's one-man execution squad. Opening my street map I wondered where I was going to live, what four walls, if any, I'd inhabit before the day was out. With two hundred and fifty pounds in the bank I was the king of kings – though not for ever. I thought of walking into a hotel, but would only do that at the last moment, if I couldn't get anything but a slice of pavement before darkfall. With so few possessions my case wasn't heavy as I walked towards Victoria, but I didn't like being seen dragging it around. A man with a case looks like a traveller, or a thief, or someone too innocent to be out on the street. You can't swagger and feel good with a suitcase. Even if it weighs nothing you're marked off from the rest of the people into which you should be able to melt for cover if you feel like it.

So I dropped it in the left-luggage at the station and strode on through streets that hadn't yet lost their freshness and interest. The market in Soho was out, an abundance of barrows lining the streets, now packed with mid-morning shoppers. I bought a Spanish newspaper, which I couldn't read, and sat in an Italian place for a cup of black coffee, sipping it down between puffs at a cigar. Whenever I did a bunk or otherwise left anywhere, I always wore my best suit. Why, I don't know, but it made me feel good when I had nowhere to go. And because it bolstered my spirit at such a time, it was also plain to me that I wasn't feeling easy in such a state of homelessness, and that I had to get out of it quick. The sensible thing, in view of Moggerhanger's hostility (I had no way of knowing whether this morning's threat was only the beginning of it) would be to get out of town for a few weeks, so as to avoid being seen in the area where he owned half the clubs.

Yet I couldn't tear myself away, and I'm glad I didn't, because when I went into an Italian place for lunch (I was hungrier than usual when on the loose) I sat down and saw the back of a head farther up the room belonging to somebody who'd taken a small table all to himself, and it was of a shape that caught a snipe of recognition in me. I waited for him to turn, but he casually faced the other way as if not caring to show his face too openly. Sometimes he seemed on the point of doing so, out of boredom at looking at the wall, which was the only thing in front of him. For a second I saw a little to the side of his face, and his way of moving convinced me that I had seen that turnip-head before. All through the minestrone I plugged my mind in every place to bring back some memory with the label of a name stuck to it. I searched all over the place, even going through every film I'd seen in the last ten years in the hope that some far-off face in one might lead me to the actual face I was trying to remember.

Thinking he'd never turn, I picked up my knife and dropped it, but too many other people were talking and eating around me, and he didn't hear a thing. There was a rack by his side, on which hung a good-quality light overcoat, a hat, and a cashmere scarf. I looked down to eat when my veal came, but noted that he was ahead in his meal, and that the waiter was taking his coffee. Cigar smoke drifted above his head, which was now bent at the table as if he were reading a newspaper. He called for his bill, and the waiter treated him like a regular client who left good tips. I tried to catch some words, but they were lost. He stood for the waiter to help him on with his coat, and as soon as he half turned my heart jumped at the sight of him.

When I called his name, not too loud but only so that he would hear me, he looked in my direction as if I'd sworn at him. It was Bill Straw, the knowledgeable glutton who'd come down to London with me from the North. He wore a light grey suit, a silk shirt, and a small-knotted dark tie, and still had the cigar in his teeth. I remembered his face as having been prison-pale and unshaven, but now it was lean and tanned, and full of vigour so that he looked ten years younger. But there was no mistaking old Bill Straw, my erstwhile friend from back on the road.

He came closer, looked at me with his grey eyes, and smiled: 'Well, my old flower, I thought you'd been swallowed up. It seems that long ago to me.'

'Centuries,' I said, shaking the offered hand. 'Sit down and have some more coffee.'

'I will,' he answered, 'If you'll have a brandy – on me.'

'You don't look the same any more.'

'I'll never be like that again,' he told me. Even his way of speaking had changed. A far-off look came into his eyes: 'No, you'll never see me as I was when you picked me up on the Great North Road.'

'Not old Bill Straw,' I said, too jocularly by half, because he flinched from it.

'You want a bit of smoothing down,' he said. 'You're too rough. And by the way I'm not Bill Straw, so do me a favour and forget that. I'm known as William Hay – to all my acquaintances and to my employers. It's also written in my passport. I'm a company director by profession. This is just to get the record straight, though don't think I'm not still a human being, because I am. I've succeeded in doing away with the life I had before coming to London this time. But I don't forget you, because you helped me. I say,' he said suddenly, with a bit of old mateyness, 'you haven't seen that June on your wanderings, have you?'

Over a couple of brandies I told him honestly all that had happened since we parted at Hendon on our way in. He was impressed at hearing that I'd actually succeeded in getting on the wrong side of Moggerhanger. 'I know blokes who have nightmares about that,' he said. 'He's dangerous, so don't tangle further with him. You'd better take a few hints from me.'

'You've done so well by the look of it,' I said, 'that it might not be a bad idea.'

He looked deadpan at this: 'You are a bit green. Right from

when you gave me that lift, and let me con you out of so much grub on the way down. I don't know how you've survived this long. More by luck than experience, from what you've told me. But I suppose it's about time you were taken in hand. You'd better bunk up at my place for a while. I kicked my umpteenth girlfriend out last night, so you can stay there till I get another one. I've got a flat over in Battersea. Small and quiet, but it's convenient. You remember I told you on the A1 that I had a few thousand to collect from a job I'd done bird for? Thought I was lying, didn't you?'

He laughed, and lit another Havana. 'I wasn't. I've often told the truth to people who think that with a face like mine I can't help but lie. An old trick. Well, it was stashed away safely for me, and what's more it had been piling up interest the years I was in prison. A tidy sum of five thousand three hundred! Couldn't believe such loyalty from the others. But I'd stood by them, you see, right through everything, and they knew it. So it's still getting interest for me. Invested in good old British industry by a broker I was put on to, curling in as much as eight per cent. The fact was, I hardly needed to touch it, just three hundred to fit myself out, because I was put on to some very profitable work, just the stuff for the likes of me, because it takes me off the island, to the hot spots of the mainland, and a bit beyond at times. I won't say too much yet, but I didn't get this tan potholing in the Pennines. Still, I don't forget somebody who helped me when I was down and out. Not me, not the new man nor the old. When you picked me up, I don't know whether you knew it or not, but I was ready to die. I was done for and finished, inside and out, stomach and heart. I felt I was trudging towards the end of the world in that rain, with cars and lorries splashing me up as they went by, the cold eating into me so that I was snatched and perished.'

He called for more brandy, as if these recollections threatened to swamp his new-found heart. 'I didn't do much,' I said. 'I just felt sorry to see this bloke, and stopped my rotten old car that I was so proud to be in.'

'You did well though, helping William Hay. That part of me has snuffed it. For ever, I hope.'

'Here's to you, then,' I said, sipping the best brandy.

'I've got a good job now, Michael. Travelling. I've become an experienced traveller in the last few months. I've been to the Middle East. I've been over the North Pole. I've been all over Europe. Mind you, I earn every penny of it. I'll tell you that for a start. Every bloody penny that gets stashed into my bank is earned by the sweat of my brow. That's why I have to eat two or three big meals a day. I've got to stay strong and full of energy for the work I do, otherwise I might break down, and that'd be no good at all, because then I'd lose my job, and worse. It's not an easy life, even though I do look well and prosperous. In fact, in some ways it's the hardest bloody job I've ever done, but it pays well.' He cackled: 'It pays well, I will say that for it.'

I didn't know what the hell he was talking about, but I was all avidity to find out. The place was emptying, and he suggested that we go for a stroll. He had to walk five miles every day when he wasn't working, to keep himself trim for when he was. 'I have to eat a lot and walk a lot,' he laughed, as we went out through the door, bowed at by the manager after William had insisted on paying my bill.

'You're not a bad walker yourself,' said William, when we had reached the inner circle of Regent's Park, as if he were putting me through some kind of test. 'I'll take it on trust that you're a good eater.' I felt we'd come too far already, and didn't exactly see the point of planing one's feet off in this way. I wasn't hungry for praise about my standards of endurance either, so began to think of cutting back to town. 'What we'll do,' he said, 'is veer towards Baker Street, and go down through Victoria to Battersea, then you can pick up your case before we cross the river.'

'You do this every day?' I said. Though he kept up a killing rate he didn't seem the least bit tired or ruffled, could have looked to any passer-by as if he'd just stepped out of a taxi, and was only walking a few hundred yards before getting where he wanted to be.

'You have to look like a gentleman,' he said, 'yet be very tough in your fibres. That was dinned into me, during training.'

'What training?' I asked, a faint regret now at the different standards of our appearance.

'Training. The first week they thought they'd never get me out of my old life. But after that I caught on so quickly that the man in the iron lung was amazed. I always was a slow starter, but that's what makes me good in the end. There's many of those chaps (and women, mind you) who've latched on with beautiful speed, but often they're the first to crack. That's what the Lung says, and I quite believe him. He's got many a tale to tell, has that pasty-faced bastard.'

'It all sounds Swahili to me. Besides, I'm hungry. We must have done four miles already. Let's go into the next place for something to eat.'

He stopped and bent down, lifting the bottom of his left trouser-leg and unclipping his suspenders so that he could roll his sock. Attached to the inside of his ankle was a multi-coloured watchface, a pedometer, I supposed, after he'd spoken. 'Three and a quarter,' he said, doing himself up coolly, and carrying on the walk. 'I wear this just to see that I don't cheat myself.'

'I don't care,' I said, 'I'm bloody famished. I could still do with an ox-eye on toast.'

'Ah!' he laughed. 'Your belly's groaning for grub already. If you aren't careful we'll take you on. There's allus room for a new hand. But I can't go into this crummy bar. Let's find a more decent place lower down. That's part of my job, too. A gentleman can't be seen in a pig-bin like that.'

'I'd like to know what you're up to.'

'I can't even light a cigar as I walk along. But it's all good discipline, and that's healthy for any man, being made to do something that your system kicks against. You're able to see a lot in life, and what more can you want than that? You might think I'm talking a bit overmuch, but that's also part of the training. You have to be able to embark on a sea of diverting and intelligible talk at the drop of a hat, because a man who talks is always less suspicious that one who can only look dumb and stand with his trap shut. You've got to say the right thing, and say it with confidence. No stammer or foot-shifting, or they're on to you right away. Those airport bastards don't think twice about tipping your pockets up if your left eyelid seems a bit out of place.'

We went into a respectable fodder bar on Wigmore Street, and sat down for a few choice dishes. 'So you're a smuggler?' A plum-coloured flush went down his cheek. 'You're worse than the man I took you for.'

'We never use that word where I come from. I'm a company director, a travelling gentleman involved in the export trade.'

'Sorry, William.'

'You'll have to curb your big mouth, that's the first thing. Until you do that you'll get nowhere.'

'Christ,' I said, making a cut so that the yellow middle of the egg ran all over my toast, 'everybody I meet makes it his job to teach me something.'

William forked into his cake. 'You were born lucky, in that case. Make sure you take 'em up on it. Otherwise you're throwing your luck away. I'm no fool, Michael, though I have been, so listen to me, and learn all you can from everybody. You didn't learn much at school, I suppose. That means you were bright. You were too full of understanding to bother with what they had to tell you. But all that's behind you now. You got through it without too much bother. They didn't succeed in training you either for a prison or a factory. But now you've got to listen to people who try to teach you something, because they aren't teachers. They do it out of the goodness of their hearts, as one human to another, and they get nothing out of it. That's like gold, so for God's sake don't scoff at it.'

I'd never known him so serious. 'All right, but I still have to pick and choose about what I want to learn.'

'Admitted, but only after you've taken it in. Come on, eat up. We've got our walk to finish. I know you eat fairly quickly, but you'll have to do better than that. A slow eater is a slow thinker, and slow thinking wouldn't be much good to me. Above all, you have to look calm and think quick, otherwise your goose is cooked, whether it's Christmas or not.'

His flat was quiet and out of the way, more in Clapham than Battersea, and I was there a few weeks before being introduced to the man in the iron lung. Out of gratitude and friendship (I didn't consider I'd earned it, though William, who had an exaggerated conscience in some things, thought that I had) he gave me the run of the place. This meant spending much time on my own, because every few days he went away on a trip.

But in between these goings away I would accompany him on long walks. Sometimes we'd go to a gymnasium or a swimming bath because he insisted on us keeping fit. As a result of this I became slightly leaner, firmer in the muscles. He also told me to use less stodge, and whenever possible we ate thick steaks and drank red wine. This treatment suited me fine, but I knew it couldn't all be free, and wanted to know the reason for it, though I realized that nothing would be told me till William was good and ready, so I didn't lose face by asking questions which would not be answered. That also was part of the training.

In his looser moments William hinted that I would become wealthy enough if I was taken on, that my standard of life would leap should I succeed in the first three trips. The only difficulty was to get me taken on, but this might not be impossible providing his own recommendations were firmly given. Fortunately, I was tall enough, and had a good face and figure for the work, which, with a bit of coaching and, later, actual training, would be quite acceptable. He himself had been so successful in the first months of initial forays that if he put up a candidate they would most likely listen to him. The fact was, also, that beginners were always in great demand, not because they fell by the wayside (though some did, of course), but because of that perpetual and reliable quality known as beginner's luck.

After one successful trip a beginner was in most cases no longer used, and he had to be content with the first handsome hand-out, and then retire to the life from which he had come. The man in the iron lung, as he lay and looked at them, was such an expert reader of faces (and handwriting, because on every occasion he would get them to copy five lines and then judge them by it), that he could tell not only whether a man had presence, courage, and nerve for the job but, above all, whether he was lucky. Like Napoleon with his generals he had to know if the candidates for smuggling gold out of the country had a built-in streak of luck that would last them for more than one trip. William, much to his own surprise, had passed this test, and now seemed to be on the permanent staff of the organization, which gave him the confidence to assume that he could get me into it for one trip at least which, if all went well, would net me two or even three hundred pounds on my return.

As soon as these definite terms and possibilities were mentioned I began to feel the stony cravings of ambition harden in my stomach. Some would call it foolish greed and they'd be wrong, because I not only wanted money but also the experience and prestige that would go with it. I saw it as a way of breaking out of a fixed imprisoning period of my life, and though there was some risk (that William played down) I was anxious to get taken on and go through with it. When I was in town, or sitting alone in William's flat listening to the foreign records he'd brought back from his expeditions, I got the black sweats because I wondered whether I'd have the backbone to succeed in something like this. I put it to William, but he laughed and said he'd gone through exactly the same doubts, and what's more it was good to have them because you were no good if you didn't. Those who didn't feel this never got through the training. They didn't even begin it because the man in the iron lung had only to see their handwriting to know that they were too brittle to have doubts about themselves, in which case he wouldn't waste time and effort training them. Of course, William said, he didn't want to push me too hard in this because, after all, I had to make up my own mind. I might be thrown out on first appearance as being totally unsuitable, but he didn't think so, and in any case the decision to make this first appearance before the man in the iron lung had to be taken finally by me and me alone.

The cunning bastard knew that by this time I was too intrigued to draw back, but I still had my doubts about how suitable I was because, as I'd always known, there's a certain idleness in me, an inability to think to the end of everything that starts for no other reason than that I can't be bothered. I think: what's the point? and the flashlight of a bright idea soon gets lost in the fog.

I started to grow a moustache, because William said it would improve my appearance, and thus my chances of being accepted. Fortunately, I looked at least twenty-five, which was also good, because no one looking too much like a youth would ever be used. I never of course imagined this might be some kind of game or trick on his part because I had the evidence of his rise to affluence before me, and I thought that if I could get on to the same railroad, then all well and good. He wondered whether I ought to start smoking a pipe, because that always creates a good impression, he said, especially if it's full but unlit when you're on the way through and they sense the opportunity to do a small kindness in the midst of their restrictive work by asking few questions so that you can get quickly to the other side and then light up. I gave it a try, but even with the weakest tobacco I almost vomited after every puff. It wasn't the strength of the weed so much as the way it hit the back of the mouth and ricocheted down the throat as soon as it came in. So he told me to go on smoking Whiffs, but that while filing through the customs, it might be better to smoke nothing at all.

Life was dull during these weeks, but I didn't mind that, because I found it interesting – as it were. In my idleness I sensed that my appearance was changing to the world, while my attitudes to the world weren't altering at all. The world saw a different man, while I saw the same world, though at the same time I saw the world seeing a different man. That made me feel good, because I became bigger to myself. Thinking I was short on cash William bought me a best-quality electric shaver for eleven pounds. 'Pay me from your first lump sum,' he said, as we came out of the shop.

'What if I never get it?' – not so stone-sure as he was.

'In that case, you've got something for nothing. But from now on get used to having it with you, so's you can shave at least twice a day. Treat it as a natural extension of your graballing hand.'

'Shall I get a bowler hat as well?'

'They'd tumble to you in a flash. For a face like yours you'll need a hat like mine. We'll go up Regent Street and buy one now. Then you can wear it every time you go out.'

The grooming was on in earnest, because on our way to the hatters I was steered into Simpsons for a haircut. Cunning old William had phoned from the flat and made an appointment, so that we went through the doors dead on time in spite of what seemed like casual and aimless progress there. He told the barber exactly what to do, how my hair should be short on top and someway down the neck at the back, with longish sideburns. I protested, but he told me to shut up, and I was on my way to his throat when the scissors scraped along the inside of my ear and the barber screamed and jumped back, thinking I was about to go berserk. 'Get on with it then,' I shouted. 'Only do it quick or I'll cut my own throat without waiting for you to do it.'

They were glad to see the back of us, though not of William, because he left a ten-bob note for a tip. 'You're more trouble than a bloody baby,' he said, and, after we'd been to the hat-shop, 'Now who's that coming towards yourself in that mirror over there?'

'Where?' I said. 'Where?' – looking straight into it, at this smart young fellow I didn't for a moment recognize. I tipped my hat to him, and wondered what the hell would happen next.

The following morning Mr Hay went on a trip to Beirut, and I was left again to wander the town. But I had been given instructions as to what I should do, each daily walk marked on a map in different-coloured pencil. William stipulated that I must carry my briefcase, which he had already filled with short lengths of lead so that it felt on lifting like a twenty-pound weight hanging from my arm. What's more, he had taken the key so that I couldn't throw any of it out. There was, of course, no reason why I should have carried the briefcase at all, but because this was an important part of my training I didn't want to spoil any chance of getting into their racket simply by being idle and unable to carry the right weight when it came to a test. The first day took me to the middle of town and back, and I don't know whether it was part of a laugh on William's part, but it so happened from the map that I was to turn around at the Old Bailey.

The idea that I was to take this weight, and wear my hat, and walk in a casual way as if I had little more than a copy of that morning's newspaper in my briefcase was, as I found after the first hundred yards, easier said than done. In the middle of Battersea Bridge I wanted to put it down and sit on it because I was sweating like a dog. When I picked it up again I wanted to sling it in the river. But I carried on, recalling as I walked how my Irish ancestors (one of them anyway) had survived the Famine created by the callous English in order to come over and build the railways for them, digging out their navigating guts as they linked up one place to another. So bearing this picture, I struggled through Chelsea, hoping I didn't look too much like a coalman about to deliver his last load of the day.

By the time I got back to the flat my arms felt a foot longer, but the second day was worse because though by then I'd got used to carrying the actual weight, I had been specially requested to put on the expression of nonchalance. If it was impossible to do this on setting out, it was even more difficult by the time I was on the return leg. The walks had been planned so that they got longer each time, and when I was putting the key into the flat door I cursed myself for a fool and swore I'd clear out as soon as I got my clothes together. It had drizzled and rained much of the day, what's more, and this only increased my exhaustion and despondency.

After a bath and a few mugs of tea I began to lose my rage. From the height of the flat I could look out, and see that the rain had stopped. The sun was shining somewhere, and softened the light, giving a rich and vivid colour to the air. It made me think of the marvellous and narrow life I'd left behind in Nottingham, though it didn't inspire me to go back there. Then I had a vision of all I could do in this soft and beautiful world if I had money, and that since I might be put in the way of getting plenty if I followed William's advice, I might as well persist in this short stretch of training he had set for me during his absence. It would be weak and foolish to give up now, and I had never considered myself either weak or foolish. I put on a record, and fell asleep before the first side ended, not waking up until the following morning, when the treadmill began all over again.

I had broken through, picked up that briefcase like an old friend, as if we'd already done a full year of days together. With a newspaper under the other arm I whistled along, even saying a cheery good morning to a copper on the bridge – knowing old Hay would approve of that. This was the longest trudge of all, but I knew I could make it. I walked from Battersea to the middle of Hampstead, changing the briefcase over now and again, but only as if to give the other hand the privilege of holding it. On the map there was a blue circle around the Tube station at Hampstead, which meant I was to have lunch there, and I made it a good one, dawdling so long at the Pimpernel that it was almost three o'clock before I left.

The day was fine, except for a bit of wind which nearly blew my hat off a time or two, and I actually enjoyed the walk, the weight no longer so oppressive that I couldn't look around me and take things in. My route led down through the streets towards Finchley Road, and I was passing a row of large houses which were used as private schools. Boys came out wearing fancy caps with tassels, and the girls with grey bowlers, accompanied by maids or parents. There was a queue of glossy cars waiting by the kerb, and a lot of honking from some that wanted to turn round and get out of the cul-de-sac. It was amusing to pick my way through, and assume the easiness of a father going there casually from the office (after a hard day since eleven o'clock) to pick up his Crispin and Felicity. But I stopped to watch a little boy with a briefcase stand outside a door at the top of some steps. He wore his cap at such an extremely cocky angle that it was about to slide off. The heavy black glasses were so big over his eyes that they almost covered his face. Compared with the rest of the kids swarming down the steps he was very small indeed, yet through this disguise of posh-school clobber I would have known him anywhere.

He jumped up on the concrete wall, which sloped steeply towards the gate-post, put his briefcase on it, and slid at a great rate to the bottom, falling off so that his cap went one way and his glasses the other. The school door opened, and Bridgitte ran down the steps, picked him up, smacked his face,

225

and collected his things together. 'You shouldn't hit a kid like that,' I said. 'It's just high spirits.'

She glared at me without recognition. 'Mind your own business. I'm his mother.'

'Are you? I must be his father, then. Don't you know me, darling?'

She looked again, but Smog cried: 'It's Uncle Mike! Have you come to take me away?'

'You!' she said. 'What do you want?'

'Thanks for the welcome. I thought we were old friends – until you vanished out of my life.'

'I'm Mrs Anderson now,' she said, 'thanks to you. And the mother of this.'

'It's not possible,' I laughed, taking it bravely.

'It is, let me tell you.' Smog snuggled up to my legs. Then he danced around me. He tried to pick up my briefcase, but stopped when his face turned purple. He kicked it, and stubbed his toe, came close to tears. Then he laughed and grabbed me again. 'Still the same old Smog,' I said, pulling his cap off and putting it in my pocket.

'He's not,' she said, 'he's worse. I took him to Holland last month and he wrecked my father's farm. He laid it waste singlehanded, and my father won't see me again.'

I was mystified at the fact that, as she said, she was now Mrs Anderson, and I tried to cover my wound by banter. 'Anyway,' she said, 'we don't call him Smog any more. It's forbidden. It's very bad for him.'

'It can't make him much worse than he is, can it, Smog?'

He looked up: 'No, it can't actually. Will you buy us some cakes?'

'You'd better ask your mother.'

'She's not my mother. My mother went away, and divorced Daddy because she found him in bed with Bridgitte.'

'Is that so?' I said. 'You can't trust anybody these days, can you? Never tell anybody that you love them. That's my motto from now on.'

'Poor you,' she said.

'Let's find a place to have some tea,' I said, taking Smog's hand and offering my arm to Bridgitte. We walked down the hill, looking as united a group as ever was.

'You set the whole thing off,' she said, as if wishing I never had, which made me see a glimmer of hope over the opposite rooftops. 'You remember,' she went on, after we'd found a corner table in a respectable place near Swiss Cottage, 'when we last met, and I told you that Donald – that's my husband's name – had been trying to make up to me – I mean make me, as you say – and you said I should slip some lipstick in his bed so that his wife would find it, and throw him out? Well, I was putting it in there, very neatly, when he was out, or so I thought, but he was in, and standing watching me. He saw me take the lipstick from my pocket and pull back the bedclothes, then bend over to set it under the pillows. When I'd done this he asked me what I thought I was doing, and I was so confused that he jumped on me and pulled my clothes off. I don't know why, but I couldn't fight him. I was shouting for help, and calling your name, but then I saw that it was no use, and he did everything to me, as well as beating me, because he saw I'd been trying to do him some harm with the lipstick.

'Then – I'm sorry Michael – but there was nothing I could do about it. I forgot everything. He did, too, because he's told me so since, and while we were there, his wife came in and saw us. She's tall and thin and has nearly no breasts, though she's very good-looking at the face. She shouted it was the last straw, packed her things, and went in a taxi. The next day she came with a vehicle and took half the furniture. I was surprised she didn't take Smog, but she didn't because Donald told me she was going to live with her own lover who wouldn't have put up with him for a single minute. Then I found out that they were divorced already, had been for a year! So we got married because he said he loved me, and we were still living together, anyway. I liked him, just a little bit, you know.'

'I phoned you,' I said bitterly, 'night after night, and I called at the flat as well.'

'We went to Scotland for a fortnight, and then we gave up the flat. We live in Hampstead now in a house.'

'Things happen too fast to me. I'm still in love with you.' It was the truth. She was no longer dressed like the gorgeous au pair girl of old, but had put on a few years of maturity with the clothes of a London wife, not to mention her added responsibilities.

'I can't say anything,' she nudged me. 'You understand?' – a glance at Smog who now had all three cups in front of him and was filling them with the remains of the tea, water, milk, and sugar, as well as the stinking contents of the ashtray.

'At least give me your telephone number so that we can have a secret word together now and again. There'll be no harm in that.'

'I hope not,' she said, smiling as she wrote it out for me. She stood up to go. 'Come on, Smog.'

'I haven't finished my chemical experiments.'

'Smog, don't be a little bastard. Come on.'

He stood up and put on his cap, backwards. 'I'm not a little bastard. I want to go with Michael.'

'You can't,' I said, 'not yet.' As I shook hands for the fare-well she said: 'You look more prosperous.'

'Changed my job. I work for the Bank of England. Just been to see a client who has an overdraft. If we can get him to settle it, England's balance of payments will be OK – for this month anyway. I get all sorts of special missions like this. Mother pulled a few strings to get me the job. I don't mind using her if I'm in an especially tight corner.'

'I don't believe you,' she laughed. 'But we won't go into that.'

I smiled, as if I thought she was being facetious, not trusting me on such a trifle: 'That's all right. So we'll be in touch?' I put an end to it rather coolly, though I feel we parted with mutual twelve per cent interest in each other.

I was too occupied in the next few weeks even to talk to any-body on the telephone. The day arrived when William, who claimed he'd put in an excellent word for me, said that the man in the iron lung would like to make my acquaintance. Before this came we went on the longest walk of all – to Highgate and back – after which I felt as fit and lean as a tiger, for the continual weight I carried was turning me into a savage, though in my face I had to show no emotion at all, unless it was that of a man mulling over some mild assignment that may possibly be fatal for others but in no way for himself.

We went to an immense block of old-fashioned flats near the Albert Hall, and William was greeted at the entrance by the doorman as if he himself had been a millionaire tenant there for twenty years. He took us up in the lift and rang the bell so that neither William nor I need take off our gloves. We were shown into the richest flat I had ever seen, a hall with pictures and vases that my fingers itched to latch upon. Then I remembered my newly opening prospects in life, and in any case they were things I couldn't properly hide on me. A butler took us into a smaller room, which had a few simple chairs around the walls and a table in the middle. There were copies of *Country Life* and *The Connoisseur* on the table, though neither of us read, but sat there without talking.

I felt my heart trying to push its way through to fresh air, and I wanted to light a cigarette, but sensed that William would have disapproved, and in any case there were no ash-trays. So I calmed myself by saying I was man enough not to get upset at this ordinary happening of being forced to wait. The last few weeks were beginning to show me that emotion must always be kept in the negative, must never be developed into a picture for the rest of the world to see. A man who shows nothing of his inner turmoil is always more formidable than one who can't help but do so and who doesn't even realize what a fool he makes of himself when he does. At the same time you have to be careful not to let this façade of calmness destroy the actual feelings inside, because that would be cutting off your nose to spite your face, as they say. I was mulling on the fact while we waited, that thought and self-examination, more than anything else, was what kept you looking as if nothing could ever break in from the outside world.

We were shown in by a tall young man with dark hair, and a soft, half-smiling face. The room was so long that the ceiling seemed lower than the one outside. There were no carpets on the floor, but a black and white design in soft lino tiles. It was less furnished in every respect, except for a few maps that had been framed, and hung in odd places along the walls. At the other end of the room a large relief map of Europe, the Middle

East, and North Africa, had been fixed to the ceiling. Red string connected various places on it, so that it looked like the sales map of some large export firm, except for its peculiar position.

What drew me most of all was a huge glass case built from the floor almost up to the ceiling, and a sort of bed inside this aquarium, with one large face – so large that it must have been in some way magnified – looking out of it at the top end. From this immense transparent construction came pipes and wires, and by the side at the other end was a huge rubber bag inflating and deflating the heart of the man inside this miracle of modern science set before my eyes. He lay under a counterpane, but with enough of his body visible to show that he was dressed in a normal suit, with a collar and tie at the neck. He sloped on a backrest, it seemed, though only a little, so that he could look sideways at the ceiling. Papers and booklets were spread over the bed, but at the moment he was mainly interested in me, as I advanced with William across the room, still carrying my briefcase. His face was pale, and rather fat, and his small brown eyes fixed me firmly. 'Good morning, sir,' William said. 'I've brought the new man along.'

'Let's see him then,' a voice replied, not from the iron lung, but out of a speaker by the side, though there was no doubt that it was the man within the iron lung who had spoken. As I went close I saw, on a built-in ledge within reach of his hand, a Luger automatic pistol. What good that would do him in a dust-up I couldn't imagine, yet I suppose it gave him some comfort to have it close by.

'A man,' said the rather cracky voice that came out of the speaker, 'must be able to carry half his own weight, without showing it. Can you?'

I made a quick reckoning. Last time, the scales had spun up to well over twelve stones, so six times fourteen came to more than eighty pounds. The idea frightened me, but instead of telling him to hire a team of yaks, I said I could, providing the packer knew his job. The speaker laughed. It surprised me that during the whole interview he asked so few questions, but I supposed that William had kept him well supplied.

'Ask Stanley to put the flak-jacket on him,' he called, and

the tall dark pansy who had let us into the flat came back with a trolley laden with long thin blocks of metal. A coat was spread over the handles and I was told to put it on. William helped me. It had long thin pockets inside, which I supposed were to receive the metal on the trolley. These were said, by running commentary from the man in the iron lung, to weigh a pound each, and one by one fifty of them were put away there, while my shoes were getting so glued to the floor that I looked down to see if I were making a hole in it. My shoulders took the weight, but I also felt it at my ribs, as if they were about to be pulled apart.

'Feeling all right?' he grinned from behind his perspex.

'Fine,' I smiled, at the fortieth bar and ready to swing over on to his floor. I pretended my life was at stake, as if I'd be shot if I weren't able to put up with it. To take my mind off the weight (which, you must admit, wouldn't make that much difference) I began to think of all the things I'd done since reaching London. Flight into London it had been, indeed and by God, and the one bright star was Bridgitte Appledore, whom it looked like I wouldn't see till I got out of this madman's den. I wanted to see her alone, and make loose so that I got through to her warm sweet nut and full white breasts and lovely astonished face that frowned but enjoyed it all by the time it was nearly finished. But maybe she'd be hotter after her months with Dr Anderson, because husbands were often good for warming up whorish wives for their lovers to get the cream of – though my wife would never be like that, for I'd settle her myself. Be that as it may, I now had sixty bars in my thick gabardine mac and it was considered enough – seeing as they didn't want to break my back first go.

A smile made his face even paler. I felt one on my own, without having put it there. It was the smile of illumination that comes before death. I was lit up inside, ready and light in weight for what came next. 'Go to the other end of the room and back,' the man said from the safety of his iron lung. I was prepared to fly, but for my sixty shackles. Maybe my convict ancestors had been laden like this when due for Botany Bay.

I knew before I started that the best trick would be not to walk too slow. That would bring me down. So I went with reasonable speed though not too quickly, one leg taking the weight of the other in an even balance, and the rhythm carried me along, though I don't suppose I looked too happy about it. But while I was going from them they couldn't see my face, and by the time I turned and started to stride manfully back the mouth was screwed shut and my gills, though in no way twisted, couldn't have been anything but purple.

Back at Lungville he said to me: 'Now write your name and address on that sheet of paper.' I bent stiffly to get at the pen and do as I was told, then stood straight again. I heard a murmur of 'Good, good,' as if Lungy had said it to himself and not into the inside mike. 'Now do *your* stuff,' he told William, who took the paper I had written on and pushed it into a tube contraption normally used in department stores for sending change from cash desk to counter. The next second it was inside the iron lung and being studied by Pasty-face through a magnifying glass. 'While I'm doing this, you can walk up and down a few times.'

'And take your briefcase,' said William. 'Just to show what you can do,' he added with a wink, dropping something in front of me that looked like a passport: 'Pick that up while you're at it, my old flower!'

'Get it your bloody self,' I said, with a look of murder.

'It's part of the job,' he told me, as if I'd hurt and insulted him.

'I haven't clocked-on yet.'

William patted me on the back: 'But you will soon, and this is one of the things you might have to do. So don't let me down. Just imagine you are carrying fifty thousand quid's worth of gold, and now that you've come to the customs bloke you've dropped your passport. You'd have to pick it up as if you'd got nothing in your pockets, wouldn't you?'

'All right,' I said. 'I get the idea.' I went out at a right angle and let my hand drop, coming up again so quickly with the passport in my hand that I astonished myself at having done it with such ease.

'He's passed,' I heard the voice say from inside the lung. 'His writing shows it, anyway. Strength, caution, speed, confidence. It's all here. Put him on that job to Zurich at the end of next week.'

'What about money?' I asked politely.

He coughed. 'When you come back you'll get three hundred. Stanley will give you twenty pounds now on account, if you need it.'

'I do,' I said, still having more than two hundred from my Moggerhanger days, but knowing that you could never have too much in hand.

The time until my first trip was spent in more training. I worked up the weights till I went into the streets with a full load of over fifty pounds, plus the briefcase, walking to a specified point, getting on a bus for a few miles, then sitting down in a stipulated café to a cup of coffee. I'd finally take a bus back to Knightsbridge, and drag a few hundred yards to the flat where I'd be divested of my straitjacket. When it came off I felt weightless and naked, and I'm sure I looked shiftier when I went out in normal gear than I ever had when loaded.

The night before the trip I phoned Bridgitte to wish her goodbye. A man picked up the phone and snappily demanded who it was, so I put on an imitation Dutch accent and said I was Bridgitte's brother. When I heard her call out that she had no brother, I raved that I had meant cousin – she must have at least one cousin. 'Who is it?' she asked. I told her I was going to Rome in the morning for a few days, but that I'd try to see her as soon as I got back. I heard a blow, a cry, a sound of quarrelling. The line went dead.

Part Five

They loaded me up at the flat and William drove me to the airport. He had only got back from a diamond trip the night before, but wanted to be the one to see me off. 'You'll do marvels. You're a bloody wonder-boy. I've never seen anybody carry so much with such a cold look in his eye. I mean it. You'll be perfect.'

'All right,' I said. 'Stop the cackle. I can't stand it so early in the morning. I still need fifteen more cups of coffee, so I hope there'll be time at the buffet.'

I'd been to the airport the day before, wearing horn-rimmed glasses and a cap as if going to wait for somebody, so I knew my way through. I said goodbye to William, then got out of the car so that he could drive home and get some sleep. I felt utterly cool and unconcerned about carrying gold out of the country, because it seemed such a harmless and easy thing to do. It wasn't stealing, and that made it all right. I was only a highly paid pack-mule.

I booked in, got on the escalator, and made straight for the departure lounge, feeling it would be better not to delay in case this feeling of righteousness deserted me. Bustling in the crowd around the newspaper and souvenir kiosk at the other end, I saw the bluff familiar head of Moggerhanger. What he was doing at the airport I didn't know, and had no wish to find out, but it made just one more good reason for getting through the formalities quickly. My ticket was checked, and then I walked towards the passport man, a real old Twitch-bollock standing behind a pulpit. Nearby was a customs officer who glanced at everybody as they went by. I looked ahead, through the door, as if anxious to get at one of the coffee urns beyond, and this disinterested craving for another dose of breakfast put a normal look on my face at a point when I was about to get nervous. There was a beautiful dark-haired girl in front of me, and after my passport was seen to I took a view of her legs when I should have been giving the customs man a dirty look. I heard no voice asking what I was taking out, felt no hand on my shoulder, and then I was through, and in, and out, and at the counter, and sweating so much under my armour-plated coat that black spots flitted in front of my eyes. I deliberately lingered by the part of the counter that was still in sight of the customs man, not out of crackpot bravado, but only to emphasize to him, if he ever had any suspicions, that I felt no reason to vanish into the crowd.

With half an hour before my plane number came up, I had two cups of coffee and a sandwich, then strolled to the newspaper counter and bought a copy of *The Financial Times*. My legs and shoulders were aching from too much weight. It was still not ten in the morning, and due to the cups of poisonous coffee, I had to go to the lavatory. I was far too clever to take my coat off before sitting down, knowing that I'd find it hard to get it on again. At the same time all was not well, because when I had finished, I couldn't get up. The coat hung around me like a cloak of rock. In one way I didn't want to get up, but to sit there and muse in my own stink till someone found me, or until I recovered my determination and picked myself to pieces, bar by bar, when I'd walk away from the airport and vanish for ever – as far as the man in the iron lung was concerned. But having followed this line through to the stupid and bitter end, I began to consider how it might be better if I got upright and went on my way. After all, I was being trusted with a big job, and if I muffed it William Hay would get his face bashed in and get sent back to being plain Bill Straw on the run from all the right-thinking criminals in society.

I stayed a minute on my knees, hand resting on the rim of the toilet. It was hard to move from this position, but at least I was mobile, because even if I got no more upright than this I'd be able to shuffle across the departure hall and up the plane steps on my knees, giving out that I was on a pilgrimage to my favourite saint's shrine at Lourdes where I was hoping to get my mother cured of a fatal illness. No, that wouldn't do, so I crawled around the wall and back again. This hadn't been part of the training, though I saw now that it should have been, and would have to get the syllabus amended when I got back, if I got back, if ever I came out of jail. I was on top of the toilet now, and by a quick but risky flip backwards my feet hit the ground in the right place, and I was shaken but standing, just as the number of my plane was announced as departing from Gate Number Thirteen. I fastened my trousers, then the coat, picked up my briefcase, and was on my way to the pressurized unknown.

The plane sagged as I stepped on board – or I thought it did, and the heat of the jungle hung over me as soon as I sat down in that long stuffy plane. I'd often wondered whether I'd be afraid of going off the earth in this way, but now I was too exhausted to care. I had no reactions at all, except a heavy pressure pushing me back towards the seat – something I didn't need because I was well bedded there already. The plane went straight into the clouds, followed the white carpet all the way. I'd got by a window, and a young girl sat next to me. Her elbow pushed into my ribs by accident, then sprang back at the touch of solid iron that she met. The central heating must have been full on, because she took off her coat, then her jacket. A bracelet hung from her wrist, but there were no rings on her fingers. There was a bump under the plane, as if we were climbing a hill, and her hand clutched the seat. It was only now, five miles off the earth, that I wondered what it would be like leaving it.

My luggage allowance was wrapped around me like solid gold armour, and I was naturally led to wonder whether such padding would be any good if the aeroplane crashed on landing. Certainly, if the wings I could see out of my window were ripped off, it wouldn't help me. We'd go down like a stone, and maybe my weight would even pull it a bit faster, and later my body would be found twenty feet under the earth, a knickerbocker glory all wrapped up in the golden handshake.

At six miles up I noticed an ordinary housefly loose in this lovely immaculate jet. Such a scruffy little surviving bastard was a sign of reassurance, made me laugh at it, something more homely and normal than myself and the eighty others lined up and down. That fly will go far, I thought, having passed the survival test this far up, the only real eleven-plus of any life. The stewardess was selling drinks a few seats away, and swayed, grabbing an overhead rack when the plane banked sharply. Again the girl by my side gripped the armrest. 'Are you nervous?'

'A bit.' She half turned her face to me, and I wondered whether other people bumped into chance meetings as often as I did. It struck me for the first time that society was formed so that they would, and nobody could escape because we were all part of a warp and weft that fitted into one homely world-wide rag. 'I've flown dozens of times,' I said, the wheels always oiled by a good old-fashioned lie.

'So have I. But I can't get used to it. I don't know why.'

'There's only one cure,' I told her. 'Talk. And drink. Be with somebody you can talk to – about anything, it doesn't matter – and have a couple of brandies, or glasses of champagne.' I called the stewardess: 'Half a bottle of dry, love. All right?'

'Thank you,' she smiled, and I felt how pleasant travelling was. It took the weight off me, back and front. I had seen her before, but only from a distance, and I doubt that she had seen me, and if she had it hadn't been long enough for future recognition. 'I was your father's chauffeur,' I said, 'until I got a better job.'

'I hate to be recognized,' she said stonily. 'It embarrasses me.'

'Sorry. I only told you I knew you in case you might recognize me first. Then you might be annoyed. Cheers!'

She drank the whole glass: 'This was a good idea, anyway.'

'Here's to you, Miss Moggerhanger.' I said Polly under my breath, for I'd seen her black smouldering hair wrinkling from always too far away, as she rode a horse to the stable when she was back from riding, her plum-coloured shirt or jumper jumping nicely as she jogged along. Or she'd be dressed in a smart suit as she got demurely into somebody's E-type for a fashionable night in town. I felt very good, as if my head had no top to it, but couldn't have said whether meeting Polly Moggerhanger was a lucky day in my life or not. Since I'd had nothing to do with it, it wasn't for me to say.

'I thought I could get into a plane at least and not be

recognized,' she pouted, 'but there's no damned hope even of that.'

'It's no use worrying,' I said, watching the colour get to her cheeks as she gobbled back the rest of the drink. The stewardess was coming with trays of lunch, but I ordered more champagne. 'Helps the food to float down,' I said. I was beginning to feel better from it myself, but only now remembered William's sternest warning: 'Don't drink, not alcohol. Not a drop. It's fatal. Don't bloody-well countenance such a thing going between your lips, Michael.' He'd repeated it over the weeks of preparation, and I'd agreed to never, never, never touch it, because I didn't need it and didn't like it. One, I suppose, would have been all right, especially since there was a meal to go with it, but two of those little champagne land-mines at thirty thousand feet and eleven in the morning put the cobwebs back in front of my eyes, notwithstanding the fact that the ice had been broken with a pretty young woman talking easily by my side. There's no doubt that the Moët Chandon helped her, for while we were smoking our cigarettes I held her hand, and she made no brisk move to get it away.

'My father brought me to the airport,' she said. 'There are times when he doesn't even want to let me out of his sight. It gets very bloody tiresome. He thinks I'm going to Geneva to see a girlfriend of mine from finishing school, and I am, but only for an hour if I can help it. After that I'll have three delicious days on my own, rent a car, drive along the lake, see who I can get to know, and have a ball.'

She asked what my work was, and I said I was travelling for a business firm. 'Ah' – her smile alarmed me because it was almost a sneer – 'it's smuggling, I suppose. How much does that coat weigh that you can't take off?'

'It's chilly at this time of the year,' I said, sweating blood.

'That coat would keep you warm at the North Pole. I've seen 'em before.'

'I had a chill all last week,' I said, 'and I'm still recovering, so I keep well wrapped up. I fell in the river. For a dare, really. My girlfriend dared me to do it, and I did, just dropped in like a stone. It's a wonder I didn't get anything worse, it was so filthy.'

'Why did she want you to do that?' Polly asked, bending her head with interest, so that some of those black curls fell on to the white skin of her neck. I wanted to touch it, but held back, though I set myself to do it some time or other.

'Oh, I don't know. We've been at sixes and sevens these last weeks. We don't really get on. It's impossible, and I'm thinking I might not see her again. I knew, when she dared me to jump into the river, that she'd be horrified if I did. So I did it, thinking we couldn't hate each other any more than we did already. But I was wrong. We did. Yet we're still together. Anyway, I've been uneasy about it ever since we've met. She's from a rich family, you see, and I don't hold that against her, but she doesn't really know how to live. It's ruined her, somehow, spoiled her. I've known a few girls who came from rich families, and they've all been the same: very difficult, and also not very good in bed. I always prefer a more ordinary girl for that sort of thing. It somehow works better. They've got less on their backs. Not that it matters to me any more. I've really decided not to see Joan again, even though I know I won't be able to make it with any girl for another few months, not till I get over it. It always takes me a while to recover from something like this. It devastates me. I'm too sensitive about it. I just can't run over to another girl and start from scratch again. I have to hide away somewhere, or busy myself in work. I'm not the flippant type, though I certainly wish I was. Not that I get too serious when I meet a girl, but if I really do know her for a long time it often takes just as many weeks or months to forget her after we've parted. You see what I mean?'

She nodded, and the curl shook on her neck, a sight that set me talking onwards so that I wouldn't pick it up to kiss it. 'I think at the bottom I don't like life, but when I'm with a person whom I consider sympathetic and intelligent, somebody I can talk to with more than polite phrases that last only a minute and a half, then I soon get on top form. I'm not talking about love, mind you. I don't think that comes into it with a person like me. I've never told anyone I love them, but I let the attachment speak for itself. As soon as love is mentioned it flies out of the window. I can just become very very intimate with a girl, so that a real bond exists when we are together, and we have wonderful tender times in bed. But love as a question or, worse, as a statement, never comes up between us, at least not from me. If a girl mentions it I feel that the end is near, and even if I still keep up exactly the same intensity of the bond, she on her part begins to grow cooler. I've seen it more than once. But if neither of us says it, the association goes on, and only ends when it is absolutely time for it to end, no sooner and no later. And it's also a strange thing, that when the girl first mentions the word love in any way, and the association ends, then whenever we meet casually afterwards neither of us feels any friendship, but when love has never been mentioned during an association and it finishes on its natural rhythm, and when the girl and I bump into each other later, we meet as the best of friends, and might even spend that night in bed together and have an absolutely marvellous time.'

'That's true,' she said, 'very true.' And though I chatted away like this I knew it was only the bubble-vat of champagne inside my gut that was doing the thinking. I had one idea at that moment, which was to get into bed with Polly Mogger-hanger. It was as if my life depended on it, I didn't know why, because in spite of all my talk, or maybe even because of it, I didn't think at all about the situation I might be slipping into. If William Hay's number-one caution had been that I mustn't drink, his second had been that I should not talk, not to anyone while I was on such a journey. But since I had started to talk, so that I was even fascinated by it myself, I went on to more dangerous ground when I casually told her the name of the hotel I would be staying at in Geneva in case she felt like phoning me up. Before I could stop her, or tell her it wouldn't be necessary, she was writing it down in a little beige address book with a diamond at the head of the pencil – a present from Daddy, no doubt. I was both thrilled and horrified, but both feelings were dulled by the after-effects of the champagne, and I was almost asleep by the time the plane settled itself on the final skid-bumps for landing, though I went on talking, never-theless, to pretty Polly, who gripped my hand.

I fastened my coat, and gripped the rail firmly so as not to slide head first on to the tarmac. I felt the need for glasses, seeing everything with less clarity than usual, so swore to have my eyes tested as soon as I got back. Something genuinely had snapped in them, not from the champagne which, after all, had been a very small amount, but due to the fact that I had never been so exhausted in my life, so racked out, as it were, and again I swore that this would be my first and last trip on such kind of work.

No one bothered me at the passport window, and soon I was lifting my arm for a taxi to take me to a prearranged office address in the suburb of Eaux-Vives. Polly, who'd gone out in front of me, was met by her girlfriend's family, and driven in a very large car to some villa along the lake.

The lift at my rendezvous didn't work, which meant an act of self-escalation foot by foot up three flights of stairs. I cursed them blind at the dead weight, step by step, sweating upwards, standing often to grunt my breath, so that a kind and elderly gentleman on his way down looked at me in alarm as if I were in the throes of a heart attack. I smiled to say I was all right, but he stood looking at me as I continued up, as if he didn't believe me, and was about to shuffle off and get one of those famous Swiss doctors to run off with my corpse. I was at my lowest gasp up the final flight, and I felt worse than I'd done since leaving William's flat, so that it was only now that I fully realized I was in a foreign country for the first time in my life. Why it only came at this point, I'll never know, but it did, and there was no great thrill about it either. I forgot all about it as soon as I pressed my sweating fingertips on the bell.

An office boy who looked thirty-eight under his rimless glasses and scrubbing-brush hair asked me what I wanted, and after I said Mr Punk he changed colour and beckoned me into a sort of waiting-room corridor. I pulled him back when he was about to disappear and told him in sign language to get me a drink of water – though he understood English as well as I did. He gave me ice-cold water in a paper cup, then went to report my arrival. There were chairs all round the room but I stood up and leaned against the wall, too weary and frightened of death to sit down. I began to have delusions that I'd landed in the wrong place, and that if I weren't careful I'd get rolled of my gold and thrown plumb-line into the gutter. I thought it best to stay on my feet so that I could run if anything threatening threatened to happen, but before I could start my looney-bin screaming from under a chair, Mr Punk himself came in, with a wide even-toothed smile on his face, which seemed merely a bigger and more genial version of the office boy's. He held out his hand for a brief shake, and said in perfect English: 'I'm pleased to see that you have arrived safely. Everything all right?'

'Good,' I said, 'except that through some strange fluke I'm dying of thirst.'

He laughed, heartily, and slapped me on the back: 'They all say that. Come into my office and get out of that coat. It's warm for the time of the year. How do you like Switzerland?'

I went before him, ignoring his inane question, and he shut the door, when it suddenly occurred to me that he was waiting for the magic-password phrase which would absolutely establish my credentials. 'I've got some good news about Sir Jack Leningrad. He's much better. And he sends his fondest wishes.'

'Ah,' he replied, with a deadpan businesslike face. 'I last met Mr Leningrad in Canterbury.'

'All right, then,' I said, 'for God's sake help me off with this coat.'

Underneath, I was as wet as if I'd been dipped into a vat of warm water, soaked from my suit down to underwear and skin. He opened a cupboard and took out an identical mackintosh coat to the one I'd been wearing except that it had no inside pockets. 'Put this on, you'll catch cold. We lost one traveller like that a few years ago – he died of pneumonia. We don't want to lose you, because according to Mr Leningrad they have high hopes of you. You're one of their promising young gentlemen.' I wrapped myself up and drank another paper cup of water. 'What I suggest now,' he said, 'is that you go by taxi to your hotel and take a hot bath. It usually makes quite a difference.'

It was a small room, looking out on rooftops and pigeons. I hung up my suit to dry, then got into the bed and didn't wake up for four hours, by which time it was dark, and I was hungry. The fact that I'd just earned three hundred pounds cheered me up no end, and I went downstairs to the dining-room to celebrate with an elaborate dinner and a bottle of rosy wine. Sitting alone, feeling relaxed and haggard, I hoped I looked interesting to the other people in the room. I hung on in the pleasant atmosphere after the meal and chewed through a few long cigars. I went to sleep that night musing on how pleasant life could be if only one had money. Nothing else seemed to matter except money, and though this came as a slow and pleasant revelation, I knew, at the same time, that I'd always known it, right from birth. I wondered if any bastard had ever wanted anything more than that. I wasn't completely rotten (not by any means) in that I wanted power as well as money. Nothing like that. I only wanted money, a desire that could do no harm to anyone, and I'd do anything and go to great lengths to get it. To want power seemed to me vile, but to want money was noble.

The desire – not that I'd needed to make it plain by thinking about it – lit a new light inside me, and, in my mind's eye, a halo around my head. I had the idea that if I kept this picture of myself clean and uncompromised, I'd never have any trouble carrying my little bits of gold through the customs. The pure of heart shall inherit the earth, and what could be more pure of heart than a simple good-natured desire for money and an easy life that would harm none of my fellow men? The wish to acquire money without working for it was a virtue that few people shared with me. They worked for it, and by this got power over others. If they didn't get power over others, then at least they got power over themselves, and I didn't want even this. For if I got power over myself it might break my innocence, put a look back in my face that would be spotted a mile off by any customs man – something which clicks within them because they can't help having it themselves.

After breakfast in my room, the telephone rang, and a girl asked to speak to me. It took a few moments to realize it was Polly Moggerhanger. Either there was something wrong with my memory or I wasn't the sort of person I thought I was. Since leaving her at the airport she had not come once into my mind, and now that she was speaking brightly into my ear I was so shocked and surprised to hear her that I didn't know whether or not I was pleased about it. She told me she'd had the most boring time yesterday with her friend and her family, and that if she didn't get out of it she'd go crazy and scream. It was a nice picture, but I couldn't let her do it, so I invited her to lunch.

I didn't know of any good restaurants in Geneva, so eating on the hotel premises might give her the idea that I did, but that I was merely being idle or pressed for time. I could hardly remember her from the desperate haze of yesterday, and thought that when I saw her maybe I wouldn't want to spend more time with her than lunch. There was a strong feeling in me to be on my own for a while in these strange surroundings – which seemed stranger the longer I was in them. It was as if yesterday's trip had taken me across an important borderline, and as usual, though I felt this strongly, I didn't quite know what the consequences would be. In fact I didn't know, in any way, at all, but when I saw Polly walking into the hotel lounge I realized that I no longer wanted to be alone for the next couple of days.

It came out over lunch that she was very unhappy, and didn't know what to do with her life – which seemed to prove that her despair wasn't monumentally serious. But when I said that unhappiness was the spice of life, and that if you weren't unhappy you were dead, she became a lot more cheerful. 'I've had an ideal life,' she told me, 'being the daughter of someone like my father, as you can imagine. He doted on me, and gave me everything I wanted, which suited me fine. It certainly kept me very content for a long time. But when I first started having men friends, he got meaner, though he didn't make too open a row about it. It got so I thought I was doing something wrong when I had it in somebody's flat or on the back seat of a car, and it stopped me getting all my thrills out of it for a year or two. Parents think they own you, just because they brought you up.'

'I hope it's different now,' I said, dipping into my water ice. 'Not for my sake, but for yours.'

'Don't worry about that,' she said.

'I won't,' I answered. 'It's not my problem, is it? But where shall we go this afternoon?' When she had no idea I said we ought to bus along the lake to the castle of Chillon, and when I went on about Bonivard and Byron's poem, she thought it an exciting plan, because though she'd heard of it herself, she was more than pleasantly surprised to find that I was no stranger to it, imagining perhaps that a born smuggler like me could never know of things like that. I didn't really, but had read of it in a tourist hand-out from the hotel only that morning. Yet I was able to tell her, truthfully and with an offhand candour, about Byron's pad at Newstead where I'd been a time or two on a bus in my childhood and youth – on one occasion with my mother who was visiting a tubercular friend in the nearby sanatorium. It gave us something to talk about, with which to break through to the comfort of more private things, whispering sugar-nothings into a sweet ear of corn as we sat on the bus, the lake glinting in our eyes at every new bend. When I ran out of topics I asked her what she wanted from life, and she said that she didn't know. 'I haven't been brought up to want anything, because I had everything I wanted.'

'There must be something you want, though, that your old man can't provide.'

'Tell me what *you* want,' she said, 'and then perhaps it will remind me of what I could want. Maybe I've been too happy to want much.'

'Or too unhappy,' I said, mixing her up, often the best way of getting the truth out of people. Since I wasn't in love with her, or even falling for her, I could try this kind of trick.

'I'm not neurotic,' she said defiantly, 'if that's what you mean. My father's started going to a psychiatrist, but I never will.'

I nearly slipped off the seat at the idea of the great Claud Moggerhanger spilling his past every Tuesday and Thursday on a headshrinker's couch. In fact, when the humorous point had gone, it actually disturbed me to think of it. 'What does he go there for?'

She took the cigarette I offered. 'Maybe to relax, to pass the time. He's nowhere near barmy, believe me. But he likes to keep up to date with the fads. All the Moggerhangers do.'

'Even you?'

'You just tell me what you want out of life,' she said, 'and then I'll tell you.'

'I don't want to have to wonder what I want,' I said, doing my best. 'I want to live so that I never have to stop to ask myself what my ambition is or what I'm going to do. That's what everybody does. They want this job or that house or a car. They want to become a foreman, a director, or a manager. They have hopes of owning this or that, or they set their target on marrying a certain woman who it looks impossible for them to get. And when they have all these things they'll want something else, and when there's nothing else for them to want, or their spirit is so broken that they can't want or strive for anything in any case, they have a convenient accident and die, or just die. To want is the Devil's own trick. To live without wanting is God's blessing – though I don't believe in God or the Devil. Yet it was a black day in my life when I switched from not wanting to wanting, and I don't know when it happened. Probably before I was born, when I was still in my mother, or during the few minutes before my first feed. But I still only swing between the two like a skinned monkey looking for its skin. One minute I want, and the next minute I'm full of innocence. It's all mixed up mostly, because often when I want so that I'm ready to die getting it, that's when everything is hopeless and there's not a chance of me getting it. When I'm in the agreeable mood of not wanting, all I want to do is to stay alive. In the wanting frame of mind I'm so much full of want that I don't know what I want, or if I do it's so many things that I don't know what to try for first, and so end up not trying for any of them. So I get blown around like a straw, and in the meantime live more or less all right by doing as little work as possible.'

'It doesn't seem to me that you're telling me the truth.'

I laughed. 'It doesn't seem so to me, either. But I'm trying, though. You tell me what truth is, and I'll give you an ever-lasting lollipop. I won't know what I want till I've got it, and that's the truth, but it frightens me. It means I've got no control over my life, and though I've no right to have any because

246

I'm so lazy, the fact gnaws at my craw nevertheless. What I often want is to have a few thousand pounds every year so that I could buy a small house and live there without worrying or doing any work.'

'That's not much,' she said. 'You could easily get that.'

'Could I?' I was encouraged.

'It doesn't seem too much to me. I'm surprised you want so little.'

This flummoxed me, and for a while I didn't know how to go on. We got to Chillon, and didn't go to the castle but sat at a café and went on talking while we held hands. First we were outside, but then a great thunderstorm burst over the lake, and we went in, to get more cream cakes and coffee down us. The sky was pink, and a flash of lightning split it like a pomegranate. Then it turned suddenly metal-blue, and a ripple of far-off thunder exploded into a great noise, shaking the floor under my feet.

'The greatest torment in life,' I said, 'is not to know what you want out of it, but I don't know what I want out of it because I don't know what it can give me. That's what education is for, I suppose. It doesn't teach you much, I'm sure, but it tells you what you can get, or expect. And the fact is that I don't want any career or job that can be offered to me. Apart from the fact that I'm not fit or qualified to get anything that might appeal to me, I don't trust any of them to do *me* any good. It's not that that sort of thing isn't for the likes of me, so much as that I'm not for the likes of them. The fact is that nothing I could do is of any value to people, though even if it were I still wouldn't do it. I don't want to be used, and I don't want to use, so you can see how difficult it is for me to tell you what I want out of life. I can easily tell you what I don't want. Maybe I won't always feel like this, but I certainly can't tell at the moment. A long-term policy isn't my cup of tea. All I'd like right now is for us to be back in my room at the hotel, so that we can be alone together.'

She showed her milk-white teeth in a laugh, which made a great contrast to her dark ringlets. 'You're just greedy,' she said. 'If you don't know what you want out of life you just end up grabbing all the small things, and getting nothing big and worthwhile.'

'That's a good philosophical point,' I said. 'But if you live well until you're ninety, then go out with a hallelujah on your lips, what bigger thing do you want than that? The best life is one that doesn't give you time to think. My life is already ruined by talking like this. Yours will be too if you aren't careful. We're birds of a feather, in a way, and after so much thinking we ought to enjoy it and not bother too much with what we want out of life. So let's get away from this view of walls and water and go back to my room at the hotel.'

'I know I shouldn't,' she said, to my surprise, putting her arm through my arm, and squeezing it so that I got the warmth of her body, 'but I feel like that as well.'

We walked back towards the bus, and I felt like a hero, as if all I lacked was a pipe in my mouth, and I was back at the age of fifteen, a firestone dip to centuries ago. If every year seemed like a hundred I really would live for ever. I was embarrassed at the tiddlywink leaping around inside my trousers, but the golden coat hit it safely till it quietened down a bit. We necked a few kisses in the bus, but the honest Swiss stared, so we left off and sat, almost glumly, not able to say much, now that we had committed ourselves.

It started to rain, and I wondered if she wanted to back down, but she didn't. Nobody said anything at the desk when I asked for the key and we went up to my room, not like in deep-blue puritanical old England, or so I had heard. As soon as we got inside and I'd seen to the lock we gobbled all over each other under the roof and the rain, to the tune of the wet pigeons warbling outside. It was afternoon and almost evening, and our naked bodies skimmed about like a couple of snakes, and I swamped her before even getting in. We didn't seem to mind which end was which, and Polly Moggerhanger did as much gobbling as I did, which I wasn't used to at all up to then. Not only I knew what I wanted (in this, at any rate) but she did too, and I hadn't met such an even match before. It was the sort of lovemaking that pulled my backbone out of place, seemed to heave my spine off centre. Yesterday's colossal expenditure of energy had put me in the way of showing Polly what was what, because I felt as if I'd been worn down to a pole so that not much of my body was left to feed off me. It had only itself to look after, and so could give all its attention to the present requirements, a perpendicular mangonel stiffening my attacks so that at some moments she was both delighted and frightened.

Four hours later we crept down to the dining-room for refuelling, both of us bruised and wacked-out, and quiet as we sat looking at each other, waiting for the food to come, which we then went into with the same gusto as had been previously used in attacks on each other, not talking much during the whole meal, as if our first prolonged time together had accounted for fifty million words that we need not now ever say.

Even so, it wasn't exactly like a church between us, and I had to keep my end up by telling her stories out of my rich past and varied family. She enjoyed those most about my drunken Irish grandparents, so once on to this line I could go on for a long time without running short of material, and I found myself making up stories, recounting them as if they were true, because she could never know the difference as long as my voice didn't hesitate or change tone. Music was playing in the background from *The Merry Widow*, or some such Viennese slop, and I said: 'Do you remember, darling, how we climbed the Matterhorn in 1905? What a lovely time we had – though it was a pity when our ten guides fell two thousand feet and were never seen again. What a beautiful view from the top! I shall never forget it, because this music reminds me of it. Fortunately, the guide carrying our portable gramophone wasn't one of those who slipped, and we put on this record and listened to it while we drank our champagne.'

I made up fantasies of what we'd done during the life we'd been together, trekking across deserts that had killed all but one of our hundred camels by the time we walked into the last oasis (where our Rolls-Royce was waiting), sweating through jungles where two of our children had been eaten by tigers (she laughed aloud at that one) and I had been brought to the edge of death by a savage dose of Blackhead Fever. We sat over our wine till the waiter brought the bill as a gentle hint that the place was about to close down, and then we went up to my room again, and made use of the night for as long as we could keep awake.

We travelled back to London on the same plane. I thought this was a bright idea in case any of the customs men remembered my face. If they did, and wondered why I was going out, they would know the reason if they saw me coming back with a beautiful young woman. And if I left through the airport next week they might think I was only off on the same dirty errand again. I felt that William Hay would approve of this bit of bluff. The long bus of a plane was only half-full, and after the light went out about removing our safety belts, and the long climb towards heaven began, I told Polly to come with me to the back of the plane. 'I want to go to the toilet,' I said, giving a wink, 'so keep me company on the way.'

There was no one around the doors, so I opened one and told her to get inside. Then I followed in, and snapped the catch behind us. 'What an idea!' she said, 'I'd never have thought of it. I suppose you've done this often with your casual pick-ups?'

We closed in a bout of hugger-kiss: 'I just thought of it. There's no other place except the baggage compartment and I don't know how to get to that – unless I ask the pilot for a key. But I'm so much in love with you that I can't bear not to be able to touch you in the right places. Anyway I've got a question, and it's the sort I can't ask unless I'm able to kiss you while I'm doing it.'

She leaned against the sink. 'What is it?'

'Will you marry me? I know it's absolutely potty to ask, but I'm doing it without too much thought, because that would spoil it. Don't answer me. I don't want to know yet. I just want to say how I can't bear for us to come back to earth after these few days. If you've no wish to see me again, I'll understand. But I don't feel like that, and don't want you to think I do, even if you decide you want to feel that way. I'm not spoiling it, either, by asking you to marry me. You don't know me yet. Maybe you never will, but you will with every minute you stay with me. I just want you to know when you walk off this plane how intensely I feel, and I can't think of any other way to tell you than this. Even asking you to marry me isn't the end of it. It's only as serious as a passionate kiss, but that is very serious with me.'

Her full and pretty face was turned to me, and I could see my own face in the mirror behind her, full of pain and confusion, greed and lies and love.

The plane dropped a few feet, and she clung to me. 'So don't answer,' I went on. 'That's not what I want, not urgently. I'm saying this so that you'll know I'm honest and am telling no lies. It's something I suddenly wanted to say. I've never said it before, and I'll never say it again, not to anyone else. Just remember it, sweet Polly, and tell me anything you like for an answer, but don't talk about what I've just said, unless you absolutely must because it's burning its way out of you. Then I'll hear it and wallow in it, because I feel about you as I never have for anyone else before.'

We went beyond speech, touched and teased each other, sometimes her eyes closed, sometimes mine, as we kissed and struggled to get our way in that impossibly furnished room. Fortunately the engines made enough noise, due to those superlative modern designs that put them near the tail, and our cries weren't heard. The door handle rattled when we were too far gone to take much notice, and presumably whoever wanted to use the place for its proper purpose had found the opposite one vacant or had waited till it was. Polly got her full coming, because she finally sat on me and worked herself up and down, and I got it too, a fountain of thick elixir shooting into the flesh-filled sky of her.

When we crept back to our places the stewardesses gave us funny looks as they handed our trays of food. One of them smiled at me on every trip up and down the gangway, and she was so much Polly's opposite that I was quite attracted by her, and wanted to take her up to the back as well in my beastly and incorrigible fashion. But we tucked into our second breakfast as if we hadn't eaten for a week, and this time I ordered a full bottle of champagne, which the stewardess presented to us with exaggerated ceremony as if we had just been married and were going to England for our honeymoon. I began to wonder whether the captain himself wouldn't be down to congratulate us and wish us long life together as part of the airline's service, because certainly the engineer gave us a knowing gaze as he went to the back of the plane, as if the girls had been talking about us up front and spilling what they'd thought we'd been doing.

Polly ate with her head down, all modesty, and I thought that maybe she was reflecting on our adventure and, caught in the public gaze because of it, was holding it against me and wouldn't want to know me any more when we'd landed. But she said: 'I remember that when we first met you said you never told anyone that you were in love with them, that it wasn't the sort of thing you did, that you just let the relationship develop, and never used the word love.'

'I've been waiting for you to bring this up. It's true. I don't know what's come over me since then. This is so new, I haven't felt such a thing about anybody before, and that's why I say it. Obviously.'

'Obviously,' she said.

'I talk too much.'

'I don't mind at all,' she answered. 'I like it in fact. All the boys I've known don't talk. Not the way you do. They say things, but they don't talk. Your sort of talk makes me feel human, but theirs just makes me feel more and more apart from them. Not that I believe everything you say. Belief doesn't come into it. But people aren't together unless they talk.'

'Or do the other thing.'

'You're mostly silent then.'

'My mouth is otherwise occupied,' I said, feeling slightly disturbed by her new mood of seriousness.

'I don't believe anything,' she said, 'when it comes to talk. I've been let down so often, except by my own father, and he isn't a man who talks very much, not to me, anyway. I only believe things when they've happened, and then I know whether I've been let down or not. I'm so mixed up, Michael, I don't know what to say.'

I felt sorry for her, and in some strange way for myself as well. Just after making love was a bad time to strip oneself down to the fibres like this, though God knows there didn't seem any other time when it might be possible to do it properly. She was right, I suppose, in choosing to do it now, though I might have been the one to start it if she hadn't. I'd noticed before that the worst quarrels, or the most intense talk, only come after a wonderful bout of love.

'I've had more of a sheltered life than you imagine,' she said. 'The people I should have been staying with in Geneva have already phoned my father to say I haven't been seen these last two nights. In any case he'll be waiting for me at the airport when we land, so maybe you'd better not come out with me, especially since he knows you.'

I was only too willing to accept her advice, not wanting to tangle with Moggerhanger a second time. I wasn't afraid of him, but I had been strenuously advised by William Hay not to get into trouble during my run of smuggling trips. It was a pity though that I couldn't go through the customs with Polly on my arm, which had been the reason for my arranging to travel back with her. I gave my telephone number, and took hers, neither of us knowing when we'd be able to contact each other again, never mind see each other. The light went on to douse fags and fasten seat belts, and we suddenly broke through the clouds to see Battersea Power Station below, without having had any time at all even to get properly stuck in to the unresolved questions that were starting in earnest to eat us away.

I went down the steps behind Polly, feeling like one of the walking wounded as I let her get far in front. But I ran and caught her up, and we kissed wildly before turning into the arrival lounge.

'I love you,' she said. 'I held back from saying it, but I do.' She went to the ladies, and I walked up and down. Half in fun I glanced at the messages rack, and saw an envelope with my name on it. I took it down and tore it open, thinking it was for someone of the same name but curious to see what it said. 'Number nine is good today. Hope you had a successful trip to Leningrad.' So I let Polly get her luggage first, and she went through the customs with only a brief question from them and a half-smile. And I went through Gate Nine as instructed, though I saw no reason to do so because I only said I had nothing to declare, which was the truth for once, and then I was through and out of the place in time to see Moggerhanger's head going down the steps to the floor below.

I hung around a while, then went below and got the bus back to town.

William was waiting at the flat, himself just back from a quick trip to the Lebanon. He sat on the living-room couch in his dressing-gown, and Hazel came in with a tray of coffee. She was a whore from Soho, with a hard face and voluptuous body, who visited him now and again, and he gave her the wink to clear out while we were talking. His cigarette smoked from a ridiculously long holder, and he sat back to hear my story, which I supposed he might deliver later to the Jack Leningrad Organization. Either that, or I had too big an idea of their thoroughness, and if this was the case then I must already be getting too outsized for such an outfit.

'You've got something else for next week,' he said when I'd finished. As he swallowed his coffee the skinbone and ligaments of his throat shook and convulsed, as if he'd been hit there with an invisible rubber sledgehammer while it was on its way through. 'They'll tell you where to in the morning.' He poured another cup, while Hazel sang to herself in the bedroom.

'What are you going to do with the money you earn?' I asked.

'Haven't thought about it yet, my old lad. Mother's coming down from Worksop next week to spend a couple of days. I'm fixing her up in a hotel. I'll shunt her round the usual tea-caddy places, like Tower Bridge and Buckingham Palace.'

'Sounds lovely. In fact it's touching.'

'Don't get bloody sarky, Michael. I'm only human, after all.'

'That's the trouble with both of us, I suppose.'

'What's splitting your tripes, though? I've seen plenty of blokes come back, and they're usually cock-a-hoop with having done it in safety, but you're a bit down in the sludge about it.'

'I'm different. It wears me out, and I can't help but show it.'

'Ah,' he said. 'You're the genuine bloody article, and that's

254

a fact. It's better you're like that, right in touch with yourself, than some of the over-confident young hotheads we could get our hands on. Just the sort we need, you are. When you decide to put on an act your soul goes into it so that nobody would ever twig. Get some snooze, then we might go out for a quiet feed somewhere. I'll pack Hazel off. She won't mind. Won't bloody-well have to.'

'Thinking of getting married?' I asked.

'Not in this game. Later, maybe.' Neither of us had our feet on the ground, but we belonged to the world, for all that. But as I lay down in the spare room and thought about Polly, I got frightened, as if only now the full trembles at passing the customs loaded with gold had come upon me. The sky seemed black and I shook in every limb. The reality of my trip seemed like a dream, and like a dream it made me more afraid than reality. I felt a coward, and thought I might not do it any more. Yet when I woke up I knew I would, because being with an aim, an ambition, or even a plan, robbed me of that final edge of courage that helped me to stand by a negative decision. All this is hindsight perhaps, but hindsight is still only part of what existed at the actual time. My memory is clear enough for me to know this. My only positive act, if it can be so called, and I believe it can, was to let myself drift with events, out of curiosity to see where it would take me, and out of lethargy because I didn't have the wit or strength to do anything else. But I told myself to fight off the black and woolly dog, not to worry, to hold on, to calm myself and let life take its course since I wasn't able to steer the crazy airship of it, comforting myself with the thought that maybe I'd be more and more able to as I got older. But this last was only half hinted at, a grain of dust in the middle of the moon that I might never be able to get out to the light of day. I wondered what was in that grain, whether I would ever catch it between my two thumbnails like a flea and split it from end to end so that blood ran out.

William was waking me up but my head felt as thin as a post. He pushed a cup of tea towards my face and the smell of it went into me like jollop. 'Get this,' he said, a wide grin behind the steam. 'It'll help you to stand on your feet instead of your arse. You can't stew in your own self all night.'

'Why not?'

'You might well ask, but you can't. Here's your wage packet from the gaffer. There's thirty tenners in it. The easiest putty you'll ever earn.'

I took the long envelope and put it under my pillow. 'It wasn't that easy.'

He sat in the armchair and watched me with his gimlet grey eyes, that were full of expression when they were trying to read me, as they were now. 'What's biting you, then?'

'The rats. They've been at me since last Saturday afternoon. Ever been in love, Bill?'

His left leg jerked back, as if the reflexes under the knee had been hit. 'It wasn't the air hostess, was it? If it was, forget it. Under their white aprons they're just like anybody else.'

'You didn't answer my question.'

'The answer's no,' he said. 'I was in love with my father, but he was killed down the pit when I was seven. While he was alive I didn't know I was in love with him, but when he died I knew I'd never get over it and love anybody else – except maybe my mother, but she's still alive, so it's still only an infatuation. There's lots of women I like, and some I wanted to marry, but as for love, I can't say I have. I've often wondered about it, when it's going to happen and if it ever will, but I've been waiting so long that I've given up hope. I broke my heart as a kid, before I could understand what was what, not altogether over my father, but over what came after. The general misery of our lives. There was nothing to live for except life itself, nobody even to say we were living like this so that tomorrow would be better. I couldn't stand it. I was made to despair too young. After that I couldn't fall in love – not at all.' He flicked his ash halfway across the room. 'I'm not moaning about it. I sometimes think that English hearts weren't strong enough to bear that much.'

'Don't you want revenge, then?' I said, thinking how much better off I'd been than he had.

'On who? Even if I knew I wouldn't want it. I wasn't so crushed that I wanted revenge. Revenge is the last resort of the dead in spirit. I enjoy life too much to think about that. As for love – we always get back to it, don't we? – well, I'm resigned to it never happening, but don't think I'm unhappy about it because I'm not. That's the way my life went, and now that I know it's settled that way, I feel easier in myself. It's no use clamouring over things your common-sense tells you you'll never get, is it? Some people I suppose would eat their own bollocks to save their fingernails, but not me, mate. I'm doing all right now, and I want it to stay like that till I decide what to do with the money I'm piling up. I'll be worth a lot soon, and do you know what I'm going to do? I'm going to buy a smallholding, go into the market-gardening business. I'll get a cottage and three or four acres in Notts with the cash I've stashed. My mother can stay with me if she likes, and if I meet a woman who'll team up and work at it the same as I do, then I'll be satisfied.'

'I hope you make it then,' I said. 'Maybe it's true that you have to be forty to realize what you want out of life.'

'I've known that since I was twenty. But I've not admitted it to myself or spoken it out loud. It's been laying low. I only yap about it now that there's a chance of it coming about, and no fucking peradventure about it. But tell me the stuff on this bint that's got your heart going up and down like a yo-yo. I can envy you that much at least.'

'It's somebody I met before I went away, but there's no point talking about it.'

'There's every point. If you don't talk you choke, and if you choke you rot. You go all black inside and explode when you're fifty. Horrible mess. I believe it's called cancer, the plague that afflicts the silent type with the stiff upper lip.'

'Well, I'll never get that disease. I'll just have to get in touch with her.'

'Let's get out,' he said, 'and get in touch with some food. I'm hollow.'

We went to the restaurant in Soho where I'd first met up with him again after our trip from the North, and drank a bottle of wine each, because William said it was his birthday. He insisted that we do no less because it was, he said, with beady eyes set on me, the first one he'd spent in affluence for a good few years. And not only that, but a birthday was always special and not to be treated lightly because it meant that you had survived another year of life, had fenced off death, maiming, starvation, and black night of one sort or another. You could put your fingers to your nose at the year that had gone, while setting yourself to greet the oncomer with respect. 'A birthday is a time to count the miracles,' he went on, 'and tot up my luck. When I was a kid nobody bothered with them. They went by unnoticed because we were too busy breathing. The fact that I've got time to remember it these days shows how well-off I am.'

'You're in a fine mood,' I laughed, 'but how old are you?'

He sliced up his escalope. 'Thirty-nine's the score, and I feel every year of it.'

I went with him to St Pancras Station to meet his mother. When he saw her come out of a second-class carriage he started shouting, 'I sent ten pounds for you to travel first class, and now you do this dirty trick on me. It ain't right, Ma.'

'Don't you talk to me like that.' I backed away because I couldn't believe all that screeching came from her. In any case she aimed it at me, and for a moment I thought she was right off her pot and that she took me for William, but then it was plain that the mechanism of her eyes was at fault. 'What would I do in first class, you great loon? You don't know who you might meet in them places. And don't snap at me like that. Nobody'd know you were my own son. After all I've been through! I've a good mind to get back on this train and go back to Worksop.'

William turned pale, but bent down to kiss her. 'Don't do that Ma,' he pleaded like a little boy, 'I wanted you to do it in comfort, that's all.' This seemed a bit rare when I remembered his own journey. He'd certainly rung a lot of changes in his belfry during this last year. 'Where's your suitcase?' he asked, when the circle of listeners began to clear off.

She was a small thin person, an absolute proud wreck, with a pale-blue coat and a powder-blue hat over her coal-grey hair. She had glasses and false teeth, and it wasn't possible to tell her age, though in spite of these trimmings she was nearer sixty than forty, shall I say. 'I forgot it. Like as not it's in the carriage still.'

'I'll go and get it.' When I came back with it, my socket tearing at its load, I saw them going towards the exit, where William had a taxi waiting. The taxi driver swore at the weight of it: 'What's in here, lead?'

'Gold bars,' Bill laughed. 'She brings her own coal with her!'

His mother pulled me into the taxi beside her: 'It's nice to have two young men with me, on my first trip to London. It *is* a big place, isn't it, Bill? Bigger than Worksop, anyway.' I got out at Cambridge Circus, not wanting to hear her comments on Nelson's Column.

I walked into the Square, nevertheless, and joined the throng. My hat was jerked off by the wind, and I ran across the flagstones to get it, under the spray of both fountains, scattering pigeons right and left. I looked at every girl's face to see if it was Polly Moggerhanger's. I don't think I was in love with her. There was too much of a bite in it for that, as if I was the apple that Eve had bitten, rather than Adam himself who'd got booted out of paradise and must finally have felt proud of it.

I bought a tin of corn from a stand and fed the pigeons, holding my palm flat and watching a bit of real greed as they jostled each other to gobble it up. I liked their button eyes, as they pecked and trusted me not to grab them while they had their fill. I bought tin after tin, and the more they scoffed the more wary they got, so that while I could have snatched them easily when they were hungry, I had only to lift a finger now and they went off in a cloud. I was a friend of all the world, in my coat of many colours, and the corn vendor gave me a couple of free tins till finally the pigeons were strutting over the corn without picking it up, because other people were podging them as well.

I went into a callbox and dialled the Moggerhanger number. A woman answered, maybe her mother. 'Is Polly in?'

'No,' she said, and hung up. I walked towards the Strand hoping to see her. A jeweller's window interested me for a few minutes, then I doubled back and went into Lyons for lunch. I wasn't hungry and left the plate spilling with cake-scraps and cellophane. I poured half a bottle of red sauce over it and shambled away.

There was a queue outside a theatre, so I followed it in and paid thirty bob for a seat. When the National Anthem played I didn't stand up, because I would have felt stupid if I had. But the rest of the herd were on their feet, and a voice behind said that I should show respect, so I called out, still on my arse, that if I did get up it would only be to push his patriotic face in. I didn't hear anything more, and the lights went down.

A man came on the stage and went rampaging through somebody's living-room, shouting how rotten the world was. His wife came in, and he shouted at her till she couldn't do anything else but burst into tears. He was well dressed and well fed, and didn't look as if he had much to complain about, but when his wife's brother came in and told him to pack it in, he went for him as well, bawling until he too sat on the settee with his head in his hands feeling like the biggest rotter in the world and not knowing what to do about it. The hero didn't tell him, but just went on raving, and when the brother's girl-friend came in he shouted at her till she went into hysterics and he had to throw water over her from the tap, still raging as he did it. When an older woman hove in who seemed to be his mother, he started on her, so that the scene looked like a cross between a looney-bin and somebody's living-room where the television set had broken down. Then the mad bastard started shaking his fist at the audience, calling us some wonderfully colourful phrases. At this I got up and pushed along the row so that people threatened me for making such a noise, but with as much disturbance as I could muster, I went out into daylight. That's what you get from joining a queue, I thought, though strangely enough I felt better than I had before I went in.

I walked to Finchley Road and met Bridgitte coming up the steps towards Smog's school. She was dressed more like her old au pair self in a set of black slacks and a mauve jumper. Her face was thin and pale, unlike her normally white and buttery Dutch skin, and she was dark under the eyes as if she'd been through a rough and sleepless time since we'd last met. She smiled and held out her hand.

'Why didn't you phone?' I said, accusingly.

'Oh, I did, but a man answered and told me you were out of the town.'

'That's true,' I said. 'I went up to the estate, to see Mother. She's had a stroke, and it don't seem she can last much longer. If she does pop off I'll come into half a million, though she threatened to leave it to a dogs' home when I was there, speaking only from the right side of her mouth. Anyway, that's unimportant. How are you?'

'I don't know. My husband went away yesterday, to Glasgow for a week, to a sort of conference. At least, that's what he said, so don't laugh. But it's true because I saw all the letters he received about it.'

A heavy weight hit me in the shoulder, and when I spun round another one caught me in the gut. It was Smog's satchel, packed with books that taught him how to read and write. I hoped it would be soon, then forgave him: 'If you were two inches taller, I'd blow your block off. Don't do it when you are older or you'll get what for.'

Bridgitte clouted him on the back of the head and sent one school cap skimming under a car. He was about to dive for it, under the bonnet of another, but I pulled him by the arm and saved his life. 'For God's sake,' I said, 'watch it.'

'I couldn't care less.'

'Well I could.' I picked the cap up and put it where it belonged. 'Let's go and stuff ourselves with cake and tea, shall we, Smog?'

'We'll go back to the house,' said Bridgitte. 'I can't face one of those awful English cafés where you get nothing but thick tea and fatty cakes.' The bus landed us somewhere on the rim of Hampstead, then we walked along a few quiet roads to the new Anderson home. The front of it looked like a British Railways airliner stranded on a hillside, and we climbed a flight of concrete steps to get to it.

She showed me into a long living-room with windows from floor to ceiling, one side looking over a lawn. Smog threw off his coat and sat on the floor trying to finish a jigsaw puzzle that Bridgitte had three-quarters done, but he lost patience, broke it up, and started to read one of his school books.

Bridgitte pressed a bell and a swarthy middle-aged woman came in and said: 'What you want?'

'Make us some tea, please, Adelida.'

'You had it already,' Adelida said, 'before you went to the school.'

'I want some more, for three, Goddamn it.'

Adelida went off, grumbling.

'A rough life,' I said.

'Impossible.' She got up. 'I'll have to see to it myself,' and went out, so that I fell to helping Smog with a page of his reading. His chaotic over-energized mind seemed to have grasped on to learning as something to steady himself by, for he read and wrote as well as I had on leaving school at fifteen. When tea was finished he asked me to play draughts, but after a couple of games he beat me at it, so I stopped thinking he was only a kid and played better, but even so it ended in stalemate. 'Do you play chest?' he asked.

'Chess,' I told him. 'No, I don't. I'll learn, though, and next time I come we'll have a game.'

'You're fairly ignorant.'

'I'll get better,' I said, 'and catch you up one day.'

'But you're old already, and that's difficult for you.'

'Who does all this to him?' I asked Bridgitte.

'His father,' she said. 'And his mother before that. He's not as bright as he seems.'

'I am,' Smog said. 'I'm top of my class at school.'

'Anyway,' I said to him, 'you shouldn't boast, or you'll turn into a monster.'

He jumped on my knee. 'Really? Then I can frighten everybody.'

'You do already,' I said.

The idea of another Swiss trip was burning me, because I hoped to see Polly on it. I knew this to be a crackpot fantasy, which could have nothing to do with Bridgitte sitting on my knee in the living-room after Smog-the-limb-of-Satan had been put to bed. Life was overflowing, for while Bridgitte was loving me I was fixed with all my wants on Polly who was God knew where. I pressed back her kisses absent-mindedly, yet firm enough for her not to suspect anything or leave off loving me. Maybe she felt I was a little distant but this made her try harder, almost smothering me, so that I was shamed into making some semblance of matching her, until this brought us blow by blow on to the carpet and rolling around at the bottom of passion's pit. When she pulled at my tie, I parted the buttons of her blouse to get her breasts close to me, for at the moment, that was the only part of her I seemed to want, and when she tried to get my shoelaces undone I eased the zip of her skirt and drew it off. Her blonde hair was down and swathed all over me, yet still I only saw the features of Polly who even in the extremes of her sexual throe kept that faint tilt of irony on the left upper lip. Our rolling drew us slowly towards the stairs, and halfway up I opened her legs wide and licked her there till she came, her head falling backwards. I was a thousand miles from her, my bowels as cold as underground moss, so there seemed nothing I could not do to her, and with me in this frosty and distant mood, she became wilder than I'd ever seen her.

It seemed impossible that she wouldn't begin to suspect we weren't as close as she thought we were, but when we got into the bedroom and I was put to it at last to strip down to my feathers, she took my diffidence to heart in such a way that it appeared only to prove an undying love, a tribute to her that no one had ever paid before. So at last, as I felt all this, I began to rise, at the moment when I thought I'd never be able to, not that night at least, and not with her. I slid in like a dream, and kept at it with her under me till she blew the walls of herself on to me, then I changed her on to her back and packed in every inch so that she grasped the pillows to try and take even more, yet at the same time escape it. The more exquisite and ferocious it got, the plainer did I see Polly and know she was the one I wanted to be with, and when every part of me finally turned into a fountain it was only in an effort to put out these sprouting flames because I was crying out Polly's name, seeing no one else, and knowing I was in nobody but her. I bit my lips, and my inside heart cried out. There was no stopping the tears, and my cheeks were wet. She noticed this, and kissed them, talking to me in a crazy mixture of Dutch and

English, and I was forced to begin returning her words, and her kisses.

'Michael,' she cried, 'take me away. Let's go off together.'

'Yes,' I said, 'all right, love' – and kissed her madly so that I wouldn't have to say any more. I began to wonder how I'd come to let myself in for this, and felt my moral fibres going rotten under the force of this tough reflection. Yet in a way I did love Bridgitte, though not all of me, not the nine-tenths in the teeth of Polly. I wondered whether Polly knew how much she was haunting me, how much the black side of her was curled up in my gut, how much I loved her, in fact. And I wondered why, if this was so, she'd put herself so far beyond my reach. I wanted to unstick myself from Bridgitte and run down to the phone, to call again in case she'd come home in the meantime. But I couldn't move, because Bridgitte was lying across me, so I rolled over her, and we went on with our kissing match, a furore growing between us, anything but talk beyond the normal words of love, when all her thoughts in that direction went on a road I did not want to go.

I grew cold again, half ashamed of those distant kisses, because she deserved more than that. Try as I could I couldn't get closer, and make our kisses properly meet. It seemed the work of only half a man, though I ploughed her up to scratch when the fire finally took hold and I could let go. It wasn't a prolonged marvellous shooting into her from the depthless part of myself, but it went in from the surface like a shower of steel dust. In spite of this and never thinking about anyone except Polly, I had the strongest definite desire when Bridgitte did finally get a look in, to make her pregnant. I don't know why, but I was detached enough to be able to think of this, and I wanted her to have a baby. It was this thought that, towards the end of the evening, more or less pushed Polly away from my mind, and though at the same time it didn't get me much closer to Bridgitte, at least I didn't feel I was being such a bastard to her.

Instead of staying all night in the haven of my love I went back to the flat, on foot, to see if there were any messages regarding the next trip. It was three in the morning, and there weren't, so

I looked forward to my next collision with Bridgitte, and went to sleep.

In the morning William didn't even have time to phone his mother at her hotel, for both of us were snappily told to get over to the flat in Knightsbridge with our passports. After a quick breakfast I went off, hoping to get a taxi before reaching the bridge. William was to leave ten minutes later so that we wouldn't be seen going into the place together.

The ten-o'clock rush hour was pouring in, though no jams were forming yet. A small souped-up car charged out of a side street and ground itself obliquely into a bus. There was a rending of glass, and a dull scraping crunch of expensive tin. People came off the bus, and the driver got down. Nobody was hurt, and I hurried on, but it was a bad omen just the same. I got into a taxi, and lit a cigarette, unnerved by the reverberation of that impact. You either believe in omens or you don't, I thought. I don't. If you don't, I suppose you believe that your fate is decided by heaven, or whatever it is, and not yourself. Believing in omens is the same as hoping that you have some control over your fate. You don't. The cigarette tasted like foul soil. Omens are there to frighten you, not to warn you. I tried to cheer myself up on this, but didn't much succeed.

I hung about in the anteroom waiting for William, looking through hunting magazines. I thought he seemed a bit flustered when he did make it, but we were taken straight in by Stanley. I had the feeling that something was not right with the world, and heard the man in the iron lung shouting into a telephone, and when I saw him through the perspex bubble he was going at that mouthpiece as if intending to eat it. When he put it down he set to rubbing and wringing his hands to get the blood back into them. It seemed to me he wouldn't be in this job much longer.

'There's an emergency on,' he said, 'a big consignment to be shifted, and I want you two to do it, a hundredweight between you, this afternoon.'

'My mother's in town,' William said, with a smile. 'I thought I'd get these few days off.'

Jack Leningrad (or whatever his name was) grimaced, his

face pale white. 'You'll have ten years off if I see another wrinkle of complaint around the sides of your mouth, my boy.' He straightened his tie. 'I want you to go to Zurich, then Beirut, Mr Hay. You'll go to Paris, Mr Cullen. Your planes leave within five minutes of each other, so Stanley will drive you to the airport. Got the shakes already, Mr Cullen?'

He was looking straight at me, and he was right, because I had, and put my arm out to a chairback to stop myself falling. 'I'll be solid enough when the weight's on,' I said. It was too sudden, though I'd expected it from the moment we were called over.

In the car we decided that William would go through the customs first, and that I would follow almost immediately, so that we could have a drink before our different planes left. He made me promise to phone his mother and take her out in the morning, and I said I'd be glad to do this if all went well.

'Don't be dispirited, old lad,' he exclaimed, with that wide false-teeth smile of his. 'You'll go through with flying colours, I know you will. It's on the cards – not to mention the tea-leaves.'

'I read my horoscope this morning, and it said my business plans would go awry.'

'Forget it,' he said, wanting to thump me on the back, but finding the effort to lift his arm too great. The weight didn't bother me so much, but I felt as fat as a Michelin man, there for the world with its X-ray eyes to see. I hung around the bookstall, then walked towards the customs hall.

I stopped, ice at the heels of my feet. William was being interviewed by two customs men, and as I turned and walked away they were one on either side and heading him into a room. This is the end of him and me as well, I thought, panic in every vein and toe. This is the black finish of our trip down the Great North Road. I felt hunted, didn't know what to do nor even where to turn. The place wasn't busy and not many people were about, but I thought they were all police and narks ready to surround and rend me. I was so paralysed that I didn't even feel enough shame to tell me to pull myself together.

I went to the nearest lavatory, intending to stand there and piss while I thought out what to do. But there was no method in me, only fear and sweat that I'd never known before, and if I'd suspected such a thing lurked in me I wouldn't have taken this job on. I locked a lavatory door behind me and opened my coat, lifting out bars of gold and with shivering rapid hands dropping them into the lavatory. I piled all forty in and covered them with half a roll of toilet paper, wishing I'd never come to London but stayed and done my duty by Claudine, worked for her like an honest man should.

I left the toilet and went back into the hall. My idea had been to dump the gold and flee, hide on a remote island off Scotland for two years and hope I wouldn't get my throat cut for cowardice, but for some crazy reason I went to the door of the departure lounge, and looked across at the customs men. There was William, talking to them, a smile across his face as if they were two old friends he'd been at school with. This sight mixed me up, but only for a moment, for I saw him wave gaily, and walk on into the departure hall, being safely through.

Shaking off my bewilderment I went quickly back to the lavatory. A man was standing at the urinal having a piss, and another was drying his hands. I went back to the toilet, but the door was locked, the engaged sign showing. I dashed into the next one, thinking I'd jump over the top or crawl underneath and strangle the bastard who was having a crap in there so that I could get my gold, but the one I was in turned out to be the one I'd used, and when I ripped off the coils of toilet paper, the gold was underneath, every bar of it still there. It was the good luck of my life, and at its sight I calmed down, and slotted every piece back into my coat. After two minutes silence I went to a mirror and combed my hair, straightened my hat, picked up my briefcase, not caring whether my fate was being decided, feeling that the excitement was over at last, come what may. I was no longer a fat man to the world, because to myself it seemed that I had sweated all the flesh of my bones away.

I walked through, and no one even looked at me, beyond a formal glimpse at my passport. William was already by the bar with a light ale in front of him: 'What kept you, old smoke?'

'I thought your number was up,' I said, feeling a tremor of

the shakes coming back, 'when they started questioning you.'

He laughed, and ordered me a beer: 'Just routine.'

'The lousy poke-faced jack-snouts.'

'They're all right. Good lads, most of 'em. Got their job to do. No use hating them. That's the road to bad breath!'

'They searched you, didn't they?'

'Just to look in my wallet. It's the travel allowance they're worried about. I thought it was getting close but they didn't get anywhere near. Still, next time I'll use Gatwick. I'm a bit known here.' His plane was called, and off he went.

In Paris I took a taxi to an address on the Île de la Cité. I was blind to Paris, except for its rain, being disappointed at not having seen Polly on the way there. The longer it got since a glimpse of her, the worse it felt. I delivered my goods, and then, as instructed, took a taxi back to the airport, and waited till seven o'clock for a leg-up to London. I sat in the airport lounge and drank black coffee, passing a bit of the time angling for a sweet look from the waitress but not getting anywhere near.

By nine I was back at the Knightsbridge flat, where Stanley put an envelope in my hand with the usual amount inside. I was then let out again, no word sparking between us. I met a taxi by the door, and got home to find William's mother waiting for me. 'He said you'd look after me,' she said, as I took off my coat.

'Had dinner then, Mrs Straw?'

'No, my duck, but don't bother about me.'

'Well, I'm hungry. Let's go and have a chop or two.'

'That sounds lovely. Can I have green peas with it?'

'You can have strawberries and cream if you like.' I hadn't expected her to be dumped on me so soon, and had meant to crash fifty thousand feet into sleep now that I was home. But after my promise I couldn't just bundle her back to her hotel. She sat in an easy chair, with a good length of brandy on the arm. 'I met some people the other day, and they want me to go to their hotel for a drink tonight, love. I wrote their address down, so I'd be glad if you'll take me there.' She fumbled in her big white handbag and passed me the back of an envelope.

'We'll do that, then,' I said, glad there was a place to go to without having to decide. When I read the name it was the hotel I'd stayed at when I arrived in London, now written in a quick and keggy hand that depressed me, I don't know why. Mrs Straw put on her glasses, while I stared at the paper, as if to help me decipher it. I had nothing to fear. In my new guise they wouldn't even know me as the one who'd left without paying his bill.

'Come on then, Mother,' I said, jumping away from my sins of the past when they started to bite at my toecaps like hungry crabs. 'It'll be too late to eat at this hotel of yours, so we'll go to a restaurant.'

'Lovely,' she said, standing up. 'We can go there afterwards. Only for half an hour. They're ever such jolly people. A man and his wife, come from Chesterfield. They'll be ever so glad to see me.'

I hoped to stupefy her with food and wine before it came to that, so helped her into a new fur coat that William had bought for her. She talked about him through the dinner. 'He's always been as good as gold to me' – that sort of thing, till I thought I'd go screwy if she said another word in this tone but then I found myself listening, and actually enjoying the way she went on. 'He was always the same, even before his dad died, and that's going back a bit, I can tell you. I know he's been in prison and all that, but he's one of the best lads any woman could want.' She looked hard at me, as if wondering what effect her talk was having. It made me uneasy, because I hadn't seen such an honest look for a long time. It was a hungry look, that threatened to black me out. 'Tell me, my duck,' she said, 'what sort of work does he do?'

'Ain't he told you?'

'Ay, he has. But you tell me.'

'He does the same as me.'

'What do you do, then?'

'I'm a travelling salesman. A group of engineering firms got together and pooled their stuff, so some of us take samples of their production to various places abroad. It pays well, but it wears you out at times, so much running about.'

She wasn't eating much of her chops, not even touching the

269

tinned fresh peas: 'That's right. He told me all about it. But I wouldn't like owt to 'appen to him. I'd die if it did.'

'Aeroplanes don't crash nowadays. You shouldn't worry about that.'

She looked hard at me, not having believed a word of what I'd said: 'No, it's not that at all, and you know it. Don't you?'

I laughed: 'What, Ma?'

'I've lived longer than you think I have. Admitted, most of my life it's been under water from one sort of misery or another, but I've got eyes and ears and a mother's heart, and when I look at Bill I know he's living under a wicked strain, and there's summat he's keeping from me. I've got all my senses right enough. Knowing what I know and feeling what I feel, it pains me to come up against somebody like yo' who won't tell me the honest simple truth that wain't do a bit of harm to me after all I've lived through.'

Her face looked pale and made of paper. Bits of powder and rouge turned her head into a lantern, with two eyes for candles. My heart was tight at the sight of her. 'It's secret work,' I said. 'I can't tell you any more, so please don't ask me. But he's in no danger, not Bill. He's doing very well with his life at the moment, so you shouldn't worry about him at all. I'm telling you.' For God's sake believe me, I added under my breath. My words made her smile with relief, because I excelled in fervour. When I remembered it afterwards I wept that I hadn't told the simple but elusive truth.

'I'd better take you back to your hotel,' I said when the meal was finished.

'I must just nip to the other place first. It can't be far and we can take a taxi. Bill gen me ten pounds last night. He's been so generous to me.' I knew that in her fur coat she felt more cared for than she'd ever done in her life, and I hadn't the heart to make a fuss about not going where she wanted, so in ten minutes we were at the door of the hotel.

The manager behind the desk still had the same sharp ulcerous look on his face. 'Hello,' he said to me, 'back again? Thought we'd seen the last of you.'

'I decided to come and settle up.'

'Better late than never,' he said.

'I didn't know *you* had pals here as well,' said Bill's bright mother, her hand crooked in my arm.

'We'll be in the lounge,' I told the manager, 'so bring the bill into me, with a double brandy, and a shandy. One for yourself, as well.'

'When you came through that door just now I hardly knew you,' he smiled. 'You've prospered a bit since you pulled out so suddenly.'

I moved on, too exhausted to make much of a night of it in the lounge with Mr and Mrs Binns from Chesterfield, but they were happy and nice enough in their middle-aged way. They weren't as pleased to see Mrs Straw as much as Mrs Straw would have liked, but it ended better than it started, for I plugged them all to capacity before we left, and paid my bill of nearly twenty pounds into the bargain. The manager had tears of gratitude on the pouches of his eyes. I'd got him to take a couple more brandies: 'Nearly got thrown out because of you,' he confessed, 'because I'd had a few bad cases only a month before. You're the first one that ever came back to pay in all my experience. It's gladdened my faith in human nature a bit.' On that slimy note, with the five of us fit to break into *Auld Lang Syne*, I pulled Mrs Straw into a taxi and back to her hotel. The same cab got me home. I was too done in to take a bath, and fell flat on to my bed like a board of lead, sleeping till midday with neither faces nor white horses to disturb my blackout.

I was wakened by the flat bell ringing, otherwise I might have stayed buried in warm wool till past teatime. I took the deep yellow envelope from the telegraph youth, still too much asleep to wonder what was in it. I dropped it on the table, then fell back on my bed. Half an hour later I got up and opened it on my way to the bathroom. As the piss piped out of me I read:

= WILLIAM IN BEIRUT COOP STOP LUNG MOVING STOP ADDRESS FOLLOWING LOVE = LENINGRAD.

I surprised myself by catching on to it so quickly. Sun was coming in through the toilet window, so maybe that helped. Bill Straw had been caught in Beirut, and the man in the iron lung was being moved in a specially built pantechnicon through the London streets to another lair. Once he was installed, I would hear from them for a further assignment, unless the repercussions of international investigation swept us all into oblivion. I wondered what charge Bill would be on in the Lebanon, whether in fact the police there could fix him on anything at all, and somehow I couldn't take it as seriously as I would if he'd been grappled at London airport, and thrown into the nick here, where he wouldn't have got out in less than five years.

I set a kettle on the galley stove, and stood in my dressing-gown waiting for it to boil. I got the shakes, realizing I'd have to wait weeks for the kettle of news to boil. I'd be the last to get information from Jack Leningrad Inc, though I decided that when next called in for a job I'd threaten to smash that iron lung to bits with a hammer unless they told me all they knew. Worst of all, I had to phone his mother, but I decided to wait a couple of days, or till such time as she began to worry. I saw no point in upsetting her, by telling her immediately. If she asked why Bill hadn't come back I'd say I didn't know. And the next time she mentioned it she'd already be half inclined to receive bad news.

If Bill was really taken in Beirut, he was done for, in which case there was no reason why she shouldn't know what was what, providing I could put my cowardice at having to spill the news to one side.

In most parts of me I didn't believe it had happened, in spite of the fact that I'd been brought up to believe that telegrams didn't lie. But I knew that this feeling was my loss, since there was no doubt that it had happened. Not only was Bill hooked, but I began to see that maybe the danger would root me out. There'd been nothing but fear since I'd started this job. But if I began to get worried at last, it wasn't out of fear, only from wondering what it meant. This wasn't the sort of work for somebody like me, certainly not what I'd come to London for. It was a load on my back, exactly what I'd intended to avoid. I'd been trapped, but how and by whom, that was the question. I sat down to some tea and bread. I was in the middle of a quicksand bog, nobody within ten miles to come and talk to me while I went down. The trouble was I had no impulse to run. Somewhere, way back in the dark, my Achilles tendon had been cut, and I didn't grieve about that but I didn't know whether this was going to turn out to my advantage or not. Was it ever better to stay still, or to run? If I didn't get the impulse to run, then it was obviously better to sit still. When the impulse did come I'd run twice as quick and to a place twice as safe than I would if I set off somewhere without being absolutely impelled. So I made a virtue out of my idleness and sloth. When strength came out of weakness it had the force of self-preservation behind it, and that was what I depended on. There didn't seem much else at the moment.

I got dressed and walked into town. On the way I put my three hundred pounds into the bank, which now made six hundred on deposit for a wet and thundery day. I took out half a crown, and flipped it up, heads I would phone Polly, tails I would try Bridgitte. It clattered healthily as it hit the pavement, rolled into a gutter and down a grate, lost for ever. You just had to make your own decisions.

There was no reply from Bridgitte, so I dialled Polly's number. 'Hello?' said a man's voice which struck me as strange.

'Is that Polly?'

'Yes, what do you want?'

'I want to speak to Polly.' Somebody went by the phone booth, with a placard saying 'The Bomb Also Kills Children'.

'This is Polly. Who is that?'

'Michael.'

'Michael bloody who?'

'From Geneva. Remember?'

'Oh, yes. How stupid. I'm sorry.'

'I've got a few days off. Can I see you?'

'Come over,' she said.

'Is that all right?'

'Mum and Dad are in Ostend.'

'As soon as I can, then.' I put the phone down. Outside, I thought I'd dreamed it, but I knew I never had such dreams. With me, it was either reality or nothing.

Half an hour later I went up the drive of the Villa Mogger-hanger, smelling the luxury of fresh hedges and growing flowers. Grey clouds were flying away from London, racing for the hills and grass. José, the Spaniard, opened the door and welcomed me like an old friend. 'Mr Moggerhanger is out.'

'I've come to see Polly,' I told him. She was in the garden, so I found her clipping roses from a row of bushes near the back wall. I intended greeting her casually, so as not to alarm her, but she took my hands, hers cold, and I don't know how it happened but both of us were kissing straight away. 'I tried to get through to you half a dozen times, but your mother hung up on me. Then I had to do a trip to Paris.'

'I've been longing for you,' she said. 'I thought it was just going to end like the others, that once you got to know me, as you did in Geneva and on the way back, then you wouldn't want to see me any more.'

'It'll take at least a hundred years to get to know you,' I said. 'Let's go up West for lunch.' I was nervous of hanging around the Moggerhanger lair for too long in case Claud himself should suddenly spring up from the ground. My instinct told me to get out of the place, though I couldn't see rationally why, since Polly said he was in Ostend – though maybe he'd only gone there for a drink.

'I'd hate that,' she said. 'I'm turned off the middle of London. You've driven Dad's Bentley, haven't you?' We walked together along the path, and she suddenly threw all the roses she had collected behind a laurel bush.

'Like a dream,' I said, my arm warm where she went on holding it.

'Let's go somewhere, then. I've got the key to one of Dad's hideaways in Kent.'

'Why not?' I said, but playing it cool.

'Sit in the lounge and pour a drink, while I go up and dress.'

'I'll watch if you like.'

She kissed me quickly: 'No, I don't feel like it now.' Her bare pale legs went up the stairs, and I unlatched a tin of tomato juice, thinking of William trying to barter his way out of some Lebanese copshop with bars of gold, and of his poor old mother worrying herself daft as she knocked back shorts with her Chesterfield friends, while I'd been talked by feckless Polly into some mad adventure with Moggerhanger's house on wheels.

We sat high in the front as I stepped on the power over Hammersmith Bridge and went towards the South Circular, the tape-recorder playing *Tales from the Vienna Woods*, and me smoking one of the Moggerhanger's big cigars kept in the glove-box for special friends. Through Clapham a bowser was blocking the road, but there was no way of overtaking. 'That Cooper just did it,' Polly said.

'I want to live. I'll do it in my own good time.'

'The exhaust's giving me a headache,' she complained.

I put on the winkers, swung out, and swept forward. The bowser seemed a mile long, and travelling fast, but I got straight up to fifty, then saw a bus coming full on towards me. It was too late to brake. Headlights flashed me, and I couldn't go back. The bastard driving the bowser was set on getting me killed, didn't slow down, or go in even an inch. I supposed he was a good honest worker who thought that rich pigs who drove around in such expensive cars should be put up against a wall and shot – or crumpled to death under a bus.

Polly clutched me, and I thought what a wonderful way to die, but by twelve inches, a single foot and no more, I was in front of the bowser and just about safe, trembling in every inside limb, my tongue hollow, Polly half fainting against her seat, wondering how other people could be so rotten.

The road was empty up ahead, and I left the bowser behind, until at a traffic light on stop he drew in between me and the kerb. I leaned across Polly and wound down the window: 'Are you trying to kill me then, mate?' I said in my best Nottingham accent.

He wore a cap, and his broad face grinned: 'Yes.'

'Better luck next time, then,' and I shot forward as the lights changed to yellow. 'His eggs were fried too hard for breakfast.'

'I was scared to death,' she said.

'That's his idea of a joke. I grew up with people like that. Worked with them – for a little while. He just wanted to see if I'd lose my nerve and pull back. I could have done, but didn't. Still, it's not often we get a thrill like that, is it, love?'

She held my arm: 'Take care, though.'

'I wouldn't do anything else with you in the car. Myself I don't care about. I'm neither here nor there. Easy come, easy go. I've had a good time up to now, and if the Big Door suddenly fell on me I might have time for a grin before the blackout made a fossil of it.' This was the last thing I felt, but I needed to say it in case she'd seen how frightened I'd been when the bus nearly got me. 'I think you must have had a fairly awful life to get into that state,' she said. 'Are you still on that gold-smuggling job?'

We were on a dual carriageway, traffic thinner: 'I gave it up.'

'Since when?'

'My best friend got caught. So now I'm going straight, waiting to meet an honest girl to keep me on the right path.'

'That's not me, then,' she laughed, and I was surprised when, instead of saying how good it would be for me to give it up, she said I shouldn't really weaken and pull out just because my best friend had been caught, that now was the time to go on, because maybe no one else would be pulled in for a long time, like it was always safest to travel by plane just after a big air disaster. I hadn't lost my nerve overtaking a petrol lorry – and she did admire me for it, after all – so why lose it at something far less dangerous? For my part, it was all talk, because I never seriously intended resigning my lucrative position, and as far as not losing my nerve between the lorry and the bus, once I got there I had no option but to go on and get out of the trap. I hadn't lost my nerve, not totally, but all my fibres had melted, and my bones had been under the hammer, I knew that now, a handshake with my final moment that hadn't been final after all. Polly was out on a limb. She wasn't in my guts. I was sailing towards trees and hills, sorry the sea was but forty miles off, otherwise I'd have driven on as far as I could get around the world. 'You don't know me,' I said. 'I give nothing up. That's what makes me stupid, and lets me, live high. I had a chip on my shoulder but it turned into a bird and it wasn't a budgerigar, either. Nor a vulture, come to that. Just a kite to keep me a few inches off mother earth.'

'You're so funny,' she said, 'have you read any good books lately?'

'I thought it would come to this,' I laughed, taking her hand. 'Ever since I told you I loved you.' We went through a traffic jam in Tonbridge with the windows down and the radio sending out Beethoven's Pastoral Symphony. I forgot for a while the sort of car I was in, but realized it when I saw the other faces looking at me. 'When do we get to this place in the country?'

She leaned over and kissed me on the mouth: 'Don't lose patience. That would be even worse than losing your nerve. Another half-hour.

'I feel like an unlucky pilgrim, caught in the trap of England's arterial lanes. We'll get a dose of arterial sclerosis if we're not careful. All those other screw drivers seem to have it already.' In my right mind I might have sung a song to them, but with Polly by my side an obsession kept twisting in my trousers, and the smell of summer grass didn't calm it beyond noticing. Where be ye, my love? She was by my side, but sitting apart and not sweetly under me, looking ahead at the green tunnel and tarmac track. 'It's a change from the lake,' I said.

She guided me on to a minor road, then along an unpaved track. 'Dad's never been here by Bentley. He usually comes in the Land Rover.'

The wheels sank into a rut. 'It's understandable.' Grey clouds made it feel like rain through the open windows. The soil on the track had been churned by tractors, and when I went too fast on what seemed a level place I hit a water-filled rut and red slosh flew as high as the windscreen, while bushes on both sides scraped the windows and paintwork. 'You should have told me,' I said, 'and we could have left the car by the road.' Even Moggerhanger didn't deserve this done to his car, though it was too late now, as we went into another dip. 'Much farther?'

'Not much.' A tractor came round the bend, a man perched on top wearing a cap and khaki raincoat, and having the smallest possible stump of fag between his lips. I crushed in the brakes, waited for the small smash, the sort that hurts no one and does no damage, until you try to stand up, when you fall down before you've had time to realize that forty blood vessels are ruptured, or the car itself drops to pieces bit by bit in the weeks that follow and you never know what was the cause of it. But I slithered up to the tractor and stopped a few inches short. The man took off his cap, and smiled: 'Hello, Miss Moggerhanger! Is your father coming today?'

'I don't think so, Bill. Everything all right at the house?'

'Well, it's still there,' he said, as I began to back away. He turned into a field and left the track free, so on I went, splashing over the humps and hollows till I came to an asphalted space in front of a plain two-storeyed brick cottage. The garden was fenced off with white palings, and had a bird bath in the middle of the lawn. At the front door Polly felt in her handbag for the key. It wouldn't fit in the lock. 'Let me try,' I said, but it was soon plain that she had brought the wrong one. 'Never mind,' I said, calmly, boiling with rage at such a mistake, 'we'll get in somehow.'

'Oh,' she cried, tearfully, 'how stupid I am.'

'Don't worry,' I said, my arm around her. 'We'll find a hotel somewhere. Everything turns out all right, as long as you never think you've made a mistake.' She laughed at this piece of suicidal wisdom, and I tried to lift up the front windows.

'I don't think it'll be much use. Dad always locks up when we leave, and he really knows how to do it.'

'Even he can slip up. Let's go to the back.' It was raining again, and through the windows it looked very comfortable. A cat sat on a soaking mat by the back door, flanked by half a dozen empty milk bottles. It got up and rubbed itself against Polly's ankle, as if happy that somebody had come back at last to feed it. The door was locked and bolted from the inside, so I tried the windows. Unless I broke a pane, nothing would come of that. 'There's a skylight window,' she called out.

'Unfortunately,' I said, 'I didn't bring my wings with me. However, I'll get up that drainpipe that leads to the apex of the roof, and slide down to it from the top. Do you dare me to try?'

The cat was cradled in her bosom, and I wanted to belt its earhole out of it. 'No,' she said, 'because I know you'll try.'

I went back to the car for a jack-knife, and opened it. 'If I fall,' I said, putting it between my teeth, 'I'll have no roof to my mouth.'

'Nor your head. But please don't do it.'

'I'm obsessed by it, I've got to do it now, but if I fall it'll be your fault. You'll have to push me in a wheelchair for the rest of our lives.'

'Oh goody!' she said, as I went up a few notches. I needed to be drunk to do this well, but there was no booze in the car. It seemed as if I was a born steeplejack, because my arms had been so strengthened by William's briefcase training. The one spoiling item was rain spitting all over me that made the drainpipe and its supports more slippery than it need have been. I straddled the roof and shuffled myself along.

Polly shouted from below: 'That window may be locked as well!' I suppose she wanted me to have a fit and fall, but I'd assumed it would be locked, anyway, which was why I had the jack-knife. The big danger was in sliding halfway down the slope of the wet roof to get to the window. I might lose control and plummet to my doom. It would have been better thatched, but Moggerhanger was always practical, preferred to see rain sliding plainly down his slates, rather than getting mushed up in thatch, where he couldn't keep an eye on it. That stretch of slate glistened, and I couldn't see much to grip on after I'd started the slide. Polly stood out in the back garden for a full view of me against the sky, and I could see her down in the weeds and rotten cabbages.

'Can you get it open?' she called, seeing that I hadn't yet reached it. I lay flat on the roof, my shoes splayed outwards and arms full length. I could feel the rain on my neck, and I seemed stuck like this for ages, lacking the cool courage and trust to let go. My shoes began sliding, and I pressed them with all force so as to slow down. This helped, for I hit the sill of the skylight, went over it, and stopped.

I was safe, but only by my nails slotted between wood and wood. Cows were moaning from fields round about, a long low gut-stirring complaint saying that I shouldn't be where I was and that if I fell it would serve me right. I was in such a plight that I actually had time to wonder why I was there, and secondly how I'd ever get back to earth if I didn't succeed in breaking in through the window. The only way down was as a human bomb of flesh and blood, to bounce at the earth like a sack of apples and oranges. Be brave, I said, and imagine how cool you'd be if there was only a twelve-inch drop beyond that drainpipe. So I calmed myself, and, hanging with one hand took the clasp knife from my teeth and dug it in the crack of the skylight. To my relief, it was loose, and after some probing I yanked it up and let it fall on my fingers – which cracked them, but I gripped by both hands and drew myself to the ample opening. The skylight frame rested on my head, then my shoulders, till I was out of the rain and able to look into the attic room below. How, though, was I actually to get into it? My scalp itched, and sweat blended with the raindrops, but it was advisable to get in feet first. Luckily there was a bed underneath, with a mattress laid across the frame. I slithered on to it like a crocodile, rolling into a ball as I landed, but spraining my ankle as it hit the end of the bed. I spun about and cursed at the fiery ache, feeling alone in the world, forgetting everything but that torment. Yet I was inside, and stood to celebrate the fact. I held on to the bed and rolled my foot around, then walked to the door, noticing on my way that half a dozen expensive shotguns were laid along a rack by the far wall.

When I opened the back door Polly said: 'I thought you'd gone to sleep up there.'

'It was quite a drop,' I told her, as we went through the kitchen, which smelled of dampness and old cornflakes. 'Is there any brandy in the place?' I found some in the living-room cupboard, and we drank a good slug of it. I put my arm around her, feeling lecherous at the noise of rain dinning against the window. 'Did you shut the skylight?'

'I suppose so.'

'Please go and make sure, love.'

I hobbled up to the attic, found an aluminium ladder, and clamped the window into place. The bed was already patched with wet. I picked up a double-barrelled high-powered fowling piece and playfully aimed it through the skylight at the piss-filled clouds. The victory at getting in, and the fact that I would soon be entangled in the warm limbs of sweet Polly, must have turned my head, for in a moment of panache I pulled both triggers. A double explosion thumped my shoulder and threw me on the floor, and the shots brought down a shower of glass and splinters, so that slits of blood joined up with marks of rain and sweat.

Polly stood in the doorway: 'For God's sake, what have you done?'

'I'm wounded. Don't just stand there, help me up. Whoever could have left a gun loaded without murder in his heart?'

'You're not wounded,' she said accusingly.

'We'd better move the bed, and put a bucket under the hole, otherwise your house will get senile decay.' I hobbled around and looked busy clearing up, while Polly said she'd never known anyone to sprain their ankle simply by firing a shotgun. I couldn't convince her that I'd done it getting in, and that she just hadn't noticed it before.

We had a shower, warm water soaking our skins back to life and sensitivity. She held me by the roots while I latched on to her breasts and soaped her between the legs, until she suddenly jerked and fetched forward as she came. Without waiting to get into the bedroom we lay on the towels and bath-mats and shocked off together, wet and raw and flushed after the difficulties of getting in. We pulled each other into the bedroom. She put on a nightdress, then opened a drawer and took out one of her father's linen shirts. 'Put this on.'

'I'm not cold.'

Her dark eyes were on fire, and I don't think she could see me at all: 'Still, put it on.' It meant nothing to me, so I did, and it was so big it was like a nightshirt, pin-striped and without a collar. She lay down, her head on the pillow and hair spread like feathers. My handle grew up, and pushed out the shirt, which she lifted till she got to it, and then I slapped her around and fucked her as hard as I could, while she moaned and whimpered about never having had it like this before, which I didn't believe, though I couldn't think of anything as my prick cut into the shrine of her and shot my life at her womb.

There was nothing to eat in the place, that was the only trouble. We found a box of matzos in the larder, and some cheese that I had to lop the rot from, so we lived on this and black sweet tea till the following morning, though we didn't need too much time to eat. Nor did we benefit from the fresh country air. Polly told me the story of her life, of how she was brought up at Moggerhanger Hall, and the adolescent shock she got when she caught on to her father's profession. She'd always been his darling, and still was, and he lost no opportunity in reminding her of that and the many times as a child when she'd said that when she grew up he was the only one she'd consider marrying. She asked me about my life, and I told her all I knew of it, and of my adventures as a gold-smuggler, on which she asked all sorts of questions about the Jack Leningrad Organization. I told her about William being caught in Beirut, and that because of this the man in the iron lung might be on the move to a new hideout.

'All this is worth nothing,' I said, while we lounged on the bed, me in her father's shirt which by this time had a bit of rank stiffening in it. 'The moon is worth nothing. The world is worth nothing. The rain can piss itself to death. All that's worth anything are your kisses.' She almost fainted into my arms at this, and my hand went down as her soft breasts flattened against me, and her eyes closed. 'We'll have lots of honeymoons, and if life tries to waylay and grab us we'll kick it in the teeth. There's only us, not life.' Her tongue and fingers were in my mouth, as if wanting me to pour out more such words, but I was half gone, then all gone as I went into her again, and got the piston of the two-stroke cycle at a regular knock. It amazed me how much spunk a man had in him, and I wondered how many times he shot in a lifetime and how many plastic buckets this would add up to, how many furrows it would irrigate, how many babies drown. These off-side thoughts kept me going, and I played her on her belly and back and side and from behind, till finally when she was spreadeagled under me and facing me, and had come at last, and I felt her velvet gobble beginning again, I calculated it was time to let go, and did, and she pulled me by the arse till I felt her fingernails must be full of either shit or blood. She cried out as if I were trying to kill her, which I swear I wasn't, and I felt a roar come out of me without knowing much about it.

As we went sadly towards the car I hoped our simple brick cottage would melt under the rain and banish back into the soil because I couldn't bear the thought of anyone ever going into it and spoiling the thick atmosphere that we had created and left there. Even to dynamite it would be better than that. I drove like a pilot towards London, neither of us saying much. There wasn't even a traffic jam in Tonbridge, and two hours later we were crossing the bridge and steaming through the mist and mire into Ealing. The thick slosh of reality was getting back at me, and I felt nervous as I drove the mud-stained Bentley up the drive of Moggerhanger Court.

I took the remaining cigars out of the glove-box and said goodbye, wondering if she expected me to match her with the tears she looked like shedding.

'Phone me,' she said.

'I will' – solid in my intention.

'Father has other places we can go to. They're all over the place.'

'We'll go to every one,' I said.

On the mat was a telegram and a letter. I opened the telegram first, and it read: PROCEED ROME TOMORROW STOP AWAIT PHONE CALL = JACK LENINGRAD. I took a bottle of beer from the fridge and put some sausages under the grill, so that the whole flat smelt like home. Whereas the telegram bucked me up and made me feel better, the sight of Bridgitte's bulky letter irritated me, though I hadn't yet opened it, because I looked forward to getting back to work with no distraction. I read a couple of old newspaper stories about foot and mouth disease, then noted that England's currency reserves were running low, and how gold was getting scarcer. Time and a pot of tea went by on this, but soon I was forced to open the letter.

'Dear Michael,' Bridgitte wrote, 'such terrible things have happened to me that I don't know where to begin.' I nearly threw it in the fire, but was compelled, like a dear reader, to read on.

'I'm so distressed that I weep all the time. You see, Donald, my husband, came back the morning after you left, and Adelida met him at the door while I was still in bed. She'd just returned from taking dear Smog to school, and must have told Donald that you had been in the bed with me, because the first thing I knew was the clothes pulled back and his wild hands smacking me. I screamed, but I was black and blue before he stopped. Then he stood there calling me all the rotten English names, such terrible things I can't tell you.

'He made me get dressed, then pushed me all down the stairs to the front door, and threw me out of it. By this time he was crying himself, but as the tears came to his own face his knocks and kicks at me got worse. As I went sobbing down the path I heard him raving at Adelida and telling her to pack and get out as well. He's a psychologist and a doctor, and he's supposed to be a man of wisdom and understanding, but he acted like a beast to me. He's never been anything but a beast.

'I had only a few shillings in my pocket so I went by Underground and bus to your flat. Nobody was in. I sat for an hour on the stairs, still not really awake, and hungry because the Beast had thrown me out with no breakfast. I went to see a Dutch friend of mine who lives in Chelsea with a student, and she gave me cheese and tea, but was too poor to put me up.

'I decided that the only sensible thing was to go back to my husband, and when I got there he wasn't in. The door was open and I caught Adelida putting my clothes into her own suitcase. I said that if she didn't take them out I'd phone the police, but she said I was a whore and could phone who I liked. When I started to dial the phone she threw my stuff over the floor and ran away from the house. So I packed my case properly and found my money purse with pounds in it. If the worst came to the terrible it was enough to get me to Holland, but I didn't want to go there because my family, who had always hated my husband, would only have said I told you so and sent me away.

'I sat on my case in the living-room surrounded by chairs, and didn't know what to do. I was stunned, and it was all my fault. And then I thought: "Why didn't I think of it before? Michael's gone to his home in Nottinghamshire." A ray of joy spread over me. Also I remembered the address, Ranton Grange, so I called a taxi and went straight to the station, where I got a ticket to Nottingham.

'It was a wonderful journey, because as soon as the train got to countryside my tears dried and troubles went, and I had a cheap lunch in the dining-wagon. The only strange incident that happened, on the train anyway, was when I was on my way back to the carriage. I was passing a first-class compartment and inside was a little old woman, who took off a fur coat and tried to push it through the window out of the train. The space was small and the coat was big, so she had a hard job to get it out. She pulled it down and rolled it up longways, to make it easier, and she was mumbling and crying all the time. I went in and talked to her, so that after a while she forgot about throwing her coat off the train, and started to tell me her life story. But it was all very quick and I didn't understand anything, thinking she was just another of your mad people in England.

'Then I went back to my own seat in third class, because the ticket man came and said I had to. Nottingham was nice and different from London, all open and good to look at, full of busy and smiling people, and I said to myself this is just the town that Michael would come from. I asked a station man how I would get to Ranton, and he told me to walk down to the bus place, so that in an hour I got there. What beautiful country! But I had to walk a long way down a lane to get to your house at the Grange. By this time I was a little bit tired, but hoped your mother would not be angry for me calling on you.

'The gate was locked, and I pressed a bell button, and down the drive came a man who I thought must be the brother you'd told me about. He looked kind, but suspicious, and asked me what I wanted. I said I had come to see Michael, and he said you weren't at home, that you were in London. This was a big blow, and I was beginning to think that it was a really bad day. "Are you his brother?" I asked. He nodded, and looked at me, hard. He was about ten years older than you, and good-looking, though his eyes were steely, and he had a small ginger moustache. "He told me a lot about you," I said. He took my case and asked me to come to the house for a cup of tea, said he couldn't possibly let me go since I had come so far. He apologized for you and said you didn't often make mistakes like this, and that you ought to be more careful where a young lady was concerned. I said I hoped I wouldn't disturb his mother, and he said, "Oh, don't worry about her. I'm afraid she recently died," and I thought it strange that you hadn't told me, but I just said how sorry I was.

'A servant took my case and we went into the house, a big mansion with paintings of dead soldiers on all the staircases, and I thought how lucky Michael is to have a childhood here. Your brother gave me lunch, and he ordered a bottle of wine to be sent up, and then another, and the more I ate and drank the better I felt about my disappointment at not seeing you. Then I felt dizzy, and your brother asked his housekeeper to show me a room where I could rest for half an hour. He then said that afterwards he would drive me to the station. So I followed this old woman into a room that looked over the loveliest green park. I stood by the window to see it all. Then I lay down on the bed, feeling small in the middle of it. I was exhausted from the events of the day that was not much more than half gone, and I fell asleep in no time.

'When I opened my eyes, your brother (I mean that devil) was standing by the bed and looking down at me. "Is it time to go?" I said. He started to undress, and I ran to the door, but it was locked. "It's even soundproof," he laughed at me. "Let me go," I cried, "I'll miss my train." "They run every day," he said. "I'll tell Michael," I said. "Who the devil's that?" he said, naked but for his shirt. "Your brother," I told him. "I don't have a brother. Only a sister, and she's in South America, I hope." I ran back to the bed. "Don't be a silly girl," he said, pulling his shirt off, "enjoy yourself."

'"Who are you?" I cried.

'"I'm Lady Chatterley's son." Somehow he didn't frighten me any more, and when he kissed me I couldn't do anything about it. I realized by now that I must have remembered the wrong address, but a few days later Clifford told me that there was no one by your name in the whole county, and he knew all the good families in it. So you are the most terrible liar, and I shall never forgive you, even though I still love you. If I didn't I wouldn't be writing this letter.

'Clifford put me on the train in Nottingham and begged me to visit him again some time. Back in London I went to my husband, thinking that we could be together again. But when he wanted to know who I'd spent my time with I wouldn't tell him. He'd been to your flat looking for you, to push your face in, he said, but he hadn't found you. We had lunch together at the house (he already had another housekeeper looking after him) and I thought things were going to be all right, because afterwards we went to bed, but then he asked me to tell him again where I'd been for the last few days, and when I still wouldn't he said he just had time to smash up the house and get rid of me before going off to Harley Street to see some patients. He threw all the vases into the fireplace, ripped the pictures off the walls, and smashed a window. Then he hit me and kicked me. He is uncivilized and savage, and I thought there'd be no end to it if I stayed with him. He kicked his wife, that's why she left him. He kicks poor Smog, and he kicked me. I told myself I'd never live with a psychoanalyst again, as I went crying down the path with my suitcase. I've got a place to live and a job. My room is in Camden Town, and I work as a shop assistant. I hate it, because I don't have any freedom, and I'm unhappy because I've been phoning you and don't get any reply. So please, please come to see me, or be in when I phone, because my life is smashed and ruined and I am so unhappy, Michael. I love you and want to go away with you. Even though you betrayed me by your lies, I still want you.'

She went on in this way for a few pages more, but I crumpled the letter up and threw it in the slop bin. What a crazy girl she was, I thought, going up to Nottingham to look for me. How can you trust someone who believes everything you say? As for the stately home she'd ended up in, it must have been the one I'd described so knowingly in my lies, the one I'd cycled by and admired so often as a youth. Some swine had taken advantage of her innocence, and now she was a serving girl behind a shop counter. What a comedown for an au pair girl from milk-and-butter land.

It was already afternoon, the livid sky filled with water, which made me feel even more sorry for her. But I had to go out in it, for the cupboard was empty and the fridge was bare, so with raincoat and umbrella I slipped down the stairs to a little man's shop on the main road, whose window was filled with orange drinks and tinned peas. I got Splendour Loaf and meatlets, choc-cake, and Tiger-eye frozen fish toes, the fifth-rate grub that dulls the brains of every Englishman. Big drops of rain dragged themselves out of the sky in an effort to wet me on the way back, but I reached the comfort of my flat in safety.

I tried on the phone to get Bill's mother and tell her the fate of her son, but the hotel manager said she'd gone back to Worksop some days ago – which was one problem less to bother me as I lay down the receiver. Only at this moment did it occur to me that she'd been seen on the train by Bridgitte, though I tried not to be dead certain of it. I put on the kettle again for tea. There was a framed photograph of Bill's mother on the sideboard, and her look went right into my heart when I took up courage and stared at her. She asked what the hell Bill was doing in London instead of earning an able living in Worksop. Come to that, she asked what I was doing here as well, but I looked at her and said nothing, thinking she ought to stick to Bill and leave me alone. Bill no doubt was guzzling typhoid sherbet in a far-off nick, so he certainly needed worrying about, far more than I did, and that was a fact.

Yet at least he was surrounded by bad breath and flesh-and-blood, whereas if my appendix suddenly burst I'd bleed to death and nobody would be any the wiser. I wasn't going crazy, but I didn't like living alone, and Bill's old mother behind that sheet of glass knew it very well, those features showing a mixture of despair with love just beneath it and trying to break through, and to succeed in seeing her love, you had to look at her with all your spirit, and with tears about to come out of your own eyes. I wanted to turn it to the wall, but didn't have enough coal in my brain for that. While filling me with remorse it also showed me there was nothing I could do for Bridgitte, that no mad rescue was possible or necessary because who, by the standards of Bill's mother, could say she was either badly-off or suffering? Certainly not me, as I looked at the tragic photograph that Bill had so lovingly framed with his own hands – and made a somewhat shoddy job of it at that. I thought of doing a rush trip to Worksop to explain the fate of her son but knew that this wasn't on the cards because I was stuck to the flat on Jack Leningrad's orders.

I was saved from the pain of this by the ringing telephone, and was surprised to hear that Appledore trill: 'Oh, you're back! Michael! I can't believe it.' I told her about my imaginary adventures in Lisbon during the last few days, but after a while she broke in and said: 'Listen, tell me yes or no, can we come over and see you?'

I was on my guard: 'Who's we?'

'Smog and I. I got him from school after giving up my job today and we've nowhere to go. Oh, Michael,' she was crying now, 'let us come over and see you.'

'All right, then.'

She laughed with joy: 'I knew you would. I told Smog you would. Oh, I'll kiss you when I see you.' All I had to do was sit down and wait, casting a rugged glance now and again at old Ma Straw. If I'd had liquor in the house I'd have drunk a mountain, but there was only a drop of sherry and I hated that.

Smog threw himself at me and started to cry, so I took him to a chair and sat him on my knee. 'Get your coat off,' I said to Bridgitte, who looked thin and wan, though it made her appear more interesting.

'You were the only one I could turn to,' she said.

'I know, love. I know. I got your letter. It was pretty daft of you to go to Nottingham. Next time you feel like a trip up there I'll give you my mother's real address.'

She pouted: 'I don't know why I did it. But it seemed like exactly the right thing to do, and the journey made me feel a lot better.'

'I'll bet it did,' I said, riled that she'd had a good time with somebody else. Smog had quietened down, and now she began to snivel. 'I'm sorry,' I said, meaning to go to her, but Smog clung so tightly that I couldn't move. His face was wet from tears. 'I want to live with you. I don't like life like I did once. Dad is rotten, and things are all mixed up.'

'Listen, Smog,' I said, 'life isn't too good for anybody. Even children have to grow up and find that out. You'll be seven soon, so you're nearly a man. Lots of things have happened to you, and lots more will happen. It's like that. You'll be safe with Bridgitte and me, I promise. As far as I'm concerned we could all live together, all the time, but I don't think your father would like that. Still, you don't have to worry, because we're friends for life.'

He looked at me, his face small but already formed as if he were fourteen. 'Can I have some tea and cakes?'

'Come into the kitchen and help me to look for them,' I said, 'because I'm damned if I can remember where they are.' I made a game of searching, and he was lost in it while I went into the living-room to kiss Bridgitte back to life: 'Let's forget about my lies,' I said. 'I'm sorry about it.' She was warm and steamy after the rain, and from our long embrace I saw Smog standing in the doorway with a packet of chocolate cakes in his hand. He forced himself between our legs, so that we made a house for him to hide and be warm in. 'You've built me a cottage,' he said. 'Let's fry some crumpets and stroke the cat.'

'I'll sing you the *Volga Boat Song* while I'm at it,' I said. 'But we don't have a cat. I used it to clean the windows down this morning and it ran away.'

I fixed him up in the main bed, since it seemed that William wouldn't be needing it for a while. Bridgitte and I sat like any man and wife at supper, when the phone rang. It was Stanley to say I'd be wanted in Rome the following day, and that I should present myself at the usual Knightsbridge flat by nine in the morning. 'What about William?' I asked.

'No news,' he said. They were doing all they could, which was a lot, but they couldn't say anything now, though they expected results every minute. I bit my tongue and said all right I'd be there.

It wasn't gold this time, but the errand of carrying a valise of true-blue British banknotes through the customs. I went out and back in a couple of days, by train and boat, landing at Dover and going through with my allowance of booze and fags so that no one could suspect a thing. It was my third time away and third time lucky, plying my trade in the mainland traffic and working with all the nerve I could muster, for not only was I fucking God's own country, through the ribs, but I was getting a fat slice of pay for it as well, and what man could be more favoured than that? The hint was dropped when I collected my divvy that the notes were forged anyway, and I didn't boast of it, even to myself, but gently let it seep down to the flowing dust of my blood in the hope that such easy tasks would become second nature to me. On the other hand, by the normal permutations of chance, I knew I could not do many of these trips without getting caught, or feeling the pressure of them break through to my face and give me away, even though to myself I might still seem to be in full control.

So I had to think about the future, and organize some plan of withdrawal, keeping an eye cocked to my own safety should Jack Leningrad Limited not want me to leave when I felt it was time to do so for my one and only good, which was the only one that mattered.

I did many more trips, and had nearly three thousand pounds in the bank. I wouldn't let my hands get to it till I'd packed the job in because if I bought an expensive car I might get caught, in which case it would rot in the street while I did my three or five years. I hadn't the ultimate confidence that I would go unscathed, and that was why I had to get out.

I seemed to live on more solid ground while Bridgitte and Smog were at the flat, as if I were a married man with full responsibility going off to work now and again to earn them cakes and meat. We assumed that Dr Anderson would be interested in the whereabouts of his son, but when Bridgitte phoned to let him know that Smog was all right, the house-keeper said Dr Anderson was on a six-week lecture tour in America – where he no doubt told his audience that they had to be kind to one another. I tried to phone Polly, but couldn't get through to her, so my love changed from the burden it had been at first, to an almost bearable pang whenever she jumped into my mind, which was still often enough to make me flinch when it hit me.

But there was work to be done, a high-stakes trip to Lisbon, and I came back first class on a beautiful Caravelle, so that I could get soaked in champagne and stretch my legs, which deserved it after the work they'd done. I intended to doze the few hours away, but I reckoned without Arnold Pilgrim, a tall thin man who sat by my side. I'd seen him sloping in, and he had the sort of face that seemed clamped tight by never having known what he wanted to do in life. He looked by now on the point of finding out, yet realized he'd left it too late to find the means for doing what he wanted to do. I talk from hindsight, but his rather staid and baffled face wasn't easy to forget, even on first sight, and I remember the journey because in one sense it was vital to my life.

We joked over the champagne, and he told me he had just

been to Portugal to negotiate the sale of forty thousand machine tools, or cars, or litres of wine – I forget which. It seemed to have been successful, whatever it was, so I said: 'Here's to it, then!' I knew I should neither drink nor talk, but these rules of William's I waived more and more, for I considered that to be too reticent while travelling only drew suspicion rather than the reverse. After all, William was rotting in jail, so he could afford to talk.

Using the soul of Gilbert Blaskin, I told Arnold Pilgrim I was a writer, and that I'd just been to Lisbon for a week's holiday. The only danger in this, I realized after he started talking, was that he would spill his heart to me for the entire flight, which he did. 'When I get home,' he said, 'I'm going to murder my wife. There's a story for you, if you're a writer.'

I was sitting by his side so couldn't look dead-on at him, but the way he said it made me want to laugh, because he sounded as if he were serious. 'You'll want to know why, I expect. Well, don't you?' he demanded, when I didn't say anything.

'Why should I? I'm not your wife.'

'I see what you mean. But I'll tell you, anyway. My wife and I married quite young, ten years ago to be accurate, and we were really in love, as you usually are when you're young, and when you get married. I hated all women, and she hated all men, so we got on like a house on fire, as it were. We started buying our own house in Putney, because I was well thought of in my job. There was a touch of ground frost in her make-up, but we thawed it out after a while. She was passionate, which meant that she realized her frostiness but did her best to overcome it. At the same time, I was cursed by a certain incompetence, which this also righted as time went on. So we got to our state of married happiness not without difficulty, but we got there, and I see now that we were happy, because we never really talked about happiness but just let the years flow by.

'But we were children, because we were inert enough to think that we never needed to do anything for each other. In a sense we were right: we could have lived in reciprocal blindness till old age, but I suppose it's always better to leave childhood behind.

'My wife made friends one day with a woman, when they were both borrowing books at the local library. I never knew what they had in common, but this other woman, as the friendship went on, was the sort who was very independent. She was married, but made a cult of being self-sufficient in her life – as far as she could. Her husband was a photographer who did freelance work for magazines, and his wife was also a sort of journalist. My wife was fascinated by her, there's no doubt of that, because she also had big ideas about women's status in the world, ideas which I'd encouraged, as long as they didn't disturb me. This other woman was the epitome then of what my wife had always wanted to be, for she had everything: a house, a good husband, a child, a job that she enjoyed, even a lover. There seemed nothing left to want. In the next two years I even became friendly with the husband, but not to the extent that Beryl was friendly with his wife, for he seemed a bit of a queer to me. I thought it was good that they should like each other, though I wasn't so stupid that I didn't see how this other woman in some way disturbed her. My wife would cite her in arguments, and hold up her life to let me know how dull and narrow her own was. Then this other woman gassed herself.

'My wife had known that she was depressed and withdrawn, but she hadn't expected this, even as a remote possibility. Later it became known that the husband had been having an affair with another woman, and that the wife had found out, but had not told him or anyone that she knew. In spite of her own lover, she couldn't stand her husband doing that sort of thing, so she quietly did herself in. It was a terrible shock to my wife, who was haunted by her friend's death for weeks, so that I really believe she even began to think of turning on the gas as well. Nothing in the world seemed secure to her any more. I did my best by way of comfort, but was pushed completely to one side. In her shock it even seemed as if she blamed me in some way for what had happened, thinking perhaps that if she'd never married me she wouldn't have been so dependent on the views that her friend held so intensely, in which case she would have been more human and open to sympathy, and it might then have been possible to fathom that her friend was going to kill herself. She may have saved her, she thought, but she was too deeply involved in her friend's principles, and too dependent on my love and support – though she claimed that this never meant very much to her. But there was more to it than that, and it was a few years before I was able to see the outcome of it. You never know where a thing begins, I know that, but I think I can see where it's going to end.'

It was hot in the plane, and he wiped his forehead and cheeks. He spoke as if telling me about something that had happened to another person rather than to himself, smiling at whatever in his story disturbed him – which meant he had a faint smile of disgust or self-pity on his face most of the time. 'I'm not going to complain for myself, or say I was full of perfect love and understanding. I'm sure I was in love with her, though she claims I wasn't and never was. Our marriage came to seem like a negation of love. It was heavy with underground recrimination, as if we were both haunted and overshadowed by a new demonic force that hadn't been there before – though maybe it had, but had taken all this time to brew itself up between us. But the lever of it had been the woman's suicide, of that I have no doubt.'

I offered him a cigarette. He didn't smoke, or wouldn't. He only drank. So I lit one: 'It was a pity though. Your wife must have had a rough time.'

His voice was caught in a laugh of irony: 'She did. No doubt about that. I was sorry for her, and did my best about it. But nothing could be enough. She had to find her own cure, which meant trying to destroy me. It was the only thing she could do, but it was too much of a price for me to pay, though I was made to pay it. The method she chose was that age-old one of having an affair, of betraying me and letting me know that she was betraying me, and continuing it to the point of trying to drive me mad. The affair's been going on for two years, though in that time she has grown more secretive about it because she has now become more deeply and seriously attached to the man she took up with. She ties me to her by saying how much she loves me, tells me she's only ever loved me, and loves no one else no matter what she does or whatever happens. This saps my resolution to clear out, but I discovered that she was put up to this ploy by her boyfriend. She is a monster, but so am I. It is easy for her to deceive me because I am away from home so often. Why did I get such a job if I can't trust my wife? We still live as man and wife, and make love often enough for us to seem so. But if the only way she could find to get over her friend's vampire suicide was to morally destroy me, my price for recovering from this attempt is to kill her. I put the matter in a nutshell, though I hope I'm not boring you.'

We had food in front of us, and it gave me the energy to go on listening: 'It's fascinating.'

He tucked into this food remarkably well, considering the ideas he had for his wife's future. I suppose a person always eats well before committing a murder, but not before killing himself – though I must admit that I still didn't believe he was serious. 'So when she grew more careful,' he said, 'I became more assiduous in finding out what she was up to. It's cost me hundreds of pounds, which in other and happier times would have been better spent on repairs to the house, in having her shadowed by private detectives. Do you know how many men are necessary to follow one person? It's a hell of a business. I only found out when I got a bill from one agency of over two hundred pounds. It takes three men to follow her. Maybe she suspects I'm having her watched and does a bit of evading. But I know exactly what she does and where she goes. So before leaving this time, after several days of vindictive skirmishes and one dreadful final quarrel, I got her to promise solemnly that she would give him up and not see him again, so that we could make a new start. All seemed set for a bright future – though at heart I didn't believe it would work for a minute. We kissed tenderly when I left for my business trip. But I called at the detective agency in Soho on my way by taxi to the airport and gave them the usual details, paid them a good advance sum in cash, and told them that if they by any chance tailed her to her lover's flat they were to telegraph the fact to my hotel in Lisbon. I made up my mind that if she went through with any more treachery, I would murder her. I would destroy her. She would perish.

'And when I left I hoped with all my heart that everything

would be peaceful and calm, that she would not betray me, that all would be forgotten and forgiven. I was in a good and optimistic mood on the way out and for the first few days, when no telegram arrived, I thought that life really could begin again. More days went by, and no news. I was happier, I think, than I'd ever been in my life. My business negotiations went very well. My brain was clear, and I bargained with more than usual firmness. I got to the stage of packing my suitcase, and I was on my way out of the hotel, with a taxi waiting by the kerb to take me to the airport, when a bellboy ran up and handed me a telegram. I read it in the taxi, lay back sweating and half fainting. I had visions of bloody entrails, while rain was pouring down the windows of the taxi. The streets outside glistened and jumped with rain – but it was a perfectly blue clear day, as you know. I felt my eyes change colour. I looked ahead and saw a huge horse lying dead in the middle of the road and blocking it, almost the whole of its side scooped out as if it had had some dreadful accident, a white horse, its head rearing in agony, as if trying to lick the vast red wound. She'd spent every night with him. I screamed at the taxi driver to stop, but he laughed and went right on through it. The white mare would be killed. There's nothing else I can do.' His hands were shaking so much that he dropped his fork. He didn't try to pick it up or get another but finished the meal with his knife alone, which began to look sinister enough to me, as more and more champagne went into my stomach.

'That's no reason to kill somebody,' I said. 'Just throw her out – with her coat on.'

'I don't have the strength to do that.'

'It's still a bit rough, that she happened to marry a man who only had the strength to kill her when she did something like that.'

The stewardess poured our coffee. 'I thought you were a writer,' he sneered softly. 'If you are, you ought to understand that there's nothing else I can do.'

'What about afterwards?' I asked.

'Time has stopped. There's no more peace, not for one minute, any time, anywhere. That's all gone and finished. No more peace, and no more love.'

'You're a saint,' I said, 'to try for those two things, the first saint I've met, on an aeroplane at thirty thousand feet as well!'

'I suppose you think I'm old-fashioned?' he said guardedly.

I thought he was drunk, but didn't say so. 'There's no such thing as old-fashioned. I have enough understanding to know that much.'

With a sudden flush of good-will he reached over and shook my hand: 'I'm glad you said that. You'll go a long way as a writer.' I held out my cup for more coffee, and got a hot spot on my trousers as the plane lurched. If it crashed, his wife would be quids in. 'I feel better now,' he said, 'after that meal, and so much champagne. Perhaps I really have got a soul. I was beginning to doubt it after my ups and downs of the last week.'

'That's good,' I said. 'Maybe you won't feel so bad when you get home.'

'Oh, no. When I feel in this mood I loathe her more than ever. I can only murder when I feel in this mood. The bottom of the ocean is in my stomach. The top of the sky is in my lungs. My spirit's flying between the two.'

He wasn't crying, but tears were coming out. I lifted my glass: 'Let's drink to happy landings, anyway.'

He smiled, showing a very good-natured face, as if all his troubles had gone.

'What I want,' I said, confiding in him, 'is to find a hideaway in the country where I can write in peace. The town is like a nutcracker crunching me. I feel I've got to get out and work.'

'That shouldn't be difficult,' he said. 'While all this has been going on with my wife, we've occasionally talked about finding a place in the country where we can go now and again, and try to get back to our old basis of love. Of course, she never meant this to be possible, but it was a good reason for her to send me out of town to look at places as they came up for sale so that she could be free to go to her lover. Well, she won't be free to go anywhere much longer. I shall be back in an hour, and then I'll do it. I know exactly what I'll do. But let me tell you what I found, an old disused railway station for sale in the Fen country. It's been empty for some time, and nobody seems to want it, so I think you can get it for about twelve hundred. I'll give you all the information on it.' He reached for his briefcase, and handed me a few sheets of paper: 'I've seen it, and you'll want nothing more remote or quiet than that. I was going to take it before I came on this trip, but you might as well have it now. There's a surveyor's report in those papers. The place is in good condition, though it needs a few gallons of paint.'

I put them in my pocket: 'Are you sure you won't be needing them?'

'Absolutely certain. I won't need peace, or any place to hide from now on.'

'Thanks, then,' I said. 'If you loathe your wife, don't you think that's a sort of love?'

'In paradise maybe, but not here on Earth. I'll never love her again. I can only love someone if I can finally trust them. Love is an extension of trust, and if you're too young yet even as a writer to finally know what that means, Mr Blaskin, then you are lucky. But trust has nothing to do with whether a person can be trusted or not, if love is involved. The normal sort of trust is only an unspoken treaty of self-preservation between two or a group of people. When this has gone, and I am forty years old, there's nothing left. The earth has slid from under me, and I am falling. There's just one more thing to do on my way down.'

'You know best,' I said. 'It's your life. But thanks for telling me about that railway station.'

I followed him down the steps when we landed, stood far enough away in the bus to the customs hall to get a further look at him in his neat shirt and tie, well-trimmed beard, stylish hat, all of it impeccable enough to warn any woman off him. He stared out of the window and saw nothing, the corners of his mouth drooping so that nobody could say he wasn't unhappy. I thought I ought to warn his wife about his intending homicidal crackdown, tell her to watch that split-level look to his eyes – that she had maybe spent all her life putting there. Still wondering whether I should do it I followed him from the bus and into the customs. By chance we went through at the same moment. I saw his head jerk, and he began to run, as if told to stop and surrender by someone only he could hear, but deciding to make a break for it against all chances.

Halfway across the hall was a woman, fair and slight in the quick view I got of her, wearing a discreet hat and a light grey suit, a faint smile of welcome on her face, as if not wanting to invest too much of a smile in case the bottom fell out of the market, and in case he shouldn't see her smile but walk right through her like his taxi had driven through the dying mare. But I was wrong again, which is what comes of being a bastard, who is too often wrong. He ran towards her, and she saw him. I watched. They latched together like lovers who had not seen each other for weeks, a murmuring groan from each that I'd swear I heard if I claimed to have invented it. They kissed openly a couple of times, his grin fixed, hers still a modest smile with half-closed eyes as if she was taken up by a great force and couldn't stop herself, but at the same time didn't want to see anyone who might be noticing them, or indeed even acknowledge the strokes of lust that taunted her for coming straight to the airport from the Christian Woman's Club. It was touching, and made me hungry for the same thing, a living advertisement for the love-shop. They walked towards the escalator, arms around each other as if they were both sixteen.

Because I'd expected him to go straight home after what he'd told me, and cleave her down the middle, I thought I didn't know I was living now that the exact opposite seemed to be on the cards. My mistake showed me what a baby I was and how little I knew of the world. All I'd got out of meeting him were the details of a remote railway station I could retire to when I decided to sever connexion with Jack Leningrad Incorporated. I supposed that the Lovers of Putney would be immersed in each other for the next twenty-four hours, so decided to steal a march on him and get to the Fens first thing in the morning to view the place, assuming that since things seemed to be patched up with his wife he would still entertain notions of getting it for himself.

I was looking forward to seeing Smog and Bridgitte, but the flat was empty. A letter on the table said she had taken Smog and gone back to her husband. He had found out where they were and had phoned them, sobbing and weeping and imploring them to come back so that they could live once more as a happy and loving family. Smog didn't want to go, so Bridgitte had to get him kicking and screaming out of the flat. What he hated most, she wrote, was having to go back to school, and no longer playing this thrilling game of being on the run from his father.

I took a shower so as to have moving water for company, and to swill off the grind of travel. Every journey pulled flesh from me and I didn't know why, though the physical cost, the fear of getting caught, and the guilt perhaps of doing this work at all, might have added up to an amount I could only just pay, and I was kicking at the limit of my capabilities. I felt as if my blood had been sucked out, but then cheered up, as I lay back and lit a cigar, at the idea of seeing the railway station. I read the timetables, then phoned the agents, Smut and Bunt of Huntingborough.

'It's cheap,' he said, 'because it's beyond the commuter belt, but it's the most beautiful little station you ever saw. Just the place, I would say, for a writer like you.' The land was flat and waterlogged, grey and green under a vast and heavy sky, metalled by the sun just breaking through. Beautiful. I felt a free man, for the first time since I'd set out from Nottingham on my old jalopy two years ago. I didn't feel like going back to London, but the trouble was that I'd no idea where to set off for if I didn't. 'It's not easy to get a mortgage for these old stations, though. Don't know why.'

'I pay cash.'

He took a humpbacked bridge over a dyke and nearly shot my throat into my brain. 'That's all right then,' he said, envious rather than impressed.

The nearest village was Upper Mayhem, and half a mile on the other side of it we turned into a cul-de-sac, at the end of which was the station, well away from the nearest houses. 'Any offers yet?'

'There've been one or two, but they've fallen through. A chap in London, from Putney, was quite firm on it, but we haven't heard from him lately. It's first come, first served. I've only got the keys to the back door.' He opened a wooden gate to get there, and it fell forward off its hinges. He picked it up and set it against the wall. 'You might find it a bit damp, but you have to expect that in the Fens. Nothing that a few good fires won't cure.'

It reeked with must as he opened the back door. There were three simple rooms downstairs, with a scullery. 'Toilet in the garden,' he said. Upstairs were four more rooms, and half a ton of soot in one of the fireplaces. I didn't tell him I used to be an estate agent. The plumbing wasn't up to much, but the ceilings looked all right. I stood at the end of the garden and trained my binoculars on the roof to make sure the slates were in place, and the chimney-stack firm. According to the survey it would need a bit of work done in a few years, but sufficient to the day is the ruination thereof.

'We'll go to the actual station,' he said, which lay across a hundred yards of asphalt, badly holed in places.

'How much does the land come to?'

'Two acres. Room to swing a cat, certainly.'

'Any rabbits around here?'

'Quite a few.'

I noticed a huge potato field beyond the track, and fruit orchards on the other side of the station. 'Not an architectural gem,' I said, 'though I expect I could make it cosy.' To the left was the booking office, and all the shelves and ticket compartments were still there, as well as a few cupboards. Across the hall was the waiting-room, with plain seats going around the walls. We strode up and down the platform, passed the ladies and gents lavatories.

'You say they want twelve hundred for it,' I said. 'Is it open to offer, or not?'

'It's a firm price. They wouldn't take less.'

I offered him a cigar. 'What about a thousand?' We lit up, and walked back towards the house. 'You can try,' he said. 'Maybe eleven hundred would get it.'

'I'll offer eleven then. I'll need the other hundred to stop it falling down.'

'It's pretty firm, the main structure. Are you married?'

'Divorced,' I told him. 'I gave my London house to my wife.'

Back in his office I wrote a cheque for the ten per cent deposit, and gave the name of William's solicitors as stake holders.

I had a meal at the hotel in Huntingborough, then got the train back to town. When I reached the flat nothing had happened in my absence. I felt let down when I saw no letters or telegrams of alarm waiting for me, so after some beans on toast I phoned Polly, and Moggerhanger himself answered: 'What do you want?'

'Can I speak to Polly?'

'She's out. Who's that?'

'Kenny Dukes,' I answered, and put the phone down. Then I phoned Bridgitte's number, and Anderson said: 'Who's that?'

'Mind your own business,' I said. 'I'm not one of your weak-headed patients who answers all your questions. Let me speak to Bridgitte.'

'So it's you?' he said, frothing.

'Yes, it's me. And if you don't mind I'd like to talk to Bridgitte.'

'You mean my wife,' he said.

'Bridgitte Appledore,' I told him, 'Mrs Anderson if you like.'

'You damn-well bet I do. You can't talk to her. And if you see her any more I'll bloody-well divorce her, and you'll be paying off court costs for the rest of your life. I'll spin you around my little finger.'

'Listen,' I said, holding the phone a few feet away and shouting into it to trample over his gallop. 'I'll see who I like when I like, so get that into your headshrinking head. And if you hit Bridgitte again, or if you kick Smog again, I'll use your head for a football all over Hampstead Heath.'

I put the phone down, and didn't feel like using it again any more, having drawn two dud numbers, but thinking I might be third time lucky I contacted Jack Leningrad to say I was back in town, at which they didn't show much interest, as if they might be glad to see the back of me now that I'd made my expected quota of successful trips. It was my honourable inten-tion to relieve them of all responsibility for my welfare, in any case, but only in my own good time. I was looking to my retreat, not wanting to end up in the next-door cell to William, which wouldn't be difficult for them to arrange, if they supposed I knew a bit too much. I suspected it was no accident that William had been caught in the Lebanon rather than in England where he would have been brought to court and may have talked too freely.

A few days later, when they loaded me up with gold for Turkey, I looked at each piece in case it was hollow and filled with poppy seed, for if I were searched at that place with such stuff on me it would mean twenty years' darkness. They noted my suspicions, and didn't like it, but when I saw them weighing me up I liked it even less. I wasn't sure I had it in me to fight a war on ten fronts. I was as helpless before the Leningrad outfit as I had been with Moggerhanger's, and if I lost my nerve it would be through this feeling, not at the brief and occasional ordeal of dodging the customs. Back from Istanbul, I spoke to Stanley, who said there'd be nothing doing for the next three days, after which there could be a bit of a rush.

Brooding on the misery of William's mother, I'd become tender enough to write to my own and let her know where I was and that I was well. A letter was pushed through the door with a Nottingham postmark and she said, to my surprise, how much she'd worried about me, and how much she missed me, and how much she loved me – love being a word I don't think I'd heard her mention before. She told me the news of my grandmother's death a month ago, which may have upset her because now, apart from me, she was alone in the world, though I thought she must be far from lonely if I knew my mother, who'd never been the person to let boyfriends grow under her feet, and I supposed she was still the same, not being too much above forty. My grandmother, she said, had left me a locked box, and nobody knew what was in it, but she thought it might contain family photos that hadn't been seen for years. So I ought to go up and collect them some time, though if I was busy they'd be kept safe for me until I wasn't, whenever that might be.

I wandered around town all day, reading the letter every time I stopped for a coffee or snack. I was touched by the fact that my mother missed me, and intrigued at the thought of what was in my grandmother's box, so the next day I got on a train at St Pancras and steamed north for Nottingham.

Part Six

I lounged among a heap of newspapers and magazines in a first-class compartment, but soon got bored with them and went to the dining-car for lunch. I'd left it late, and the only remaining place was opposite two other people. I'd felt like being alone with my thoughts, didn't even want to be asked to pass the salt or ashtray. The man's hand was on the table, and the girl by his side touched it, then rested hers on it. I was looking at the window, fascinated by beads of rain breaking and multiplying on their way down the glass as the train rushed along. Then I heard my name spoken, and, being forced to look, I saw that the loving and handsome couple in front of me were none other than Gilbert Blaskin, and my old friend June. I couldn't speak, and a wide smile came on to Gilbert's already wide mouth: 'Having a rest from the big city?'

I smiled back, but it nearly broke my face: 'Where are you two going?' I hadn't seen June since our encounter in the taxi, for which I wasn't exactly well disposed towards her. 'June and I came down to London together in my car,' I explained to him. 'And now you two are travelling north together. My head's beginning to spin.'

'It's a small world,' said Gilbert. 'We all know that. But she's going back north with me now, aren't you, darling?'

'I gave up my job at the club,' she told me. 'Gilbert and I have known each other for months, and we've decided to stay together. You know, the old "man-and-wife" kick.' They'd already had brandy, and we were served with scalding soup.

He toasted her: 'Maybe we'll even get married. We don't talk about it, though it's in the air we breathe. I'm divorced now, thank God.'

I couldn't stand their brimming happiness. 'What happened to Pearl Harby?'

He winced, but I waited for an answer. 'She left me.'

'You mean you threw her out.'

'She left me, old son.'

When the next course came I asked June how Mogger-hanger was these days, and she didn't take it so well: 'You're as rotten as your car. Why don't you drop to bits?'

'I'd like to, but I can't.'

'Not yet, you mean.' Then she smiled, too happy for many hard feelings: 'He came to the club and asked for Kenny Dukes. Moggerhanger said something about Kenny trying to get off with his daughter Polly, who's a lecherous little bitch, I might say. But he told him not to phone her again. Kenny went all flustered and tried to deny it, and when a few more words flew Claud punched him, and had him thrown out of the club.' I laughed, because that must have been the result of my casual phone call, but I didn't tell her, merely tut-tutted at Moggerhanger's vile temper and irrational suspicions. Her opinion of Polly seemed no more than a bit of feminine pique. And one good turn deserves another, I thought, remembering how Kenny Dukes had done me down in a similar way when I lost my chauffeuring job.

The meal ended amicably because we all got drunk. On the way back to the compartments Gilbert fell down, and I trampled on his hat. This made him truculent, but I told him to pack it in and not get so ratty over an accident. 'I'll scratch your eyes out,' June said to me, 'if you try anything.' She picked up the hat and put it on Gilbert's cock-head. 'Come on, love.'

In spite of our differences we sat in the same compartment, much to the disgust of an elderly parson, who told Gilbert to stop using such foul un-Christian talk in front of a lady. 'Don't worry, your reverence,' June said with a downbeat leer, 'I'm not a lady, and he's not a Christian. If he is I'm going to stop living with him,' at which he got up and walked out.

'I'll have to take you everywhere,' Gilbert said to her. 'I like space, and you'll clear every place I go into. We're made for each other.'

I asked him if he was writing another book.

'Not if I can help it,' June said. 'We're too busy living, aren't we, Gilbert my sweet?'

'Almost,' he said, standing up to do physical jerks on the luggage rack. 'I'm doing a monumental non-fiction work at the moment called *The History of Carnage*. My publisher thinks there's a market for it in these years of peace.' He was out of breath, so sat down between us. 'I should get good material living with dear June. The reason I've been so unsuccessful and unhappy with women so far in my life is because I've never found one that will stand up and fight with me. June is a real match. In a restaurant last night she threw an avocado pear, and it splattered beautifully, oil and all.'

'He kicked me under the table.'

'I wanted to see what you'd do.' Gilbert smiled: 'Whenever I did it in the past I just got a look of regret from the injured party.'

'Next time,' she said, 'I'll throw the table as well.'

'Wonderful,' he said, 'and I'll break your bloody neck.' I marvelled at the way he seemed to have altered. I could only assume that Pearl had been driven into the looney-bin. I got off at Nottingham Midland and left the happy couple to their love and kisses.

I'd sent a telegram to my mother the day before and, as I hoped, she had got the afternoon off work so as to be in when I arrived. I took a taxi from the station, craning my neck to get a view of Castle Rock as I went by, caught in the swamp of memory, and loving every minute of it, so that I could get out of it blithely any second. Nobody can feed me the crap that you can't go back, that you can't go home again, because I never believed I was going anywhere, anyway. You do what the hell you like, and don't need to believe in any such thing that ties you down and stops you moving. To go back or to go forward is better than standing still, that's all I know, though the only final moving you do is in the skinbag of yourself.

She was cleaning out my room. 'I'll only stay tonight,' I said, 'because I've got to be back at work tomorrow.'

I stood in the scullery as she lit the gas.

'What work?'

'Travelling' – adding the usual explanations.

She had her curlers in and wore a turban to cover them up: 'You've landed a good job.'

'It pays well.'

'Do you like it, though?'

'It's easy.'

She laughed, and we plonked in the armchairs opposite each other: 'You always were on the lookout for a cushy billet.'

I offered her a cigarette: 'How's your work then?'

'The same old drag. But it keeps me alive and kicking. Do you want something to eat?'

'I'm not hungry.' She made the tea, poured it, put in sugar and milk, stirred it up, and pushed it towards me. 'I'm sorry I couldn't be at Grandma's funeral,' I said. 'But I didn't know about it.'

'We tried to find you. I even went to the police, but there was nothing they could do.'

This made my stomach jump: 'I'll keep in touch from now on.'

'It's best if you do, in case something happens to me. Not that I'm likely to be a drain on you, because I'm getting married soon. Albert and I have fixed it for about three months from now.'

'Albert?'

'You'll meet him tonight, if you come out down town.'

My grandmother's box was upstairs, and I was given an envelope with the key in it. It wasn't full. There were the rent books she'd kept right through her life, all the lapsed insurance policies, birth certificates, a family Bible which, when I opened it, had the births and deaths of several generations of the family written in the fly-leaves, not only by her but by others before her. There were character references from people she had worked for from the age of twelve – packs of that useless detritus that old-fashioned half-literate people liked to hoard. I tore up a few of the rent books and stacked them in the fireplace, piled them on and got a good blaze going with my lighter, for the room was damp and cold. Some fifty-year-old newspapers came out, and these I put to one side to read later, curious as to why she had saved them. Then a pack of ancient photos, a few of them daguerrotypes, members of the family who had steamed over from Ireland.

I compared the dates on the back with the notes in the Bible, and one photo was particularly interesting because it was of the first Cullen to come from County Mayo at the time of the Famine. He'd brought six sons and a wife with him, and the photo showed a man who looked very much like photos I'd seen of myself. It gave me a shock. Polly Moggerhanger had taken one of me in Geneva, and the same stiff self-conscious pose was there. The man of eighteen-forty wore a fine suit, with a waistcoat that had a watch-chain looping across it. He was just above middle height, about thirty years old, and wore a derby hat (or was it a billy-cock?). But he had my thin lips and straight nose, the same arching of the back as the head looked superciliously into the air as if expecting trouble from that quarter. It gave me a pang to realize he'd been dead eighty years, and that maybe in another hundred years someone like me would be looking at a photo of me and saying the same thing to himself. Time has no meaning, I thought, when it comes to photos hoarded by an old woman. I tried to picture his life in the England of those days, but I couldn't. He'd worked with his sons on the railways in Cambridgeshire, and I supposed they'd earned good money with it. He certainly looked well dressed in this photo.

I put it in my wallet, continued digging in the trunk. There was a bonnet, a few embroidered handkerchiefs, a hymn and prayer book, a man's yellow necktie or cravat, and a gold watch that didn't go when I wound it up. Lower down and beneath everything was a small leather bag with something inside that weighed heavily. I opened the string, and gold coins fell out. There were fifty altogether, and I'd never seen golden sovereigns before, that must be worth four or five quid each. The sight and weight of so much gold made my mouth water, and for several minutes I ran them through my fingers like a miser. I was so long up there my mother must have thought I'd laid down and died, so I put all the things back except the gold and humped my way to the living-room.

She looked up from her novel. 'Get anything?'

I clinked the bag down: 'Photos, rent books, and this.'

'What the hell is it?'

'Fifty gold sovereigns.'

She stood up: 'Do you want any more tea?'

'If it's fresh. There's half for you, and half for me. It's over a hundred pounds each.'

'It was left to you,' she called from the scullery.

'I insist on going halves.'

This obviously pleased her: 'All right. Albert and me might go to Paris for a few days with it. I've always wanted to go there.'

'That's a good way of spending it,' I said, pleased that she hadn't wanted to fritter it away on sensible things like clothes or the house.

I met Albert that night, and we hit it off together, which was just as well because my mother wanted me to 'give her away' when the time came, and we both knew I wouldn't give her away to just anybody. She looked so young dressed up that if I'd met her in London and she'd not been my mother I could imagine wanting to get off with her. As for Albert, he was about fifty, and had been a factory worker most of his life. But from being a boy he'd been in the Communist Party and had educated himself, so we had a lot to talk about. Before the war he'd actually been sent to Russia by his trade union, and in those days, being so young, he'd thought it was great. Even now, he wasn't one of those who'd opted out. He knew all about what had been going on, but still kept his faith in a better world and all that. I didn't see eye to eye with him on some of this, but there'd always been a tradition of religious tolerance in our family, so there was no reason why I shouldn't respect him for it. We drank steadily, as if we'd never stop talking, and I could see how pleased my mother was that we took to each other. I certainly wouldn't mind him going to Paris on part of the Cullen gold. My grandmother must have got her hands on so much during the Great War when she was working at the gun factory. I'm glad to know that somebody made something out of it apart from the millionaires. She must have gone out of her way to get gold so that it wouldn't lose its value, and I was glad that at least one member of the Cullen family had shown a bit of wisdom for once.

I left my twenty-five sovereigns locked in the box, and went back to London, an ideal journey in that I neither met nor spoke to anyone. Sunshine came warmly into the musty compartment as I left Nottingham, but two hours later the train passed St Albans and entered the drizzle. My mother had packed sandwiches so I didn't need to go to the restaurant coach. As for drink, I never got thirsty. I don't know why but I could go a whole day without liquid of any kind, not even feeling uncomfortable for lack of it.

On St Pancras Station I bought a newspaper to pass my time on the Underground, and when I unfolded it I saw a headline which made me feel uneasy, not to say queasy. HEADLESS BODY FOUND IN RIVER. POLICE LAUNCH SEARCH ON PUTNEY REACH. HUSBAND GASSED. I read it several times. Her head had been discovered in the mud, and my friend on the plane from sunny Portugal had done it after all, in spite of that loving reunion I'd witnessed at London airport. The gory gossip was given, and all the office girls were reading it up. I chopped my vomit back and saw his face before me, mad and vivid in its details, when even on the plane during his spiel I hadn't got a good look at it, and so could never have known what was really behind those amiable, intelligent, grotesque eyes.

His story had fixed me, there's no doubt of that, because who isn't still gripped by tales of medieval jealousy, mother-love, and spite, even though it can be seen as rockingly funny? But I couldn't see that far behind his eyes and believe he'd really meant what he said. I decided that from now on I'd accept what people said as being part of their true interiors. They are incapable of lying when they are desperate, and in any case your intuition has to tell you when they were in this state. If I had taken the pains to see, which wouldn't have been that far beyond me, to the deepest recesses behind his eyes in which that picture lurked in black and grey and red, of his wife's head tilted in the mud and staring at some innocent barge going by in the moonlight, I might have saved her, and him. But I didn't, because somehow my feet were no longer plugged into the earth, and my aerial was withered in its contact with heaven. It seemed I had been living underwater not to have known the truth of what was so obvious, and been able to do something about it. I saw everything sharp and clear with the bare eye, but a lazy idleness inside kept a permanent cloth-bound foot on the deeper perceptions that blinded me from action. Some explosion was necessary in my consciousness and I didn't know how to bring it about before something happened due to this inadequacy that would be fatal to me.

The train rumbled under the earth of London. I was packed in with office workers, my eyes uncontrollably reading all the inane advertisements that even such thoughts as I was having could not blot out. I took my eyes away and set them on someone's blank back.

I was relieved on reaching the flat to find a letter from the estate agents saying that my offer of eleven hundred for Upper Mayhem station and house had been accepted. I was asked to instruct my solicitors to proceed as quickly as possible with a view to exchanging contracts. I didn't want telling twice, so in the morning called up Smut and Bunt asking them to get a move on in case someone should now come and pip me by a bigger offer. The man from Putney was out of the running, but as far as I knew there might be others, and in view of my precarious situation I was now more set in my heart than ever at getting that bit of property.

I dialled headquarters to see if a trip was lined up for me. Stanley was in an expansive mood. 'No,' he said, 'not for a couple of days, Michael. We've got Arthur Ramage going to Zurich in the morning and he's so good he can do two men's share. So stand by the day after tomorrow.' Before I could say Arthur Ramage ought not to be such a graballing bastard, he hung up. Ramage was a legend in the smuggling trade, king of the job. William had called him champion, held him in awe because he'd been on it for years without getting caught and had exported more gold than Cunard – making himself so rich by his earnings that he owned a prosperous farm in Norfolk. He got good prices for all his jobs because they were the trickiest, and William said that if he wrote a book about it it would be a bestseller except that he'd get three hundred years in jail for endangering Britain's economy. Every time the Prime Minister got up in Parliament to try and talk his way out of a financial crisis you could bet Arthur Ramage had been in action. Whenever Britain got its neck saved by a massive loan from overseas to reinforce its gold stocks, Arthur Ramage set to work again (with the connivance of the Jack Leningrad Organization) to wittle them away. In fact if you took all such talk seriously you might honestly begin to believe that those who made the massive loan were the ones who got the gold back again via Jack Leningrad in order to keep the pot boiling and their commission and profits piling up. It was all so dirty I could only laugh at it, because if I took it seriously and wept I might not have earned the money to buy my station.

I went out to have a meal in Soho. Before going in I phoned Polly, and by the breath of luck she picked it up herself. There was a tone of gladness in her voice at hearing from me. 'Are you working tomorrow? If not, why don't you come and see me?'

A bloke outside hugged a girl to him and waited to come in. 'I was on in the morning,' I said, 'but somebody else is going to Lisbon for a change.'

'As long as it's not you, love,' she said softly. 'I *have* missed you. What unlucky man is taking your place?'

'Oh, a bloke called Ramage will be doing it for the next two weeks, on the same day. You don't know him, though. I've only seen him once myself. A champion.'

She broke in, as if I might go on boring her for half an hour over it. 'The house should be clear by ten. Phone me, and then come over. You can help me pick roses.'

'As long as I don't get pricked.' She laughed, and hung up. I did likewise, pushed my way roughly by the bloke and girl struggling to get in.

The head waiter bowed as he'd previously done to William, and I didn't like the omen of it, though just the same I was pleased because when I couldn't think of what to order he'd pamper me with the dish of the day, or suggest something special that might tempt me in my jaded mood. So in order to bring my fragmented mind to heel I treated myself to a good feed and washed it down with half a bottle of champagne. My dreamprint for the future, in so far as I hoped it would work, was to leave my gold-smuggling profession, put a certain proposition to Polly Moggerhanger, and retire with her to a life of bliss at my railway station. Yet none of this seemed real or possible, because I knew that no matter how fondly I mused on the future, it was all worked out for me, in spite of my wants and hopes. Still, this part of reality didn't suggest itself strongly enough to douse my appetite. I looked around the room for a girl who might interest me, but it was an off-night, for not many people were there.

I walked in the rain down Charing Cross Road, on my way towards Hungerford footbridge, meaning to wend home along the south bank. Near midnight I met Almanack Jack, with a sheet of plastic over himself, holding two carrier bags. 'What's in there, Jack?' I asked. 'You've done another job?'

He told me to eff-off, and shambled on.

'It's me,' I said.

'Who's me?' he growled.

'Michael, of bacon-sandwich fame. Remember?'

A breeze sent drops of rain from him, and his breath was tainted with decay, and pure steam-alcohol he'd been floating down himself. 'I'm grovelling,' he said, coming close. People passing thought he was tapping me for a bob or two, so hurried on in case he should turn to them, though they made it seem as if they were merely trying to get on out of the rain. 'Grovelling,' he said, 'can't you tell?'

'Is it like that, Jack? I can't see it though. You've never done that.' A vivid picture came to me of my grandmother dying and I didn't know where to turn my head, wanting to get away from him like those people and buses going down Whitehall. 'I can't escape it,' he said, 'and that's the truth. A hundred million people are standing on the moon holding up the Earth, and they're going to throw it on my belly. They want me to burst. It's the world's end, the only way it can end.'

I lit a fag but didn't offer one, wanting him to ask so that I could see he was coming back to his right mind. Maybe he's in it already, I thought, and has spent most of his life trying to get there. 'They won't be able to lift it,' I said, 'so you'll be safe enough.'

He laughed: 'They will, don't you worry. I sleep under a

bridge. Even then, I try to keep awake. But I sleep. Can't help it. When they throw it the bridge will break. Bound to if you think of the weight of the world. Straight through and on to me.'

'You can't live without hope,' I said, as much for myself as him, wishing I hadn't bumped into him, because I didn't feel as safe and callous as I'd always thought I was.

'You'll never do it,' he said, out of nothing. 'No, you'll never do it.'

I tried to laugh, but my throat cracked: 'Do what?'

'Never,' he said.

'Do what, Jack?' He stared at me, grey eyes through grey beard. 'Do what?' I asked. 'You're cracked, you stupid get. You've had too much plonk down you.' I wanted to go, but hung on to him like an old friend, as if he were the last person in the world I knew in London. 'None of us will do it,' he said, leaning against the wall. 'We haven't got the stomach. Too much heart and not enough stomach. No brain either. The world is an apple with a maggot inside, so even half a man could hold it and put his foot on it.'

I could stand here listening all night, but he wouldn't know who I was. He was too far back in the attics of his own mind. 'What is it you want then, Jack?'

'Eh? Who are you?'

'I'm asking you what you want most in the world,' I said, feeling the rain eating its way through to my shirt collar despite an overcoat.

'Bread and jam,' he said. 'Slices of bread and butter, spread with jam. And tea. Tea. Hot.' He clutched his carrier bags: 'You can't have my almanacks, though, so don't try it.'

'I don't want them,' I said, taking a few pound notes out of my wallet. 'Has anybody been bothering you? I'll break their heads.'

'Rotten fruit,' he said. 'They'll bury me in rotten fruit.'

'Bollocks,' I said, 'take this money and have a binge on bread and jam. It'll make you feel better.'

He stared at the notes. 'Take it,' I said, then had to dodge, because with great strength and cunning he swung both heavy bags of almanacks at me, one of them catching me sharply on the hip. He screamed, and kept swinging, and both bags burst so that almanacks went flying all over the pavement and into the wet road, blown open by the wind. He rushed at me, kicking so that I had to fly for my life from his madman's strength. I didn't run far, turned, and saw him leaning against a wall, his face pressed to it. I walked back and he went away, but I caught him up and touched his elbow. It was impossible to leave him, not only for his good, but mine as well. 'Jack,' I said, 'it's me, Michael.'

He stopped and looked hard: 'Oh, it's you,' he said, calmly, but with great weariness.

'Where are you going?'

'To hell,' he said, 'unless somebody gives me a couple of bob.'

'Hang on Jack. Here's three quid. In a month or two I'll be getting a house in the country, and if you want to, you can live there. It'll be quiet, and you'll like it, an old railway station neat Huntingborough.'

'You can say that again.'

'I mean it,' I said, giving him the money.

'I'm down on my luck, but I'll pay you back.'

'Don't worry about that. I'm earning it at the moment.' I found a five-pound note in my wallet, and gave him that, too. 'Take care of it.'

'Yes,' he said. 'I will. Eight pounds. It's years since I had that much.' I left him, hoping he'd survive the next month or so, then I'd let him come to the station till he got his strength back. Plans altered as you made them, though to make plans was the only way to get anywhere.

After languishing with Polly in various beds of the Moggerhanger household, and in the cottage hideaway in Kent, I knew what I wanted at last, and though it seemed crazy and catastrophic for someone like me to marry her, yet that is exactly what I set my heart on. I told her about my railway station, embroidering on its beauty and solitude, until it seemed the most romantic retreat in the world for two people as much in love as we were.

Driving back from the country, she said that even though

she was in tune with all my proposals regarding Upper Mayhem, she didn't really want to make too violent a break with her father, whom she loved, and whom she wanted to reconcile to our elopement sooner or later. She would abide by her own passionate wish to stay with me for ever (she was an even more eloquent talker than I was, at times, it was beginning to seem) but I would have to be patient and help her to make the break at the right time.

This plea delighted me, being definite proof of how seriously she took our planned departure. At the same time passionate and sensible, she made her way to the deepest part of my heart, and the least I could do was help her to make the break at the time of her choosing, because whether I stayed another few months with Jack Leningrad made no difference to me when a whole future of bliss was involved.

She was the first person I'd ever been completely open with. My natural bent to tell lies became submerged, and if I did feel the fever of fantasy coming on me I meshed it into a story so ridiculous that there was no chance or danger of her believing it had any connexion with the truth. I thus discovered that love makes people honest, but the only trouble was that in the subterfuge world of smuggling, such honesty might be a disadvantage, a race against time between Polly coming to Mayhem with me, and me giving myself away in one of my passages through London airport or Gatwick. She knew of all my techniques as a bona-fide traveller burdened by impossible loads, for I told her when I was going on a trip and where, and who as far as I knew would be going that evening or the following day. Confiding so easily helped me to carry on the work till she decided it was time for the lovers' flit. And doing it longer than I'd contemplated didn't faze me because with every journey I was piling more money into the bank.

I asked Polly to come with me on one of my trips to Paris, but her parents were going to Bournemouth for a few days and wanted her to go with them. There was nothing she'd like more than to stay with me in Paris, she said. 'I'll tell my parents to go to hell. It isn't right that I'm forced to spend three deadly dull days in Bournemouth when we could be in Paris together. You mean more to me than my parents, so

I'll come, even though it might mean the break taking place sooner than I'd thought.'

'No,' I said, 'it's all right. Let's wait. We might not spend a few days in Paris now, but we'll have all the time we want later on, and we won't need to disturb anyone about it either.' When I talked her out of doing anything so rash as making a break now, she had tears in her eyes at my solicitude. I said I didn't want to be responsible for such a thing, in case she found it hard to forgive me later. In any case I hoped that after we'd eloped, and set up house at Upper Mayhem, her father would see his way to forgiving us and letting me once more into his protection and confidence.

It always came back in the end to care and cunning and patience and nerve, so that at last I was beginning to get the pattern of my life, and the feeling of these qualities became so intense that my strength increased to a height wherein I had to watch it so that I didn't become slipshod. I sensed myself acquiring the confidence that could ruin me, but because I saw it, I thought that was sufficient protection against it. A man did not stop being a fool merely by knowing he was one. This was even less likely than being clever by simply realizing that one was clever. If anything, the knowledge that I was a bastard had stopped the appropriate distillation of bitterness entering my view of things. If I'd been like everyone else with a married mother and father, the iron in the soul might have bitten into me sooner and given me that extra veneer of protection against the world.

But Polly was my brilliant star, my beautiful heavy-breasted love whose sweet cunt turned into a morass as soon as I touched her. In the cottage bedroom we turned on Moggerhanger's high-powered radio and danced naked to Arab music. Sometimes she brought a few hash cigarettes that put us into such a high trance that we could dance and fuck all night.

One evening I took her to my favourite eating-place. We hadn't met for three days, and our hands, mine warm and hers cool, joined over the table, glasses of Valpolicella not yet touched. 'Let's drink to our departure,' I said. 'All you have to do is say the word. I'm ready. Contracts have been exchanged for my country seat, and in a couple of weeks I'll actually have the deeds. Michael Cullen will be a property owner!'

She looked anxious, worn by some inside trouble: 'Do we just run away?'

'Isn't that what we agreed on?'

She took her hand back and lifted her glass a little higher: 'Let's drink, then, to when we are together, properly.'

The wine went into my stomach like sour ice: 'Not well warmed.'

'Oh, Michael, I hope you won't think I'm stupid at what I'm going to say.' The temperature of my stomach dropped, and met the chill of the wine. 'What is it, love? I could never think such a thing about you.' The waiter asked what we wanted to eat. 'Let me order,' I said.

She smiled. 'I like it when you take charge.' I asked for smoked eels to start with, followed by ravioli, brought up by escalope, then sweetened by zabaglione. The waiter floated away and she took my hand again: 'You know we're a close-knit family at home, don't you, Michael? I couldn't do anything to make my parents too unhappy.'

'I'm not asking you to,' I said, not caring about them one way or another, until after we were married: 'It's good that you don't want to hurt them. I like you even more for it, if that's possible.'

'Well,' she said, and I expected the worst, 'I've told them about us.'

I held myself from keeling over. 'What did they say?'

'They took it very well. Father knows you, of course, and Mother remembers you, but they want to meet you again. They'd like you to come to dinner on Friday, if you aren't working.'

'Really?'

'I was very nervous, but I couldn't help telling them because we've never had secrets from each other. Not for long, anyway. And just going off to live with you would upset them terribly. I just wouldn't have been able to do it when the time came.'

'That's all right, love.' I looked to see if any of Mogger-hanger's hoods were keeping me under watch and key.

'I said how much in love we were. Father was very kind about it, and told me I wasn't to worry.'

I regretted ordering such a big meal, but when the food did come I began filling up. I would have liked to trust in God at that moment, except that my optimism had been strangled at birth. I was afraid that Moggerhanger would now get his claws into me, either to do me in without more ado, or make my life so miserable that I'd have to flee even beyond England to keep breath in my body, out of sight and mind both of Polly and my railway station. Yet I ate so much that fear seemed to have a peculiar hunger of its own.

'It's a lovely meal,' she said, noticing my appetite, and stroking my wrist while we waited for the second course. 'It'll be all right, Michael. I know Father and Mother will take to you.'

'I hope so,' I said bravely. 'I can be charming when I like, you know that! Being in love stops me being nervous.'

She touched my arm and gave a luminous loving smile: 'Wait!'

It didn't get through to me: 'Most of what you wait for never comes.

'You waited for me tonight,' she said. 'We can call at your flat on the way home.'

I was certainly nervous at going to the Moggerhangers' for dinner. I felt I had need to be. It was a simple physical fear of being set on, because Moggerhanger was no fool. From his point of view I intended robbing him of a daughter. Of course, at the same time he would gain a son, let us not forget it (I said to myself in town, as I bought a large expensive lot of flowers for the household, knowing that there was nothing he liked more than to see the right thing done), though this seemed unlikely to console a man in Moggerhanger's shoes who saw sons as being available at ten a penny. So I considered myself a big enough threat to set him into back-handed action. Nevertheless I still saw the position as hopeful, and had a feeling that perhaps after all things would turn out well for Polly and myself. I respected Moggerhanger for the way he'd got on in the world, but I didn't have much human sympathy for him. It's no use saying I wanted him to perish, because I did, but I knew also there was no hope of this, and neither did I think the bunch of flowers would do any good, though I carried them just the same.

José opened the door and took my raincoat. Mrs Mogger-hanger came into the hall: 'I'm so glad you could come, Mr Cullen. My husband and daughter are out strolling in the garden. Do join us. It's such a pleasant evening.'

We walked through the living-room and made an exit by the french windows. She was taller and thinner than Polly, but dark-haired, and must have been even more good-looking, though at forty-five I still wouldn't have said no to her. There was a soft pink light over the lawn, meshing with green, and in the distance by the lilac bushes Polly was talking to her father, a hand on his forearm. I should have been happy at meeting my future in-laws, but there was something I didn't like about this evening.

'Hello, Michael, I'm glad to meet you again,' he said, and sounded so friendly that for a moment I thought his remark was genuine. I very much wanted to tell myself that he did mean it, but a protective manifestation of my scurvy spirit prevented me from doing so, and this troublesome nagging caution stayed with me most of the evening. Moggerhanger said he'd like to show me the garden.

'I'm interested in horticulture,' I said, 'because I like flowers, especially roses, but I don't know much about them, though I suppose I should because Harry Wheatcroft comes from up my way.' Polly smiled, as if to say I was doing very well indeed.

'They're a man's best friend,' said Moggerhanger. 'I only say that because I could never stand dogs.'

'I'll have to study a few gardening books,' I said, 'since I have a few acres with my country place near Huntingborough. It'll take a bit of getting in order.'

'I taught Claud all he knows,' his wife said, with a touch of homely pride.

He left Polly's arm, and took hers. 'She did, Michael, that's quite true. It's saved us a few arguments, this garden. Whatever house I buy I always make sure it's got a good piece of ground that I can turn into a riot of colour. I don't get much spare time in my sort of work, but I'm never bored when I do. We've got a penthouse in Brighton, and there's a beautiful roof-garden we've created there. We are a bit naughty when we go abroad, aren't we, Agnes?' he chuckled. 'We can't resist smuggling a few plants back into the country. We get them by the customs all right. Not that those chaps bother me. I suppose they know what's going on, really, but I tip them the wink. A few fivers in the benevolent fund goes a long way.'

Agnes laughed: 'Now then, Claud, you know you've never done such a thing.'

His voice turned a shade sterner. 'Not as far as you know, Mother.'

'It's getting chilly,' she said, 'I don't want Polly to catch cold. Do we, dear?'

'Oh, don't fuss,' she exclaimed, while giving me a wide and loving smile in front of them.

I sank into a deep armchair. It was too low and soft. My feeling was to get up again and stand at my own height by the mantelshelf where I could be seen to greater advantage. But I sat, and accepted a heavy cut glass nearly half filled with whisky. 'What kind of work do you do now?' Mrs Moggerhanger asked with a smile.

I told her the same old lie, but it went down well, for I embellished it concerning some upgrading I was in for because the firm was opening new branches in Europe, even as far afield as Turkey, and I was coordinating this new scheme at the moment so that while extending operations I was making it possible for us to economize at the same time. 'I don't want to bore you with it, though. I'm likely to talk all night if you don't stop me.'

In any tight spot about my job I threatened to go on for hours rather than be reticent, so that any listener was only too glad to drop it. Moggerhanger cut in: 'Well, we don't want to spoil your inspiration, and that's a fact. I often find it doesn't pay to talk too much about your work. It waters down your ideas without your noticing it. If I'm taking a man on, I decide whether he's much of a talker, and if he is he don't stand a chance.'

I swigged his plonk: 'I can talk for hours, but I never give anything away, and neither does it dilute my ideas, if that's what you mean.'

He laughed. 'You know, Michael, I think I believe you.'

Seeing that she had set us going, his wife went to check the dinner. 'Polly tells me you're in love,' he said, at which Polly stood up and said she was going to see if there was anything she could do in the kitchen. He had pronounced the phrase *in love* as if I'd been caught by him trying to blow a safe in such a clumsy fashion that I wouldn't even have buckled the hinges. I stood up.

'Sit down,' he said.

I walked to the mantelshelf, and finished off my whisky, refusing to sit when that bastard told me, even if he was Polly's old man, and one of the richest men in London – or Ealing. 'I am in love with her,' I said, 'and have been from the moment I saw her.'

He smiled: 'You don't have to spit the words out like rusty tacks. I wanted to hear it from your own lips, that's all. But you've been going about things like an elephant trying to be cunning. I've always admired tact, and don't particularly like somebody who's sly and devious from his toenails up. I believe you when you say you're in love with Polly and want to marry her, but at the same time I love her as well – and never you forget it – so I don't want her to get into the hands of the wrong person. The fact that we both love her gives us something in common. Don't let that go to your head, though.'

'I'm sorry if I spoke too sharply,' I said, 'but you can be sure I'll do my best to make her happy.'

He got up and went to the whisky pot. 'Another drink?'

'Yes,' I said.

'Don't think you're in much of a position to make a bargain,' he said, hovering over me. 'Not yet, at least. I know you're a sharp person, so I'd like a few words with you after dinner. We'll go to my study and let the ladies go about their own business. In the meantime. let's drink this. I'm not supposed to, but I will for once.'

He took only a sip of it before we went in to dinner. It was the most stultifying meal I'd ever been at. I weighed every word carefully in my brain-pan before letting it out to do its best, or worst, and the same seemed true of the adult Moggerhangers, even of Polly. She was particularly subdued, and that I liked least of all, though occasionally she did try to open some new road of conversation. But everything seemed to die in its tracks, and I thought Moggerhanger himself was responsible for this. In fact he seemed to exult in it, as if showing off in front of me the power he held over his family. But I had my pride too, and was by no means inclined to start an entertaining stream of talk. To do so would have pleased him, for he would know himself responsible for it, and congratulate himself on having broken my nerve. There were moments when I didn't know what I was doing there, until I looked across at Polly and managed a smile of complicity out of her. Worst of all, as if even that was planned, the food wasn't up to the standard I'd been stuffing myself with at the Italian place.

Towards the end of the meal we were comparing the merits of the various holiday spots in Europe, such as Klosters and Monte Carlo, Majorca and Cortina, none of which places I'd been to. But pretending that I had gave the conversation a more jumpy and natural rhythm, which caused a slight melting of the ice between us. When we stood up to go back into the living-room things became quite affable. But the deep armchairs felled me again. They were like fox-holes, from which we couldn't talk but only snipe each other. I'd never imagined I could have landed so deeply into the household of such a bourgeois racketeer, but I supposed it to be just another proof of my unworldliness. Though I'd previously worked for him I'd thought this middle-class nook was only a front to face anyone who might accuse him of being a criminal to the core – which he certainly was.

I'd been curious during most of the evening to know what he wanted to talk to me about. After an hour of brain-dragging small-talk he stood up and asked Polly and her mother to excuse us. I took the hint that I shouldn't see Polly again for a day or two, so wished them goodnight and followed Moggerhanger into what he called his library. It's true, there were books in it, a stand of five shelves full of novels I wouldn't be seen dead, or even alive, reading, though I did have time to notice a couple by Gilbert Blaskin, one called *Vampires In Love* and another entitled *The Seventh Highway*.

Happily there were no deep armchairs in this room, otherwise I'd have gone berserk with the table knife I'd slipped into my pocket at the end of the meal. The room was walled in panelled oak, and Moggerhanger stood behind his desk, neither of us being inclined to sit down.

'Brandy?'

'A noggin,' I said.

He pushed it over, as well as an opened box of Havanas: 'Only one,' he said.

'Sorry,' I said, unwrapping it.

'And hand that knife over. Nobody goes out of this house with one of my knives, unless it's in his back.' He laughed at this joke, and even I thought it funny as I slid the knife on the desk. I wished I hadn't stolen it now because some gravy had congealed inside the pocket of my best suit. 'I just wondered whether you'd notice it.'

He sat on the desk itself: 'I don't like pissed-up young tiddleywinks making tests on me, so watch it.'

I certainly watched him, because I knew him to be as savage as a shark, a wild man who wore gold cufflinks and stank of after-shave lotion. 'Tell me what you want, then.'

'I don't know where to begin,' he joked. It was obvious to me that Polly had made a big mistake in letting him in on our secret. He was her own father but she didn't know the first thing about him, taking his career for that of an honest property dealer when the only property he'd ever dealt in had been other people's. There was not a hope of Polly and I ever marrying under his vicious auspices, so it didn't matter to me whether I showed him any respect or not. 'It was a pity you stopped working for me.'

'You gave me the sack,' I told him.

'Yes, so I did.'

'In any case,' I said, 'I didn't feel like being a chauffeur all my life.'

'There's worse jobs.'

'And better.'

'I'm glad you think so. I would have had something better for you, by and by.'

'I can't help it if I were headstrong,' I said, 'but I'm getting over it.'

'There's hope for us yet, then, as far as I'm concerned.'

'What sort?'

He sat down in the swivel chair behind the desk. 'If you want to join the family, I might ask you to prove your regard for it by getting you to show a bit of loyalty. I think I can safely say that my wife likes you, and I know Polly does. As for me, I always considered you the sort who would get on in the world – as you've shown by the job you've landed yourself in. I was pleased to hear it when Polly told me about it.'

He gave me a hard look, and half a smile, and I knew he knew what was cutting through my mind. I'd have walked out, if I could have covered my retreat with a Molotov cocktail. The effort not to smile, twitch or say any halfcock joke made me sick at the stomach. 'In my experience,' said Moggerhanger, 'the hardest thing for any man to do, including myself, is to keep his business to himself. You're still young, though if I were at the butt-end of your flap-mouth I wouldn't consider it much of an excuse. But I can understand you not thinking it too bad an indiscretion, because a man often tells things to his girlfriend that he'd never tell anyone else, not even his mother. And you weren't to know that Polly has never had any secrets from me. She may hold back a while with some, but sooner or later she'll confide in me or her mother, and I might say here and now that I find that sort of thing a great virtue. Anybody who confides something to me that's in any way profitable can rely on me to stand by them for as long as they'll be able to stand themselves. And that's saying something. It's saying a bloody lot, Michael, in fact, and I want you to know it.'

He became quite emotional, more so than I'd ever seen him. And he shall reign for ever and ever, I thought, looking at him. 'Loyalty,' he said, suddenly calm, 'there's nothing to better it, Michael.' Loyalty to whom? I wondered, as if I didn't know, but I grew shakier by the minute, as he went on: 'I've been familiar with the Jack Leningrad Organization for a long time. In fact I was a founder member, you might say, but I got pushed out by a little piece of chicanery just after the war – when I wasn't as strong as I am now – by that bastard in his iron lung, who at the time was all hale and hearty. The organization, you see, began early in the war, and I was the lynchpin and mainstay of it, because in those days the danger was great – we had the Germans to put up with as well as the British. In spite of the occupation of France and everywhere else, we had couriers travelling all over Europe, and sometimes to Soviet Russia. Our offices were in Lisbon, London, Gibraltar, Zurich, and Madrid, and how we got gold from one place to another is just nobody's bloody business. And at times it was a very bloody business indeed, with our chaps getting picked off by British or German officers who considered that they hadn't been paid enough to leave well alone. There was near damn-all profit in it at times. Still, business picked up after the war when we booted Churchill out – the only trouble being that I got booted out as well. Not that it was a bad thing, because it put more strength in my elbow to push other affairs along, and I made more money than if I'd stayed with the Leningrad gang. That's years ago, and I'll tell you Michael that in the last year I've had a mind to get the organization back into my fold.'

I was about to reach for another cigar when the canny bastard pushed them over. 'The obvious way to begin, without using too much push, was to get a man in who could reconnoitre the situation. And this I did.'

I nearly choked on smoke: 'William Hay?'

'Right. You're too sharp already. But he got nabbed in the Lebanon. At first I thought the Lung had got him picked up so as to get rid of him. But that wasn't the case, because if they'd got him pulled in for that reason, they'd have had you in the same black hole of Beirut because he was the one who got you into the set-up. See what I mean?'

'You've got me sweating,' I said. 'Internally. Blood.'

'But they haven't tumbled to a thing. You're in the clear, my boy! So I can go on with my campaign.'

'Why are you going back into their organization? Is there that much profit in it for you?'

He gave a great laugh. 'Not a bit of it. I've got so much I can't want any more and keep my self-respect. I'm doing it because I'm bored for an hour every day, and I've got to put my brains and talent to something, otherwise the capital investment will run down.'

'And now you're proposing that I take William Hay's place.'

'Oh, Michael! If only I'd had a son like you! As well as a daughter, of course! And now my fondest hopes may come true, because you might be my son-in-law. What more can I want?'

'Things are looking up,' I said.

'They'll look up even more if you tell me you'll do it.'

'What, exactly?'

'Just keep me informed on who does what, and what they take where, and when. I'm sure that's not too much for you. You've got the talent for it.'

'If you don't mind,' I said, 'I'd like a couple of days to think it over.'

'Better and better. If there's a thing that'll ruin a man quicker than a loose mouth it's hurry. But you realize that this conversation is so secret that to mention it anywhere would be a personal disaster for you?'

'It's engraved on my heart,' I said. 'But how would you break up such an organization as Jack Leningrad's? It's very tough and extensive, I might tell you.'

'That's my worry. I've got it all worked out. Say you'll come in with me, and when I take over you'll be my operations chief. You'll have a house, an American car, a boat – and Polly as your wife – and I'll tell you that you won't get a better wife, or a better father-in-law come to that.' His face grew hard: 'With someone like you working on the inside of Jack Leningrad's lousy set-up I'll have his couriers disappear so fast into the nets of the law that he'll wonder why God's turned against him. Then I'll pay that paralytic a personal visit, I'll smash his lung to pieces and watch him die like a fish on his own floor. So think it over, Michael. We'll do great business together.'

'Promise me one thing,' I said, 'and I'll think very seriously about it.'

'Anything,' he said.

'Find out where William Hay is, and help him.'

'Done. Expect him back in a week or two. Don't ask any questions, but welcome him like a brother and a hero.'

He offered his chauffeur to drive me home, but I wanted to walk, to stop the crazy spinning in my head by pitching my eyes against the night air. I hadn't the least intention of working for Moggerhanger, even though it seemed against my own best interests not to do so. I not only didn't trust him but I disliked him intensely. True, I was caught up with Polly, but the idea had been to go off and live with her at Upper Mayhem, where I hoped he wouldn't track us down. I'd never had a father and I didn't want one now. The idea of it made me sick. How could any self-respecting man want to laden himself with a father? Not me, certainly, I told myself as I walked along, rattling two silver forks together in my pocket, and smoking another of the half-dozen cigars I'd lifted from the box unbeknown to the all-seeing Moggerhanger. Even if I decided to give up my cushy job with Jack Leningrad, it wouldn't be to get entangled with Moggerhanger, because his promise of an eminent career for me as a racketeer didn't bode well for my head staying on my shoulders. And I knew for certain and for sure that even if I helped him to get Jack Leningrad back into his grip, he'd never in a million years agree to me marrying Polly. All his rhetoric about loyalty and standing by people who'd done him a good turn was nothing more than wind and piss. He'd kick me aside when he got what he wanted, and then make Polly forget me by having her marry somebody else.

I sweated at the thought of what she had told him. It seemed to have been quite enough for him to be going on with for a while. I wondered why she had done it, because such a thing wasn't necessary in order to explain that we were in love and wanted to get married. My suspicions took me home through a series of nightmares, one being that Claud was already on the board of Jack Leningrad Limited, and was playing this bit of theatre only to find out whether or not

I was loyal to the organization. Also, it had probably started months ago when he'd seen to it that Polly and I were on the same plane to Geneva, knowing we'd get acquainted on board like any two young people would. Even my socks were sweat-soaked. Maybe she wasn't his daughter, but someone he'd taken from the club to work for him in this way. One minute I felt unborn, the next I was going crazy, and though I knew that these fantasies were mostly unjustified, the one about Polly being specially set on to me in order to get information for her father lingered and bothered me.

It was a relief, once I was back at the flat, to get a call saying I was to take a consignment to Zurich on the next morning's plane. I was so locked in with thoughts about Moggerhanger's proposition that I walked through the airport customs as if in a dream. Lines of weary people at the beginning of their holidays straggled from each counter, and I joined them patiently, obviously not one of them, almost expecting a smile of recognition and commiseration from the officials when I went through the eggtimer into the crowded departure lounge. As always, I looked for friendly recognition from some old acquaintance, for though in a risky situation, I felt exposed without friends, one fly among many but unlike any of them. There was a smell of sweat, tea, coffee, mildewed fag smoke, make-up, booze, boot-polish, and nondescript dust, and a scattering of displaced faces staring dreamily in all directions, tourist-agency labels fastened on their lapels. In spite of my nonchalant air and familiarity with the procedure of separation, I knew that in my heart I felt the same as they did. It only seemed in all truth that my heart was buried a bit deeper than theirs, that's all, as I stood looking at them like an experienced traveller – though I wasn't at that time to know by how much.

I came back from Zurich next day and went straight to the man in the iron lung's flat to collect my pay and report the success of my trip. Stanley opened the door with a sombre look on his face. 'What's wrong?' I asked. 'Has the firm gone bust?'

He let out a cry: 'That's just not bloody funny, Michael. Come quickly. The boss wants to see you.'

'I've got to see him,' I said, 'because I've some bad news.'

I had the satisfaction of seeing him jerk back from me:
'What do you mean?'

'Just this,' I shouted. 'I'm fed up with doing these trips at
three hundred a shot. I'm one of your most experienced men,
and I think four hundred would be nearer the mark, so from
now I'm putting in for a raise. This bloody *Volga Boat Song*
has gone on too long as far as I'm concerned.' I threw my
smuggler's coat at his feet for him to pick up himself or leave
there to rot.

He tried to calm me down. 'All right, Michael, maybe you'll
get it, but for God's sake be careful and break it to him bit
by bit because I tell you he's in an awful state today. Arthur
Ramage has been caught on the Lisbon run.'

He looked closely at me as he broke the news. 'How do you
expect me to feel?' I cried. 'He was the champion, the best
man ever known in the trade. What do you expect? A smile
because it wasn't me? Goddamn it, somebody couldn't keep
their mouth shut.'

As if full of grief and rage, because that was my only
chance of not being killed as I walked through that door, I
knocked Stanley aside and barged into Jack Leningrad's pad
with as much violence as I could muster. Cottapilly and Pindarry, two men I hardly knew were standing by the iron lung,
but I rushed the whole length of the floor screaming that
Ramage had been sold down the river, that Leningrad himself had done it, had picked up the phone to make an anonymous call to London airport because he thought Ramage had
gotten too big for his elastic-sided boots and had wanted
to split the organization so that he could take charge of part
of it with the idea of one day snapping up the lot. So he'd
gone the way of all flesh, just the same as William Hay, who
Jack Leningrad had also framed.

'It'll be my turn next,' I ranted on, 'I can feel it coming.
I'm working for a nest of vipers. You're hand in glove with the
customs men yourself and you can do what you like with us.
Cottapilly and you, Pindarry, you'll go after me, don't worry,
and that fat pasty-faced paralytic slug knows it. We're puppets
to him, wax figures that he'll throw into the deepest jail as soon
as he sees fit or gets frightened enough. He's paranoid. We're

loyal, but he thinks we're all set on doing the dirty on him. And if it's not that, he now and again gets a spiteful little fit of sadism and thinks to pass the time on and gratify himself by getting a few of us caught. And when this happens he makes sure that the one he's going to have pulled in has three-quarters of his load in false gold.'

I was on my knees, screaming all the preposterous things I could think up, then on the floor, then standing up against the wall only ten yards away from him, sobbing, keeping him in good view all the time. His pale face grew yellow, and I could see a twitch at the temples under the border of black sleek hair that went thinly over his head. Out of the speakers came his raging voice, from every side of the room in stereo. 'Stop it, you lying vandal. It's not true.' He held a heavy revolver and pointed it at me.

'I've been loyal,' I said, calming down, 'I've worked hard, Mr Leningrad. You can rely on me to do my utmost. Maybe I said too much just now, but the news went through me like a knife. It's terrible. I'm blinded by it. I can't go on.'

He actually smiled: 'You have to, Mr Cullen. We're in a tight spot. We've got a rush job on, urgent. If you're loyal, as you say, you must stay with us.'

I stood by his lung: 'If I do I've got to have four hundred a trip. I can't do it for less because I've bought a house, and my overheads are appalling.'

His eyes narrowed. He hated my guts, but wouldn't at the moment say so: 'You're not getting married, by any chance?'

'Never. But I've got to have a quiet place I can go to between trips, if I'm not to have a crack-up.'

'Where is it?'

'Berkshire,' I told him. 'A cottage, but it cost the earth – and a bit of the sky.'

He chuckled and put down his gun. 'All right. Four hundred. But you're off to Athens in the morning.'

My only thought on the way out was to hope the plane to Greece crashed with me on it so that all my troubles would come to an end. Because was I in trouble? I knew who'd arranged for Arthur Ramage to be caught. It was Claud Moggerhanger, either by an anonymous phone call to London airport, or because he wanted to give his old friend Inspector Lantorn an easy job to do, in the hope that Lantorn would keep his claws off the Moggerhanger operations for a week or two. And who had told Moggerhanger that Ramage went to Lisbon every Friday laced-up with gold? His darling daughter. And which unthinking love-crazed flaptrap had told Polly? Me, not imagining that she'd even take it in, never mind relay it so accurately and with such deadly intent. And why had he done it? Not only to play havoc with Jack Leningrad, because that seemed rather an obvious thing to do, but precisely to warn me to go in head and bollocks with the Moggerhanger conspiracy-takeover, or vanish the same way as Arthur Ramage. It was as plain as the dismal day, that the great intriguer of the age had been caught in a vast and sticky web, with a murdering spider ready to come from each corner and scoop out his guts. All this went through my mind when Stanley broke the news, and I knew that the man in the iron lung would have it in for me as being the only person who could have published Arthur Ramage's itinerary. Maybe he would kill me on the spot, such was his ugly mood, and for that reason I threw my medieval fit and ranted for a higher wage. It had worked, for the moment. He was almost bound to have me followed or watched from now on. I had to take care even of the air I breathed, and that was no sort of life for me.

But to abandon everything would mean slipping into oblivion, and that was not part of me. I had come too far through the keyhole of myself to do that. I wanted Polly, in spite of her absolute and rotten treachery. She had been set on to me from the first, and of that I could only be certain. But I wanted Polly more than ever, even because of her treachery, for by that alone I felt we were made for each other, that she had more depth and dimension than I'd ever dreamed of. I had fucked her countless times, and she had now monumentally fucked me, so that while I had made us one flesh, she had made us one spirit, an element of fatal cooperation I had never encountered in anyone else nor was likely to. She seemed so much larger now that I couldn't have noticed her before, but I knew I was as far from having her – or her having me – as I'd ever been, because even if I threw in everything and worked for Moggerhanger, it would mean little in the end. I thought I was fit enough to live in a jungle, but now I was certainly beginning to doubt my ability to survive in this little corner of it. How could I go off with an easy heart to Athens when I expected any minute that Moggerhanger would think to pick up the phone and stop me?

I went. And I came back. I could only assume he was giving me more time than I'd expected or even hoped for. The one consolation of this cat-and-mouse game was that my bank balance continued to grow. I paid the cash for Upper Mayhem station, then took the bundle of deeds and a spare set of keys to Nottingham, where I stowed them in my grandmother's chest. Whatever happened, they would be safely hidden there. Work had slackened off. Maybe there was no more gold left on the island, though this would not stop the Jack Leningrad machinery dead in its oils because they also *imported* it. As fast as I took it out, others brought it back. Profits were made both ways, and everyone was happy.

So I had a few days in Nottingham. My mother wouldn't take time off work, but I was quite happy going around on my own. On a cold windy day I was muffled up in my overcoat, and warmed by a cigar as I walked along Wollaton Road. I'd been away a long time, but none of it was foreign to me. I was born here, and it swam in my blood. All other places were a swamp I had to stop myself sinking into, but here my feet were on solid ground – even though the pavements were uneven and there were often potholes in the roads. With a place like this I didn't need a mother or father. Say what you like, the place where you were born and brought up is bread and butter for the rest of your life, no matter where you go or what you do. If you deny it, you stamp on your own feelings. If you don't have it, you can't see other places with the freshest of eyes. I speak from hindsight, and I speak from youth, and I speak from myth, and the trio will always meet when you're feeling low and desolate. At such times, if you're far away you know you can't go back there, and don't even want to, but to think of that solid indestructible land soothes your eyes for a few hours.

I walked along, my thoughts spinning as if in a milk-churn making cheese. Up the hill from the weighing house and Horse Trough and White Horse pub was the railway bridge, and Radford station whose booking hall we used to raid as kids for a handful of timetables to push through letterboxes or scatter in the streets as if they announced the coming of bloody revolution. We'd hide in the timber traps of the goods yard and run from the railwayman who didn't give a damn whether we got away or not. If I hadn't been a long time in London I don't suppose I'd have had all these memories flopping up into my brain like wet fish. Beyond the station was the tobacco warehouse on one side, and the Midland pub on the other, then newer houses and the Crown pub on the corner of Western Boulevard. We used to swim in the old canal on hot days, and once I remember a boy of five falling off the lock gate and hitting the concrete edge fifteen feet below which stopped him going into the water and getting drowned but didn't prevent him from getting a savage dose of concussion that sent him running after skylarks for the next few years, though he eventually recovered so well that he went to grammar school. And when I was fifteen I remember a mate and I went up the canal one dark night with Connie Ford who sat between us on a lock gate and wanked us till we shot into the moonless dark. I laughed through my cigar smoke. This was the only place where I could feel free of all the Moggerhangers and Leningrads of the world, where sentimentality was realistic, and memory meant safety, and familiarity strength. I coined my happy phrases, not taking much notice as to where I was going but knowing that all these thoughts were false and not worth a farthing.

I turned up Nuthall Road, and smelt the first undying smell of evening mist coming down from the collieries and Pennines. I caught it so strongly in the nostrils of my heart that it even warmed my penis and made it half stand up. I'd got something very bad, but it didn't frighten me at all, just made me know I was still prone to it and therefore still alive.

It softened my soul for when I saw Claudine coming out of the supermarket and putting a basket of groceries on top of a baby sleeping in the pram. She saw me first, but even so I wouldn't have backed away if I'd been the one to spot her. Her face turned pale, as I'm sure mine did as well. I looked at the baby, about a year old, pink, fat, and peaceful. 'You might well stare,' she said, 'you rotten bastard.'

I smiled: 'He looks as if he'll thrive.'

'It's a she.'

I took another look: 'Are you pleased with her?'

'Of course I am. Alfie is as well.'

My mouth dropped: 'Alfie?'

'It's his. We got married over it. Just in time as well.'

'That lets me out, then. I was on my way to ask you to marry me. I've earned a lot of money in London, and I've spent the last three months fixing up a house for us both near Huntingborough, a marvellous place in the country that I paid cash for. It's got a marvellous garden, full of flowers, just the sort I thought you'd like. I even got a job there, as manager of a car-hire firm. But nothing goes right with me. My life's in ruins. Always was, and always damn-well will be.'

'I hope so,' she said. 'You swine. I sincerely hope so. You're rotten with lies. I hate your guts. Alfie's worth fifty of you, and I'm glad it's him I ended up with. At least he loves me and doesn't only think of himself. As for you, I don't care how well you're doing in London, but you're heading for a fall, and that's a fact. I should think even that place will get too hot for you before long, if it isn't already. I expect you've only come back here to get out of trouble there, if I know you. Or have you just come out of prison? You can stop looking at her, even if it is your baby. I only hope she'll grow up with none of your rottenness in her, though thank God I'm pregnant again, and by Alfie this time.'

I lowered my head, tried to look affectionate: 'I'm sorry you feel that way. I didn't mean to make you bitter. I just thought we might be able to get together again. That's what I came up specially for. I've always been in love with you, you know that, and still am, even though you've gone and done the dirty on me by getting married to Alfie. It wasn't my fault if you couldn't wait.'

'Oh,' she wailed, 'how rotten can anybody get?' She

shouted, and women coming by laden with fish-fingers and Miracle Bread stared at us.

'I can get a lot rottener,' I said, 'to someone who's betrayed me.' I hated saying all this, but couldn't stop myself, wasn't even enjoying it, didn't know why I was doing it, at least not then. She went away sobbing, and even the kid began kicking up a row from under the basket of groceries.

I walked backwards, watching her go, grieved at what I had done to myself more than to her, because even though I knew how lousy I'd been, and regretted it to my core, she at least had a daughter and her husband. My gall felt as if about to burst. I was sweating, and walked with the wind behind me.

When Mother came home from work she told me to cheer up. 'You're always full of troubles and worries. Can't you store up that experience till later on in life?'

I split my face into a smile: 'Maybe I want to get it over with now.'

'Don't hurry it. There's plenty of time.'

'I'm worn out.'

'At your age? Stop feeling sorry for yourself, that's all I can say.'

'I'm not bloody-well feeling sorry for myself,' I snapped.

'Well,' she said, 'I'm glad you're showing a bit of spirit at last. Eat your steak and chips before it gets cold.'

'I'm sorry.'

'Sorry? That's new, coming from you. Still it's a start. A thin one though.'

'It's all I can do at the moment,' I said with my mouth full. She was reading the newspaper, and I went on eating.

Albert was working late, couldn't come out with us, so we got on a thirty-nine and went down town to sit a few hours in Yate's wine lodge. I put her on to port, while I stuck to brandy. 'Are you and Albert really going to get married?'

She laughed: 'Are you jealous?'

'No, I'm not. I've got enough of that on my plate. It's just that life's so long.'

'A good job it is,' she said, 'or we'd all be dead.' She looked young enough for any devil's work, with her perm that had come out well, and her lipstick that drew your eyes to it and away from the few wrinkles at the corners of her temples. 'I'm not even too old to have another kid,' she grinned, 'if I put my mind to it.'

This remark gave me a funny feeling which, if it came about, and I couldn't believe it would, showed me with a little brother playing uncle to any newborn bastard I might have of my own. 'Life's not only long,' I said, 'it's a stew.'

'As long as it's tasty, and doesn't get cold on the hearth. I don't know, Michael, you're a funny one. Sometimes I think you're just like your father – when I remember him.'

I poured my brandy down, but it tasted like soda water: 'You told me I never had a father,' regretting such a stupid phrase when she replied: 'Who do you think you are, Jesus Christ? I'll get a cross for you from Littlewoods if you like, or maybe I'll rent one for three days.'

'Stop joking, can't you?'

'I'm in that sort of mood. Get me another port, duck.'

I called the waiter, couldn't speak till he'd brought the drinks and I'd annihilated my brandy and asked for another. 'You'll go corky inside,' she said. 'He used to knock them back like that. And he used to buy me port. Funny. The cheeky bastard said he thought all working-class women liked port, and he was right, because *I* did, anyway. We even came to this place, when there was any booze, and staggered away in the blackout at closing-time. Maybe port's good for the memory. He was younger than me, though I was young enough, God knows. A young sergeant, though he spoke like an officer. Oh, we had a good time, till he got posted somewhere else. He even wrote me a letter or two, then they stopped after I'd told him I was pregnant. I was so mad I burnt the letters and a photo.'

I felt white and avid: 'Why didn't you ever tell me this before?'

'Didn't think to, I suppose. You know me: memory like a sieve. He wasn't what you'd call good-looking, but he was lively, and had an educated way of talking – though he used the most terrible language – awful, mixed it with everything he said.'

'Go on. Go on.'

'Let me get my breath, then. I don't often talk about old times.'

'You're telling me,' I said. 'Once every twenty years, I suppose.'

'Don't get like that with me, or I'll throw this drink up your nose.'

'All right, Ma. Let's have a good time. It's a long while since I got drunk.'

'You're not very like him, though. There's too much of me in your face. He had the funniest shape of head, and even though he was only twenty he was already going bald. But what a marvellous man he was, because in spite of his flash talk he was very gentle at times, almost shy, and maybe that's what I liked most about him. He practically lived with me for a month, thought it a great thrill to be in a house like ours, but he'd always come with a bottle of whisky to make himself really at home. We had some good times between us. I could earn good money because of the war, and it was easy to wangle a house of my own, especially with Gilbert's help. He forged anything. Used to get a bus from his camp and make straight for the house. Sometimes he'd wait for me outside the factory, and I remember how happy this made me, though I never told him so. He'd laugh and say I was sentimental, rubbing it into my face like broken glass, so that I'd get into a paddy and throw pots around if he didn't stop. He often liked that sort of thing, and just sat there goading me. He was a real devil when he got started, though I was as bad. But we had some times together. It seemed to go on for ages, and now it seems like no time at all. I can't always remember it, even. He didn't get drunk, he just got dangerous, though at the sound of a cup smashing he'd smile and be happy again.

'I always missed when I threw things, but he liked the sound. Some people *are* funny. I used to call him Blasted Blaskin, and this would make him laugh more than anything. I can't tell you all the things we got up to, you being my son. What are you looking so white for? I thought you could take your drink?'

I felt the slab of concrete in my stomach lifting up, as if it were suddenly trying to get out of my mouth. 'I've got to get into the air,' I said, standing. 'It's killing in here.'

'You do look bloody pale,' she said, taking my arm. 'What's got into you?'

The concrete flagstone lifted: 'Come on, let's go.'

'Oh, all bloody right then.'

We went down the stairs and the fresh air pulled me round a bit. She was flummoxed, as if I might be going odd in the head and she had no idea what was expected of her, no cups or glasses being handy to throw at me.

We walked into Slab Square, the illuminated front of the town hall looking so tall I hoped it was about to fall flat on its face and bury us. That cock-headed tripehound seemed not to have altered in all his waking life, still on a mad career from one dripping slit to another. He threw up his women left and right and centre, and just as quickly others came back to him, flocking towards the same unwholesome fate. He was a bastard right enough, a real travelling trickster if ever there was one, and if my mother's memory served her right, this sky-licker, this grub who rubbed his prick along the bare earth so that wheat and sunflowers shot up in abundance and gave him a great and lazy life, was my one and only unsuspecting father.

We made for the Eight Bells, and managed to get a seat: 'Look,' I said, 'I know this bloke you've told me about, and from your description of him he hasn't altered a bit.'

'Oh, dear,' she said. 'Don't go on about it or I shall begin to get upset. It's so long ago, but now you've brought it all back I'm getting sentimental. You make me feel as though I'm still in love with him, the rotten swine. I was, for years and years. When I was with another chap I used to make believe he was Gilbert, to try and bring him back to me. Not that it was much good, but it was a game that helped me to bear it. Ah, well, it's more than twenty years, but it's only a minute when you lost somebody you thought a lot of. I told myself he'd been sent to Egypt and got killed. I lived with that, till the war was over and I forgot him. But you never forget. For a woman to lose a man she loves is only one bit less than losing a kid.'

I was almost in tears, not only from shock and brandy, but from realizing what a hard life she'd had, all because of Gilbert

Blaskin, and of having me without being married, a fact that didn't let her forget the man who gave me to her, and at the same time made if difficult if not impossible for her to get somebody else. I thought how the world was a million times harder on women than men. Blaskin had gone his own sweet screwing way, though from what I knew he'd been miserable, except that he hadn't really suffered in the way my mother had because he'd never had the honour and torment to really fall in love. To bring her back to life I told her a little of what I knew about him, just to give him reality and, if possible, rob him a little in her mind of the sentimental glory she attached to him. 'I know it was only a dream,' she said, 'and that if we'd had much more time together we'd have started to drive each other round the bend and halfway up the bloody zig-zags.'

'Still,' I said, taking her hand, 'you had your dream.'

She drew it away, as if I were Blaskin: 'You *can* say that, I suppose.'

'You should see him now. He don't look up to much.'

'Neither do I,' she said.

'You do,' I told her.

She got angry: 'Pack it in. When are you going back?'

'Tomorrow,' I said. 'I'd go tonight, but the last train's gone. 'When are you marrying Albert?'

'In six weeks,' she said, as if I'd changed the subject.

'Don't you think you ought to marry Gilbert Blaskin instead?' I asked, and she laughed so long and loud that people in the pub began looking at her and wondering what was going on between us, as if we'd cracked some dirty joke about them all.

I took a lunchtime train that punched its way south through the steel fallopian tube of Trent Bridge. Cows stood in fields under the sousing rain, stock-still as if they were actually made of rain and wanted to grow bigger from it. I'd had no breakfast so went to the dining-car for a meal, shaken so much to bits on the way that I was almost not hungry by the time I got there.

I thought of the worry and trouble waiting for me when I got to London, but when food started to slide in, no worry seemed too difficult to sort out, and my chopfallen state soon left me. The train was so fast it seemed to gallop, swaying soup over the lip of the plate, so that it was difficult holding a newspaper at the same time. I looked to see if anyone of my name had died or got married, or was to be remembered in gratitude for having given their glorious lives in any of the world wars, or whether any he or she was getting engaged or had had a nice new legitimate baby between them. But there was no sign, so I stared at the houses or motorcars for sale, and saw nothing to suit my exigent tastes.

When I smoked a cigar no one stared at me and thought I shouldn't be smoking it, as they might a couple of years ago, and when I paid my bill the cashier wasn't surprised at the five-bob tip I left for the waiter. Then I looked at the news part of the paper to see if Ron Cottapilly or Paul Pindarry, those ganglions of Jack Leningrad Limited, had been nabbed at the customs in the last twenty-four hours. They had not, though if I had my way it wouldn't be long now, because as soon as I got to St Pancras I went into a box and got through to Moggerhanger.

'*Who* is it?' he said. I told him I'd thought over his proposition. He laughed: 'I knew you wouldn't come up in a hurry, Michael, for which I always admire a man, but when you left it so late I thought you'd had an accident, like getting caught or something. It struck me as unlikely, but you never know in your sort of game. I hear they did have rather a nasty jolt in your firm, didn't they? Man called Ramage. Fate strikes pretty hefty blows from time to time, I must say. It was all I could do not to send a message of condolence to the Iron Lung. But I never do anything in bad taste. I'm not that sort of person. What have you decided, then?'

I'd worked myself to a sweat of rage while listening to his two-faced banter: 'I'm joining you,' I said, 'and that's straight. I'll go on working for Leningrad, and I'll phone you any time I've got information. Or I'll phone Polly, it's just the same, I realize. In any case I'm only doing it for our future happiness. Do you understand?'

His voice sounded right in my ear, as if he was no farther than the next telephone box. I looked nervously that way, but it was empty. 'If you're to work for me,' he said, 'you'll have to alter that tone of voice. I'm old-fashioned, I am. If you talk in that voice it's obvious who you're working for, and since we don't want anybody to know, you'll have to moderate it a bit, won't you, Michael? I expect you to understand that, just as I'm to understand that you're doing it for Polly's future happiness – as well as your own. Are we on the same wavelength, or not? Tell me that, and the deal's on.'

'It's on,' I said, trying not to breathe hard or curse. 'I phone you. You don't phone me. It'll work best that way.'

'I'll tell you how we'll do it, Michael,' he said, as if I hadn't spoken, 'phone me whenever you know anything. I'll never try to contact you – unless you find a note under your plate at that Italian restaurant where you eat. Old Tonio's in my good books there, and I sometimes let him help me.'

'That sounds all right.' I was going to say goodbye, but the line went dead, meaning he'd hung up on me. Moggerhanger never said goodbye in case it brought him bad luck. He looked upon it as an unnecessary waste of breath.

My next move was to call on Blaskin with the idea of getting him to marry my mother before she could throw herself away on that worthless Albert. I didn't care whether I stayed a bastard or not – I'd be one of those till my left foot was tipped into a soily grave – but I wanted Blaskin to make an honest woman of my mother. He'd had his own runner-bean way too long, and it was time one of his sins came home to roost, namely me, because I was beginning to see how serious it was that he'd rampaged through the world, and God knows how many innocent women, without anybody having lifted a finger against him. I took the Underground to Sloane Square, then walked a couple of corners to the block of flats where he lived. It was his divine luck that he wasn't in, so after ten minutes' ruminative smoke outside his door, I walked over the river and home.

I saw William sitting on the settee when I went into the living-room, listlessly thumbing through the *Evening Standard*. Beside him were two suitcases. 'Get away from me, you treacherous bleeder,' he said, when I went up with a big smile of welcome to shake his hand.

'What?' I yelled back.

He stood up, half a grin. 'Don't take it so bad. It'll happen to you some day. Not by me, though. Never by me.'

'What sort of a swamp am I in?' I said, pouring two drinks. 'I've never betrayed anyone. You were hooked by working for Moggerhanger. The Leningrad group of British Industries found out, and you got pulled in.'

He took the whisky: 'I've been all this time with the corsairs, boy, in a Moslem slave-hole, and I'm out of the habit of taking raw booze.' But he drank it as if it were Jaffa Juice: 'If what you say is true, and you may be right, then they'll be on to you next, because I recruited you.'

I was sweating again. 'You got pulled in because the Beirut cops wanted Moggerhanger's ransom,' I said, fishing for any old explanation.

He laughed bitterly. 'You can take your pick, that's all I'm saying. But I'm back now, thanks to Claud. I've called for my things. I'm off, Michael, on the run again. The Leningrad lot don't know I'm back. When they do they'll nail me. I know they will. To tell you the truth I don't know where to go. They'll get Cottapilly and Pindarry on to me, and they're like Dobermann Pinschers. They'll tear me to pieces. Moggerhanger won't hide me. He laughed on the phone just now when I reported in, and told me to steer clear. I've got a taxi coming in twenty minutes to get me to a railway station. Don't even know which one yet.'

'Make it King's Cross,' I said, 'and stop worrying. I've got just the place for you.' I told him how I'd bought the railway station: 'It's in the middle of nowhere. Nobody'll trace you. You'll have to buy a bed and table, that's all, but you'll be safe as houses and as right as rain. Stay as long as you like. I hope to be up myself in a month. Are you all right for money?'

'That's no problem,' he said. 'But you're a real comrade, Michael. I shan't forget this. I'm really in the shit this time, because the man in the iron lung is bound to smell a rat once he knows I'm back.'

'He'll never know.'

'That's what you think. His snoops already know I left

343

Beirut. Moggerhanger's man got me to the plane without 'em knowing, but they'll start looking for me by tomorrow, though I'm sure nobody tailed me here.'

'When they know you're back without reporting to them, they're going to suspect me more than ever. It's a very awkward moment.'

'I'm afraid it is, lad,' he said, looking at me with those sad eyes that at times permeated his whole spirit. Without his briefcase and smart clothes, his good haircut and stylish hat, and after his time in the sink-hole, he looked very subdued, already hunted and dodging from hedge to hedge. 'Why don't you come to the station with me?' he said. 'I've got a couple of revolvers and some ammo. Two's better than one when you're on the run. We could hold 'em off a treat if ever they find us. Believe me, it'll be the wisest thing in the end.'

I saw the sense of it: 'Can't. I've got too many things to wind up here. I'll see you in a month, though.'

'I hope so,' he said, as the doorbell rang. 'Don't say I didn't warn you.'

I managed a smile, and helped him with his luggage: 'I shan't.'

I was sorry to see him go. He took some of my courage, though I kept enough of it to phone headquarters in a very jocular mood, to which Stanley reacted beautifully. I wanted to put my foot down as a brake and stop things tilting along so fast, but that would only draw unnecessary suspicion on me, so I had to learn to roll with it, and look out for myself as I went along. The tell-tale bead of sweat could be my ruin, a stray hair in my nose, a shoelace about to come undone. I had to be careful not to lose too much weight in case anyone should imagine I was afraid of the thin ice under me.

Stanley said it was business as usual. I was to be on a plane the day after tomorrow, late afternoon, so as to give Pindarry and Cottapilly time to get off first to Switzerland. After that there'd be a week's rest. I said I'd get there at three o'clock, but Stanley told me to make it an early lunch that day, and get to headquarters at two for loading. 'I'm ready for anything,' I said. 'The firm seems to be looking up these days.'

'Our clients have confidence in us,' he said with a laugh, and hung up in the middle of another.

At seven I walked over the river and made for the Blaskin pad. Pearl opened the door, and showed no surprise on her small face, made even smaller by short hair that came in a fringe over her forehead, so that she looked more like some TV riverbank animal than ever.

Gilbert looked at me: 'What the hell do you want? I thought you were stuck for ever in that city of sin, Nottingham. Didn't I last see you dropping off the train there? Not that I remember much. I was so drunk.' He wore a plum-coloured dressing-gown and had a cigarette in his wide mouth. He had no hair to go grey on his pink bald head, so his face had taken over that role. 'Sit down and get some alcohol.'

'You don't look good,' I told him, throwing down my coat. Pearl curled up on the rug at his feet, and I thought she was going to take off his carpet slippers and start kissing his toes. But she merely nestled her cheek on them.

'I've had a few upsets,' he admitted, his head right back and canon-mouths of smoke going up at the ceiling.

'June?'

'Right,' he laughed. 'She couldn't take it, I suppose, so she ran off with that phoney poet called Ron Delph. That's one way to get rid of her.'

'Poor, poor Gilbert,' said Pearl. 'He hadn't eaten for days, and he was lying near the gas stove when I found him, trying to turn the taps on, drunk and crying.'

He jerked forward, and lifted her face sharply with his feet: 'That's your sorry tale, you lying bitch. Don't re-write my history, you Kremlin-faced pug, or I'll throw you out of that window and down into the dustbins.'

'Naughty Gilbert,' she said, looking as if she were about to cry. 'You're such a novelist, my love.'

'To hell with that,' he said. 'You are, not me, with your sycophantic thesis. Those that live by the novel shall die by the fucking novel, you trollop. Remember that, or your life won't be worth living.'

'Does this go on all the time?' I asked, hoping to stop them.

'Only when you're here, or somebody else is.'

He smiled: 'We're like two lovebirds in a cage when we're on our own, aren't we, pet?'

'Yes,' she said, her cheek back on his foot.

'She's trying to drive me crazy,' he said, 'but I'll get her first.'

'I'm glad to see you so happy,' I said. 'How's *The History of Carnage*?'

'Bloody. I'd only done fifty pages when I cut my finger slicing a lemon. So I threw it aside. I'm back on the novel now. It's going very well, the best thing I can remember doing, in fact. Thank God I got rid of that whore June. She went on to Ron Delph, the Concrete Poet. Too much sand in him, I expect. God's a bloody awful builder.'

'She had a kid by him when she was eighteen,' I said. 'Maybe they'll get married now.'

He walked to the door and back again: 'She never told me whose kid it was. Never mind, one more down the chute.'

'Don't get depressed about it,' said Pearl soothingly.

He poured half a pint of whisky and held it up to the light: 'Piss. But hot piss. If I drink whisky, I'm just plain randy – and it doesn't take long to get it over with, does it Pearl Barley? Go and make us some black coffee for Christ's sake. When I drink vodka I get brutal, and take my pleasure that way, so I can't say whether it's enjoyed by both parties because it depends who I'm with. Best of all is when I drink champagne, because then it goes on for hours.' He gulped his whisky. Pearl shook her head and went to make coffee. 'You know what, Michael?'

'What?' I said, watching him.

'I should have been born without a penis. Not only would I have been a happy man, but there'd have been lots of happier women in the world as well. As soon as the doctor pulled me out of my mother he should have told the nurse to chop off my cock. It's not fair to man or beast. It's the curse of mankind, sex. If a man goes with a woman ten years older than himself he's humping his mother. If he goes with a girl

346

younger than himself he's raping his daughter. If he pansies after a young man he's buggering his son. If he keeps pets he's a bit of a sod. If he gets off with an older man he's being bummed by his father. Hallelujah! If he gets a woman of the same age he's perverse because he's normal. The only answer is to be indiscriminate, hump into what hole you can get and as the mood takes you.'

He fell silent, but I knew it wouldn't be for long, so I asked him if he'd ever been in love. His bald head wrinkled. 'Love? Way back in the swampy mists of time, I vaguely remember it. Adolescent infatuation. There was nothing between that and a lifelong attack of satyriasis which is still going on only because I can't stop breathing.'

'Or boasting,' I couldn't help saying.

He looked hard at me. 'Don't be impertinent, sonny boy.'

'You were in Nottingham during the war, weren't you?' I said.

'Stop me drinking, Michael.'

'Why the hell should I?'

He sent his glass splintering against the wall. 'I'll stop myself. What mercy can one expect from the hungry generation? I was the hungry generation twenty years ago, and I haven't stopped being hungry. The trouble is that I don't see why I should. But another hungry generation is coming up on me, and I don't like it.'

'You'll have to,' I grinned.

He flopped back in the chair, but I could see he was a man of great strength: 'The hungry generations tread you down all right. That's what keeping up with the young is – allowing them to trample on you with impunity. If you get weak about it and try to keep up with the young, you only succeed in doing their job for them by trampling yourself down. To keep up with the young is a refusal to grow old, but by doing that you let them eat you up. If Pearl weren't so busy sweating over her hot stove she'd write down that priceless aphorism. The thing is, Michael, I was everywhere during the war, except where I could pull a trigger. But I was in Nottingham – the soldier's kiss from which he got the clap. We used

347

to fight to get posted there. Nottingham was the Rose of England. I suppose it still is, what?'

Pearl came in and set a tray on the floor by Gilbert's feet. 'Don't you remember anything pure and virtuous about it?'

'I'm tired of masochistic women,' he said, 'but that's the only sort I attract. When I get the other kind we fight on equal terms all the time, and then we part.'

'Have you had many children?' I asked.

'None that I know of. It would have been jolly to have two or three, then I could have ruined their lives as well. I could hate myself even more. I don't think there's anybody in the world hates himself as much as I do. That being the case what else could I have done in life but write novels? I've got to pass it on to somebody, and who else but the great inert mass of the British public? A few thousand of them, anyway, but that's better than nothing. I hate myself so much I don't even have a personality – just a novel in my heart and a cock in my hand. Pearl's writing all this down while the coffee gets cold. Get up you tripehound and pour me some.' He clutched his forehead. 'Oh, God, she's even writing that down before she does it.'

She poured it so quickly that grounds slopped into the saucer. I thought that if life was made too hot for me by the Jack Leningrad gang I could always go into hiding again here, providing I was able to stand the stream of Blaskin's mediocre self-pitying commentaries. It frightened me that I was his son, though I was heartened by the fact that he didn't yet know that he was my father. I was beginning to think that marrying off my mother to a beaten-down old prick like this would be the worst favour I could do her. Coffee spilled on his dressing-gown, and at the same time I felt sorry for him, because his easy ways had got him nowhere, and there seemed nothing more terrible to me at my particular time of life. I realized how possible it was that if I did want to hide here he wouldn't let me do so, whether or not he knew me to be his son, though I was tempted to try it out, just to see how finally rotten he was.

Pearl brought in other trays, and laid a cold supper before us. 'There's nothing in this house if not hospitality,' said

Gilbert. 'Food comes first and love second, and the Devil take the hind leg of the chicken' – at which he tore it in half, putting a stringy piece of carcass on my plate, and a solid piece of back-meat on his, while Pearl helped herself to fish and salami. 'I'm beginning to remember rapey old Nottingham now,' he laughed.

'What about a girl called Alice Cullen?' I asked.

'Rings a bell. There was only one girl in Nottingham because I was shy in those days, though I don't suppose she noticed it. Used to send out poems to little magazines, long before I descended to being a novelist. When the war ended I went into my first disastrous marriage. It lasted seven years, and my wife thought she was looking after me, saving me from myself and for myself. Poor woman died of a broken heart, and I was hooked again in six months. After seven years of this second go, my wife found refuge in the arms of someone of her own intellectual level, a man who talked twenty hours a day and didn't say anything at all – a much younger man, which gratified me because it kept her out of my way while I went after my much younger women. The only trouble was she wanted me to go on loving her while she went on loving her psychotic, and I couldn't do that, because while in some ways I didn't mind being her husband – until now – I refused to give up playing that part only to become her father. Anyway, it staggered on for eleven years altogether. Where she is now I've no idea. Probably staring straight in front of her in some provincial looney-bin being consoled by her bourgeois intellectual drop-out. We quarrelled for years, on and off, but it didn't come to anything because the only time I used to say I was going to leave her was in the middle of the night when I was too tired to get up and pack. When I woke in the morning I just had to face myself and the normal ordinary world again, and such things as leaving your wife no longer seemed important. It's all sad, really, but making love is second nature to me. My first is self-preservation, and that's my one real failing. But nowadays I just enjoy life with my little Pearl.'

He turned to her and said, in a dangerously tender voice: 'Will you marry me, love?'

Her face reddened, lifted from her page, then turned pale: 'Are you serious, Gilbert?'

'You see,' he said to me, 'even she's found out how to torment me. Life gets worse instead of better. I'm even beginning to have headaches.'

'That's cancer,' she said, getting her own back.

'If ever you marry, Michael, stick to her for life, because the next one is always worse than the one before. Pearl was gentle and obedient when she first came, but she's a rotten little tiger now. Yes, my young days in Nottingham and sundry other places were the best times of my life. I've often thought of going back to find the girls I knew in my youth, and maybe marry one of them if they're still eligible. But I suppose they've all got false teeth, and I couldn't stand that, because mine would be on one side of the bed in a glass saying HIS, and HERS would be on her side, and while we went into a loving and oblivious sleep they'd be in the air above snapping viciously at each other like crocodiles. If not that, then she'd wear those horrible heavy steel curlers that would gnash my eyes out in the night. I couldn't stand that sort of thing. But I do remember Alice Cullen – any relation of yours?'

'She's my mother,' I said. He spewed chicken-shreds all over the table, as if about to have a seizure. 'Last time I was up there,' I went on, 'she told me all about you. I'm your son, right enough.' I filled in the puzzle, and he listened, hands stretched across the table so that I could have driven nails into them, or the bread knife – one at a time.

'Now shall the eyes of the blind be opened,' he said, his gills white nevertheless.

'She never married after that,' I told him. 'I think you were the love of her life, though she was too proud and independent to say so. I don't suppose she'd look at you now. In any case, she's getting married in a month to a bloke who's worth a hundred of you, a Communist. I'm sure she'll do well by him.'

He stood up unsteadily, though he wasn't drunk: 'Pearl, go to the kitchen and get a bottle of champagne from the fridge. We must drink to this. I didn't have children in either of my marriages. Thought I was sterile – which it seems I was, in the married state. But now I find I had a son from the first real love of my life – though I didn't know it was going to be that at the time.' He came round, and I stood up as well, knife in hand: 'Put that down,' he said.

I didn't even know I was holding it. 'Why did you abandon her?' Memories of Claudine crushed me, and I couldn't say anything else. What could I do but shake his hand firmly if I was to be true to myself?

'It's no use saying I'm sorry,' he said, 'because I am.' He stared at me, and I stared at him, wondering why the hell I'd let myself in for this. Pearl, holding the champagne, glared at us both as if we were pulling some fast trick on her, and at me in particular so that I knew she finally didn't like me at all. My one ambition was to get into a simple situation, but no sooner had this deep wish struck than I knew it to be impossible. I couldn't even hate my father for what he'd done to my mother, now that I'd found him, meaning that he was no use to me at all. And I was glad I couldn't put him to this use, for he was unable, because of this, to sap my strength. At the same time he had none to give me. Meeting him like this was just one more experience for me to mull over from time to time. While we drank the champagne he looked at me, a strange glimpse, almost as if he were afraid in some way. He was certainly shocked, and I had the feeling that he might go off and hang himself in an odd moment of boredom or emptiness at some time in the near-future. But this crazy idea passed off, and he asked me all about my life. I refused to tell him anything at first, saying he only wanted to know so that he could put it into one of his novels. Then he started to cry and said this was true, which made me laugh, while Pearl ran for some pills, so I told him what I thought he wanted to know about myself, which had no connexion whatever to the truth. Some time later I said I was going to the toilet, but I picked up my coat and walked out of the flat, not even bothering to say goodbye.

I went round Sloane Square a few times, then got into a phonebox and dialled Moggerhanger. The line was dead, and when I looked down I saw that the paybox had been ripped out. At the next one I phoned Blaskin's flat, listening for him while two men stood outside waiting to come in after me. 'Hello?' said Blaskin.

'This is Michael.'

'I thought you were in the toilet?' he shouted.

'I left. I'm in Hampstead. Listen, I never want to see you again. I'm not your son and you're not my father, so get that into your stream of consciousness.'

I slammed the lid down before he could reply, and pushed my way out of the box. Halfway to the World's End I realized I'd yet to phone Moggerhanger. At the next booth I got straight through to him. 'I'm going to Geneva the day after tomorrow,' I said. 'Pindarry and Cottapilly will be off to Zurich in the morning.'

'I shan't forget you for this. You've got a place in my heaven from now on.'

'Can you put me on to Polly?'

'I'm afraid I can't,' he said, and I could see him trying to laugh, 'she went to Geneva, to see her old schoolfriend. I expect she'll be back in three or four days. If you're lucky she might be waiting for you when you get there.' This was the best weather forecast for some time, and wishing him good-night I got back into fresh air and headed for the river. The thought of a few days by the lake with Polly put my head above the clouds, made all my mix-ups seem very small indeed. I thought that if I kept my nerve, watched myself, played my cards right; if I was patient, cool, and prayed for the upkeep of my luck, repeated all such clichés as if they were prayers, then I'd sail out of this tricky patch unscathed and happy. I'd haul down the skull and crossbones and henceforth live at Upper Mayhem under my purple banner of bliss with sweet Polly Moggerhanger for ever and ever.

Sleep was deep and dreamless that night, and it's as well that it was. I'd expected a quiet and uneventful day on my own before the trip to Geneva, but during breakfast the phone rang. I didn't want to answer it, no matter who was trying to needle through. I counted the times it rang, thinking it couldn't go on to more than fifty, but at the thirteenth I lost patience and picked it up. 'Hello?' I said sharply.

'Michael? It's Bridgitte.'

I'd expected Polly, Leningrad, my mother, Blaskin, Mogger-hanger himself, but not Bridgitte. Why couldn't I expect everything, even the unexpected? 'How are you, my own sweet darling? I've been phoning you for days and days.'

'You liar,' she screamed. 'I've been trying to get you.'

'What's wrong?' She was crying again, and her sobs went through to me. I was getting used to women crying, and was beginning to feel sorry for them when I heard it, no longer feeling just annoyed. 'What is it, love? What can I do for you?' I almost pleaded, till I pulled myself together and stopped it.

'Come over to the house,' she said, 'now. It's Smog.'

'I'll be right over on the number-two helicopter,' I said. 'What's gone wrong?'

'Dr Anderson was killed last week, in a car crash on the motorway. Oh, that's all right, don't be sorry. He was buried the day before yesterday. I don't care. But Smog won't eat. He's curled up in the dark, and won't open his eyes.'

I slammed the phone down without giving her time to finish, picked up my coat and ran.

I flagged a taxi at the end of the street, and told him to get up to Hampstead like a jet because I'd just heard that my son was ill and in danger of his life.

'Leave it to me, mate,' he said, and drove over the first junction with the light just changed to red. 'I shan't kill you,' he laughed, 'just rest back and try not to worry.' He went up through Chelsea and Kensington, over the Park and through St John's Wood. I offered him a cigar. 'Light it and pass it in,' he said. I couldn't see much of his face, but he wore a cap and seemed about forty, and had glasses on. 'Whatever you do,' he said, 'don't worry. Things'll be all right. Take it from me. Kids often go off a bit, but you'll pull him round. How old is he?'

'Seven.'

'That's all right. Under five, and it might be touch and go. What's wrong with him?'

'Don't know. Wife just phoned. Can't get much out of her.'

'Women!' he said. 'Never mind, mate. They do their best.'

'And more,' I said. So we went on, and soon he was pulling up by that open flight of steps climbing the green bank of the garden. I gave him two quid, but he pushed one back. 'Don't skin yourself. Just get going.'

'All the best,' I shouted, going like Batman, but feeling sick.

I called for Bridgitte. She wasn't in the living-room. Half the furniture had gone, and there were suitcases all over the floor. Of course Smog was upset. How could he grieve in an atmosphere like this? I had a sudden vision of the brutality of the world towards children, and ran down the stairs into the kitchen. A saucepan of milk was boiling over on the electric stove and causing a great stink. She wasn't there so I ran upstairs, on to the bedrooms, looking in each one till I found her.

She stood by the window, staring outside: 'I saw you on your way up.'

'Then why the bloody hell didn't you come down and let me in?' I was full of rage, then saw Smog in the bed, curled up. He seemed to be asleep. 'What's the trouble?' I lowered my voice in case he was. I knew she wanted me to kiss and comfort her, but I was too concerned about Smog to feel much sympathy for her distress. She wore a black sweater, and a black skirt, black stockings, and black carpet slippers with black pompoms in the front – as if she'd really fitted herself out for mourning day and night. I suppose she had a black nightdress, and stuffed herself with black wadding if she was having a period.

Smog groaned and turned over, facing me without opening his eyes. 'He's drunk warm milk,' she said, 'for the last four days.'

'And you haven't got a doctor?'

'Not yet. His mother came to the funeral, then went off and left us. She's gone up to Scotland.'

'I suppose he sleeps all the time?'

She lit a cigarette, and nodded.

'Go down and make him some Quaker Oats,' I said, 'and cool it with milk and butter. Put plenty of sugar in. I suppose you can do that?'

'Of course I can.'

She went out. I stroked Smog's face, and he looked at me. 'What's all this?' I said. 'I've come to see you, and I wanted to take you out.'

'Daddy's dead.'

'I'm your dad. I thought you knew. I always told you I was.'

'You're Uncle,' he said.

'I'm your dad now, as well.' He was pale, his lips thin and pink as if somebody had tried to doll him up with lipstick. His feet kicked under the clothes. 'How are you feeling?'

'My head keeps ringing.'

'Like a telephone?'

He smiled. 'No, like a big single bell.'

'I suppose that earwig got loose, and started swinging on it. Everybody's head has got an earwig in it. But you know why they always get on that bell and make it ring?'

'No,' he said. 'Why?'

'To tell you that they're hungry. They want you to stuff some food into your mouth for them.'

'I don't feel hungry.'

'But they do. Your earwig must be getting very restless, ringing that bell like that. If you want it to stop, you have to eat something.'

He leaned on his elbow, but fell back. 'Really?'

'Really.'

He thought about it. 'What do earwigs like best to eat?'

'Depends. Some of 'em are like tigers, and only want raw meat. Others eat bacon and eggs. Mostly they like a nice breakfast if they haven't eaten for a while. I should think yours is that sort. A bit of porridge to start off, warm, with some milk stirred in it. That'll keep him quiet for an hour. Then try a bit of scrambled egg.'

'I don't believe you.'

'Listen, Smog, I've never told you a lie, have I? A few stories maybe, but no lie. So you try it, and if the ringing doesn't stop, then you'll know I'm telling a lie. Either that or the earwig wants scrambled egg.'

'Where's the porridge, then?' he said.

'I don't know that there is any. I'm about to have my breakfast, starting with porridge. Bridgitte's bringing it up to me on a tray so that I can talk to you while I'm eating it. There was only a bit left in the packet, but maybe I'll give you a spoonful of mine, just to keep the earwig quiet. The thing is that if he doesn't get fed soon he'll call on his pal the hedgehog to get on that bell and help him to ring it a bit louder. Here's Bridgitte, and I'm starving for my breakfast. I always eat porridge to start with, so you'll have to look sharp if you want any of it from me.'

I was able to feed him nearly all of it. He wanted some scrambled egg as well, but I gave him a drink of water, then lay down with him on the bed so that in two minutes he was asleep. 'It's half past ten,' I said. 'We'll wake him at one with some toast and egg. I'm sure he'll eat now. If I stay all day, he'll be back to normal by the morning.'

I was sweating with the effort of getting him to eat, and went down to the kitchen so that we could make coffee. 'I knew you'd do it,' she said. 'That's why I didn't call a doctor.'

'Thanks for having such blind faith in me, but it was Smog's life you were playing with. Why all the packing in the living-room?'

'I'm going to Holland, with Smog, for a couple of weeks.'

'Then what?'

'I'll come back here. This house is mine.'

'You'll live here?'

'I'll sell it.' I made the coffee myself, because first she dropped the milk, then tipped over the sugar.

'Stay with me, Michael. I need some help.'

'I'll stay today. Tomorrow I'm working. I'm going to Switzerland for a couple of days. I'll get in touch when I come back. We must pull Smog around. After coffee we'll go to the living-room and put the cases away. We'll arrange the furniture and clean the place up a bit, so that when I carry Smog down this afternoon he'll see we're all orderly and settled. I only care about him at the moment. I never believed it was women and children first, only children.'

We set the living-room to look more or less the same as it had before Anderson was killed. Bridgitte sat in one armchair, and I was in another by her side, both looking through the big windows and down over the lawn.

'I'm sorry I'm such trouble,' she said, holding out her hand.

'Your trouble seems like calm to me,' I said. 'I'm sorry Anderson died. This is the first moment I've had to tell you.'

'I hated him,' she said, pulling her hand away.

'He couldn't help being what he was. He was Smog's real father, so I can't finally damn him.'

'He was Smog's father as far as we know,' she said.

'I don't give a bugger who his father was,' I said sharply. 'That's never been a big point with me,' She didn't say anything, and neither did I, content to rest in this little calm whirlpool we'd unexpectedly made. Then I took her hand again and stood up, so that she did the same, pressing herself to me. Scalding tears ran on to my face.

'What are you crying for? Don't cry, love.' I saw the picture of her when we first met, when she had been plump over the bones and pink-cheeked, when the eyes had been ingenuous and wide at my lies, and her hair fresh and too young to be tidy. Now the natural shape of her face had come out, the oval skin over the bone pear-shaped head, and eyes blank with misery she never knew how she'd got into. I took her face between my hands and kissed all parts of it, saying nothing because the time hadn't yet come to use talk on her. Whenever I kiss someone I can't help telling them that I love them. The words come as soon as the flesh of my lips touches theirs. A kiss with me was never only a meeting of skin, but something that reached right to the middle of me, where it releases those three words out of their box that lead either to pleasure or trouble. They were evidently the words to say now, because it certainly seemed as if she'd been waiting for them. I knew it always paid to tell a woman that you loved her, because unless she was unnatural and had a heart of stone she was bound to respond. But that wasn't the reason I said it now, for it came spontaneously out of me. Her response was scorching, and we moved in on each other so that I knew we had to find a flat surface somewhere, even a bit of old board, though in such a house it was bound to be more luxurious than that.

'You're the only person who's ever cared about me,' she said.

'I can't help it. What else can I do if I love you? We've already been to bed together, and I'm bound to love somebody I've been to bed with, aren't I?'

'I don't know,' she said.

'I'm not asking you,' I told her. We went upstairs, but I was disturbed because she could not stop weeping, as if she didn't know who she was or where she belonged. I couldn't do any more than lie down and hold her close. 'Did you tell your parents about it?'

'No,' she said. 'Yes. I wrote a letter yesterday.'

'Yesterday? A letter? Why didn't you phone?' I stood up and lit two cigarettes. 'Or send a telegram?'

She smiled, as if pleasantly astonished at her own thoughtlessness. 'I don't know. Really I don't.'

'You're crazy.'

'I know,' she said, weeping again.

I held her. 'You're not. But stop it.'

'I don't like my parents.'

'What's that got to do with it?'

'I came to England to get away from them.'

We made love, and she clung to me as if I were a tree and there was a gale trying to blow her away. When she came it was as if an electric shock had gone through her, and she nearly snapped my old man off. It was one o'clock, so we got dressed and went to see Smog.

He was lying with his eyes open. 'I heard you,' he said. 'What were you doing?'

'We were lying on the bed,' I said, 'loving each other.'

'Was it nice?'

'Are you hungry?' I sat him on my knee: 'Bridgitte's getting you some more breakfast.'

'That earwig's gone,' he said. 'The bell doesn't ring any more.'

'We'll give you some egg then, otherwise he'll wake and get up to his tricks again.'

'I'm hungry,' he said. So we fed him, and he ate well. Afterwards I read one of his books, then another, and he didn't want to go to sleep, but eventually he did.

I walked alone for an hour over the Heath, up to my ankles in mud and rotten leaves. It started to rain, so I hurried towards the Tube station, and wandered around till I found a bookshop to browse in. I saw an old copy of a Gilbert Blaskin book marked at two bob but I thought it was expensive so didn't buy it. Nothing interested me. Smog seemed to be getting back into himself, so I was worrying about tomorrow.

Kids were coming out of school, and I made my way back. I didn't seem to be connected to anything solid. I floated. The present bore no relationship to what was about to happen. This made me think that the world was going to end soon, or that something big was coming to pass. I felt an impulse to cut and run. My instinct told me how to cut and where to run to, so there was no excuse for not obeying it. And because I knew I hadn't an earthly chance of doing what it said, I felt that something even bigger than my instinct had me in its power. It was having a game with me. I felt an impulse to get away from the rain which was covering the trees and bushes of the Heath in mist.

I got Smog down to the living-room for tea, and he sat near the window, joyfully watching the rain painting its glass. His eyes had grown larger since morning. His skin was fragile, as if made of porcelain; until it moved when he smiled or turned to ask for more food. I told him I would be going away for a few days, that I had to go because it was to do with earning my living. 'Why don't you just go to the bank?' he said.

'That's not how you get money. You've got to earn it first.'

'But I'll make you some,' he said, jam all over his mouth. Full of energy, he ran to look for felt-pens. I cut paper into small pieces, and he covered each one with designs, but he sensed that something was wrong and made me cut more shapes. Then he asked me for a five-pound note, which he wanted to copy. When he'd done, he wouldn't give me the note back. So I let him borrow it, but said he must give it to me when I came home at the weekend, adding that if he was a good boy and ate all his meals, I'd take him to Hamley's, where he could spend it on toys. He went to sleep happy.

I said to Bridgitte that I would see her soon, telling her to look after Smog first, and then herself, which she promised to do. 'I don't like people to travel by aeroplane,' she said. 'They crash.'

'Not with me on it. I'm not worried about that. I have faith in those marvellous pieces of machinery.' Her black clothes were thrown off, and she lay on the bed in a flowered dressing-gown, while I had nothing on. A small bedlight glowed at us. I got dressed, saying I had to go. But I was afraid something might happen to her and Smog, as if only I could look after them, as if without me they were at the mercy of I didn't know what. I knew it was a stupid fear, which only came because I thought I was more powerful than I was, and that they were weaker than they were. Bridgitte was perfectly strong and competent. Yet I was also scared of what might happen to me after I left, and it had nothing to do with any plane taking a nosedive.

The rain had stopped, and stars were out, gaps between the clouds blown out of shape by a strong wind. At the bottom of the steps I hesitated, and wanted to go back. But I walked away, my footsteps sounding as if they carried someone in a hurry. If they did, I didn't know what for, because I felt frightened for the first time in my life. I imagined ambushes as I walked along by the Heath, so that I was glad to reach the Tube station and traffic lights, and make my way down Haverstock Hill. I intended walking home through the middle of town, not willing yet to try my hand at sleep. Even a passing car gave me comfort, and eventually the exhaustion I felt put me into a more hopeful mood, and I knew that I would not feel nervous in the morning.

It was a fine cold day, and I started it with a bath and a shave both to freshen me up and to get me clean for Polly when I met her in Geneva that afternoon. I boiled an egg, then phoned Bridgitte to say that I loved her and Smog, and that they were to wait for me at the weekend. When she promised I could almost feel her hot breath going into my ear. Smog was well, she added, and had eaten a lot for breakfast. Right now he was playing in the garden with a neighbour's boy, the son of an architect whose wife had just left him. He was already talking, she said, of what he would buy with the five pounds when I took him to Hamley's. That made me happy, at any rate, and I put down the receiver.

I stood looking along the rooftops and backs of the blocks of flats, and I didn't want to go out, a desire I put down to idleness. But soon I thought of the good lunch I would treat myself to before going to the Jack Leningrad depot for the ritual of loading up, so got my coat and hat on, picked up my briefcase packed with overnight things, took one last look at the den, and departed for a walk into Soho. The river flowed green and oily at the bridge, and I looked into it for a message. I found none, yet felt satisfied by the patterns and movement there.

Tonio greeted me like a compatriot when I went into his dining-room for lunch. I no longer liked him since Mogger-hanger had mentioned that Tonio kept in touch regarding the activities of his customers. But I smiled and asked how he was, kept my lips to their accustomed style of action. When he went to give my order I thought (and only knew later how right I was) that he had gone to phone Moggerhanger about my movements. I would have stopped eating there, except that the food was good, though if I had done so Mogger-hanger would have become suspicious of me, and in any case when things got complicated I preferred to do what I wanted to do in the first place, because usually it made no difference. On top of having my own way, I got a good meal as well, which I was going to need for the long trip before me, which was none other than to Brazil.

When the Jack Leningrad outfit loaded me up with gold I would sell a bar of it in Geneva, and then make connexions as fast as possible to Rio de Janeiro with the rest. From what Moggerhanger had said I didn't expect Polly to meet me at the airport, so I would be in and out before she thought to contact me. My plans were in as shaky a condition as I could expect if I hoped for them to succeed. I would send for Polly when I got to Brazil, and imagined in the present euphoric state of my intentions that she'd be delighted to come, but if it turned out that she played hard to get, or was too much under

Moggerhanger's thumb to slip away, then I'd make a similar proposal to Bridgitte and Smog, and I was sure they'd take up the idea like a shot. Everything was in a fluid condition except hope, and that's all I needed, because hope and luck usually went together with me.

Halfway through my zabaglione Almanack Jack came in, one of the few people I didn't want to see at that moment. I pushed my sweet away quickly, so that I wouldn't have to offer him anything to eat, and lit a cigar. Tonio came to ask whether I wanted coffee, but really to grab Jack by the beard and collar and frog-boot him out of it. 'Leave him alone,' I snapped, 'or the pair of us will get hold of you.'

He looked at me as if wondering whether I'd gone mad, then went to get the boiled dandelion root that he called coffee at two bob a thimbleful. 'What's the score then?' I asked Jack. 'You might as well sit down. I won't be coming here again.'

The grey coiling beard grew around and under his coat, but he looked fairly clean and didn't smell too bad. 'The score's ten to them and none to me, but I'm not complaining. I'm off the plonk. I'm not even hungry. Young people give me money now because I'm part of the scene. It's changed. I don't ask them, but they want to be generous, especially if they're poor. Some of 'em look worse off than I am, but they push a penny or sometimes as much as a few coppers into my hand.'

'That's good,' I said. 'You were in the front line.'

'Aye,' he said, 'but I want to pull out and go into a rest area for a month or two. If I can manage that I'll get enough strength to go on till I'm ninety.'

His grey eyes were turning yellow, and the skin visible through his beard was like painted asbestos. 'I know a nice quiet country place less than a hundred miles from London,' I said. 'Might do you a lot of good. It's that railway station I mentioned.' Tonio put our coffee down, then looked at us from the doorway to the kitchen. In case he could hear us, or the table was bugged, I wrote the address for Jack, and told him that somebody was there already, but mentioned no names. Then I scribbled a few words to William. I didn't imagine they'd get on well together, but asked him to give

Almanack Jack the waiting-room, where he could fend for himself. 'I'll be up myself in a few days,' I said, 'just to see that things are functioning. Do you need money to get there?'

'I'd like a quid if you've got it.' I gave him two, then said I had to run because I was going to work. When I paid the bill I didn't leave anything at all for a tip, which was something else Tonio could tell Moggerhanger, if ever he felt like it. Seeing nothing by the plate he didn't come forward to help with my coat, and so I buttoned up and went outside. A taxi stopped to let someone out. I jumped in.

It was a treacherous day, the sky high over the town, with small clouds in it, and a cold wind when I opened the slit in the taxi window, a very good day that sharpened the brain and woke you up before you wanted to be out of bed. But I was on my way, feeling optimistic and full of perception, captain of my own rotten rowing-boat.

Stanley hung my own coat on a hanger and put it into a cupboard where it would stay till I got back. 'Cottapilly and Pindarry off?' I asked casually, getting into the tailor-made over-mac.

'Without a hitch.'

'They're good men,' I said. 'Very handy people.'

He looked overworked, stooped a little as he went in before me to the big hall. 'The ticket to Geneva,' he said, pushing a plastic wallet into my hand. 'Return.'

'I hope so,' I laughed. 'Never play that trick on me.'

He stopped, and turned. 'Listen, I'm sick of your jokes.'

'Don't the others ever chaff you?'

'Never,' he said. 'So don't you.'

'No wonder they got caught, then, if they haven't got that much sense of humour.'

He was sweating. 'Who were you thinking of?'

'Ramage,' I told him. 'Who else?'

'Who indeed?'

'We'd better get in, or I'll be too late.'

I felt as if I'd been cast among a nest of madmen, instead of a bunch of cool and persevering smugglers out to beat the British Government's paid servants of Customs and Excise. To wonder what I would do with fifty thousand pounds' worth of gold when I finally sat cackling over it by the shadow of Sugar Loaf Mountain no longer seemed to concern me, for my only thought was to act in good faith, as if I were still set on carrying it to the specified place for Jack Leningrad Limited who were known throughout the city as a business firm of the highest integrity.

I walked across the hall towards the iron lung. 'Good morning, Mr Leningrad.'

He was listening to a record of Chaliapin singing one of his Russian songs, but he turned it down so that it almost faded away. 'It's afternoon,' he said, 'It's past two o'clock.' I must have been out of focus, for he swivelled his mirrors and periscopes, then smiled and asked if I was ready.

'You know me,' I said. 'I hope I get a gold watch at the end of twenty years' faithful service.'

I heard his dry laugh: 'We'll put it before the committee. In the meantime you'll be a bit closer to it if you start loading up.' Stacked on the purple cloth of a nearby table were fifty slender bars of the best gold, the fortune of my life that would set me up with a vast ranch in Brazil or the Argentine and make me king of all I surveyed. I held my coat open, and feeling Stanley slot the first bar's definite weight and warmth in one of its pockets, it seemed as if during some past time my guts had been pulled slowly out of true by the worries of life, and that now, one by one, they were being stuffed neatly back again. The second bar went in. Stanley, like a skilled craftsman-packer, always started from the top so that no tell-tale wrinkles would be left in the coat when he had finished, and the whole weight was in. I regretted that Smog, Bridgitte and myself weren't travelling together to South America by boat, for then Smog could while away the long hours by playing with these golden bars on the cabin floor, making his own squares and pyramids, triangles and palisades, his eyes glittering over it all. I was smiling at such a pleasant picture, which vanished when I noticed Leningrad looking at me, his fat face and beady eyes behind that battery of equipment surrounding his iron life-saving lung.

Stanley slotted in the third bar, when the telephone rang. As he picked it up, the man in the iron lung lifted his extension at the same time. 'When?' Stanley cried. 'Oh, my God!'

I didn't like the shocked tone of this, but thought I might as well go on with the loading while Stanley and Leningrad continued their business conversation at the phone. 'Don't touch it,' a voice screamed at me.

The phones were down, and Stanley's face was dusty with horror as if I were part of a bad dream he'd been having all through his life that had suddenly turned into reality. 'What's wrong then?' I demanded, as superciliously as I could, looking from one to the other.

'Cottapilly and Pindarry have been caught,' Stanley said.

'That's their hard luck. What's it got to do with me?'

'I'll kill you,' Leningrad screamed.

'You're lying,' I said. 'You told me they were off already.'

There were tears in Stanley's eyes. He was crying with rage. 'They were fetched from the plane when it was already taxiing to the runway.'

'We'd better get on with the loading,' I said. 'If they've caught those two they won't be looking for me. I'll be as safe as houses.' A gun was beamed on me, and I knew that Stanley had another ready under his coat. I had the terrible and empty feeling that I was going to have my light put out, and all I could do was go on talking, get in as many words as I could before blackness came, as if under those guns and at the end of it all words were the only thing left.

'You informed on them,' said that thin voice, cracking out of speakers all over the room.

'What's in it for me?' I said. 'They must have given themselves away, somehow or other, so keep your accusations to yourself.'

Stanley's eyes were almost out of his head. 'Who else then?'

'You,' I said, 'That's who else. Load me up and let me go, or I'll tell Mr Leningrad all I know about you, or maybe we'd all better get ourselves out of here in case Cottapilly and Pindarry talk. And they will, those two, don't you worry,' I added, as if I was dead certain of it, traducing all and sundry so that I'd go blue in the face and stamp out my guilty look. 'I've never seen such double-crossers. None of us are safe, so we've got to stick together and trust each other. That's our only hope. If we don't, we're done for. It's certainly a lousy world I've landed in when as soon as trouble comes it's dog eat dog. Worse than a jungle. I'm the best man you ever had, and you're throwing my faithful service away as if it was an old banana skin. Even if I do do this trip and get away with it, I'm finished with the likes of you lot. There's not even honour among thieves any more. I'm disgusted to my marrow.'

I was overflowing with honest irrepressible indignation, but this time it wasn't working. Leningrad turned a knob that increased the volume of every loudspeaker in the room, so that he drowned me out. 'You scum, liar, traitor. You've double-crossed us. Tell me who it was to, or I'll kill you on the spot.'

I was going to tell him the truth, I swear I was, when the door snapped open, and a revolver shot spattered across the room. I felt it sizzle past my head, a lurch of hot wind that sent a scorching breath at my ear. It must have disconnected some line of the iron lung's communications system, because the man inside was shouting, and no sounds came out.

Claud Moggerhanger stood at the closed door, while Kenny Dukes, gripping a huge cosh, and Slasher with hands in pockets obviously holding down some threatening weapon, rushed across to the iron lung. Slasher took whatever it was from his pocket and tackled Stanley, who was struggling with a gun. They went down at my feet, and I stepped back so that they wouldn't dirty my boots or crease my trousers. They fought like lions and I was pleasantly surprised to see that Stanley had a lot of strength and courage in him. They rolled over, blood spurting between them, because Slasher had his blade out and was managing to weave it from time to time.

The table capsized, and forty-seven bars of gold slewed across the floor. Kenny Dukes was getting to work on the equipment of the iron lung, and a loudspeaker had come on again because Leningrad was waving his arms about inside, yelling at him to stop. But Kenny worked like an expert demolition man wanting to prove to a new employer how efficient he was at smashing iron lungs. Under the tangle of splintered equipment Jack Leningrad was firing a revolver across the room at Moggerhanger, and Claud was dodging about the floor with the agility of a man in his prime.

Screams and shots were pitching all over the place, and Stanley who seemed to be bleeding in several places at once was pleading for mercy from Slasher, but just as it seemed that Slasher was seriously thinking about it Stanley got in a kick that sent him flying across the room. Windows that had been painted over with thick black lacquer were shattered by bullets, and the whole tangle of iron lung was on the floor with the man buried in it, and Kenny Dukes still bashing away at the wreckage from above.

I lay on the floor, watching the gold, waiting my chance, and while the chaos was sweeping round me I stuffed another couple of bars in my pouches. Moggerhanger's hand jabbed into the air when one of Leningrad's last bullets clipped him, and for a moment he was too dazed to guard the door. With all the jack-rabbit strength in my legs I leapt out of the room, leaving yells of murder, and the heartening sound of more breaking glass behind me. My briefcase was in the vestibule and I grabbed it in a last inspired frenzy of possessiveness – before getting clear of the place for the last time.

Rather than fumble with the lift, I ran down the stairs, calming myself before reaching the exit. I walked into the street, buttoning my coat as I went up by Harrod's and on to Brompton Road. People passed me, noticing nothing unusual, but I was bewildered, not knowing to which point of the compass I should flee. I had a vision of Upper Mayhem station, of William Hay with his boots off mashing tea in the booking office, then with his feet propped up and a novel bent back in his hands. But to go there would betray him, for I knew they'd trace me soon enough. The wild woods and open fields didn't appeal to me, either, and neither did I care to head for Nottingham because that would bring trouble on my mother. The one person who could help was my grandmother. She'd defend me against all the gangsters of heaven and hell, never let them get near me. But my grandmother was dead, so no help could be expected from that quarter. The fine day had turned to drizzle and low cloud. At last I got a taxi and sat inside.

'Where to?'

'London airport,' I said, not thinking about it. My instinct took over, though by now I was beginning to hate its guts. I felt cut off from the roots of my intuition, and that being the case, because it definitely seemed so, I sensed a sort of resurgence coming out of the shock and panic, a hope that once more my organism would reform and provide me with the ability to grapple at the unexpected. I didn't want to think. If you think, I told myself as the taxi made a fair lick west along Cromwell Road, you cut yourself off from luck and the benefit of action.

There was still time to get the Geneva plane, and I had the ticket in my pocket, as well as five bars of gold that would see me right for a year or two. I was already planning my future. I'd sell the gold, open an account with the money in Zurich, buy a few old clothes and a rucksack, call myself a student of languages, then hole up in some quiet town and wait for what came my way. I'd grow a moustache and a beard, and as long as I paid my bills and lived an uneventful life no one would bother me. With only five bars of gold Brazil was out, for a bit of travel there would eat up most of it. In any case I'd feel safer not too far from Moggerhanger's claws than I would if I were to drop myself conspicuously in some such exotic place. Later I'd get in touch with Bridgitte, though not for a while. As for Polly, it seemed as if she was out of my life for ever.

I sat back calmly as we reached a bit of green on the edge of London, smoked a cigar, and checked my ticket. It was real. My brain settled itself into accepting this new and unexpected future. I certainly hated Moggerhanger's guts, and couldn't wait to get a good distance between us. The last information I'd passed on had set him working so hastily to get Pindarry and Cottapilly cooked that he'd nearly caused a bullet to be put through my own head. His sense of loyalty was even worse than mine, so we should never have met, and all I could want in my eternal hopefulness was that he'd now be glad to see the back of me.

I dropped a fiver to the taxi man and hurried in to have my ticket checked. There was exactly enough time. It was a quiet day in the Airline Transit Camp, and I walked calmly into the departure hall with ticket and passport ready. The idea of saying goodbye to the island for a long time boosted my spirit because the morass would be behind me and emptiness in front, just as it had been when I'd set out from Nottingham and tried my luck down the Great North Road. Perhaps someone like me needed this shot-launch into the wide-open spaces every few years.

My ticket was clipped, and I walked across the space to show my passport with a smile. The customs man was watching me, but I went by him without trouble into the waiting-room. A sudden great hunger scooped a hollow in my stomach, and I stood looking at the cafeteria counter, wondering whether to knock down a couple of double brandies and a few cream cakes before my number was called, or whether to sit calmly and contemplate the last of England from the plate-glass windows beyond which a misty rain smoked across the runways. I felt a pang at leaving Polly, though I couldn't believe I'd absolutely seen the last of her, hoping that at some future time kind Fate would enable us to meet again. Then there was Bridgitte and Smog, who in some ways I thought more softly on, and I wondered how the three of us would ever meet. I saw matronly Bridgitte in ten years' time travelling with a sixteen-year-old youth through a north Italian town, the pair of them getting off a bus in some sunny and dusty piazza. I would be lazily painting at an easel on which a few pigeons rested. I'd go over to them, and Smog would be very protective to Bridgitte and wonder who the hell I thought I was, trying to get off with her, but Bridgitte would recognize me, and I'd invite them back to my simple room, by which time Smog would have remembered me perfectly and with great affection.

I asked for a cup of coffee, when a hand rested on my shoulder. The long pale face of a customs man said: 'Will you come with me, sir?'

No one was to call me that again for a long time. We went back to the passport counter. He asked, now with two more customs men looking on, how much money I was taking out of the country. I told him, and was asked to open my wallet. With the legal amount of currency I had nothing to fear. I stepped out of my existence so as to watch myself being calm, smile, open my briefcase. I expected to be released, as William had been on one of his former forays, and was already congratulating myself on the fact that this little interview did not matter because I wouldn't be coming through here again.

'Would you follow me, please?'

I walked into another room, out of the gaze of honest or lucky people who were asked no questions at all. Two policemen were waiting, as well as a lamp-post of a plain-clothes detective whom I recognized as none other than Chief Inspector Lantorn. 'Take off your overcoat.'

I knew that it was all finished. Lantorn himself lifted out the five bars of gold, and I was cautioned that anything I said might be used as evidence against me, while the customs men outlined the laws under which I was charged.

On my way to the police station I knew that Moggerhanger had arranged for me to be picked up at the same time as he'd mentioned Cottapilly and Pindarry. When he threw out his net, he cast it wide.

My legs trembled, but I had no wish to sit down. They offered it, but I still stood up, as if I didn't want to be obliged to them for anything. Lantorn pushed me on to a bench. My iron lung was also smashed, and the light that flooded in frightened me so that I could hardly breathe. I wondered when Moggerhanger's lung would smash, and smiled at the possibility of helping to bring it about. But in spite of everything I couldn't think of what he'd done to deserve it, because with Inspector Lantorn gripping my arm as we went to another part of the police station, how could I prove Moggerhanger to have done anything wrong at all? If he'd thought there was any good chance of my doing so, he wouldn't have had me picked up with such alacrity.

Epilogue

Moggerhanger had used me to bust Jack Leningrad, knowing that when I was in the hands of the police there'd be nothing else I could do but talk, in the hope of getting as little prison as possible. I didn't accede to Moggerhanger's wishes out of weakness, but from a position of strength, because having decided what my policy was to be, I stuck to it so that Moggerhanger got the best results as far as he was concerned. So did Lantorn, for this became one of his celebrated cases Moggerhanger had confidently fed me into the police machine like a spanner, and I didn't disappoint anyone, so that any other case against him simply came to pieces in Lantorn's hands.

I was so busy saving my neck that I hadn't the time or emotional energy to brood about the way Moggerhanger had used me, but in the months before my downfall he must have had a huge diagram on his wall, with a series of pins labelled *Cullen* that he moved from place to place until I was sucked into the final trap he had laid for me. It had been so well plotted that if I didn't hate him so much I would have admired him. There were a hundred places where his assumptions could have gone wrong, but such was his knowledge of human nature in general, and of mine in particular, that I had chosen exactly the right turning at every fork of the way, simply because he took care to make sure that I'd see each decision to my own advantage. He'd laid such a string of traps that after the first few I ceased to think or take any precautions.

I admitted carrying gold for Jack Leningrad Limited, but pleaded ignorance regarding the seriousness of what I was doing. Smut and Bunt the solicitors helped me, and it wasn't till afterwards that I found out who paid them. They got an expert barrister of the old school to stand up and say I was a 'man of good character though in many respects naïve, who has never been in any sort of trouble before'. They could say that again, and again, and I smiled inwardly to hear it, though it didn't stop the judge from yapping out that he would have given me more than eighteen months but for the fact that I'd been such a fool.

At the moment of being caught I'd expected ten years, but between then and the trial I became more optimistic and saw myself getting less and less, being so puffed with hope and the barrister's claptrap that I thought I'd get off with no more than a fat fine.

But no man is a real man, or a hero, unless he's been in prison, and I was about to qualify for that honour. I had lots to think about, including the surprise of seeing my mother appear in court to testify what a loyal and loving son I'd always been. An even greater shock was to hear Gilbert Blaskin, described as a well-known author from the best of families, say what a good character I was, in such a way that I began to believe it myself. I seemed to have lived in a different world till then, been in fact one of the few saints in it to hear some people talk, though I was dropped abruptly back on to the scruffy earth when the verdict of eighteen months was announced from the mealy-mouthed old bastard stuck up on high. I was in such a state of rage and despair for the next few weeks that when I came out of it I was quite used to the conditions of prison. It was like a new country that I had learned to live in during a dream.

One day I had visitors, so stopped my sweeping-up to get marched off and see who they were. Beyond the double thickness of wire-meshed glass I saw my mother and Gilbert Blaskin. I leaned forward, but said nothing. They peered through the glass, and I wondered why they looked at me. For some minutes I couldn't understand why they were there together. People were shouting and making signs all along the line on either side of me, and when my mother opened her mouth I realized that though she was talking I couldn't hear a word. Gilbert smiled and lifted a hand, not even bothering to try. I smiled, put my head closer, and sneezed.

They wanted to tell me something, but I didn't see what could be of sufficient importance to break through the overwhelming fact of me being locked away from them like a monkey on a wet day. Blaskin wore a trilby hat, looked healthier than I'd ever seen him. My mother also had a hat on, and seemed by her looks and figure to match well by the side of Blaskin. She had gained a little stoutness.

Her voice broke faintly through, but I couldn't make out what she was saying. The visit was going on too long. I could understand why she had come, but not Blaskin. He leaned as far forward as possible, put both hands to his mouth and bellowed. From the look on his face, and the anxiety on my mother's, I tried to hear the words because it seemed particularly important to them both. I didn't get it, so he made one more attempt. I conquered my stupidity by a force of will that in the outside world wouldn't have needed any will at all. The words came as if from the bottom of the sea: 'We got married last week!'

It was a blow under the heart, but maybe I needed it, because it knew where to go and went straight there. I said it aloud, repeating it, and though they couldn't hear they read my lips, and both laughed and waved and kissed and held hands against the glass so that there could be no mistake. They even showed me the ring. I heard later how Gilbert had gone to Nottingham, after my last call at his flat near Sloane Square, and found my mother, wooing her till she'd agreed to marry him. After their visit I began to notice my surroundings, and to accustom myself to the new world, so maybe it did me some good after all.

One day as I was walking round the exercise yard a face floated by that I knew very well, and recognized as that of Stanley. 'Oh,' he said, when we talked later, 'they brought me here from the Scrubs.'

'So I see. If they want you to nark on me, I don't know anything.'

His face was fatter, and two of his front teeth were missing. A smile made him appear sadder than when I'd last seen him. 'I say,' he sneered, 'we have lost our good-natured trust, haven't we?'

'If you get like that with me, you're going to perish while you're here, make no mistake.' This calmed him, so I cooled off as well. 'They caught me at the airport, in case you didn't know. I was trying to get the five bars to Geneva, but that bastard Moggerhanger had them waiting for me. And I suppose you were the one who told Moggerhanger to get your own back, because I know you blamed Cottapilly and Pindarry's capture on me, not to mention Ramage, but how could that have been possible when I'd got nothing to gain by it, and in any case went out and got bodged straight away? I wanted to get that gold to Geneva for the good of the firm, and a lot of bloody good my great sense of duty did me. I even got there in time for the plane we had planned for. That's why I ran out of the flat so suddenly. I'd seen that Moggerhanger was hit, so I was sure our side had the upper hand. And look where it got us. We're all in the bloody iron lung now.' I don't know whose good books I expected this virtuous testimony to go into, so I laughed and ended it.

Over the days and weeks I got the rest of the story out of him, of how, as anyone ought to have known but me, Jack Leningrad wasn't paralysed, and conducted operations from his iron lung to fool everybody. It was full of radio and electronic devices which, unfortunately, hadn't warned him of Moggerhanger's last great break-in. Maybe it had and he was too busy with me to notice it. The battle had gone on after I left, and Stanley made a fighting retreat with Jack Leningrad out of the building, leaving all the files and some stocks of gold in the hands of Moggerhanger, who must have been satisfied at the way the day finished up. The police arrived to find the flat empty, for Moggerhanger had two estate cars waiting outside into which he piled all the clues and every scrap of loot.

Stanley and Jack Leningrad found a hiding-place in Highgate, but the police surrounded it an hour later. Nevertheless, they escaped the net, and Stanley broke into a car. No sooner was it started than they were topped and tailed by the blue flashing light. Stanley was captured, but Jack Leningrad got away, and now, months later, nothing had been seen of him, and it was assumed he'd gone to Canada. For the man in the iron lung was agile and elusive once outside his trappings – though they had served him well for a long time. It looked as if he'd live to do more work in one guise or another.

The unluckiest person of all was Stanley, who got sent down for four years. I did my best to keep out of his way, but one day he came at me from behind and tried to stun me with his clenched fist. It was a hammer-thump, but it didn't work, because I was able to turn and strike him back, not once, but too many times. I was disciplined for it, and lost my remission, which was why I had to serve every hour of eighteen months. This exploit made me more respected among the roughs of the place, for what that was worth, which wasn't much.

I had several visits from Bridgitte, who said she was waiting for me, and who pressed a photograph of Smog against the grille so that I could see how tough and well he looked. I had no feeling for her at first because my two eyes were still full of Polly Moggerhanger. I burned for her, saw her as the one great love of my life whom I'd run to as soon as I got out of prison. The fact that she would in no way be waiting for me, that she would laugh at the idea of me even thinking about her, and that it was in other words clearly impossible for us to be together ever again, made her more real to me, brought her so close that at nights I woke up startled, thinking she was in the cell and about to put her hand on to my shoulder. It went on for a long time, till the emotional cost of keeping her in front of me began to wear me out, and she eventually faded with my absolute loss of spirit and energy. This landed me in a state of emptiness I would rather forget about, but when I came out of it, Bridgitte took her place, and never left it.

There were three men to a cell, sometimes four, and often in the middle of the night I'd feel that I wasn't able to stretch myself out on the bed. What's more, I clung to it, as if it were vertical and I was in danger of falling off into oblivion. In order to get the illusion of laying full length and finding more peace, I'd go down on the floor, and it gave me great comfort, even when it was bitterly cold, to press my limbs against the solid concrete, which was the nearest I could get to real earth in that madhouse. I would have given my right arm, and even taken another year of prison, to have been a coalminer for a few hours and gone a thousand feet under into the dark.

I got messages from William Hay that my station was being taken care of, and when I was released I found that he'd planted beans and potatoes in the garden, rose bushes and sunflowers along the borders and platforms. Bunting was hung across the station entrance saying: WELCOME HOME STATIONMASTER, when my taxi drew up from Huntingborough.

Wedding bells were ringing from the moon, because while I was inside, Almanack Jack, who stayed on at the station, got married to William Hay's mother, who heard he was back from his adventure in the Lebanon, and came down to be with him. William lived in the booking office, while his mother and her new husband had taken over the waiting-room. The entrance hall that lay between was a sort of no-man's-land in which they occasionally fought great fights over such insignificant items as a bucket of coal or a cup of sugar.

Almanack Jack became a man of many colours, for he smartened himself up at the station, though he still keeps a bushy spade-shaped beard. In an old cupboard he found and commandeered a railway guard's uniform, which he makes Mrs Straw press and spruce up for him every week, so that with the hat, whistle, and small red flag, he strolls along the platform and on to the rusty railway line, anxiously looking at the fob watch of Clegg's that I made him a present of. He keeps the business end of the station clean, makes his wife polish the brasses and lamps, sweep the platforms, and wash out the lavatories – though she does it swearing and grumbling. The palings have been reconstituted, and flowerbeds planted with pansies and jillivers. All it needs to make his life complete is to hear an engine whistle, and to see an old locomotive steaming down from the main line. But if ever it does (and it never will) he'd die of a heart attack, because we've known for a year or two that poor old Almanack Jack has a dicky ticker.

The travelling library van comes round once a week and brings him books on astrology, for he spends some of his spare time casting horoscopes for all of us. He says I'll have a quiet life up to when I'm thirty-five, and then all hell will fly loose, sending me out on the wild again. I'll believe it when it happens. Not that I have long to wait, because I'll be at the gates of that age in a couple more years. Bridgitte isn't pleased by such talk, but doesn't otherwise mind, because Smog, who is fourteen now, has always been so fond of him.

Bridgitte and I got married soon after I came out of clink, as if I'd at some time promised faithfully to do just that. Both of us wanted it when it became possible because it seemed the only thing to do. She sold the house in Hampstead (which Dr Anderson, in spite of his addiction to kickshins, had taken care to leave her) for thirty thousand pounds, which, being well invested with her good Dutch sense that had surfaced at last, brings us enough money in to live on modestly. She's got fuller now, redder in the face, and is no longer the glamorous and flighty au pair girl from the London days of old. But I've put weight on too, though not much, because I do plenty of work and walking around the place to keep me fit. She cooks haunches of meat and Dutch butter-dumplings for me and the kids, while Almanac Jack and his wife do their own catering. In summer they build an outdoor fire by the railway line, putting a pot on it like two old gipsies. That's when they are happiest, and cause least trouble around the place. Bridgitte and I live in the house, which became big enough, since we had more children, only when William and I built two more rooms on the back of it.

Almanack Jack is also good with Julie and Ray and Jake, because in the morning he wakes them up and gives them breakfast, then takes them down the road to the village school. At first the local children jeered at him, but now they like him because he gives them sweets and brings them on conducted tours of our railway station. At harvest time he used to do a few weeks' labour with the local farmers, and because he worked well they gave him milk or eggs, and tried to persuade him to stay on longer, or even permanently, but he never would, liking his freedom above all else.

William came and went, and came back again. Although he still had money his dream of getting into a market garden somewhere in Nottinghamshire, with his mother as his bond-maiden, never came off. He found new strength from somewhere with which to face life, never having been the sort to let death touch him in the form of early retirement.

A year or two after the Lebanon setback he found himself once more in some shady trade or other, maybe even smuggling, because his obvious prosperity couldn't have stemmed from honest work. We were out for a drink at the village pub, and I asked how he got such a big car and dressed so well, at which he lost his good humour and told me to mind my own business. 'Don't worry,' I said, 'I shan't ask you to get me some of the same work.'

He relaxed, and laughed: 'Not like last time, eh?'

'Never. I'm set up for life here.'

'Better you than me.'

It was a warm summer's evening, and the pub was still empty. 'I know when I'm well off,' I said, taking a good drink of my pint.

'Still,' he said, 'if ever you do find yourself in need of a bit of employment, let me know. You're cool. You've got nerve, and that's always a marketable commodity.'

'I've not got so much as I once had.'

He jeered: 'Just because of a bit of bird?'

'Keep your voice down. I'm known as a respectable house-owner around here.'

'That's just another part you're playing,' he said, 'and like all the others you play it very well. It's lasted a long time, this one, but that doesn't mean it's permanent.'

'It is as far as I'm concerned.'

He winked, and lifted his double brandy: 'You've had a good long rest, that's all. You'll get back to work soon. Cheers, mate.'

'Cheers,' I said, smiling.

My mother and Gilbert Blaskin seemed reasonably happy for a few years. She went to America with him on a lecture tour, and this was a wild time because they played at making each other jealous, and by the time they got back they were in emotional rags and tatters. I don't know how it came about, because my mother was well over forty, but she produced a baby daughter, and Gilbert thought this the best thing that had ever happened to him – after he got over the shock. They came down in his new Jaguar to see us, staying two nights at the hotel in Huntingborough.

I'd never got used to the idea that Blaskin was my father, and never would. I'd pumped myself so long with the fabrication that the only shadowy father I'd had was killed in the war that all my pipes and connexions of filial piety had atrophied and finally snapped. And yet here *was* my real father, coming towards me from his Jaguar and leaving my mother behind to struggle out with her newborn baby. He was tall, his face lined, his eyes slackening down from the fire they used to have. Blaskin dominated the small living-room, until he sat down. We set them a good winter's meal for that evening, and sitting at the table were me, Bridgitte, Smog, Gilbert, and my mother, five of us surrounding a dumpling soup, and a side of beef, with egg-custard and apple fritters to follow. Gilbert was in a bad frame of mind, as if he'd just been unsuccessfully poisoned and was slowly getting over the illness of it.

After the meal he rolled a cigar at me across the table. I'd bought a bottle of brandy for the occasion, and poured everyone a shot after the blow-out dinner. The baby was asleep in Julie's room, but we could make all the noise we liked because my mother said that once Lucy was asleep nothing could wake her – just like I had been in fact, when I was a baby. Gilbert was getting restless under this particular dome of conversation, so he asked whether I ever felt like getting down to any sort of work.

'Not particularly,' I said. 'How about you?'

'He does a lot,' my mother said, 'and I get bloody bored at times.'

I watched him looking at her, and he knew I was watching, which encouraged him to think of something rotten to say because of it. 'You weren't bored in New York. You just vanished for twelve hours at a time.'

'I couldn't hang around with your friends, that's all. They weren't interested in me, and I wasn't interested in them. They were all poofs and drug fiends.'

Bridgitte and I laughed at this, and Smog, who was eight at the time, smiled, which didn't help to calm things down.

'So you went off to find a real man,' he sneered.

'No, love,' she said. 'I'd got you, so I didn't need one.'

She was being sincere (at least I thought she was) but he took it as a slash of sarcasm: 'And that little Lucy upstairs came out of it, I know.'

I stood up, ready for a fight. 'Lay off my mother will you? I thought we were all here to have a good time.' This stopped him, but it was a very uneasy peace that came out of it.

They left next morning. A year later they were divorced. My mother wasn't too upset about it, because she still had a daughter to spend the next twenty years of her life on – unless another unexpected adventure stopped her dead in her tracks. A neighbour's wife looked after Lucy while my mother went to work again at the factory. Blaskin made her some allowance, thinking perhaps of all the years he hadn't provided for me, so that she didn't absolutely need to work. But she used the money to get a flat, take driving lessons, and buy a Mini on the never-never, which means that every month or two she drives down with Lucy to see our mob at Upper Mayhem. Smog is very partial to Lucy, despite the difference in their ages, which pleases me very much.

The last thing heard of Gilbert Blaskin was that he lived at his Sloane Square flat with Pearl Harby. She'd tried to gas herself while he was married to my mother, but a girlfriend had pulled her head from the oven in time. This attempted suicide so impressed Blaskin that when he heard of it, just after leaving my mother, he went straight back to her, probably in the hope that sooner or later she will do it again, preferably while he is around to watch, so that he can write about it in a novel.

I wear a waistcoat now, and never go out unless there's a golden sovereign in one of the pockets. While we till our garden, I love Bridgitte and the children more and more, being linked to them for ever. Smog is a tall, thin, dark boy who'll need a shave in the next six weeks. He never says much, though we talk now and again about various things. He plays chess at his grammar school in Huntingborough, and collects botanical specimens. For his last birthday I bought him an expensive microscope, and for his twenty-first I've promised him ten of the golden sovereigns my grandmother passed on to me. My mother had given me back the twenty-five I'd offered her, since she had never needed them for her honeymoon with Albert in Paris.

From time to time I find myself getting interested in Almanack Jack's prophecy that I'll be on the wild at thirty-five, and though these flashes of interest only show my inborn Blaskinite stupidity (because there needn't be anything in such crackpot prophecies at all, no more, in fact, than there is ultimately any truth in me), yet it snaps at my neckstrings now and again, because no one, finally, can spend all of his allotted span in an iron lung.

GOOD TIME COMING

A New Shocker

by

Edmund Schiddel

author of

The Devil In Bucks County – the outspoken bestseller that sold over a million copies.

GOOD TIME COMING

Never before such a fascinating exploration of the sexual obsessions, frustrations, and antagonisms in the bizarre world of America's jet-set men and women.

GOOD TIME COMING 45p

'Written with a compulsive pace which makes it difficult to put down' – THE GUARDIAN.

R. F. DELDERFIELD

This celebrated author writes his first crime novel and provides a whole new reading experience for a faithful public.

COME HOME CHARLIE AND FACE THEM 35p

A gripping story of crime and lust, in a little Welsh seaside town of the 1920s, which demands to be read at one sitting.

'Highly recommended. Combines tension with a splendid sense of atmosphere and vivid characterization. An excellent read' – SUNDAY EXPRESS

'There's a savage climax to this fine novel by a born story-teller' – SUNDAY MIRROR

A SELECTION OF POPULAR PAN FICTION

These and other PAN Books are obtainable from all book-sellers and newsagents. If you have any difficulty please send purchase price plus 5p postage to P.O. Box 11, Falmouth, Cornwall. While every effort is made to keep prices low, it is sometimes necessary to increase prices at short notice. PAN Books reserve the right to show new retail prices on covers which may differ from those advertised in the text or elsewhere.